Dorian was still standing so, so close, right here, in her bedroom.

And even as she was being engulfed by this ridiculously unexpected and totally unwarranted attraction, her rational mind reminded her that this was the same man who had been getting on her very last nerve just an hour before. But the warm, woodsy scent of him made those thoughts irrelevant.

Why didn't he do something? Why didn't he make a move, say something or lean forward and...touch her? Rita felt her body sway toward him a little. She lifted her eyes to his and found that he was not looking at her, but was staring at the ceiling, in the attitude of someone praying, or at least consulting the heavens for guidance....

"Rita," he began.

"Yes?"

"I'd better go before..." His eyes were on her mouth again. "I'd better go now."

Without another word, he turned abruptly and headed out her front door.

SIMONA TAYLOR

lives on her native Caribbean island of Trinidad—a
fertile place for dreaming up scorching, sun-drenched
romance novels. She balances a career in public relations
and a family of two small children and one very patient
man while feeding her obsession for writing.

Simona lives under the spell of her muse, or, as they'd
say on her island, the writing "jumbie." At the end of the
day, when her son and daughter—her little matched set
of salt and pepper shakers—are safely in bed, after school
bags are packed, the laundry done, the kitchen cleaned
and the toys put away, she indulges in her latest writing
project with a sense of anticipation usually reserved for
chocolate.

A sensual setting is half the pleasure to be found in
reading—and writing—a book. While Simona loves to
show off the charms of Trinidad and its sister island,
Tobago, she has also set her romances in the south of
France, Barcelona and the fictional city of Santa Amata
in the eastern United States.

When not dreaming up drool-worthy heroes, she updates
her Web site, www.scribble-scribble.com, which, as
thousands of visitors have found out, is a fun place to
visit, read her novel excerpts and her blog and have a
good laugh.

She has also published three works of women's literary
fiction under her real name, Roslyn Carrington, but it is
her passion for romance that most consumes her.

Dear Rita

TAYLOR Simona

KIMANI™
ROMANCE

 KIMANI PRESS™

ISBN-13: 978-0-373-86062-3
ISBN-10:   0-373-86062-5

DEAR RITA

Copyright © 2008 by Roslyn Carrington

www.kimanipress.com

Printed in U.S.A.

Dear Reader,

Dear Rita was one of the hardest books I've ever had to write. Why? Timing, timing, timing. I started it on August 16, 2005—when my daughter, Megan, was eight weeks old.

I vaguely remember starting that first chapter, sitting in a haze of exhaustion. Snatching half an hour while my baby slept.

And that's how *Dear Rita* has been shaped. In dribbles and bits; in stolen half hours and precious whole hours that were too few and too far between. I wrote on my lunch hour, dividing my attention between the book and my ringing phone, my boss passing by my desk to have a word and the *blip* of e-mails.

At night, while Megan slept and my three-year-old, Riley, read quietly in his bed (or hollered at the top of his lungs for Mommy), I wrote a little more.

The days in which I was able to write ten, fifteen hours a week are gone. Now, 4 or 5 hours a week are a miracle. But I don't begrudge my babies the time they've taken from me. They've added a whole new dimension to the person that I am, and I love them dearly.

I hope you enjoyed *Dear Rita*. In spite of the constraints, I enjoyed writing it.

I look forward to hearing from you. You can e-mail me at roslyn@scribble-scribble.com, or drop by my Web site at www.scribble-scribble.com. My snail mail address is:

Roslyn Carrington
8190 NW 21st Street
Suite T-926
Miami, FL 33122

Dedicated to Mrs. Leeba Deo La Roche

Thanks for your enthusiasm and your encouragement. Thanks for being you. You make me laugh every time we meet. And thanks for the loving care you've shown toward my children, and, very importantly, for keeping them out of my hair long enough for me to write this book.

Chapter 1

Spam.

Delete.

Spam.

Delete.

Spam... How in the world did people dream up half this stuff? And who in the world was crazy enough to buy it? Rita held down the Delete key and shook her head. She had no intention of buying chcap aphrodisiacs onlinc, had no cellulite to speak of and was quite happy with the extra eight pounds or so she carried around on her five-foot-six-inch frame. After all, on the scale of the universe, what was an extra eight pounds?

But spammers certainly made life difficult, especially when her job involved spending hours online each day. People out there relied on her, women who were hurting and confused, who needed her help. Clearing junk mail took longer and longer every day, and when you worked freelance, time was money.

She settled into her Starbucks seat, glad that she had come

early enough to bag her favorite, a comfy, funky one near the window, and slurped on her thick, aromatic White Chocolate Mocha. Rita knew her frailties, and coffee was one of them. She could start the day without food. She could start the day without air, if it came to that. But caffeine? Noooo.

She patted her mocha mustache with a napkin and got down to work. A dozen e-mails down, she found a likely prospect.

Dear Rita,

My husband and I share a computer. Last night I was surfing the Net when I began to type in the address of a Web site I wanted. Guess what? The Auto-complete feature was on, and before I could finish typing, another address popped up. It was a singles Web site specializing in girls under thirty. My husband is fifty-two, and we've been married twenty-nine years. Rita, I'm devastated. My husband's registration dates back almost a year, and he's been using another name, claiming that he's only forty-one, and single.

What do I do?

Is it just a phase?

Hopeful

Washington D.C.

Dear Hopeful,

What do you do? Try to figure out his password (it usually isn't all that hard), go into his account with the Web site and cancel it. Then look through his History, dig around in his cookies and Temporary Internet Files, and try to find out where else he's been. If he has memberships in any other sites, cancel those. Then sit back and wait.

Next time he tries to access the site, he'll know you know. The measure of the man is what he does next. Either he'll stay quiet, in which case he's a coward as well as a cheat, or he'll 'fess up, in which case he's honest—for a stinking cheat, that is.

Either way, any man who passes himself off as being ten years younger just to chase women has issues. Is it a phase? Probably. Should you sit back and accept it? No. Either thrash it out before he gets lost in cyberspace, or toss him in the Recycle Bin. Your choice. But I've got to tell you, honey, in your shoes, I'd cut the stinker loose and go find a Web site that specializes in *men* under thirty... Rita

Rita took another swig of coffee and sighed. Every day she was confronted with the pain of other women's love lives. They claimed they were coming to her for advice, for her to steer them in the right direction, but most of them knew, deep down in their hearts, what to do. What they were coming to her for, more than anything else, was a sympathetic ear.

And that was why she loved the Dear Rita job. *Niobe*, a glossy, chatty magazine for women, came out in hard copy monthly. With a wide ethnic base and a decent print run, it was chock-full of everything a women's magazine should have: fashion, makeup, financial advice, contests and giveaways and an advice column. Her advice column.

Even better, her column ran weekly in the online version of *Niobe*, creating four times the income for her, and four times the chances to provide a sympathetic ear for sisters in need. It didn't get much better than that.

She opened up another e-mail.

Holler at ya Rita girl!

Big-ups on your column! You're a hoot! I have to ask you something. I'm seventeen and still in High School. I've been going with a college junior for five months, and he is totally phat!!;-) I'm a virgin and I want to save myself for marriage. (Don't laugh, my Grandma is a preacher and she'd kill me!) He says he understands.

Thing is, he's been having sex with other girls. He told me so himself. Not a whole lot. Only once a week or so. He says he loves me and all, but he's a grown man and has needs.

My girlfriends say he's a dawg and he could get me sick and I should kick him to the curb, but I love him so awful much, and plus he is so, so cute!! ;-)!

What d'you think?
Desperately in Love,
Miami

Rita tapped out an answer, wishing she could thump the girl on the head while she was doing so.

Dear Desperate,
I think your friends are right.
Rita.

She hoped the silly little girl took the hint, but she wasn't banking on it. What was it with these young women nowadays? Why were they in such a hurry? Was there no more room in the world for friendship rings and promise pins, she groused to herself, feeling a good sixty years older than the twenty-seven she really was.

From deep in the recesses of her coat pocket, her cell phone rang. She fumbled, trying to fish it out, and dropped it on the floor. It survived, but by the time she retrieved it, it had stopped ringing. She recognized the number at once. Beatrix.

She took a few deep breaths. The right thing to do would be to call her mother back. But the idea of it brought a twinge of anxiety to the pit of her stomach. She hadn't spoken to her mother in, what, a week, maybe two?

She could ignore the call, at least for a day or so, and then plead deadlines, but that would be a bug-eating lie. She was on top of her deadlines for the time being, and it wasn't as though her social calendar was all penciled in. Besides, the daughter's rulebook said that a mother's call had to be returned, even if it amounted to buying an economy-sized bag of trouble at the discount store. She hit Recall.

Her mother picked up. "Rita! Sweetheart! Are you all right?"

"I'm fine. I just—"

"Glad to hear it. I thought you'd fallen off the edge of the Earth. And you didn't take my call just now! Did I catch you at a bad time?"

"No, I was—"

"Sure I'm not interrupting anything?"

"No, Mom, I was just—"

"Bea," her mother corrected her automatically. If there was one thing Beatrix hated, it was being called Mom. It made her feel old. She'd been discouraging Rita from doing that since she was fourteen.

Rita started over contritely. "No, Bea, you weren't interrupting anything. I'm in the coffee shop, actually."

"With someone?" Beatrix sounded hopeful.

"No." Rita tried not to sound too sharp. It was just that whenever she and her mother—or her father, for that matter—talked, the conversation always swung around to Rita's rank among the unattached. Every time she asserted her loner status, the response was surprise and disappointment. Beatrix, especially, seemed to think that Santa Amata was a metropolitan version of Temptation Island, throbbing with sexy young singles just waiting to hook up. It was downright ridiculous. In spite of all evidence to the contrary, Beatrix remained hopeful that once, just once, Rita's story would be a little more titillating. She was like an older sister who sat up on a Saturday night waiting for her younger sister to come home from a date with the boy next door, hoping that the news would be juicy.

But neither of them was a teenager, and there was no boy

next door, or high school sweetheart, or football hero, or break dancer or biker boy. As far as Rita was concerned, Beatrix needed to grow up.

"I hate to disappoint you, Bea, but I'm alone."

"Well, a coffee shop's not so bad. Lots of young business-men fueling up on their way to work. Nice and creative ad execs. Pinstriped suits from Banker's Row. Yummy. You should start up a conversation with one or two. They're not as stuffy as you'd think, you know. Trust me." She could almost hear her mother wink.

"I'm writing," Rita answered pointedly. "It's how I get paid. I haven't got time to throw myself at strangers."

She thought she heard her mother mumble, "Might do you some good."

"What?"

"Nothing, kiddo." Bea went quiet for a while, then sighed. "Well, if ever you need—"

"No, thanks," Rita said hastily. She wasn't sure she wanted to know what Beatrix had on offer this time.

"Because, you know, speaking of writing…"

Rita braced herself. Moving from her dismal, manless state to her abysmal writing was only the second verse in an all too familiar song.

"I read your column last week…"

"Uh-huh."

"And I was thinking…"

"Yes, Mom?"

"Bea," her mother answered impatiently. This time, Rita didn't correct herself.

Bea went on. "I was just thinking, you know, sweetheart, if you ever need a few pointers… For example, what you said to Fidgety in Phoenix? Well, I don't agree with you. This poor woman was having serious sexual issues, and I don't think you took the right approach. You had the wrong perspective. Not that you probably could have had the right one, given the fact that you choose to live your life in cloisters."

"I do not," Rita managed. "And there's nothing wrong with what I said to Fidgety." Her throat was tightening up, and it was the kind of automatic response that even a swig of her favorite coffee couldn't fix. Being a relationship writer, seeking out the right words with which to say the right things, was enough of a challenge. Being a relationship writer, and living in the shadow of parents whose two blockbusters on sex and relationships had taken up permanent residence on every bestseller list in Christendom, and whose names were buzz words on the talk-show circuit, was a different story. Beatrix was a sexologist with a collection of erotic art that made her cocktail parties a hit. Her father was an anthropologist whose doctoral thesis on the primal nature of human sexuality was still one of the most requested documents in half the universities on the East Coast. As proud as she was of them, it didn't cheer her up to know they scrutinized every word she wrote.

Beatrix was undeterred. "Feel free to run your column by me next time. It wouldn't be a problem. Torrance and I—" Torrance was her father. He insisted that Rita call him by his first name, too "—we'd be happy to help. And by the way, when're we seeing you? We're home for a whole week. After that, ah…"

Rita jumped on the small conversational bone. "You're off again?"

"As usual. No rest for the wicked." Beatrix laughed. "We've got a whole week of signings in the southwest. Three or four radio programs, couple of TV spots. Most of them cable," she added dismissively. "But we are looking forward to being back in Vegas again. You know how much your father loves the cabaret. He finds it…inspiring."

Ick, Rita thought. *Here it comes….*

"Last time we hit the clubs, your father ordered champagne and strawberries up to our suite the minute we got back. I don't have to tell you, most of the champagne wound up in the hot tub—"

"Mom!" Rita pleaded. Beatrix relished regaling strangers with stories about her erotic adventures with her husband, but it wasn't the kind of thing a daughter needed to hear about her father. Why couldn't she just have a mother who played mahjongg and a father who liked golf?

"All right," Bea gave in. "Have it your way. Wouldn't want to traumatize you. But that offer still stands, okay?"

"Okay, Bea. Thank you. I will," Rita promised, scanning the sky for flying pigs. "But I really have to go. I've got a deadline."

"Say no more, I read you loud and clear. I'm hanging up, okay? But I'm aching to set eyes on you. Don't forget we live in the same town, all right?"

Rita smiled. "All right. I'll see you soon. Maybe over the weekend."

"Looking forward to it. Love you, baby." And before Rita could return her mother's air kisses, the line went dead.

The conversation left her feeling as though she'd done two rounds in the ring with Tyson. Rita slumped forward, resting her forehead on the cool tabletop, and took several deep breaths. Ah, parents. Couldn't live with 'em….

But there was work to be done. She went back to her e-mails. Junk…more junk…and then the next few messages in her In-box made Rita pause and frown. There were five e-mails, all coming from the same address, all sent within the space of three minutes, sometime yesterday. The first thing that came to her mind was that they were more of the much loathed spam, but something stopped her before she could wipe them off her screen. The subject lines of all the messages were identical: Dear, dear, *dear* Rita. That was puzzling. Spammers didn't yet have the ability to identify each of their targets individually. That technology just did not exist…did it?

Cautiously, she opened the first message.

Dear Rita,
Bet you think you're real smart.
A.F.

Rita pursed her lips. A lot of her mail came from readers, rather than people with questions. Fan mail. Some were complimentary, even fawning. Some were from men wanting to date her. A lot of it came from men in prison—all wrongfully convicted, of course—who swore they had nothing but love and respect for their "strong Nubian sister."

But not all of it was that good. Frustrated individuals, readers offended by a column or bored Web surfers looking to start a flame war—she'd had to deal with them all.

She moved to delete the other four, assuming they'd be more of same, but stopped in mid-action, morbidly curious to see what else this person had to say. She opened up another. I bet you think you're all that.

Someone needed to lighten up. Resisting the other three e-mails was impossible; she opened them all up at the same time. *Don't you?* read the third, and the fourth, in bold caps, **DON'T YOU???**

Unease replaced amusement. She opened the final message with a mixture of curiosity and apprehension. It was cryptic— and a little too threatening for comfort.

Are you afraid of heights?
A.F.

Rita felt her skin crawl. If this was a joke, it wasn't funny. She took another look at the e-mail address, but it was simply A.F., the same as the writer's signoff, coming from one of those generic mail hosting Web sites that everyone used when they preferred to keep their regular one private. She had one herself. That wasn't much help.

She hit the Delete key a little harder than necessary, sending the offending messages into the ether, and leaned back in her chair. This called for another chug of coffee. She lifted her cup, but it was empty. She left her possessions where they were. After all, she'd been a regular here for years. It wasn't as if she thought anyone would touch her stuff for the few seconds it took to go to the counter and back. She ordered another coffee, keeping it simple this time. Plain, with the tiniest squirt of hazelnut in deference to the aforementioned, lamentable eight extra pounds. She went back to her table, sat and downed half the steaming cup before returning her attention to the glowing screen before her.

A new e-mail had come in.

It was from A.F.

Even the coffee wasn't enough to keep the chill out of her blood. She opened it at once, and stared at the unblinking words before her. How's the coffee?

Chapter 2

Rita felt the hair at the back of her neck snap to attention. She put her hands to the base of her skull, tugging at the long, dark brown double-stranded twists that fell about her shoulders. *How's the coffee?* How could this man, whoever he was, know where she was, and what she was drinking? The possibilities nauseated her. Either someone knew her habits so well that he could make an educated guess as to her whereabouts at seven every morning, or she was being watched. Right at this very moment.

Wildly, she looked around, unable to keep the movement casual and circumspect. Had she been followed? Could someone be right there, in Starbucks, quietly watching her? She glanced from table to table, her heart feeling uncomfortably large in her chest.

But all she could see were the regulars, caffeine addicts just like her who turned up every morning, just as she did, to sit in companionable, familiar surroundings while they had their morning fix. Rita knew them so well, she even had names for them.

Across from her, there was the tall, agonizingly thin man who wore business suits and smelled of expensive cologne. Every day he carefully withdrew the financial section of the papers to read over his coffee, then left as silently as he came, abandoning the rest of the paper in a neat heap for whoever occupied his seat next. She privately called him William Wadsworth, Senior.

Closest to her was an older man, who wore a cable-knit cardigan and tweed jacket whatever the weather, and who took plain coffee and a cheese sandwich every morning. No variations. No substitutions. He arrived at the same time, had his breakfast and left at the same time. Sometimes he timidly invited her or one of the other regulars to sit at his table, but whenever she accepted he never said much, just had his coffee and threw her the occasional shy smile. He always left a fifty-cent tip on the table. Rita felt sorry for him. She thought of him as Uncle Harold.

Then there was the strange Goth girl who, like her, always took the same seat if she could get it, near the window. She was about eighteen, although it was hard to tell under the mass of black, greasy hair that fell over her face. Her skin was the color of oatmeal, and the thick, smudged kohl rimming her eyes made her look as though she was losing out on a lot of sleep. She wore the same black hoodie, dark gray jeans, black socks and black high-top Converse sneakers every day. The only hint of color about her was the dozen or so plastic bracelets on one arm, and an oversized silver pendant, representing some arcane symbol, between her small breasts.

She was hunched over her PDA, thumbs flying as she moved the controls to her game, head bobbing to the rhythm of the music being piped into her ears via noodle-thin wires. Rita had decided that her name was Drucilla.

A few joggers were buying drinks at the counter, and a young couple she hadn't seen before were wrapped up in each other, sharing a chair made for one. Otherwise, the coffee shop was quiet.

The staff, then? Could someone behind the counter have discreetly shot off an e-mail, and were they now covertly watching her, enjoying her reaction? That would be hard to believe. She glanced in their direction, but they were engrossed in their duties, hurrying to and fro in their green aprons, getting ready for the morning rush. Unless the brace-faced youngster fiddling with the digital register was also logged on to the Net at the same time, the scary note hadn't come from inside the coffee shop.

That left someone outside. The prickling of her scalp morphed into a throb at her temple. She looked furtively out the window, wondering queasily which of the dozens of pedestrians hurrying down Independence Avenue could be the one. But nobody so much as glanced inside. Served her right for sitting at the window. Making a sitting duck of herself. Tomorrow she was sitting against the farthest wall, facing the door.

The coffee tasted bitter and cold to her now, although it was neither. She set it down and packed up her computer.

Outside, in the mild autumn air, she turned west on Independence and followed it a few scant blocks before turning north onto Jubilee, where her apartment sat midway along the short street. It was an aging building, a sedate brownstone that only rose to a height of five stories, so that the nearby buildings towered over it, cutting out much of the natural light. Carved busts of angels once adorned the facade, but, after the first one worked free of its moorings and fell, the landlords took the rest of them down. Pale, angel-shaped scars remained on the wall, ghostly outlines etched into the grime.

Real estate agents euphemistically described the building as "reminiscent of its former glory," but she liked its charm. Elaborate brickwork decorated the doorway and windows, the tilework throughout was spectacular, and the hot water worked most of the time. Besides, when you considered what they were charging for rent in Santa Amata, she was getting a bargain.

As she ran up the five steps to the main door, she glanced at her watch. She was ten minutes late for her daily jogging date with her best friend, Cassie, thanks to her distraction back in the coffee shop. Hurriedly, she took the stairs to the third floor, not bothering to wait for the elevator, opened up her apartment, tossed her computer and newspaper onto the couch and left again. There was no need to change as she was already in her sweats.

By the time she made it to their regular meeting place, the convenience store around the corner, Cassie was there, leaning against a parking meter and doing stretches, bringing her knee up to her chest and holding it for counts of twenty. Considering her more-than-generous bustline, which dwarfed Rita's fairly substantial C cups by several sizes, this was not quite as easy as it seemed.

"You're late, Steadman."

Rita began her leg bends. "I know. Sorry. I was, uh…." She wondered if she should say anything about the nasty e-mails. Was it worth getting into? She did get them from time to time, so it wasn't a big deal. Although there was the eerie possibility that A.F. had known where she'd be this morning, she decided to forget it. "I was answering mail," she said instead, quite truthfully.

"And pumping your body full of poison," Cassie countered. As a penance for keeping her waiting, she loped off, not affording Rita the time to warm up.

Rita caught up with her, even though the mild throbbing at her temples persisted. Maybe a jog was just the ticket to make the beginnings of a stress headache go away. Cassie was one of those health food evangelists who took pleasure in pointing out the dietary transgressions of others. She thought eating red meat was a crime and *had* to know exactly which spring her water came from. In spite of this, her curves were not those of a fervent dieter, but Cassie dismissed her bustline and bottom as hereditary, and left it at that.

Rita defended her drug of choice. "The detrimental effects of coffee are greatly exaggerated. It's good for you, actually."

"Says who?"

"Says the May issue of *Niobe*. If there's anybody who should remember that, it should be you." Apart from being Rita's best friend, Cassie was also a senior editor at the magazine.

Cassie blew a raspberry. "The opinions expressed therein are not necessarily those of management."

Both women laughed.

"Speaking of which," Rita said as they found their stride, "how's work?"

Cassie rolled her eyes. "Don't ask. I had the awfulest, awfulest day yesterday. The art department sent up the new cover layout, and it's a joke. The model weighed about twenty pounds! Does anyone around there ever listen to what I say? *Niobe* is a magazine for *real* women, not scarecrows! I sent it back and told them to get me a model with some flesh on her bones. Someone who looks like she's had a meal this month. You know?"

"Just wait 'til the scarecrows' union gets on your back."

"Oh, yeah? Ha! Your mom'd be proud of me. You know how she's always raving on about a positive body image for women— never mind she's still a perfect size six at her age."

At least that would make her proud of *someone,* Rita thought. "She called me this morning."

"Yeah? Speak of the devil. What are Ma and Pa Kinsey up to this time? Nude boogie-boarding in Ibiza?"

"Close enough. They're off to Vegas. Signings, lectures, interviews, the usual."

"I heard Bea on the radio the other night. She was a riot! Is it true she had male strippers at her book signing in Denver?"

"That's what she told me. And I wouldn't put anything past her."

"Aw, Rita, don't be like that. You have no idea how lucky you are to have them as your parents. When I was young, my folks threw a fit if I bought a skirt that showed off my knees. Yours have got to be two of the most modern, forward-thinking sixty-year-olds around. It must have been so cool growing up in their house."

So you'd imagine, unless you actually had to do it, Rita thought. But she trotted along, pretending she had to take her pulse. Cassie didn't push it, and they both fell silent.

They jogged in perfect synchronicity with the ease of two

people who had done this for a very long time, dodging commuters and other joggers, keeping up the rhythm by running in place at traffic lights, all the way down to De Menzes Park, the pride of Santa Amata. The spread covered several acres of prime, gently undulating land. At the turn of the last century, it had been a horse farm, owned by one of the founding fathers of the small east-coast city. After the grandson of the patriarch died in the late 1950s, his widow donated it to the city. They turned it into the site of choice for a host of community activities, from Girl Scout bake sales to Little League games to summer kite-flying contests to outdoor yoga classes.

They entered by the eastern gate and took their favorite footpath, the one that led to the enormous man-made lake that took up almost a quarter of the park's area. The trees that ringed the lake had begun shedding their leaves, which crunched under their pounding feet like musical accompaniment.

Cassie cleared her throat. "Rita…" she began.

Rita was too engrossed in the pleasing rustle of the leaves to pick up on the note in her friend's voice which, under other circumstances, would have set off alarm bells. "Yeah?"

"You know how I'm always saying you should get out more often?"

"You know how I'm always saying I'm happy with my life just the way it is? Dateless?" she joked back.

Cassie didn't laugh. "Well," she began, and then stalled. She tried again. "Well…"

This time, Rita heard that note loud and clear. "Well, what?"

"I have a favor to ask you."

She didn't like the sound of that. "Tell me you're going away for the weekend and need your plants watered."

"No, it's not that."

She was almost afraid to ask. "What, then?"

"I need you to go out on a date with me."

"Sorry, I'm not that sort of girl."

"You're being deliberately obtuse, and you know it. I need you to go on a *double* date with me."

Rita halted, shoes scraping on the footpath. "You're kidding, right?"

Cassie, who had stopped a few yards farther down, turned and jogged back to her side. "No, I'm dead serious." She jogged on the spot, keeping her rhythm, even though Rita was standing stock still.

"Cassie, we're two sane, adult women. I haven't been on a double date since I was seventeen. Why, for heaven's sake? Is my lack of a love life that pathetic? Because, let me tell you, I'm perfectly—"

"Perfectly happy being single. I know. It's not that. I need you." She stopped her on-the-spot trot and faced Rita.

"Okay," Rita gave in wearily. "Out with it."

"Remember last week how I told you about this guy who chased down a purse snatcher for me?"

"Ah, yes, your knight in a three-piece suit."

"His name's Clark."

"Okay, Clark. What about him?"

"Well, he asked me out."

"You talked to him for ten seconds and he asked you out?"

"Well, uh, it was more than ten seconds. After this total stranger chases down my purse for three blocks and brings it back, I feel like I owe him a few moments of my time, you know? So I thank him, and the next thing I know we're chatting. About the weather and the news and the Middle East and what we do for a living. Then what d'ya know? We've been standing on the sidewalk for more than half an hour. He apologizes for keeping me, and says he'd better let me go. I say, nice meeting you. And then we go on talking for another fifteen minutes."

"You stood on the sidewalk in rush hour traffiç talking with a stranger for forty-five minutes?"

"He brought me back my purse!"

"Thank him, slip him a twenty, and go your separate ways."

Cassie was scandalized. "You don't slip a twenty to a lawyer in a fifteen-hundred-dollar suit!"

"Lawyer, huh?" Cassie and a corporate man? Could've blown her down. Cassie's idea of a thrill was a galaxy away. Her men tended to sport do-rags, wear way too much bling, and drive hand-detailed, ten-second rides. Most of them had jobs that paid by the fortnight.

"Yeah. His name's Clark. Got his own company, on Temple Street. Niiiice. He's involved in the negotiations for that new mall they're putting up on—"

Cassie had a tendency to ramble. Rita reeled her back in. "What about the date?"

Cassie came back to the subject without any further prodding. "He called me up and asked me out."

"You gave a stranger on the street your number?"

"Not exactly. I told him I was a magazine editor, and he tracked me down. Not many magazines come out of this neck of the woods, I guess."

"Not that many. But don't you think that someone tracking you down, calling around blind and asking for you, was kind of creepy?"

"No! It was romantic!"

"Ah. Romance."

Cassie pouted. "Well, it was!"

Rita didn't bother arguing. "So, you like him?"

Cassie's dark skin glowed prettily. "Uh-huh."

"Go out with him, then." It wasn't the kind of thing she herself would have done, but Cassie was different. Cassie walked around with magenta hair.

"I will, but you gotta come, too."

"Why?"

"Because he could be wacko."

"What makes you think he's wacko?"

"I don't *think* he's wacko, I said he *could be* wacko." Cassie's large brown eyes were pleading. "Rita, please. You know how things have been with me. After what happened and all…"

Rita softened at once. The left sleeve of Cassie's lime-green sweat top hid a long, ugly scar, inflicted a little less than a year ago by an ex-boyfriend just days after she'd tried to call it quits. The man had begged her not to end the relationship, peppered her with calls and unwanted visits, before his passion turned to rage. He stormed into her office drunk, calling her every name he could think of for dumping him, while at the same time begging for a second chance. When Cassie refused, he went after her with a letter opener. Only the intervention of a security guard had prevented a tragedy.

The fact that her jealous lover had been put away did nothing to erase Cassie's fear. It killed Rita to watch her, a natural flirt who gravitated toward men and loved going out, withdraw from male company. Her friend hadn't been on a date since. Now she'd met someone she liked, and was afraid.

"Let's walk," Rita said gently. She didn't much feel like running anymore. They fell into step along the footpath. "Tell me more."

"Well, he calls me up at the office yesterday and apologizes for hunting me down like that. I say okay, no problem. He says he really wants to see me."

"And you said?"

"I say I'd like that. But if he wants a date, it's got to be a double. He says okay, he understands. Please, Rita. Just one date. Just so I can get to know him better. And you can give me your opinion on him. You know I value your advice."

"Dear Rita," she quoted, smiling, "can you tell me if I should see this man again?"

"Exactly."

Rita stopped walking again and looked out onto the lake, buying herself a few seconds. The reds, oranges and yellows of the changing leaves were reflected in the rippling water, and the clear blue of the sky filled the middle. Why not? It was only one night. That was what friends were for.

"So," she said, "who's the frog your prince is bringing along?"

"He's not a frog. He's a very good friend of Clark's. His partner, in fact."

"Another lawyer?" Ick. She wasn't one for the corporate type, either.

"Uh-huh. Clark says he's smart—*and* good-looking."

"Ah, a smart, *good-looking* lawyer. Let me at him."

"Rita!" Cassie protested. "You never know, you might like him. Like your dad says, sometimes serendipity doesn't just happen. Sometimes you have to hunt it down."

"My dad says a bunch of things," Rita said briskly. "But I don't need to like this guy. I don't even care if I do or not. I'm in, but just for you, okay? Does this catch of a guy have a name?"

"Dorian. Dorian Black."

"Dorian *Black?* What, is he Dorian Gray's evil twin?"

Cassie made a face. "I know! Sounds like a joke, but that's what Clark said."

"Does he have a cursed painting in his basement, too?"

"Attic," Cassie corrected.

"Huh?"

"Dorian Gray's cursed picture was in his attic."

"Oh. Right. And when and where are we going to have the pleasure of their company?"

"Tonight." Then Cassie added, sheepishly, "Clark suggested Vimanmek Palace."

"You hate Thai food. You think curry is a toxin and coconut milk causes heart attacks. You told him so, didn't you?"

Cassie gave her a level look. "I told him that sounded lovely."

Rita tried not to roll her eyes. "So my favorite feminist is willing to gulp down cuisine she thinks is sure to kill her rather than admit to a new guy she doesn't like it."

"That's pretty much it, yeah."

"The sisterhood of feminists will miss you," Rita couldn't resist teasing, but put her arm around her friend. "Don't worry. We'll have a nice evening. I'll scope out your guy, and I'm sure that by the end of the evening his report card will be glowing."

Cassie hugged her gratefully back. "Thanks, girl."

"Don't ever say I don't love ya."

Chapter 3

Dorian Black set his mouse down on the polished surface of his desk. The desk was the most imposing thing in his office. He only kept it because it had been a gift from his father who had spent way too much money on it the day his son began to practice. It was massive, made out of dark oak, with brass handles on the drawers. His dad had half-seriously called it "a power desk for a soon-to-be very powerful man." It was hardly the kind of furniture he would have bought himself, but it was a gesture born of paternal love and pride, and that made it precious.

The rest of the office was less daunting. It was painted a warm honey, with a few line drawings Dorian had brought home from a trip to the Sudan a few years before, comfortable visitors' chairs set around the low coffee table where he held most of his conversations with his clients, a small bar that contained, instead of alcohol, a variety of coffees, plain and flavored teas, cookies and Fig Newtons (his favorite snack), all to be served to his guests on simple stoneware. He understood that a visit to a lawyer's office was probably one of the most traumatic experiences most people had to face. Anything he could do to make that experience a little more bearable was worth it.

He swiveled in his chair to face his partner, Clark, who was staring out of the widepane glass window of his office, down onto Temple Street. He didn't know whether to laugh or cuss. "*This* is my blind date?" He pointed at the *Niobe* Web site up on the computer screen.

Clark tore his attention away from the view. He had covertly been watching Dorian, reflected in the glass, waiting in silence as he read. "What's wrong with her?"

"Apart from the fact that I don't do blind dates, and I especially don't do double dates, I've read through the last few months of her archives and I've arrived at the only possible conclusion."

"What's that?"

"This Rita woman hates men."

"Why do you say that?"

"Oh, I don't know," he drawled. "Maybe because every single bit of advice she's given is anti-man."

Clark came over to perch on the edge of Dorian's desk, gently moving aside a sheaf of documents. "Maybe it's not so much anti-man as pro-woman," he suggested.

"Nice try." Dorian shook his head. "Have you read this stuff? For every woman that takes her advice, there's one more man out in the cold. She's just one more love guru who isn't about love at all. She's about a woman's need to always be right."

Clark peered at the screen and read the correspondence open in Dorian's Web browser. "Seems to me, a couple of these guys had it coming. Look at this one—stealing from his poor girlfriend…."

"Maybe this one," he conceded, "but—"

"Dorian," Clark interrupted, "it's just for one night. Just one meal. I'm not suggesting a marriage of convenience. If you don't like Rita, just stick out the evening and you two can go your separate ways. I'm asking this as a favor."

To Dorian, it sounded like madness. This was the twenty-first century. What woman over eighteen insisted on dragging her best friend along on a first date? And Clark hardly looked as though he were trying out for the lead role in *The Texas Chainsaw Massacre III*. He was one of the most buttoned-down men Dorian knew. He had his hair cut once every three weeks, did his nails every fortnight, bought new suits twice a year, owned three or four identical shirts in each color and had his underwear dry cleaned. Clark was as harmless as it was possible to be and still be breathing. "Why's she so insistent on this gruesome foursome?"

Clark shrugged. "She didn't say much, other than that she was naturally cautious. I don't blame her. It's a scary world out there."

Dorian snorted. "I'd have thought that chasing down a purse snatcher half your age on her behalf would have been enough of a character reference for any woman."

Clark looked bashful. "It was just one of those things. She was standing next to me when this guy knocked her over. Next thing I knew, she was yelling about her purse. I just reacted. If I'd thought about it, I probably wouldn't have run him down. He could have been armed."

"But he wasn't, and good won out over evil."

Clark peered at Dorian for traces of sarcasm. "I guess." He took on a more optimistic tone. "So you're doing it, right?"

Dorian smiled. Clark was his friend, partner and mentor. What was one evening? He'd have done much more, if Clark had asked, and they both knew it. "Of course I will."

He took another look at the screen, examining the small photo that accompanied each article. "Dear Rita" was a good-looking woman with skin that made him think of warm cinnamon. She looked less than thirty, with a mass of fine, dark brown corkscrew twists pulled back into a bun at the top of her head. He wondered if that, together with the stylish glasses she wore, were merely affectations in an effort to look more mature and agony-auntish. The glasses did nothing to obscure the clarity of her honey-colored eyes. Even in the tiny photograph, those eyes were disarming. They at once drew him in and made him squirm. Her cheekbones were wonderful, and her shapely lips tinted by a conservative but attractive shade of lipstick. It was little more than a head and shoulders shot; just enough to enable him to see a hint of cleavage under the beige blouse.

From over his shoulder, Clark observed, "She's cute."

"She is," he agreed. He added slyly, "As cute as your Cassie?"

"Nope," Clark said immediately. "But you could do worse."

Dorian laughed. "I suppose I could. You can drop the sales pitch now. I said I'd go. You picked a restaurant?"

"Vimanmek Palace, that new Thai place. It got rave reviews in the Food and Beverage section of *The Register* last month. We have reservations for seven-thirty."

Dorian let out a bark of surprised laughter. "You're kidding, right?"

"Nope. Dead serious."

"But spicy foods make you sick. You can't even take Tabasco in your Bloody Mary."

He looked abashed. "I don't know what got into me. One minute I was asking her out, the next minute I was suggesting a Thai restaurant. I guess I wanted to sound more adventurous. I'm a boring man, Dorian. My idea of a culinary adventure is dinner at TGI Friday's."

Dorian was quick to leap to his friend's defense, even from a self-inflicted attack. "You're not boring. You are one of the most intelligent and educated human beings on the face of the Earth."

"If that isn't boring, I don't know what is." Clark smiled wryly. "But at least she sounded keen. Said she'd been dying to try it, too."

"That's all that matters. Chug a bottle of antacid before you get there, and you'll be all right."

"Want us to leave together, from here?"

"I doubt I'll make it back into the office today. You go ahead, I'll meet you there."

"Seven-thirty, right?" Clark still looked anxious, despite Dorian's promise.

He must really like this girl. Dorian did his best to reassure him. "My word is my bond." He glanced at the heavy platinum watch on his left wrist, rose, took up his jacket from over the back of his chair and shrugged it on. "Got to go now."

"Elcroft Green?" Clark guessed.

"Yep. Gonna be a long one."

"Good luck."

"Thanks." He'd need it. Although the name Elcroft Green sounded like a day spa, it was, in fact, a large medium-security men's prison in the worst part of town. There was nothing green in it or around it, just a forbidding expanse of concrete walls, watchtowers, twisted barbed wire, gun turrets and metal bars, all designed to keep the dregs of society inside while they paid their debts. Dorian did eight hours there every two weeks, taking on some of the toughest cases pro bono.

The law he practiced was not criminal law, though, but family law. In the case of these men, he mostly handled custody battles, visitation rights and other unjust situations regarding their children. It was a sad fact that many of these men, the vast majority of whom were black, lost not only their freedom but access to their children as a result of their sentencing. Disgruntled and often vengeful mothers sought to deprive them of their parental rights not just for the duration of their sentence, but even after their release.

This was wrong. Just because a man made some mistakes, it did not mean that he should lose the right to be a dad. There were too many children in the world growing up fatherless. That, in itself, was a tragedy. As long as a prisoner had never been convicted of a violent crime or a crime against children, he was willing to take on any custody or visitation rights case for free.

In fact, he had single-handedly lobbied the warden, and later the governor, to ensure facilities for non-violent prisoners to meet and play with their children in a simulated home environment, just as women prisoners were allowed to do. The visiting house on prison grounds, with a playground that featured swings, slides, jungle gyms, and even a basketball hoop, was the result of his badgering. Dorian considered it the finest victory of his career. His work at Elcroft Green was not a job, it was a calling.

As he put his hand on the doorknob, he sought to reassure Clark one final time. "I'll see you there tonight." He couldn't resist adding, "I can't wait to meet this Cassie you're so entranced with. And I *certainly* can't wait to meet Dear Rita!"

Rita woke up with a start, sitting bolt upright in bed. The apartment was in darkness, which was a good thing, because even a sliver of light right now would be a dagger between her eyes. The nagging headache that had begun that morning had exploded into a full-on migraine sometime during the day, with all the pain, nausea and light sensitivity the devil could visit upon her. After popping more than the recommended dose of pain pills, she'd given up the battle and taken to bed around three in the afternoon, and lay there moaning, with a cold compress on her forehead and her face pressed against the wall.

Now something had woken her up, an inner alarm clock that would not be silenced. Still under the bewildering effects of sleep, she searched her mind for that thing, that very important thing she needed to do right this minute, but came up empty.

Why was she up? Was it a sudden noise, a vicious jolt of pain or the subconscious knowledge that she was supposed to be doing something? She put her hand to her head, and the touch sent waves of pain through her.

Then she remembered.

Cassie.

Oh, God.

She threw herself to the other side of the bed and her fingers frantically sought the clock. Turning it around, she could see the green glow of large digits. It was ten to seven. Cassie was coming to get her in about ten minutes, and Cassie was never late.

She toyed with the idea of calling to say she was sick, but the thought itself was a betrayal. Cassie meant everything to her. If Rita had been lying in the woods with her leg caught in a bear trap, she'd have gnawed it off in order to make it tonight.

She clicked on the bedside lamp and winced. She stripped, dashed into the shower and was out again after barely getting her skin wet. Her legs needed shaving and her hair could have done with a quick shampoo, but neither project was plausible. She toweled herself down, dragged on mismatched underwear, and threw open her closet door, cursing herself for not having decided in advance what she would be wearing. She chose a faithful old standby: a slim-fitting, warm burgundy skirt that reached mid-calf (thus solving the problem of the unshaven legs) and a sheer champagne top with a neckline that showed cleavage without plunging all the way to her belly button.

She didn't have time to pile her twists up onto her head as she liked to do when dining out, so she satisfied herself by smoothing them so that, at the very least, they didn't look like a fright wig. Now, for makeup—

Her phone rang. Rita snatched up the receiver. "Cass?"

"I'm outside, babe," Cassie chirped.

Rita glanced at her dresser, strewn with pots of color, lipsticks and brushes, and hesitated. "Uh…."

"Ready, right?" Cassie asked, but her question was not a question. It was a statement that demanded an affirmative response.

Rita hesitated. Her reflection in the dresser mirror wore no makeup. Her brows needed neatening and her forehead was just a tad too shiny. She was going out on a blind date looking, if not like something the cat dragged in, at least like something the cat would have given serious consideration to.

But Cassie was a bundle of nerves and a tangle of excitement, and Rita didn't have the heart to keep her waiting a moment longer. After all, it wasn't as if this was a real date, with prospects for dates in the future. This was a favor for a friend, an evening to be endured, to be ended with relief. Her "date," this Dorian Black, was probably as reluctant as she was to be dragged along as third and fourth wheels. If he wasn't, if he thought this was anything more than it seemed, he was a bigger nerd than she expected him to be.

"Rita?" Cassie's anxious voice was tinny in her ear. "You there?"

"Uh, yeah." She regained control of her scrambled thoughts. "I'm here. I'm on my way down."

"Good." Cassie sounded relieved. "I was afraid…." She didn't finish.

"On my way," Rita repeated, and hung up. Pausing only to slip on a pair of pumps that were almost the same shade as her skirt, and to snatch up her purse and a light coat for the cool evening, she darted through the front door and raced downstairs. Her head pounded with every footfall.

Someone had tried very hard to create an ambience of soothing, almost trance-like calm at Vimanmek Palace. As soon as Rita and Cassie walked in, they were greeted by the tinkling of brass and the trickling of water through bamboo pipes. The interior was decorated throughout with shades of avocado, gold and a warm red, with rich wall tapestries and rows of bronze statuettes, the largest of which, a benevolent Buddha, dominated the lobby.

They were escorted into a reception area by a Thai girl clad in silk wraps of hummingbird colors: gold, emerald, turquoise and rose pink. Despite her headache, Rita was entranced by the grace with which the girl moved, and the butterfly flutters she made with her slender hands as she gestured to a corner of the room before she bowed and disappeared.

Standing there, looking nervous, was a slightly-built man in a silver-gray suit, with sandy, thinning hair, pale gray eyes and a hopeful half smile. He had been staring intently at the doorway, and when he saw them, his face brightened.

"That's him," Cassie hissed.

Rita's brows shot up. "You didn't tell me—"

"That he's white?" Cassie interrupted defensively.

"That he's *old*," she responded, just as quickly.

"He's fifty-one," Cassie retorted. "That's not old."

Your dad's fifty-four, Rita would have reminded her, but they were within earshot now and Clark stepped forward, both hands outstretched. "Cassie! I'm so glad you came. You look lovely!" He blushed madly as he said it and grasped Cassie's hands in his.

Rita looked at Cassie properly for the first time this evening. She did look lovely. Her short natural hair gleamed as though washed in sunshine. Her makeup was flawless, as was her manicure. She wore a deep green wrap dress with long sleeves and a high collar, a surprising choice for the normally unconventional Cassie. She even had a large silver brooch pinned over her left breast. Although it did little to disguise her outrageous figure, it made her look several years older. She tried not to feel too weirded out by the fact that Cassie was disguised as her own mother, and allowed herself to be introduced.

"This is my best friend, Rita Steadman." Cassie indicated her with a sweep of her arm. "Rita, this is Clark Burrows." She added unnecessarily, "He's the guy I told you about."

Clark engulfed her hands in both his warm ones. "Rita. Delighted, delighted! Cassie has told me so much about you."

"Really?" Rita murmured the standard response. "I hope it was all good."

"Oh, it certainly was." He beamed. "We talked on the phone for hours yesterday, and trust me, half the conversation was about what a great friend you are, and how much you've been through together."

Rita cast a glance at Cassie, who was doing nothing but standing there, smiling. She'd known that Clark had called yesterday, but she had no idea that the conversation had gone on for hours.

There was an awkward silence, where everyone seemed to be waiting for someone else to say or do something. Clark rushed in to fill it. "I think we'd better have a seat, ladies. Dorian called—that's Rita's date." He smiled reassuringly at Rita. "He said he'd be a little late. He suggested we go ahead and order, and he'll be here as soon as he can."

She couldn't help but feel a bit irritated. She'd made the effort to come along on this little caper, even though she was halfway through death's doorway. So why couldn't this Dorian guy?

Their table was large and ornate, laid with gold-rimmed china and bright silk napkins, and brushed by feathery fronds that hung down from potted plants on the wall. A water feature tinkled nearby, and small brass chimes swayed idly overhead, even though there was no discernible breeze. Rita accepted the chair that Clark held out for her, and, glad for the distraction, began to peruse the menu. She listened with mild amusement as Cassie and Clark discussed the choices, knowing full well that Cassie was doing rapid calculations in her head about fat grams, sodium content and such. She pitched in with suggestions of some of the more innocuous items on the menu for their communal dishes. Eventually, they agreed upon several simple dishes, although Clark did persuade her to order a spicy green curry to share with Dorian, promising that Dorian was a more adventurous eater.

Over hot lemongrass soup, the conversation became more relaxed. Rita found herself liking Clark. Though hardly a sparkling wit, he was charming in a Midwest farm boy sort of way. Even his nervousness was endearing.

But by the time the main courses arrived and there was no sign of Dorian, Rita's irritation rose again. It was an awkward, left-at-the-altar kind of situation, made more uncomfortable by the fact that Cassie and Clark kept trying to draw her into their conversation, as though they felt sorry for her sitting alone like the cheese. She was thankful, but inwardly she seethed. If this Dorian

Dear Rita

person thought she'd be all sugar and spice when he did turn up—
if he turned up at all—he had another think coming.

As sweetly as she could, she asked Clark, "Are you sure
nothing's happened to Dorian?"

He frowned slightly, as if the idea hadn't occurred to him.
"He's usually not this late, but you can't always put a time frame
on legal matters. If you forgive me for using the phone at the
table, I'll give him a call." He withdrew a small cell phone from
his breast pocket and was just dialing it, again murmuring apologies, when he looked up, past Rita's shoulder, and smiled. "There
he is now."

In spite of herself, Rita turned in her seat, toward the entrance,
wondering if she would be able to guess which of the patrons
entering through the doorway would be him. Would her date for
the evening turn out to be another soft-spoken, homegrown Idaho
farm boy old enough to be her father? But there was just one man
standing there, and this was no Idaho farm boy.

The man in the doorway was so tall, he had to dip his head
slightly in order to clear the low-hanging silken ropes curving
down from the lintel. His skin was darker than dark, and as he
drew closer she could see that so, too, were his hair and eyes.
One image ran through her caffeine-addicted brain: coffee…
black. The man's skin made her thirsty.

Rita sat up straighter in her seat.

The breadth of his shoulders gave balance to his height, and
the sedate navy of his suit was offset by a shirt the exact color
of a cloudless winter morning sky. He walked quickly without
seeming rushed, and made his way directly to their table, where
Clark was already on his feet with his hand extended. The two
men shook hands warmly, with Dorian uttering apologies as fast
as Clark could brush them aside. Introductions were quickly
made, and Rita found her hand engulfed in Dorian's huge one.
Closer now, she could examine his features in greater detail.

His brows were dense and arched, and unbelievably black

eyes were framed by lashes as thick as moth's wings. A shapely nose drew her eyes downward to a wide mouth that was saying something she could not hear, as the tinkling of the fountain nearby had become in her ears as loud as a pounding surf.

Unfashionably late or not, Dorian Black was easily one of the best looking men she had ever met.

This was not a good thing.

Chapter 4

Dorian looked down into the face of the woman he had been shanghaied into having dinner with. Her eyes were even clearer and more honeyed than they had appeared in the little photograph that accompanied her column. With her hair let down (and a little messier than he would have expected for such an occasion) she looked younger, too. She appeared flustered, almost as though she hadn't expected him to actually turn up. He was, after all, forty-five minutes late. For someone who didn't understand how trying his prison visit day could be, and how insane things got behind those high stone walls, such lateness would seem unforgivably rude.

He repeated his apologies, this time, directly to her. "Sincerely sorry for keeping you waiting, Miss Steadman. Please forgive me."

She looked even more flustered. "It's, uh, Rita."

He cocked his head to one side. "Rita, then. It's a lovely name," he added, more for want of something pleasant to say than out of any particular affinity for the name, which was a perfectly run-of-the-mill one, as far as he was concerned.

"Thank you." She accepted the compliment as though she knew he hadn't really meant it.

There was an awkward moment, the kind that usually falls between two people who have been thrown together against their wills. She motioned for him to sit. As he sank onto padded satin, he wasn't even aware he was sighing. He was drained, not just from the pressure of having to discuss so many different cases with so many different prisoners in one day, but from the emotional toll that delving into the lives of these men took on him. He needed to remind himself that it was worth it. Sometimes his work brought disenfranchised fathers joy. Often, though, in spite of everything he could do, all they suffered was more heartache and rejection. Most nights after leaving Elcroft Green, all he wanted to do was go home, sip a solitary drink, shower and pull the covers over his head.

But the occasion demanded good cheer, so he listened attentively as Rita led him through the array of dishes, describing each one as though she had memorized the menu. Tofu rolls, fish in cucumber sauce, steamed seafood salad, roasted duck smothered in cashews, chicken in green curry, wild boar simmered in coconut milk, assorted vegetable dishes, two kinds of rice, two kinds of noodles and cups generously filled with rice wine. He wondered how poor Clark was managing. His joking advice about chugging antacid seemed inadequate. After a meal like this, Clark would need a medic.

"Are you sure there aren't four more people coming to help us finish this?" He piled his plate with food kept warm by small heating trays under each platter.

Rita smiled, and he noticed how perfect her teeth were and how white they appeared, even though she wore no lipstick to throw them into contrast. Alluring, he mused, but as he glanced at the perfectly made-up face of her friend, he wondered how it was that she had not used so much as a little lip color or blush. He wasn't the sort to expect that women be exquisitely painted at all times, but he was an observant man, one who made his living trying to get to the bottom of a person's personality, discerning their motives and characteristics. Was the lack of makeup a matter of artlessness, disinterest or a political statement? His mind went back to her columns, and the men-are-dogs, women-are-goddesses spirit of them, and decided that the reason was probably behind door number three.

Again, he glanced across at Cassie, trying to get a handle on her without being too obvious about it. He'd known Clark for ten years. First, Clark had been his professor at law school. Then, when Clark grew bored with teaching and returned to private practice, Dorian had moved from summer intern, to wet-behind-the-ears employee, and finally, to full partner and trusted friend. In all that time, he didn't remember Clark ever acting so impulsively.

She didn't seem to be his type. The racial difference between the two was not surprising, even though he had never known Clark to date black women, because Clark was one of the most unbiased and unbigoted people he knew. It was more a matter of the age difference, which was twenty years if it was a day, and the vivacity that rolled off her in waves. Even though it was obvious that she was trying to dress older than she really was, he could sense by the way she moved and talked, the arresting color of her hair and the aura she had about her that she was much more unconventional than she was trying to look.

But the two were entranced by each other, chatting away and laughing as though they were alone. He couldn't remember when last he'd seen Clark so animated. Even though from time to time he remembered his role as host and tried to encourage Dorian and Rita to take part in the conversation, it was obvious that he had eyes and ears only for the lovely, curvaceous young woman across from him.

Dorian wished him well.

He returned his attention to Rita, who was staring intently down at her plate, and kicked himself for having the bad manners to let his mind wander and leave her out of the loop. He tried to initiate some idle chatter. The only thing he knew about her was her work, so he decided that that was as good a place as any to begin.

"Do you just write your column, or do you do other things as well?"

She seemed relieved to have something to talk about. "Mainly the column, but I write commentaries and investigative pieces for *Niobe* as well, when I come up with an idea they're willing to buy."

"Pieces about what?"

She shrugged. "Women's issues. Relationship articles, stories about families, and the difficulties they have staying together. Or how hard it is when things go wrong."

"So, your background is in counseling or psychology?"

She looked at him in surprise, as though she had never considered that. "No. Actually, my college degree is in classical literature."

He thought again about some of the cutting remarks he read from her that morning, and his brows lifted. Shelling out advice to the lovelorn without a solid backing was like dispensing medicine without a permit. What made her think she had the right to tell other people how to conduct their love lives? Unable to stop himself, he probed. "I always thought of agony aunts as being matriarchs in their sixties, who have a whole lifetime of experience—good marriages, bad marriages, kids and grandkids, fights and breakups—to rely on when they give advice. What do you base your advice on? You hardly look old enough to be a shoulder for the lovelorn to cry on."

She bristled visibly, and he couldn't help but notice how cute she looked doing it. The color in her cheeks made the absent blusher unnecessary. "I'm not that young!"

Maybe not, but she was hardly the Oracle of Delphi. Her indignation was endearing. Like a cat with an irritated mouse, he tweaked her some more. "Besides, it seems to me that your advice hardly ever gives the man in question a fighting chance. Women's magazine or not, I'd have expected a column like that to be less biased."

"Most of the women who write me know that their men are bastards. They don't need me to tell them that. They just want someone to agree with them."

"So you think your role is to confirm their poor opinion of men, rather than to provide them with a more balanced view?"

She twirled her noodles around her fork, but didn't bring it to her mouth. "They want confirmation, not balance. And anyway, if their men were nicer to them, they wouldn't need to write me."

"Don't you get letters from women who, despite the problems they're having, beg you to help them find a way to keep their men?"

"Sure."

"And what do you do?"

"Help them see the light. Try to show them that, if they're being disrespected, they need to assert themselves. And their men need to shape up or ship out. No sense clinging to something if it's only going to do you harm."

"And do you ever get letters from men who are the injured parties? Men whose women have done them wrong?"

She thought about it. "I guess."

"And what do you do?"

"I try to be fair."

He doubted it.

She added hurriedly, "Look, I don't hate men."

"I didn't say you did."

"You're thinking it," she insisted.

"I'm thinking nothing of the sort," he assured her smoothly, although that was pretty much the idea he was forming. "I was just trying to get an idea of what your work was like. It's not often I get to meet a real writer. I'm fascinated."

The flattery worked. She seemed mollified. "Okay, I just didn't want you to…" She didn't finish her thought.

He pressed again, curious to penetrate her mind even further now that her defenses were down. "And what about the men, these husbands and boyfriends who were put in their place on your say-so?"

She looked perplexed. "What about them?"

"Do you ever get letters from these rejects? Doesn't anyone ever complain or react to your role in their downfall? Hasn't anyone ever threatened to get even?"

She flinched as though she'd been hit, and immediately he regretted his flippant question. "I…I guess so. Sometimes they're… angry…" She rubbed her temple as though it were sore.

Dorian immediately sensed that he'd gone too far. "I'm sorry. Did I step into something I shouldn't have?"

"No," she said shortly, but he knew she was lying. "Nobody's ever reacted in a way I can't handle. I get a few ugly letters, no big deal. You can't be a writer if your skin's not thick enough to handle a few bad reviews." She swirled her rice wine around in its little cup, took a sip and switched from defense to attack. "What about you? Is your name really Dorian Black, or did you make it up because it sounds interesting?"

He'd endured enough teasing about his name not to mind a little more. "It's all mine. My mother had an unusual sense of humor. But I promise you there's no cursed picture hidden away in my house, getting old and gray while I stay young and beautiful—" at that, she cracked a smile "—and I certainly haven't sold my soul to the devil for a shot at immortality."

"That's good to know. That devil is one tricky fellow."

Dorian nodded. "You said it. I'm sure even I couldn't find a loophole in one of his contracts."

His work was as good a conversational gambit as any when two people had run out of other things to say. "So, property law must be as rife with drama as the agony aunt business, huh? Buying and selling buildings. I bet you've made a whole slew of enemies."

He took no offense at her sarcasm, but set her straight on one point. "Actually, property law is Clark's specialty, not mine. My area is family law. More specifically, divorce and child custody cases."

She squinted a little. "You're a divorce lawyer?"

She said the word *divorce* as though it tasted bad. He was used to the reaction, so it rolled off his back. "I guess you could call me that. And before you even think about it, I think I've heard just about every lawyer joke in the book."

"I wasn't planning on joking," she informed him. "I don't think breaking up marriages is funny."

He shook his head. "We don't break marriages up. We try to find ways to dissolve marriages that have already broken down, as equitably and as painlessly as possible."

Rita snorted. "Equitably? Painlessly? If I had a buck for every woman who's written to me to complain about her husband using a fancy, high-priced lawyer to shaft her out of what's rightfully hers…"

His calm before the courts was legendary, but this unwarranted attack in the most innocuous of places, the dinner table, by a woman he'd known fifteen minutes, got under his skin. He answered sharply. "I can't speak for every lawyer out there, but I can tell you that I have never shafted anyone—".

"Nah. I'll bet you fall all over yourself to make sure that every woman who walks into your office walks away with a nice, cushy settlement…so long as you get a big cut, right?"

Her distrust for his profession was one thing, but her personal indictment rankled. "Actually, our fees are quite moderate by industry standards, and we offer the best service we can to every client. We work very hard, and we're entitled to be paid for our labor, just like anyone else."

"I'm sure you must charge a whole lot of *very* moderate fees to be able to afford a suit like that."

He looked down at himself in surprise. He'd almost forgotten he was wearing a suit. He'd been toying with the idea of stopping home after he left the jail to change into something less stuffy and more appropriate for the evening, but was running so late that he'd decided not to. He could have explained that, but perversely said, "I don't need to apologize because our practice is performing well, and I certainly don't need to feel bad about what my clothes cost. I dress appropriately for my job. My clients expect me to be well groomed. It's no different from a surgeon wearing scrubs or a fireman wearing his gear."

She was as intent on needling him as he was on needling her. "Sure, your practice must be performing well. You people look out for yourselves. Just yesterday I got a letter from a woman whose husband, and his *lawyer,* practically ruined her. They're probably divvying up the loot right now."

"I'm sorry to hear that. But there are as many men out there who have been ruined by wives set to break them, more out of malice than financial necessity. A last shot fired at the end of a bad marriage."

"So, you're saying your male clients suffer as much during a divorce as your female clients?"

He thought about that for a second, wondering how to respond, and then said, "Divorce is painful for everyone, but to be honest, I don't have a whole lot of female clients."

Her eyes widened. "You're saying you don't represent women?"

"I represent anyone who walks through my door. But I've developed a reputation for being receptive to men and their special legal needs."

She put her knife and fork down and scowled at him. "What exactly does that mean?"

"It means," he explained slowly, even though it was obvious to him, "that I have many more male clients than female clients." He couldn't resist reminding her, "Men *are* entitled to legal representation under our constitution, you know."

"So you spend your days huddled with other members of the

Boys' Club coming up with ways to make sure that, after years of devotion to their husbands, women are left without a penny after their husbands dump them?"

Dorian's head hurt. He resisted the urge to rub it, wishing he had an ibuprofen tablet or two in his pocket. It hadn't been a good day. He'd been battling one cause or the other since he'd set foot in Elcroft Green, and now he was sinking deeper and deeper into a new battle with a stranger.

It made no sense, but instead of calling a halt to the madness, he fired back irritably. "Not all divorces are the fault of the man, and if you think so, you're sadly deluded, sweetheart. And furthermore, despite what your readers might tell you—and Lord knows why they'd want to spill their guts to an inexperienced slip of a girl like you, except perhaps because they're sure that they're only going to hear what they want to hear, and not necessarily something that makes a lick of sense—not all wives are devoted. No divorce I've ever worked on was the sole fault of one party. It takes two to tango."

Indignation at being called "an inexperienced slip of a girl" was written all over her face, and the result was comical. He pressed on. "Furthermore, if there is a Boys' Club, I'm not a member, and I don't sit around scheming with other men to rob women, either of their money, or their children—"

She gasped. "Children?"

Maybe she hadn't been listening. "As I said, I specialize in divorce and *custody* cases."

"You take children away from their mothers?" The look she threw him could have bent steel.

"Most of the time, I negotiate for fair sharing of custody and visitation rights, depending on what's best for everyone involved, especially the children. I've won custody battles for my male clients, but I've won them for my female clients, as well. I don't win them all—nobody does. But I'd like to think that I help families adjust to a rocky period in their lives."

"Help? How, exactly, does it help, tearing children out of their mothers' arms?"

"No child is ever 'torn out of their mother's arms,' as you put it, and I'm sure that even someone as biased as you would admit that not every woman is Clair Huxtable. There are mothers out there who aren't at the stage of their lives where they can raise children as they deserve to be raised. Some can't because they're unemployed, or holding down too many jobs, or drink too much, or have issues to deal with. Some are simply bad mothers. And there are fathers out there who are aching to raise their kids right. Don't tell me that you think it would be wrong to award custody to the man under those circumstances?"

When she hesitated, he knew he had her cold. It was a minor victory, but as sweet as any he'd won under judge and jury. He waited for her to say something, anything, to demonstrate that she was giving up her unwarranted attack in the face of his inescapable logic.

She did say something, but it certainly was no concession of defeat. "Lawyers!" she grunted, and attacked her cashew-covered duck.

"Feminists!" he threw back, and stabbed his pork.

It was several moments before he noticed two pairs of eyes on him. Clark and Cassie were watching with open curiosity. "Is everything okay?" Cassie asked.

Their spat had been louder than he'd thought. Tom-toms banged in his head, but he fibbed politely. "Everything's fine."

"Peachy," Rita agreed, but didn't look up from her plate.

"Good," Clark said, but sounded doubtful, making Dorian feel ashamed of himself. Rita was getting on his nerves, but it wasn't his night out, it was Clark's. And in spite of her prickles, she was a cute little thing. Maybe he should lighten up and not spoil the evening for everyone. He smiled warmly at Cassie to put her at ease and tried to smile at Rita, as well, but she was studiously avoiding looking at him.

"What about dessert, then?" Clark suggested with forced heartiness.

Dorian tried not to groan. Although Cassie and Clark had finished their meal, neither he nor Rita had eaten much. He looked down at his plate. On one hand it would be a relief not to have to finish it off, on the other hand, he was reluctant to move on to the next course. Thai dessert would certainly not consist of something light and frothy and easy to slide down into the corners. It would be along the lines of sweet dumplings in sticky sauce or something equally filling. He was wondering if he could get away with suggesting just coffee when Rita spoke up.

"Actually, Clark, Cassie, I feel really awful about this, but I have a terrible headache, and I don't think I'm being good company." She threw an apologetic glance at Dorian. "I hate to duck out on you like this, but it really would be best if I just went on home."

Good one, Dorian telegraphed. A graceful way to make a speedy exit. Who challenged anyone on an imaginary headache? It would work out best for everyone. Cassie and Clark were obviously having a great time in each other's company; whatever Cassie's little hang-up had been about being alone with Clark was overcome. They'd probably relish the idea of finishing their date as a twosome instead of a reluctant foursome. And he and Rita could sneak out, end this disaster, and go their separate ways.

Cassie was immediately solicitous. "Oh, poor baby! Is it really, really horrible?"

Rita grimaced and nodded. "It really, really is."

Cassie threw a wistful look at Clark. "Maybe I should drive her home, Clark…"

That, he wouldn't stand for. Just because he and Rita hadn't hit it off didn't mean his friend should cut his date short. He stepped in smoothly.

"Rita, if you haven't any transport, I'd be happy to drive you home."

Rita looked so aghast he wondered if the idea of a few more

moments in his company would really be as bad as she thought. She blathered, "No, no! I won't think of it. I can get the doorman to stop a cab—"

"But you're sick," Cassie interrupted, looking as concerned as if Rita had announced she'd contracted the Hanta virus. "You can't go by cab if you're sick!"

"I can, and I will," Rita began, but Dorian decided to put an end to this silliness once and for all.

He got to his feet. "Nonsense. If you're not feeling well, it would be stupid to try to get yourself home. Not to mention unforgivably rude of me. Come on, let me make sure you get to your door okay. It's not often I get to play the knight in shining armor."

Before she could protest, he reached out and took Cassie's hand in his. "Cassie, it was a pleasure to meet you. Now I see why my partner was so taken by you. You have my word that you're in good hands for the rest of the evening." She beamed at his compliment.

He turned to Clark and the two men briefly shook hands. "Enjoy the rest of your meal, Clark. See you in the morning."

Clark nodded. "Take care, Rita. I hope you feel better. Sorry you had a bad time."

"I had a lovely time," Rita said wanly, but was unable to keep herself from shooting a dark look at Dorian. It was so baleful, he tried not to laugh. "I hope we meet again."

Clark glanced at Cassie. "I hope we will," he said fervently.

Dorian took control of the situation by slipping his hand under Rita's elbow and guiding her away from the table and out to the main doors. She kept pace with him silently, not even looking his way, until they had retrieved their coats and were standing on the sidewalk, under a crisp, bright autumn sky. Then she wrenched her elbow out of his grasp and spun on her heels.

"My car's this way," he told her, somewhat perplexed. "Where're you going?"

"As I said, I'm going to have the doorman stop a taxi." She

signaled to the doorman, who was elaborately costumed in a silk tunic, pants and small hat. The man nodded, understanding her request, and stepped off the curb, peering down the street in search of a flash of yellow.

She couldn't be that anxious to get away from him. "Don't be silly," he said firmly. "I said I would get you home, and I will."

"Thanks," she answered primly, "but I can take care of myself." She ignored him for several moments, until a cab drew near. The doorman, a broad smile on his face, held the door open for her.

He could have let her get in without another word, but for some indefinable reason he hated the idea of it. They'd snarled at each other for the brief portion of the meal they'd shared. She'd gotten on his nerves virtually from the moment he'd taken his seat. But something, *something,* made him want the evening to end differently. Not this way, growling their goodbyes and parting company on a street corner. Maybe it was vanity. Maybe he was loath for her to leave with a lousy opinion of him, just because he'd had a bad day and had been all too happy to take it out on her. He put one hand on the door of the cab just as she was about to climb in. "Rita, don't."

Her eyes were wide. "What?"

"Let me take you home. There's no reason for you to take a cab when I'm parked right here."

She looked doubtful. "My apartment's a long way off," she said falteringly.

"All the more reason why you shouldn't be making the trip alone. Come on. I promised Cassie I'd see you home safely. Don't make a liar out of me." He couldn't resist adding with a smile, "I know you probably think that, as a lawyer, lying would be second nature to me, but it's harder than you think."

To his surprise, she smiled back, and the smile actually reached those beautiful eyes of hers, setting them afire. "But I've already hailed him…"

"I'll handle it." Moving quickly to deflect the cab driver's impatience, he withdrew his money clip from his pocket and slipped him a bill, apologizing as he did so. Bored, the driver shrugged, accepted the money without a word and pulled away. He tipped the doorman, who was observing the entire exchange with a slightly perplexed look, and then gestured. "This way."

"Thank you," she said quietly, and was silent while he led her to his vehicle. To have called it a car was a bit of a stretch. It was, in fact, a hunter green four-wheel-drive twin-cab piece of space age engineering that came with just about every doohickey an outdoorsman would crave, from the tow-bar at the back to haul around his fishing boat, to the rack on top that could hold everything from a white-water raft to a tent. Her look of surprise pleased him.

"Teach you not to judge a book by its suit-and-tie cover."

"Consider me schooled."

Her humorous response made him relax. Maybe the drive back to her place wouldn't be as tense as dinner. He helped her inside, as the running board was a little high, and her slim skirt, though it showed off her attractive curves, wasn't much good when it came to climbing. He made sure she was comfortable, then came around to the driver's side and hauled himself in with ease. The engine started with a soft murmur, and as soon as she gave him her address, he pulled away from the curb.

Rita still wasn't saying much. Out of the corner of his eye he noticed that she had closed her eyes and was massaging her temples with the tips of her fingers.

"You can drop it, you know," he told her gently.

Her face was the picture of puzzlement. "Drop what?"

"The I've-got-a-headache act. I know neither of us was having a great time back there, and you did manage to get us out of it without hurting anyone's feelings, but really, you don't need to go on for my sake. I understand. We didn't hit it off. No hard feelings."

Then he noticed something he hadn't before: a glimmer of moisture in her eyes. "Are you crying?"

"Not exactly," she answered sharply.

"What the—why?"

"Nothing. It's not an act."

"What?"

"My headache. It's not an act. I get these migraines some-times, and this one's…pretty bad. I feel like I've been stabbed in the head. And the nausea…it's awful…"

He felt like a genuine heel. He'd all but accused her of lying, when, if he'd taken the time to really look at her, he'd have seen that she was in real pain. "If you feel like you need to throw up, let me know. I'll pull over."

"Don't worry. I won't throw up all over your precious Weekend Warrior Mobile."

"That's not what I meant at all!"

She covered her face with her hands and slumped forward in her seat. "Fine, whatever you say."

Still ashamed of himself, he fiddled with the stereo. "Anything you'd like to listen to?"

"Silence would be great," she told him from between cupped hands.

He snapped the stereo back off again. "You got it."

Silence was just what he gave her, all the way to her apart-ment. He liked this part of town. It was old-fashioned and nos-talgic without being run-down. It reminded him of the neighborhood he'd grown up in. He pulled up before her building, squinted at the brass plate fixed to the wall to ensure he had the right place, and alighted before she could bestir herself and try to get out without his help.

They stood on the sidewalk, solemnly regarding each other. "Got your keys?" he asked her.

She looked perplexed for a moment, as though seeing him through a blur of pain, and then rummaged in her purse. "Yes, got them." She held them up, jangling them as proof. Then she turned toward the stairs. "Thank you for bringing me home."

She wasn't getting away that easy. He fell into step with her, locking his car and shoving the keys into his pocket. "I'm walking you inside."

"You don't have to," she began hastily.

"Oh, yes I do. You're not feeling well. I'm not driving off and leaving you until I know you're safely inside."

"I don't need—" she began, a spark of indignation rising out of the mist of her pain, but just then she stumbled, and he caught her deftly and righted her.

"See? You can't even make it to your own door." He took her hand, which was limp, clammy and unresisting, in his. "Come."

"But, Dorian…!"

Her protest was half-hearted, and he ran over it effortlessly. "But, nothing. A promise is a promise. I'm seeing you inside." She gave no further resistance, so he unlocked the door to the main entrance and led her to the elevator. "Floor?"

"Third."

He punched in the number. Once on the third floor, he looked around. There were just four apartments on each floor, and she wearily pointed out her own. By now, pity was consuming him, and he wanted urgently to get her inside so that she could rest. He selected the key that looked like it would fit the lock to her front door and began to insert it into the keyhole…

But the door yawned open before them without any further bidding.

Chapter 5

Rita stared in shock as her door opened at the lightest touch of Dorian's hand. A creepy sensation overcame her, like worms crawling along the back of her neck. How could that be?

Dorian gave her a wary look. "You have a roommate?"

"No."

"Boyfriend?"

"No!"

"Anyone have a key to your place?"

She frowned, her migraine making it difficult for her to think. "Cassie keeps my spares for me, but…."

"Stand back," Dorian instructed, one arm moving her protectively to one side, with her back against the wall so that she was screened off from the entryway by both his broad body and the door. He bent forward, inspecting the keyhole and the lock. "Not even a little scratch," he commented. "Nothing to suggest that the lock was picked." He lifted his head to look at her. "You certain you locked up securely?"

Normally, she would have bristled at the suggestion. Did he really think she was enough of a knucklehead to have left her front door unlocked? But as memories of the evening tumbled upon each other, she tried to piece together their fragments. She'd left home in one heck of a hurry. Too much of a hurry to do her hair or put on some makeup, even. That thought made her run her fingers self-consciously through her messy corkscrews. Cassie had been downstairs in the car, waiting. Lord knew, Cassie had enough lip on her to make it very clear that she didn't like to be kept waiting. So she'd hurried. But had she left in such haste that she had forgotten to lock up?

Dorian was still looking at her, waiting for an answer. "Rita?"

It was ridiculous. There they were, standing in the hallway, with her door agape, nothing inside but quiet darkness…and, perhaps, something, or some*one* else. She shivered again.

Dorian called her name again, more softly this time.

She looked at him, foolishly wasting precious seconds thinking how awesomely handsome he was, in spite of the concern that was wrinkling his brow. She found herself stuttering. "I…I…have no idea. I wasn't feeling well, and I'd been a-a-asleep when Cassie came to get me. I rushed out to meet her." She laughed self-deprecatingly. "I didn't even have time to do my hair. I know I look a mess."

His onyx eyes swept over her, once, and then again, more slowly, but if she was expecting a compliment, she was sorely disappointed. "Enough of a rush to forget to lock up?"

She was stumped on that point, but forgetting to lock the door was the better of the two options. "I don't know."

He straightened up and expelled air through his nose, shaking himself determinedly. "In any case, it's pointless for us to stand here staring at the lock. I'm going in. Wait here."

Was he serious? "I'm not waiting anywhere. I'm coming in with you."

He gave her a long, sober look. "If someone broke in to your place, they could still be in there."

A scary thought, but she insisted, "It's my place. I'm going in with you."

He sighed again. "Well, stay behind me. If I say to run, run all the way downstairs and outside, and don't look back."

She stifled a nervous giggle. "You planning to take a bullet for me?"

He threw her a dark look. "That was *not* funny."

She had to concede that it wasn't. "Sorry."

She followed him inside, heart thumping. Her own apartment seemed alien to her, lit throughout only by the eerie glow of the bedside lamp she'd left on. Shapes loomed as their dense shadows made bogeymen out of everyday objects. To still her lurching stomach, she flicked on the lights as she followed Dorian from room to room, taking his advice and staying well behind him, even as she cursed herself for her cowardice. For once, she was willing to admit that if there was one thing that men were better at than women, it was hunting down skulking burglars.

They made their way to the last room, the study where she did most of her writing, and stopped. Dorian's eyes were bright, his nostrils flared from the tension, and his deep chest rose and fell heavily. He stated the obvious. "Nobody here."

"Maybe I did leave it open after all," she mused. "You said yourself there were no marks on the lock or anything."

"Not necessarily. They could have got in somewhere else, and used the door to leave."

He was making no sense. "Got in where?"

"We'll see." Her study and her bedroom, which were side by side, faced the street. Along the far wall, which she had painted a deep teal, a color that helped her to relax and write, were three small windows. He checked them; they were all securely locked. Without saying anything, he returned to her bedroom, also painted teal. Three identical windows lined the wall, interspersed with small framed sepia drawings of men and women making love, their limbs so intertwined that it was almost impossible to tell where one body began and the other ended. Their huge, kohl-lined, almond-shaped eyes, full berry-colored lips and glossy black hair made them so exotic that he did a double take. His lifted brow asked a silent question.

"Those are, uh, recreations of ancient Buddahist drawings. It's supposed to represent Tantric, uh, sex." She felt fire in her cheeks. "My mother bought those on a trip to Calcutta. They're not exactly my type of thing, but I, uh, didn't want to offend her. So I put them up in here."

He gave the drawings a slow once-over that left Rita squirming, before saying, "Your mother's very progressive."

"If only you knew," she couldn't stop herself from saying.

"What's that mean?"

"Nothing." She wished the damn drawings would spontaneously combust. It wasn't every day a girl found herself standing in her bedroom with a stranger who didn't like her, examining erotica on her walls. She wondered how to diplomatically remind him of his reason for being in her room in the first place. "Dorian…"

He took the hint. "Sorry." He cleared his throat and focused on the windows, checking one lock, and then the next. The third was not only unlocked, but slightly ajar. He gave her a significant look. "You keep these locked?"

"Usually," she said defensively. It was growing clearer and clearer to her that she'd screwed up and forgotten the door. She wasn't happy about admitting that she went about leaving windows unlocked, too.

"Maybe they got in through here," he suggested.

"From three floors below?"

As he shrugged, that suit she had so criticized pulled against his broad shoulders, drawing her attention once again to his heavy, beautifully shaped chest. He pointed downward at the old, elaborate columns decorating the facade of the building. They were old and worn, dating back to the same era as the carved angels that had been stripped off. "Somebody crazy enough to risk it could use that scrollwork as footholds."

Maybe. She looked at the window again. It was divided into four-by-two metal bars in the shape of a cross. She pointed at the small spaces left by the bars. "A trained monkey might be able to get through there." She pointed. "But not a person."

He nodded speculatively, inspecting the lock and the window. "A trained monkey or an eight-year-old kid."

"What?"

"Determination can make quick work of little obstacles like a narrow opening."

"Even so," she argued, "what would an eight-year-old kid be doing in my bedroom?"

"Whatever the grownup that's controlling him forces him to do." He said this with a grimace of bitterness.

"You've got to be joking!"

He gave her a glance that said she had no idea what she was talking about. "It's a mean, nasty world out there, and people do lots of mean, nasty things to each other. Including children."

"Why would anyone want to do that to me?"

"Simple burglary, most likely. Unless…." He stopped, thought for a while, and then went on, "Unless someone has it in for you. As we were discussing over dinner, your writing stands a good chance of making you enemies."

Her mind was yanked backward several hours, past their disastrous dinner, to that chilly online encounter back in the coffee shop. *Are you afraid of heights?*

The look on her face must have told him something, because he stepped forward and placed both hands gently on her shoulders. He had to dip his head somewhat to look her in the eye.

"Do you?" he asked, very softly.

Her stutter was back again. "D-d-do I…what?"

"Have any enemies?"

"I…." *How's the coffee?* But that was ridiculous. Someone at the coffee shop, or maybe across the street from the coffee shop, was yanking her chain for his own amusement. It had nothing, *nothing* to do with this. "Not that I know of," she said stoically.

He didn't look as though he believed her, but he gave in gracefully. "Okay." He still hadn't taken his hands from her shoulders.

To cover her confusion, she added, "You're a pessimist."

"It's a professional requirement. If you fail the half-full/half-empty glass test, you can't get into law school."

She laughed, ashamed of the way she'd lit into him over his profession. She was about to apologize, but he gave her the sweetest, most genuine smile she'd seen all evening, and the icky, crawly feeling at the back of her neck went away. It was replaced by a delicious, all-over-the-body tingle. The silence that fell between them, one of many this evening, was not uncomfortable, but weighty with expectation. Again, she was unable to stop her tongue from curling out to moisten her lips. Dorian's black eyes followed the gesture.

A crackle and a squeak in the corner were loud enough to shatter both the silence and the moment. They both jumped. Rita knew exactly where the sound had come from: a long table upon which she had put together a convoluted series of plastic cages, featuring exercise wheels, water bottles, tunnels, windows, lookouts and even a rodent bath. The sole occupant of the cage was wide awake and staring at them curiously, beady eyes glowing, velvety nose twitching.

"Oh," she said with a laugh, "it's just my gerbil."

"You keep a gerbil?" He was both surprised and amused.

"Yeah." Then she added, as though that explained everything, "Since college."

"And how long ago would that be?"

"You trying to determine my age?" She was well aware that she was flirting, and surprised that she wasn't embarrassed by that fact.

"Yes."

"Well, put it this way, I've had the little beast for seven years."

He was already moving over to the corner to peer into the cage, where the small, fluffy orange creature had come over to get a better look at *him*. Man and animal stared each other down. "I didn't know they lived that long."

"Me, neither, but there ya go."

He tapped lightly on the wall of the cage. "What's its name?"

"*His* name is Wallace."

"Wallace?"

She rolled her eyes. "Don't ask. I can't even remember where that came from. You know how college rolls by in a sort of haze."

He grinned. "I know." He straightened up, and then, God help her, he was standing before her once again, and that all-over tingle struck up once more, like a marching band that had paused for a break but had taken up instruments with new vigor.

She floundered for something—anything—to say. "What about you?"

"Did my college days pass by in a haze?"

"No, I mean, do you have any pets?"

He was looking down at her, eyes sweeping her hairline and moving slowly down, along her nose, to her mouth. He didn't seem interested in her line of questioning, but answered anyway. "An aging basset hound called Angela."

"Angela?"

"Angela Basset."

She groaned. "Oh, Lord."

"She doesn't have Tina Turner legs, but she's pretty good company on camping trips. And she's an amazing fisher…um, *dog*."

He was still standing so, so close, right here, in her bedroom. And they were jabbering on about gerbils and dogs with fishing skills. Even as she was being engulfed by this ridiculous, unexpected and totally unwarranted attraction, her rational mind was reminding her that this was the same man who was getting on her very last nerve's very last nerve just an hour before. But the warm, woodsy scent of him made that irrelevant. The Tantric drawings on her wall looked down on them.

Why doesn't he do something? Why doesn't he make a move, say something that doesn't involve ghost burglars or animals, lean forward…touch her? Rita felt her body sway toward him a little. She lifted her eyes to his and found that he was not looking at her, but was staring at the ceiling, in the attitude of someone praying, or at least consulting the heavens for guidance.

"Rita," he began.

"Yes?"

"You're tired."

"What's that supposed to mean?"

"It means I'd better go before…." His eyes were on her mouth again. "It means I'd better go." Without asking her to see him out, he turned abruptly and headed toward her front door.

Humiliation burned in her face. She'd flashed him a come-hither signal, almost without being aware of it, and he turned tail and ran as if the Hound of the Baskervilles were after him. That was so not like her. More than he could even imagine. It was desperately important that she tell him so. She hurried in his wake, protesting. "I wasn't…I didn't mean to imply…." Damn him, damn him, *damn him.* She felt gauche and clumsy and stupid and—

His fingers came up to touch her cheek. "Don't."

"What do you mean, don't? Don't what?" She was working herself into a fine lather. At any other time, if this had been happening to any other person, it would have been funny.

"Don't do this to yourself. We didn't exactly hit it off. We've both had a lousy evening. We said a couple things we probably shouldn't have. And then you come home and have to deal with a scare, false alarm or not. We're keyed up and tired. Let's just cut our losses and put this evening to bed."

The word *bed* hung suspended between them in the air like a sweet-smelling wisp of smoke.

"You have a migraine," he reminded her.

"I remember."

"You have anything you can take for it?"

"Yes, I do. I'll take it right away, and go straight to…sleep."
She knew her face was flushing crazily once again, partly from
the embarrassment of rejection and partly from the image that
had leaped to her mind as the word *bed* had been on the brink of
falling from her lips, too. The whole thing was ridiculous, especially considering her unique personal situation. If he knew the
truth about *that,* he'd laugh her out of her own apartment.

"If not, I can run around the corner to the drugstore and pick
something up for you," he suggested.

All she wanted right now was for him to go and leave her alone.
"That won't be necessary," she said brusquely. "I'll be fine."

She was certain he was about to ask something else, but
instead he nodded and opened the door. He gave her one last, long
look. "Good night, then."

"Good night." She put one hand on the door and began to
close it on him.

He gave her an impish grin, and a dimple she hadn't noticed
before showed in one cheek. "It was a pleasure meeting you."

"I'll bet," she said, and shut the door. Once he was gone, she
felt her whole body slump. The headache she'd almost forgotten was back, in full intensity. She didn't bother rubbing her
temples; it wouldn't have made a difference.

What a day. First, she's threatened by someone who may or
may not be stalking her. Then she gets roped into a blind date
she wouldn't have agreed to in a million years for anyone other
than Cassie. Then she endures a torturous dinner with a chauvinist pig whose very life's work violated everything she believed
in, and then gets home—driven at his own insistence by that self-
same chauvinist pig—to find that she'd left her front door open.

And if she needed further proof that she was losing her mind,
the pig turned out to be significantly less piggy than she'd been
led to believe. He had, in fact, shown himself to be a pretty nice

guy. Nice enough for her to all but throw herself at him. Waiting, wishing, wanting him to kiss her, and flashing mad signals at him, like a chimp in heat. She should be ashamed of herself. Especially considering the fact that there were things about her that he didn't know, obviously couldn't know….

Beatrix would have been delighted, or, at the very least, amused by the whole scenario. That made her situation even more untenable. And, oh, those awful drawings. He'd studied them, as though they were stuck up in some art gallery. Studied her, too, at the same time, and come up with the wrong conclusion.

Oh!

She stepped away from the door. Dorian was right. She'd had a lousy evening, and the best thing she could do right now was to end it. As she started toward the bathroom, there was a knock on the door. She looked at her watch, perplexed. Who could it be at this hour?

"Yes?"

"It's me," came a deep, immediately identifiable voice. And then, unnecessarily, "Dorian."

She unlocked the door quickly, and he was standing before her again. He still smelled wonderful. "Forget something?"

"Not exactly."

"What, then?" She was slightly irritated. He walks out leaving her feeling like a first-class idiot, and moments later he's banging on her door again? What's his problem? "What'd you come back for?"

"This."

His mouth was upon hers before she could say yea or nay, before she could duck, demur, take a breath or voluntarily kiss him back. Her mouth was all his, and in a flash, any thought she might have harbored about ducking or protesting or running away became moot, because it was good. So damn good, and over so damn quickly, that when he was done with her she staggered back, nearly tripping over her own feet. She brought her hands to her mouth where the warmth from the unexpected pressure still tingled. His kiss had been fast and light, but shockingly sweet. A hit-and-run bandit attack that left her head spinning. "What'd you do that for?" she asked accusingly, and her body tried unsuccessfully to get her to add, *And why don't you do it again?*

He twinkled at her. "I just thought we needed to get it out of the way."

He read the puzzlement on her face and added reassuringly, "Not in a bad way. I just thought if we're going to see each other again, we might as well get our first kiss over and done with. It has an annoying way of hanging in the air, waiting to get noticed, putting everybody on edge, don't you think?"

Their *first* kiss? That would imply that there would be more. Which made him stupendously presumptuous. *If they were to see each other again?* Uh, yeah. After needling her half the night, and then walking out on her like that, what could possibly make him think—

"See you soon," he promised, cutting across her self-righteous indignation with a grin, and disappeared through the door.

Chapter 6

Dorian could have done the standard keep-'em-waiting-and-wondering thing and let two or three days go by before he called Rita again, but he was in no mood for games. Sure, she'd gotten his back up at dinner, just as he had hers, but in spite of that, she intrigued him. She had a wide chip on her shoulder, but he liked her anyway. She was a pretty little thing when she wasn't scowling at him. Once she wasn't dashing out of her apartment with a migraine for an unwanted blind date with her hair in disarray and not a lick of makeup on her, she'd clean up quite nicely.

And she could kiss. It had been a sneak attack on his part. He'd gone for that full, delicious-looking mouth of hers without even sounding a warning bell. He supposed he should have apologized, but he didn't feel a shred of regret. That brief taste of her sweet mouth was the best thing to happen to him all month. So much so that he'd opted to beat a strategic retreat before he forgot about his noble gesture of a few moments before and said or did something physically satisfying but inadvisable.

He called her up the next morning, having cadged her number off Clark, who, in turn, had cadged it off Cassie. According to Clark, Cassie was thrilled that he wanted it, especially since Rita and Dorian hadn't exactly enjoyed each other's company at dinner. Deciding that silence was golden, Dorian chose not to comment. He thanked Clark for the number and left it at that.

He called Rita at breakfast, while he was still lounging in shorts and dressing gown, with orange juice in one hand and his paper folded, half-read, on his lap. He'd learned over the years to make personal calls, whenever possible, before he climbed into his lawyer suit. Somehow, being dressed for work put him into attorney mode. His analytical brain kicked into high gear, his conversation became more clipped, and his voice tended to be a degree or two cooler. Another hazard of the job, but it was a hazard better avoided if you were intent on coaxing a young lady out on a date, one-on-one, without the buffer of a second couple.

Especially if that young lady didn't like you.

Rita's phone rang long enough for him to entertain second thoughts. But just as he was summoning the memory of those flashing toffee-colored eyes as an incentive to persist, she picked up. "Hello?"

She sounded rushed, and slightly irritated, but he chose to be cheery in the face of it. "Sorry," he told her.

The silence on the other end told him that she knew at once who it was. "Sorry for what?"

"For any and all comments that might have offended you last night, as well as for any gesture, covert or overt, any vocalization, glance or look, that might have gotten your dander up in any way, shape or form…."

"Dorian?"

"Yes?"

"It's too early in the morning for you to be drinking."

He smiled. "I wasn't, actually, unless you count O.J., which, I assure you, might have been in the deepest recesses of my fridge for a few days, but hasn't attained anywhere near the level of fermentation necessary for me to get a buzz."

"Then what was all that about?"

"I just called to apologize for getting on your case last night. I believe that at one point, I made a derogatory reference to your youth and possible lack of experience."

"You called me a little slip of a girl."

"I must have been out of my mind. You're very much a grown woman."

"You need to apologize for more than that," she told him, but she sounded slightly less irritated.

"What?"

"You got me out of the shower."

"Oh. Want me to call you back?"

"Not necessarily. While you were going through your spiel, most of the water dripping off me evaporated."

He laughed out loud. "Didn't mean to bore you."

"Not at all. It's not often a lawyer hurls fifty-dollar words at me without billing me afterward." She paused. "You aren't planning to bill me for this call, are you?"

He took that in good humor. "I assure you that this entire conversation is free of charge. In fact, if you play your cards right…."

"Uh-huh?"

"It comes with an invitation attached."

"To do what?"

"Whatever you like. Dinner, dancing, drinks, a concert, a movie, a walk in the park."

"I jog in the park every day," she informed him. "Just got back from it, actually."

"Hence the shower I interrupted?"

"Hence the shower you interrupted."

"So, for lack of originality, a walk in the park is out."

"For lack of originality, everything you just suggested is out." She had him there. "Good call on the dinner and dancing, though. You'd have wound up with sore feet. I can't dance worth a lick."

She sounded genuinely surprised. "A brother who can't dance? Doesn't exist."

"He does exist," Dorian insisted, "and you're talking to him."

"However do you court the ladies?"

"I get by on wit and charm." She was nice enough not to scoff, so he pressed his luck and asked, "So, what shall we do, then?"

"Assuming I do want to go out with you."

"Assuming."

She paused, and then said, "Well, I've always been a fan of Angela Bassett movies…."

"Would you like to meet her?"

"Who'd give up the chance to meet a dog that can fish? Can she run, too?"

"Like the wind."

"Can you?"

"Fish? Yes, and I frequently do. Would you like to go fishing with Angela and me?"

Rita snorted. "I don't know if I'd feel too comfortable with the idea of luring poor innocent fish onto a hook with the promise of food. It seems kind of underhanded, in a way. Not to mention painful."

"Can't argue with you about the underhanded part, but as for the painful bit, I assure you they barely feel a thing. Primitive piscine nervous system."

"Well, maybe." She sounded doubtful. Then she added, "And worms make me queasy."

"I'd put them on the hook for you. *They* barely feel a thing, either."

She laughed. "Actually, what I was asking you was, can you *run?*"

His brows lifted. Was she challenging him? "I've been known to do a fairly decent five- or six-minute mile, with the right motivation, but America's Olympic hopes are hardly pinned on me. Why? What you got in mind?"

"There's a Fun Run to raise funds for breast cancer research on Sunday, starting at De Menzes Park. They left a whole bunch of fliers at Starbucks. Got one right here. It says all you have to do is make a donation, get a T-shirt and follow the route. There's a free concert afterwards."

He looked down at his lap, and, strangely enough, the newspaper was opened to a feature about the charity run. He considered it a good sign. "I was just reading about it," he told her.

"It's five miles for the wusses, and ten miles for everyone else. Which are you?"

A broad smile spread across his face. "I may be many things, but wuss has never been one of them."

"Think you can handle going the whole hog?"

He scoffed. "Ten miles? Without breaking a sweat."

"Can your dog?"

"She could probably outrun you."

"Good. It's a date, then. At the registration table, at 7 a.m."

"Broad daylight, huh?" he asked softly. "Nice and safe."

"I hardly know you," she returned. "Cassie isn't the only careful one."

"No problem. You're entitled to be cautious. I won't take offense. But are you sure you wouldn't like me to pick you up?"

"So I'd have to clamber into that monstrosity you drive? Last night I nearly ripped a seam in my skirt."

"I'd give you a leg up," he offered soberly.

"Bet you would."

She was flirting with him, he was sure of it, and he liked that. "Besides, if you're wearing really short running shorts, it wouldn't be a problem."

"I'll be wearing track pants," she retorted. "It'll be cold out."

"Only for the first three miles or so."

"I'll hedge my bets, thank you."

"Damn."

She chuckled, accepting his compliment, and then a not-too-un-comfortable silence fell between them. "Well," she said eventually.

"Well," he echoed.

"If you'll excuse me, now that I'm completely dry, I think I should go get dressed."

To distract himself from the delicious mystery of what she looked like naked, he said graciously, "Okay, then. Sorry again for interrupting that shower."

"Don't mention it."

"I need to get going, too. Busy day ahead of me. Lots of babies need their candy stolen."

"And I've got lots of innocent men to bad-mouth in print," she responded spiritedly, "so I guess I'll see you Sunday."

"Sunday," he agreed, and hung up. When he rose from the table, he was grinning. He had a good feeling about this.

Are you out of your ever-loving mind? Rita demanded of herself as she wound her way toward the registration desk that Sunday. Runners of all shapes and sizes milled around her, most of them in sweats against the coolness of the morning, a few more daring ones in shorts as brief as Dorian had suggested. Most of them were in the midst of some warm-up routine: swinging their arms and bending their knees, trotting around in tight circles and performing stretches with intense concentration etched on their faces. Rita barely saw them. She was way too busy questioning her own sanity.

Whatever had made her get all flirty on the phone with a man she kinda-sorta didn't like? Whose professional beliefs she disapproved of, and who clearly disapproved of hers, but who, she was prepared to admit, was as cute as all get out?

That thought made her smile. He *was* cute, wasn't he? So dark and smooth, like a cup of java made just the way she liked it, with a single dimple thrown in as an extra treat like a squirt of hazelnut syrup.

Mmm.

Certainly worth a second look. In which case, if she were to question her motivation for asking him to join her on the run, it probably pointed less in the direction of lunacy and more in the direction of an unauthorized attraction to a good-looking man. Which made her a little pathetic, perhaps, but certainly not mad.

She spotted Dorian easily. He was standing a few yards from the registration desk, holding two pieces of paper in one hand and a leash in the other. At the business end of the leash was a large, droopy-eared basset hound who was nonchalantly chewing on one of his shoelaces.

Dorian looked fighting fit and ready for a good, long run in expensive (and delicious, if his dog's opinion was worth anything) running shoes, slim-fitting, deep green track pants and a white T-shirt with a faded Army Reserve logo emblazoned on the chest. The moment he saw her, he lifted an arm and waved, making the muscles of his chest and shoulders ripple under his T-shirt. He was smiling broadly, and that hazelnut-syrup dimple was very much in evidence.

As she came close, she felt her pulse and respiration rise—and they hadn't even started running yet. She hoped he'd think that it was the walk clear across the park that had done it. It would be unbearable if he could guess by looking at her how their one kiss was still on her mind. She became unsure about how to greet him, and stuck out her hand awkwardly. "Dorian," she began.

He ignored her hand, and instead gave her a peck on the cheek, setting her skin instantly aflame, and making her throat go dry. She glanced around. These races usually had tables laden with bottled water at the start, finish, and everywhere else in between. She could do with one—or two—right now.

But Dorian was saying something. "Glad to see you again." He looked like he really meant it.

"Same here," she confessed. He was so tall the Army Reserve logo on his chest was directly in her line of vision. Something told her he wasn't wearing it as a fashion statement. "I don't suppose you picked that up at the army surplus store, huh?"

He shook his head, smiling. "Nope."

"You really in the Reserve?"

"I, two of my brothers and my dad. Family tradition."

"Ever seen active combat?"

"No, but I've rebuilt a few dams and dug through rubble for disaster survivors in my time."

"Oh." She'd never given any thought to doing volunteer work, and in the face of his cheerful sacrifice, she felt small.

He must have seen a shadow cross her face, because he made light of it. "I figured I needed to make it up to my country for being America's only non-dancing brother." That made her smile. Then he changed tack. "You look very nice." His eyes moved slowly along her body underlying his appreciation.

I do *not,* she wanted to groan. She had originally intended to wear her new running suit, which was cherry-red and made of space-age material that wouldn't sag or bag and would hug her in all the right places while letting her skin breathe. At the last moment, she decided to put on an old pair of black track pants, a plain gray discount store T-shirt, and topped it off with a worn purple velveteen track suit top that was a decade or two out of style and bagged in places it had no business bagging. She'd pulled her hair back with a scrunchie and wore just a hint of lipstick, deciding that applying any more makeup to go running was ridiculous. Now she found herself half-wishing she'd accepted his invitation to dinner and dancing, whether he was a lousy dancer or not. At least an evening out would have given her an excuse to make herself a little more presentable.

To hide her embarrassment, she squatted before his dog, holding out her hand to allow her an introductory sniff. Dorian dropped down immediately and they were eye to eye.

"Excuse my bad manners. I should've introduced you two. Angela, this is Rita. Rita…Angela."

"The famous fish-catching dog." She fondled the long, floppy ears, enjoying the feel of them. Angela was the least doleful-looking basset hound she had ever seen. In fact, the dog had a huge grin plastered across her face, splitting her slightly graying muzzle from ear to ear.

"You should see her pitch a camping tent."

"What?"

He laughed. She liked the way it came from deep inside his chest. "Never mind."

"You know she's eating your shoelace, don't you?"

He shrugged. "That's okay. It doesn't serve much of a purpose anyway. It's the Velcro that really keeps the shoe on. Lord knows why anyone would design a shoe with both laces *and* Velcro."

"Just an excuse to add another fifty dollars to the price, I'm sure," she murmured.

He gave her a quick look, probably searching for some indication that she was having another crack at him for his expensive taste in clothing. She literally bit her tongue, wondering whether she should clarify, but he took her comment at face value and held out the pieces of paper he was still holding. "Here, your registration sticker."

"You registered me?"

"I got here early, so I figured I might as well."

"But I was supposed to make a donation…."

"I made one for you," he said easily.

"You didn't have to do that," she mumbled.

He shrugged. "It was no big deal. It's for charity, after all."

Still, she protested. "But you shouldn't have had to go through that expense on my behalf…."

"Don't be ridiculous. If we'd gone out for dinner or drinks, I'd have bought. So forget it." His eyes told her he wasn't prepared to accept any further opposition. He added, "Besides, it's tax deductible. You know how we attorneys are always looking for a loophole."

He was needling her again. "Dorian—"

He cut her off by proffering the sticker once more. "You're supposed to stick your number on your chest." He gave her the sweetest smile. "Would you like me to do it for you?"

She snatched her sticker from him, peeled off the backing, and stuck it on herself before he could offer a second time. "Thanks, but I can handle *that*."

"Cool." He was holding something else in his hand, and held it up for her to see. It was a small pink loop of ribbon, the symbol of the Breast Cancer Awareness Drive. This time he didn't ask her permission, but instead deftly and quickly pinned it to her jacket on the left side, fingers lightly brushing the skin at her throat. He affixed his own sticker and ribbon, and rose. "I guess we should make our way to the starting line."

She followed, silent.

"I thought your friend Cassie was big on jogging," Dorian commented.

"She is. She's a total health fanatic."

"So she's around somewhere?"

Rita shook her head. "She was planning on it, but it seems she and Clark were out late last night...."

His brows lifted. "You're kidding. That's every night this week."

"Nope, not kidding. They're hitting the town like they're about to get shipped out to war. Cassie's totally—" She stopped. She was about to say totally taken with Clark, but she remembered how close the two men were. It was one thing for Cassie to be running around giddily, totally bushwhacked by a new man, and another thing for her to be blabbing about it to his best friend.

But Dorian was right there with her. "They're totally into each other," he commented. "Who'd have thought it? I wouldn't have thought Cassie was his type."

Rita bristled. "What's wrong with her?"

"Nothing," he responded patiently. "I think she is a beautiful woman and a delightful person. But you have to admit that they're a bit of an odd couple."

Rita was no less offended. "For that matter, *Clark's* not *her* type, either!"

"Exactly. He's a middle-aged, childless widower who's been out every night this week with a woman half his age, with twice his energy. Don't you find it a little strange?"

She stared at him. "He's been married?"

"Yes. His wife died several years ago. He's kept pretty much to himself since. Clark's not exactly a party animal."

"And Cassie is?"

"I never said that."

"You implied it."

"I didn't. You inferred it."

"Justifiably. It was there in your tone." By this time, Angela was turning her head back and forth from speaker to speaker, like a patron at a tennis match. It would have been comical if Rita wasn't so irritated.

"There was nothing in my tone except concern for a man who means a lot to me." Dorian was trying to maintain his equilibrium, she could tell, but she wasn't letting him slander her friend like that and get away with it.

"Well, Cassie means a whole lot to me, too, so your buddy better not be coming off all sweet and harmless, and then skunk out on her…."

"Skunk out?" He was half puzzled, half amused. "What's that mean?"

"You know what I mean. Anyhow, she's been through a rough patch lately, and I don't want her getting herself hurt."

"I don't want either of them getting hurt. Hence my concern. I wouldn't have bet much more than a quarter that the two of them would've hit it off as much as they have. I sure hope they don't crash land."

As much as she privately agreed with him, the urge to be

contrary made her say, "Who knows? Maybe it'll be good for both of them. Opposites attract."

He studied her for a long, lingering moment, and then said softly, "They sure do."

Rita's gaze was caught in his. She read his meaning, felt a rush of heat, and wondered again where the heck was the table with the bottled water.

"Let's not fight," she heard him say. "We're on a date, remember? To get to know each other?" He gave her a cajoling smile. Even Angela seemed to be trying to persuade. She was laying it on thick: tongue lolling out, big brown eyes fixed on her in that beseeching way dogs had.

As reluctant as Rita was to admit it, getting to know Dorian seemed a very attractive prospect indeed. She simmered down. "Okay."

"Okay," he echoed, and took her hand in his as though it were the easiest thing in the world. He led her to a comfortable spot within the crowd. Rita kept busy by telling herself, over and over again, that the resultant tingle was all in her head, but the immediate cessation of the tingle the moment he released her was proof that it wasn't.

With five minutes to the starting gun, the runners were ready and waiting. Even in the thick of the crowd, she recognized a few faces. Fellow runners who beat the path through the park alongside her and Cassie, day in and day out. Casual acquaintances, familiar faces from around town. Quite a good turnout of coffee shop regulars, no doubt through the efforts of a waitress who, herself a cancer survivor, had made it her mission in life to press fliers for the run on anyone and everyone. There were a bunch of construction workers who always arrived and left together, and she spotted the buttoned-up financier type, the one she called William Wadsworth, Senior, disappear into the crowd. Seeing him in casual wear for the first time ever brought a shocked laugh to her lips.

"Medal?" Dorian was asking her.

"What?"

"Are we going for a medal, or are we going to be laid-back about this and let some other lucky dog get it?" There were trophies for the first man and woman across the finish line at both the five-mile and ten-mile markers, and medals for the first one hundred runners at each. Rita cast a doubtful look around at the size of the crowd. Her, come within the first hundred? He was kidding, right?

"Ha, ha."

"No 'ha, ha.' I'm serious."

"Dorian, there are real runners here. People who run ten miles every *day*"

His dimple was showing. "I know. What do you say we give them a run for their money?" When she looked doubtful, he provoked, "You were saying something on the phone last time about wusses?"

She began to regret her taunt, recognizing it now for idle bravado, but she wasn't having it flung back in her face so easily. "I'm not a wuss," she defended.

"Good, then let's—"

Bang! went the starter's gun, and the crowd was off, Dorian, Rita and Angela with them. But as the mass of runners surged forward, Angela, in her excitement, zigged instead of zagged, tangled her leash around Rita's legs and brought Rita down.

And someone else down right on top of her.

Runners parted around the human heap on the ground. Amidst Angela's anxious yaps, and Dorian's efforts to bring her to her feet, she was aware of a tangle of limbs that weren't hers. She heard Dorian say, "Are you okay, young lady?" Since she was still in a crumpled pile, she had a feeling he wasn't talking to her.

She allowed him to help her up, and as he was fussing over her and checking her for bruises, she looked past his bent-over form to determine who had rear-ended her. Whoever it was certainly wasn't big on the theory of personal buffer space.

It was the grunge princess from the coffee shop, dressed head to toe in black as usual, from the plastic beads on the ends of each of the odd-looking little two-strand corkscrews into which she'd coaxed her dead-straight, thin, greasy hair—that's new, Rita thought—to the uncomfortable-looking black faux-patent-leather boots, with silver clasps in a row from calf to ankle. She'd have been better off running in her Converses.

The girl's ash-pale face was aflame, and her kohl-rimmed eyes looked about to spill tears. "I…" she began, and then covered her mouth with gray-gloved hands. "Um…"

"You okay?" Dorian asked, addressing Rita this time.

"Fine," she said easily. "Don't worry about it." Tumbling tail over elbows onto the ground in front of thousands of strangers, a speechless teenager and a new date wasn't all that bad, was it?

"Okay." Mercifully, he could see for himself that she was fine and didn't fuss any further. His black gaze fell upon the teenager, who was standing there, looking abashed, almost afraid, as people streamed past. "Miss?" he inquired politely.

"Uh," the young girl said, leading Rita to wonder at the extent of her vocabulary. "Yeah."

The awkward silence that followed desperately needed filling in, perhaps with an introduction, so she gestured at Dorian. "This is my friend, Dorian. And this is…." She faltered. This girl was so much a fixture at the coffee shop that she was practically furniture, but Rita didn't have the slightest inkling of her name. What should she call her? Coffee shop girl? Her private pet name, Drucilla?

"Lauren," the girl supplied, and ducked her face again to hide what could have been a smile.

"Nice to meet you, Lauren." Dorian shook her limp hand gravely. "Are you running this morning?"

"I don't…know." The girl looked down at herself, as though she had only just discovered that she was wearing a race sticker on the front of her shirt.

"Because the race is getting away from us," Dorian pointed

out good-naturedly, although Rita could tell that he was itching to be pounding the road with everyone else. When Lauren didn't say anything, he suggested she join them.

Lauren looked startled at the invitation. Her eyes shifted wildly from Dorian's encouraging face to Rita's curious one, down to Angela and the leash that had started all the trouble, and back at Rita again. Then she ran.

In the opposite direction.

They watched her disappear into the onrushing crowd, like a salmon swimming upstream in mating season. They each had their hands on their hips and identical expressions of bemusement on their faces. Dorian was about to comment, but thought better of it. Instead, he turned to Rita and said, "This is supposed to be a race, right?"

"Supposed to be."

"Bang," he said, and was off.

Rita pursued him and Angela relentlessly, but damn him, he was both merciless and fast. To give him credit, he waited up for her from time to time when she lagged too far behind, fetched her water at the watering stations and encouraged her to regularly check her pulse to ensure she didn't keel over. But otherwise, he was unapologetically competitive. He egged her on with encouraging words and taunts, spun out ahead with his inexhaustible hound so that she had no choice but to keep going, even when the temptation to abandon the race and give in to the lure of a nice iced coffee became almost too great to resist.

By the fifth mile, when more than half of the runners ended their course, she contemplated offering to catch a cab and meet him at the ten-mile finish line, but he sensed her failing courage, and a warning look made her swallow the suggestion.

In a glimmering moment of chivalry, he held back at the finish, waiting on her, putting his arm around her and all but hauling her past it. She collapsed in a sweaty, panting heap, and he fell beside her, laughing. "Think you'll survive?"

"I'd better."

"You will," he assured her confidently. "I've faith in you."

"Somebody has to," she grouched, rubbing her sore calves.

"Need help with that?" he flirted.

"Nope."

"Pity."

She was half regretting her refusal herself, as his big hands looked as if they could give a killer massage, but she shooed him away nonetheless. "Your dog probably needs more of a massage than I do. Just look at her."

She was right. Angela was little more than a floppy, boneless bundle of happy fur, lying on her back and regarding them both. Dorian humored her, giving tired canine limbs a thorough rubdown, finishing up by feeding her a pouch of liver and rice treats fished out of his pocket.

The post-race festivities kicked off with a live band, and barbecue grills fired up all around them. Fairground treats such as hot dogs, corn dogs and popcorn were perhaps antithetical to the spirit of running for health, but looked delicious all the same. Dorian left to speak with one of the officials, and returned with the results. Among the men, he had come in one hundred and twelfth, and she had come in one hundred and thirty-fourth in her category.

"You'd have won your medal, if you didn't have me as an albatross."

"Nonsense," he denied the truth gallantly. "Besides, what would I do with another medal? I've only got so much storage space back at my place."

She punched him in the shoulder. "You dog! You run competitively, don't you!"

"Well, not on a national scale, or anything," he answered modestly, "but I did do track in high school and college. And in the Reserve, of course. But otherwise, nah."

"And there I was on the phone like an idiot, calling you a…." She put her hands up to cover her mouth.

"Forget it. You didn't know." He was smiling broadly. "There's a lot you don't know about me."

Evidently, she thought weakly, but then he was leaning closer, and saying, so softly that he had to bring his lips to her ear, "But we've got time."

The sun moved slowly across the sky. Bands played, and those who still had energy left danced. She and Dorian ate much more than they should have, and moved around less than they should have, as their little spot on the prickly grass was perfect for lying back and staring up at the cool blue sky and watching the clouds form and dissipate. Perfect for talking, and they did a whole lot of that, too.

It was a simple, enjoyable way to spend the day, and Rita was surprised at how pleasant it was for her to do nothing but lie there and listen to Dorian talk. She was happy. She was happy!

And at some point during the day, he leaned forward and kissed her again.

Chapter 7

Cassie was still talking. Rita wanted to glance at her watch to get an idea of how long Cassie had been raving on but that would have been rude. She hid a smile and listened. The subject that held Cassie's attention was, of course, Clark.

"Everything in the basket was organic. Right down to the candy. Wasn't that thoughtful?"

"It was," Rita agreed, although she was hearing for the third time about Clark's ten-pound gift basket. By now Clark was well aware of her health fetish, since on their third date they'd confessed their mutual disdain for Thai food, and vowed not to try to impress each other anymore by pretending to like things they didn't.

Not that Cassie had kept up her end of that bargain. So far their outings had included a night at the opera (which Cassie contended was slightly preferable to slivers of bamboo driven under the fingernails) and a leisurely Sunday afternoon paddling around the lake in the middle of De Menzes Park, even though Cassie had a morbid fear of drowning and got seasick in her own bathtub.

Love, Rita mused, made people do stupid, stupid things.

Because, make no bones about it, Cassie was in love. Bafflement by the suddenness of it all didn't minimize it in any way.

"What about you?" Rita heard Cassie say.

She dragged herself back from her thoughts. "Come again?"

"What about you and Hunka-Hunka?"

Rita stopped jogging so suddenly her sneakers squeaked on the hard path. "Who?"

"You know who. Dorian! Bright eyes!" She rose on tiptoe and stretched her hand overhead to indicate great height. "The Tall One. What about you and him?"

"What *about* me and him?"

Cassie eyed her slyly. "Clark says you two are an item."

"Clark says wrong. We aren't, quote, an item, unquote."

"Oh, girl, puh-leeze!" Cassie blew a raspberry. "Who're you trying to fool? It's me, remember? Your BFF. I hear you two're all over town…."

"We've been out three or four times, if you don't count the Fun Run, which was hardly a date anyway, because half the time he was concentrating on beating the pants off me." *And kissing me on the grass in front of about two thousand people, give or take, like a schoolboy in the ballpark while everyone else is distracted by the game. And making me heat up more in five seconds of lip-on-lip action than I had over the ten miles we'd run. But that's all.* "So I wouldn't call it being an *item*."

"Perish the thought." It was Cassie's turn to be amused.

Rita added defensively, "And he's not that much of a hunk."

Cassie slapped her hands over her mouth. "Oh, my God! What are you taking for it?"

Rita was genuinely puzzled. "What am I taking for what?"

"That vision problem you have."

Cassie had her there. Dorian really was all that. But that was as far as it went. "His gender politics stink," she commented, as though that explained everything.

"Pulse rate dropping." Cassie started jogging again, leaving Rita to catch up with her. When they were running in concert once again she said, "What d'you mean, his politics stink? He's a perfect gentleman."

"He's a chauvinist. He's all about men's rights this, men's rights that."

"That's like accusing a pro player of passing the ball to his own team."

Cassie's reasoning was inescapable, but Rita insisted petulantly, "Well, I still think he's biased. And on top of it all, he has the nerve to say that *I'm* biased toward *women.*"

"You are."

Rita sputtered. "I'm what?"

"You're as biased as a left-handed can opener. Your columns don't cut men any slack, and you know it. The one you sent in last week was particularly harsh. You could've given that guy in Wyoming a break, you know. He was being a butthead, but that ain't a hangin' crime in these here parts. You could've told that girl to keep him and try again."

Sometimes it was easy to forget that apart from being her buddy, Cassie was also her editor. "You hated my column?"

"I never said I hated it. I said it was unfair."

"So, why didn't you say anything?" She was both taken aback and pained; her work was a source of great pride to her. She didn't like to hear it criticized, but she disliked even more to hear that criticism come from her editor *after* the column was put to bed. "Why didn't you say something? I'd have changed it. Or toned it down a little. Or—"

"Tone it down?" Cassie waved off the idea. "You tripping? You know how many people you're going to tick off this month? The angry letters are going to be rolling in. Pollyannas don't sell magazines, sweetie."

"I know, but...." Rita fumbled, then finished, defensively, "Anyway, I don't hate men."

Cassie gave her a surprised look. "Where'd that come from? Who said you…." She stopped, and laughed. "Ah, right. You and Dorian were squabbling about that that night at the restaurant, weren't you?"

"I don't know if squabbling's the right word—"

"Forget it. He doesn't think you do, either. And you know when I criticize your work it's nothing personal. I love your stuff, for the most part—"

"For the most part?" Rita echoed.

The reassuring smile Cassie gave her leaned slightly in the direction of a grimace. "It's just that…."

"That what?" In spite of herself, she was bristling. "For the love of Mike, Cassie, Spit it out!"

Cassie said carefully, "It's just that, you know, if you were a mechanic, you'd put in as much time as you could working with cars, right?"

"Huh?"

"And if you were a doctor, you'd make rounds every day, lay hands on your patients, and keep up with the journals, right?"

Rita began to see where she was coming from. "Cassie…"

"Well, you're a relationship writer. When was the last time you had a relationship?"

"*Et tu,* Cassie?"

"What's that?"

"You sound like my mother. She thinks having a man would do me some good."

"She's got a point. And apart from the fact that she's your mom, she's also a professional. You should listen to her."

"I don't need my mother to tell me how to live my life."

"Everybody's mother tells them how to live their life. It's in the job spec."

"Well, mine goes beyond the pale."

"Maybe, but that doesn't mean she's not right. But this isn't about Bea. We were talking about your articles. All I was saying was that you can't hole yourself up and watch life go by, especially if you want to advise people on what to do with their problems. You've got to live life to write about life. I bet even Dear Abby didn't hang around and molder on a Saturday night."

Molder? She defended herself. "You know I haven't got time for—"

"Oh, baloney! What're you so busy doing, you don't have time for men? What d'you do when you're not working? Hang around moping and making kissy-face with that hamster of yours?"

"Gerbil," she corrected without even thinking about it. "He has a tail…."

"Midget rat." Cassie sniffed. "Whatever. It's not about the little fuzzball. It's about this drought you're going through."

Rita hung her head. If Cassie had so much as an inkling of the extent of her drought….

"You're stuck in a rut. Both your writing, and you. As your editor and your friend, my prescription for both those ailments is easy to come by. And—" she grinned wickedly "—it so happens you've got a doctor waiting in the wings to administer a dose. And let me tell you, sweetheart, you don't need a spoonful of sugar to make that medicine go down!"

Rita was scandalized. "You think I should sleep with Dorian to improve my writing? That's your solution?"

"Wasn't thinking about your writing. I was thinking about your mood. And did I say you should sleep with him?"

"Well, you hinted…."

"Oh, no, Missy. You arrived at that conclusion on your own. I was just thinking you could go out with him a few times, do a little canoodling. See where it leads. No harm in it."

Lots of harm in it, she could have said, but Cassie didn't give her half a chance.

"And the fact you'd think that was what I meant shows me it's on your mind anyway. A Freudian thing. You know you wanna. You like him, right?"

"Mmm."

Cassie threw her arms up. "So what's the problem? Call him."

"I saw him two days ago."

"And?"

"And if he wants to see me again, he can ask."

"Augh! Is that you speaking?" She addressed her next question to a tree they were jogging past. "Is that the famous feminist, Dear Rita? Tell me that's not Old Miss Vinegar and Spit, hard as rusty nails, hanging around waiting for a man to call her?"

She spun back and was in Rita's face again. "Ask him out. He'll love ya for it. Have fun, drown in those deep, deep eyes, and enjoy the man. Stop acting like a dumb old virgin." She swatted Rita's behind. "And wear something hot for a change. Dragging around in them ugly clothes. I know nuns with hotter outfits. Buy yourself something brazen and shake what ya mama gave you, girl."

Rita couldn't think of a response, so she just kept on running. Mercy of mercies, they made it around the lake. Cassie sailed away on the good ship Loveswept, leaving Rita to schlump back to her apartment, mind buzzing.

Ask him out, Cassie said. Enjoy the man. With everything that concept entailed.

As if that would be so easy. Rita looked at the phone on the kitchen wall. The phone looked back at her. To get out of its span of influence, she took a shower, but once she was in the bedroom, the wall extension was calling her name.

Rita felt like a four-year-old with a problem, and, like any four-year-old, the person she wanted to turn to was her mother. Where would Beatrix be? Still in Vegas? Somewhere else? Wherever she was, she wouldn't be hard to catch. Bea's cell phone was grafted to her ear. But once she got hold of her, what would she say?

What she was contemplating, and the nervous knot that had formed in her stomach at the prospect of it, was way too embarrassing to admit, even to someone as open-minded as Beatrix. This one, she'd have to wing on her own.

She pressed the towel against her breasts like a bulletproof vest. Dorian's business card was propped up against the alarm clock. It was nearly nine. She assumed he'd already left for the office, but she couldn't be sure if he'd made it there yet. She picked up the phone and dialed his cell.

He answered almost immediately. "Rita." His voice was as warm as a double espresso.

Now that she had him on the line, she wasn't sure what to say. "Hi," felt like a good start.

"Hi!" Still warm, making no effort to hide the fact that he was glad to hear from her.

"Am I disturbing you?"

"You could never do that."

Unconvinced, she was still hesitant. Her brain was screaming, *Stupid, Rita. You're a grown-up. Say something.* She came up with a gem. "On your way to work?"

"Been here since about six-thirty. Lots to get through this morning."

"Then I am disturbing you," she said hurriedly. "If you'd like, I could call back."

"Don't you dare. Your call is the nicest thing that's happened around here all morning." His voice grew softer, more inviting. "Talk to me."

His reassurance made her relax. "I was calling to get all feminist on you."

He sounded amused. "Feel free."

"You've done all the asking so far, between…well, us." Mad flush. "So I thought I'd return the favor and ask you out."

She had a vision of his dark eyebrows shooting upward. "Ask away."

"Dorian! That *was* asking!"

"Then, I accept. When?"

Might as well go for broke. "Tonight?"

"Well…."

She hastily offered him an exit route. "Doesn't have to be tonight, if you're busy. We could do it tomorrow, or over the weekend. Or—"

"Hold on, hold on, honey. I'd like nothing better than to see you tonight. It's just that today's my day to visit Elcroft Green, and that's always a long one. If we made plans, it would have to be fairly late. I wouldn't want to almost stand you up a second time." He added, "If you're up to it, we could do something around nine. Would that be okay?"

"That would be just fine."

"What'd you like to do? I could call in reservations somewhere nice…."

Impulsively, she said, "Come here. I could cook."

She knew by his voice he was smiling. "Can you?"

"Can I what?"

"Cook."

She smiled back, never mind he couldn't see her. "I've had a guest or two ask for seconds."

"In that case, I'd be delighted."

Now she was grinning like a mad fool. "Okay, then."

"I'll be there with my stomach in my hands." Then he was all business again. "Got to run. Lots of cases to handle."

"Good luck." Which was pretty big of her, considering her opinion of the cases he was handling at Elcroft.

"Thanks. And thanks for calling. You really made my day." He ended the call.

Only twelve hours to go, and she'd offered to *cook* for the man. There was shopping to do. And not just for food, but for something to wear. Nothing scandalous like Cassie had suggested, but sexy enough. She remembered that she was naked, and moved to rectify the problem.

The phone rang.

She flew to it and snatched it up, heart growing wings. "Hi!"

There was nothing but a black hole at the other end of the line. "Hello?" Nothing. Then some sort of buzz, and a click.

Odd. She put the phone down and turned away to get dressed. Panties on, bra on, jeans and a T-shirt, and the phone rang again. "Hello?"

Silence.

Her skin crawled, with that same sensation she'd had when she'd returned home to find her front door unlocked. The day those e-mails first started coming. Since then, she'd had half a dozen more, all from the same person, A.F. Some were fawning, complimenting her on her column. Some were creepy. This guy always seemed to know where she was. Could he have her phone number, too?

Ridiculous. Her mind was playing tricks. Someone was trying to contact her, and was getting cut off. There was a ghost in the machine. That was all. "Dorian?" she asked tentatively.

Quiet echoed. The line went dead.

With a feeling of dread, she hit Redial and listened for the series of bleeps that signaled her call going through. The now-familiar, deep voice on the other end of the line said, "Hello?"

"Dorian?"

"What's up?"

"You busy?"

"No, but I'm driving. I'm on my way to…." He sensed something was not right. "You okay?

"Did you just try to call me?"

"No. What happened?"

She felt stupid. "Nothing. It was probably just a bad line, or a wrong number."

"What'd they say?" His voice was wary, hard. "Did someone say something to you?"

"No. Nothing." At least, that was the truth.

"They said *nothing* to you?" He sounded protective, the way he did when he'd volunteered to go into her place and find out if someone was hiding there. Protective in that hunter-defending-the-females-of-the-tribe way he had. It was part endearing, part irritating. "Just silence? No cursing, no obscene suggestions?"

"No."

"You sound rattled. Did he scare you?"

"Not really," she lied.

"I'm coming over."

"No!" She hastened to stop him. "Don't. You don't have to. Please, forget it. It was nothing." She wished she was sure of it herself, but she'd feel even worse if he deviated from his course just to calm her jittery nerves.

"Sure?"

"Positive." She felt more assertive now. "Go to work. I'll be fine."

"Okay." He was still doubtful, but mercifully cooperated. "I'll see you later, then."

"See you." That thought cheered her up.

"Gonna be a long twelve hours," he told her softly.

That was just what she was thinking.

Chapter 8

Dorian was more excited than he should be at the thought of seeing Rita again. A dinner invitation from a woman was a good sign. It was one thing to get her to go to dinner with you. She might do it because she was curious, or hungry, or had nothing better to do. But when a woman cooked for you, that was different. Nine times out of ten, it meant that she liked you.

He was getting to like her, too. He chuckled when he thought back on how much she'd gotten on his nerves the first time they'd met. He was sure she still held to the opinions she'd expressed that night, as he did to his. But they were both wise enough not to reopen that can of worms—so far.

He dressed carefully but casually in jeans, a hand-knitted sweater and a jacket. He selected a new, but very nice wine from his small collection, regretting that he hadn't had time to pick up a bunch of flowers. On a whim, he detoured into his den and pulled down a book from a shelf, smiling. At least he could offer her a gift that meant something to him, even if it was a tattered old book.

She'd either get the joke, or she wouldn't, like it or hate it. He hoped she didn't hate it. He sensed with an unerring masculine intuition that their relationship was going to go deeper tonight. The idea warmed him up so much his jacket was almost redundant.

She opened up her door on the second knock, looking flushed—hopefully not just from her labors in the kitchen—and beautiful. Like him, she'd dressed casually. She wore a long, flowered skirt and close-fitting blouse in cheery, citrusy colors. Both garments had an aura of newness that pointed to the flattering possibility that she had gone shopping for something to wear…just for *him*.

As he leaned forward to kiss her, he smelled the soft sweetness of her perfume. It was citrusy, too. She willingly tilted her head back to accept his kiss, none of the familiar fight in her. She tasted even better than she smelled, making him feel that they had fast-forwarded through winter and spring was here.

They kissed for a long time, standing on her threshold with the door open, the bottle of wine still tucked under his arm, the other stroking her hair. For one hot minute, he was close to losing his desire for food, even though he hadn't had anything to eat all day.

Would it be inappropriate to sweep her up off her feet and carry her inside? Very. He reined himself in, broke the kiss and regarded her seriously. "Wow. What a welcome!"

She looked slightly abashed, catching his gaze for a second and then looking away in that way she had. "Well…I was…um…."

"I'm glad to see you, too. Is dinner being served in the hallway?"

She looked blank. "What?" Then she laughed. "Oh. Sorry. Come in." She took the wine from him and studied the label appreciatively. "This looks delicious."

"It is. Want me to open it?"

"Please." She stepped aside to allow him to pass. Whatever she was brewing in the kitchen smelled excellent. The table was set with orange, lemon and white placemats and dishes, bright blocks of color against the pale wood. Glasses and cutlery were buffed up to a glow, and in the center of the table, instead of flowers, was a basket of autumn fruit. He was pleased she'd taken as much time with the presentation of the meal as she had taken with herself.

Smiling, he draped his jacket over a chair. He withdrew his utility knife from his pants pocket, opened the bottle and poured generous portions into two glasses.

"Always prepared, huh?"

"A Boy Scout to the last." He folded the knife carefully. It was a big, ugly, ungainly object, not the easiest thing to carry around, but he wouldn't dream of swapping it for a smaller, more convenient model. "I can dig pebbles out of horses' hooves with this."

She humored him. "The horses of Santa Amata must be very relieved."

"And the fish are all very nervous. It's got a little thingy on it that I use to make some wicked lures."

"You and that fishing dog of yours must be the bane of all the lakes and rivers within a hundred miles."

He reiterated an earlier invitation. "That offer to bait your hook still stands."

She laughed. "Ick. I'll pass."

It felt good to make her laugh. He offered her a glass. "What'll we toast?"

"To second impressions." She lifted her glass and her caramel eyes engaged his over the rim. "They always seem so much better than first ones." She was flirting like crazy.

"Perfect." He was flirting back. "To second impressions."

They had a long sip, then she bustled into the kitchen. To pass the time, he strolled around her living room, taking in the eclectic mix of art on the walls, and the books on her coffee table and low, laden bookshelves. His eyes were drawn to a long silk rectangle, most of which was rolled up around a length of bamboo to form a scroll. The rest was open upon a wooden stand. Large black characters, probably Japanese, ran down one side. It was graced by faded, explicit erotic paintings. The silk looked so old, so delicate, he was afraid to touch it, lest it fall apart.

Then there was a small wooden African sculpture, crudely made of dark, aromatic wood. It was a figure of a nude man— in an obvious state of arousal.

Dorian didn't know what to think. Rita was a conundrum. Just as he was becoming used to her demure conduct and chaste kisses, she meets him at the door with a kiss hot enough to take the curl out of his hair. And this penchant for erotic art. What other surprises were in store?

A sound behind him made him turn. He was still holding the sculpture in his hands. She spotted it, and squealed. "Oh, God, you found that stuff!"

"Kind of hard to miss."

She took it from him hastily and set it down on the shelf— facing the wall. "It's a fertility idol from Mozambique."

"Well, he sure looks fertile," he chuckled. "Interesting taste in art you've got."

"It's not mine," she said hastily.

"Not your art?"

"Not my taste."

"Ah, was this a present from your mother, too? Like the Indian paintings on your bedroom wall?"

"Actually, it's a present from my dad. Two birthdays ago. The Japanese scroll, *that* was from my mom."

"Congratulations. You officially have the coolest parents on the planet."

"I guess," she murmured, but she didn't sound so sure. She changed the subject. "Ready to eat?"

He let her off the hook. "Lead the way, sweetheart."

The ruins of their dinner sat between them. Butternut squash soup with almonds, Angus beef, string beans sautéed in olive oil, sweet potato pie and flaky, melty garlic bread. Apple crumble drunk with amaretto.

She couldn't stop herself from asking him, "How was it?"

"Marry me."

Despite her evident pleasure, she waved off the compliment. "I don't cook like this every night…."

"Once in a while is all you need, darlin'." He reached across and took her hand. It was warm and unflinching. "Seriously, Rita, thank you. It's been a long day. This is just what I needed. I only wish I could…." He trailed off, thinking. Wasn't he forgetting something?

"Oh, snap," he muttered. "Almost forgot." He removed the hand covering hers and stood up.

She tilted her head back to look at him. "What?"

"Nothing," he soothed. "I just forgot I brought you something."

She didn't try to hide her curiosity. "What is it?"

He fished deep into his jacket pocket, suddenly feeling that his impulse was, to put it mildly, quite idiotic. Talk about muddying your own water! He hesitated, but as she egged him on, saying "What? What? Is it bigger than a bread box?" he pulled out the heavy, worn book, hastily dusting off the battered jacket. She was standing at his elbow. He handed it over.

She read the title on the cover. *"The Old Curmudgeon's Complete Compendium of Lawyer Jokes."* She lifted her questioning eyes to his.

Bang, he thought. *Think of the headlines tomorrow—Lawyer shoots self in foot.* "Like I told you, I know all the lawyer jokes ever written. I thought you might want to have a few on hand to hurl at me," he explained lamely. Then he began to hedge. "Sorry, dumb idea. It was a gift from my father my first semester. He said I should develop a thick skin." He half expected her to throw it back at him.

But to his amazement, she had already flipped it open and began reading one aloud, at random. "Two lawyers and a duck walked into a bar…." He watched the smile as it was born on her lips. Two jokes later, she was laughing out loud.

Whew.

She set off toward the living room, so engrossed in the book she had to avoid bumping into a coffee table. Instead of sitting on the couch, she dropped cross-legged onto the rug, modestly arranging her skirts, denying him a glimpse of a fine length of leg, but he was so elated that she liked his unthinking present he didn't mind the loss. Instead he sat next to her, as close as he could without becoming painfully wedged between the coffee table and the couch.

"You've read this whole thing?"

"Most of it," he understated. Truth be told, he knew the book six ways from Sunday, having read and reread it over the years. But he didn't want to spoil the freshness of it for her.

"Did you read the one about the lawyer and the devil?"

"Which one about the lawyer and the devil? He's practically our patron saint."

She paraphrased for him. "There's this lawyer, right? He goes to the devil and asks for success, money, fame, fortune and wild sex. So, uh, get this, the devil says he can have all of that, and more, but that when they die, his wife, children and his children's children will, um, rot in hell for all eternity, right?"

God, she's an awful joke teller, he thought.

"Know what the lawyer says?"

The punch line came easily and silently to his mind. *So, what's the catch?* "No."

"So, what's the catch?" she read, and laughed uproariously, clutching the book to her breasts. He didn't want to leave her laughing alone so he joined in, but as he did so, he was thinking how tempting her mouth looked when she laughed. He'd only kissed her once since he'd got here. He wanted to do it again.

She was thumbing through the pages, totally into it. More peals of laughter. Watching her have a good time—even at his expense—felt better than it ought to. He let her rip on him for several more minutes, and then she put down the book and wiped away tears of laughter. "Oh, Dorian, that was too good."

"Glad you enjoyed it." He smiled indulgently. He poured the last of the wine into a glass and offered her a sip before taking one himself. "I was afraid for a second there you'd be ragging on me," he added mischievously.

Her face sobered up. "Oh, my gosh. Did I…I hope I didn't offend you."

She looked so serious that he regretted wiping the smile off her face. He hastened to reassure her. "Don't be silly." He pinched his forearm, hard. "Thick hide, remember? Besides, you should hear my father and my brothers have a go at me." He pointed at the book. "*The Old Curmudgeon* is practically love poetry compared to them."

"Tell me about them." She pushed the book away, closing the comedy segment of the evening.

He settled closer to her, feeling the warmth of her hip against his. She didn't move away. Her desire to delve beneath his surface pleased him. "My father's a semiretired bus mechanic from Indiana."

"How does a bus mechanic become *semi*retired?"

"He teaches two days a week at Arlo Tech. Can't help himself, he's mad about machines, and he loves working with youngsters. Says he'll retire fully when he's ready to take the dirt nap. His words, not mine."

"And your brothers?"

"Three of them. I'm the eldest." He counted off on his fingers. "There's Heathcliff—he's an eye surgeon, working out in Zimbabwe with Doctors Without Borders. There's Titus—he's got a farm down in Arizona."

"What kind of farm?"

He laughed ruefully. "Well, this year, it's ostriches. But he's tried his hand at goats, sheep, and, for a while, alligators."

"Alligators!"

"Yep. Titus is always coming up with a scheme to make a million bucks. And finally, there's Oberon. Still in high school, but he's getting into college next yea—"

She interjected, holding her hand over her mouth to contain her surprised laughter. "You have a brother called *Oberon?*"

"Puts the whole Dorian Black thing into perspective, doesn't it?"

The connection between the four names clicked. "Your dad sure must love reading the classics."

"My mother, actually. She's a voracious reader. I don't think it occurred to her when she was naming us, especially poor Obie, that she was giving the class bully a damn good reason to kick our butts. There's fifteen years between Obie and me, though, so by the time he was old enough to fall victim, I was old enough to march down to the principal's office and raise holy hell."

"Nice brother to have."

"I am." He grinned. "Especially with Mom not being there. Obie's become pretty dependent on me."

A shadow flitted across her face. "Oh, Dorian, I'm sorry. When did your mother pass away?"

"Mom? Dead? Far from it. Last I heard, she was sipping hot buttered rum in Aspen, with whatever young admirer she's dangling from her little finger this month. What I meant was, my parents are divorced."

"Oh. I'm still sorry."

He shrugged. "No need. They were mismatched from the start. It's a wonder they stuck it out long enough to have four kids. Mom's a trust fund baby who ran off to marry my father. She never got over all the things she could've had if my Average Joe father had what she called 'more ambition.' After Obie was born, she went back to her family and picked up where she'd left off."

"And you never saw her again?" Rita looked so sorry for him he was quick to reassure her.

"Of course we saw her. She still jets into town three or four times a year, and these days she stays with me. Mom and I get along. It's my father she doesn't see. There's enough bitterness between them to spoil milk. She played a mean trick on him."

"What?"

"She sued for alimony. She didn't need the money, naturally. One of my grandfather's cars was worth more than our house. She did it because she knew it hurt him. Every month, when he wrote out that check, he'd have a reminder of her and how he'd let her down. To her, what she got was pocket money. To my father, it meant half of what he had to raise his boys on. It meant moonlighting for him, and substitute dad duty for me."

"Didn't she see that she was hurting her children, too?"

Dorian sighed. He wasn't quite sure why he was telling her all this. It wasn't the kind of thing he got into with women, no matter how much he liked them. But there was some kind of pressure building inside him.

"Maybe. My father was too proud to let her know the strain she was causing. To admit to being hard up just felt unmanly. So he pretended it didn't matter. He never defaulted on his payments, not once. But we got by. Between my father and myself, I made it through college, and I've put two of my brothers through. When Obie's ready, he knows I'm willing."

"Is that why…." She stopped.

"Why I spend my time huddled with the other members of the Boys' Club, making sure that ex-wives don't get their due?"

She flushed prettily at her own words. "I'm sorry, I…."

"Don't be. I wasn't throwing anything at you." He rubbed his chin, thinking hard. "But that's what you're asking. And the answer is, I don't know. Divorce law isn't something a young boy dreams of, not over becoming an astronaut or a fireman or something cool like that. But even back then, I could recognize miscarriage of justice when I saw it."

Her eyes were soaking in his face, her lips slightly parted, and he became intensely aware of her and of how fast the night was slipping away. He cleared his throat. "Forget it," he advised her. "I love both my parents, and deep down, they probably still love each other a little. I had a great childhood. Don't feel sorry for me." Then he added, more decisively, "And let's not waste any more of the evening on that nonsense."

She took the hint and rose gracefully. He found himself mesmerized by the curve of her calves and the small, protruding bones in her ankles as she walked across the rug. She fiddled with the CD player. Jill Scott breathed life into the air.

Rita dimmed the lights, and put her hand on her hip. "Well?"

He pretended he didn't know what she was getting at. "Well, what?"

"I'm waiting."

Inwardly, he groaned, but played it cool. "Waiting on…?"

She lifted her arms from her sides, holding them out before her. "You don't expect me to dance alone, do you?"

"Aw, come on. You know I'm the world's…."

"…only non-dancing brother. I know. But I like to dance. And I want to dance now. It's mighty cold out there tonight. It'd be a terrible thing to cast you out…."

"So, for clarification, it's strictly a case of put up or you show me the door."

"That's right."

"And you admit you're openly threatening me."

"Correct again, counselor."

"Just building up a defense against any claims you might level against me when I step on your feet."

"I'll risk it." Her hips were already swaying, fluid, undulating under that long, flowing skirt. He was pulled to his feet by the power of her influence. He approached her, and the way she curled her arms around him made him glad he did, even though he was about to make a complete ass of himself. He was getting to touch her, and that made it a bargain.

"Now, you do know what a beat is, don't you?"

"I have an inkling."

"And you know how to count them?"

"I can count beats. Just because I'm spatially retarded doesn't mean I don't listen to music."

"Then we're halfway there," she soothed. "And you aren't spatially retarded. I've seen you run, remember? You go like a great, long-limbed leopard."

"You're saying I should drop down and sprint around your living room?"

"I'm saying listen to your body. Or, at least, listen to mine."

He was listening. He pulled her closer until her hips were brushing against his. He swayed with her, trying to match movement to beat. Jill Scott's voice guided him, whispering urgently in his ear like a woman in the heat of lovemaking. He responded as if they were moving horizontally rather than vertically. His clumsiness forgotten, he found his groove. Pretty soon, her body was all he was hearing.

Chapter 9

Have you totally lost your sanity? You've done nothing all day but plot and plan how to throw yourself at this man. The only thing you haven't done is wriggle out of your half-slip and wave it under his nose like a red flag. "Are you nuts?"

"Hmm?" Dorian's voice was in her ear, his lips pressed against a few loose strands of hair that had fallen out of the roll she had wound them into. Music dripped from the CD player, but she barely heard a note. Had she spoken out loud?

She rushed to cover up her lapse. "Nothing."

"I thought you said…."

"I didn't say anything. Forget it."

He was happy to forget it, and she was happy he did, because it meant he wouldn't have to let her go, to pause for an explanation. Although she would admit that an explanation—a complex, embarrassing explanation—would soon become necessary. Because the way he was touching her, and the way she was touching him back, told her the evening was whirling toward its inevitable finale. If it did—when it did—would she have the courage to say something?

Dorian had had enough of letting her take the lead. He'd given in to her guidance when it came to dancing, but now to call what they were doing dancing was like calling Godiva chocolates a little snack. His body was as hard as hers was soft, as unyielding as hers was pliant, and the arm around her waist pulled her ever closer, until her breasts were in full contact with his chest, her hips with his. Reason took a hike.

He kissed her. He'd kissed her before, at least once or twice every time they'd gone out. But never like this. Once, and then again, his tongue requested entry. Permission granted. She opened her mouth and he invaded her defenses. As their teeth made contact, there was a muted clink, the sound their wine-glasses had made earlier when she had coquettishly proposed a toast. He sipped their own private brand of wine from her lips, her neck and from that hollow at the base of her throat, where her collarbones met. Every touch made each tiny hair along her skin go mad, snapping into erection like sensitive plants under the curious touch of a child.

Her breath came faster and heavier. His hands sliding up and down her back robbed her of speech.

Dorian had plenty to say. "I've kissed you before," he mused. "How come you've never tasted like this?" Soft fabric rustled, and up came her blouse out of the waistband of her skirt. His hand slid under it. His exploring fingers skimmed the lace cup of her bra, until he found the hard bump of her nipple. He ran the tip of his finger in circles around it, making her want to yelp, bite, pull away. Anything to stop the sensation. "I've touched you before. How come you've never felt like this?"

"You've never touched me quite like that," she managed to point out.

"That makes me a fool." All pretense of dancing was abandoned. His body still moved, as did hers, but they were hearing their own internal music, sweet and heady, beckoning to them in the way the bottom of a well beckoned to someone looking into it, or the ground to someone leaning over the balcony of a tall building. Beguiling and dangerous. Seductive. Scary.

Say something.

She remained mute.

Her arms rose in compliance as he eased her blouse over her head. It fell at their feet. She didn't care. His genius fingers found and undid the catch on her bra without him having to look. That, too, fell.

Tell him.

If the color of her skin had allowed it, she would have turned red. As it was, there was merely a darkening, a tint that spread across her skin in waves, from the inside, deep in some hot spot in her tummy, out to her navel, and then up to her breasts as they suffered under his black gaze.

She wished he'd say something, anything, recite his grocery list if he had to, anything to minimize the impact of the shattering seconds as he simply looked at her.

She put her hands up over her pebble nipples.

"Don't cover yourself. You're amazing. I'm sorry I stared. I didn't mean to make you uncomfortable. It's just that…you're…" He floundered, trying to find the right word, but, for once at a loss, settled for the one he had used before. "Amazing!"

His kisses went lower, leaving her jealous mouth and neck for her breasts. There it was: that urge to scream again. To silence it, she wrapped her fingers around his head, feeling the roughness of his freshly cut hair. Her hands slipped lower until she could feel each vertebra in his neck and between his shoulder blades, like large beads strung together.

He began to undo the buttons on his own shirt. The floor was becoming littered with abandoned clothing. "Touch me back." His voice was as raspy as a cat's tongue.

She wanted to, and that unfamiliar desire almost knocked her flat. She put her hands up between them, palms out, like someone feeling her way across a darkened room. Under her fingers his skin was hot, and under that skin, a wall of hard muscle rose and fell. His nipples were like dark, flat old pennies, but when she scraped them lightly with her fingernails he had to grit his teeth to keep a groan from escaping.

Power. What awesome power. To be able, with just one finger—no, just one finger*tip*—to force this large and powerful man into submission. Experimentally, she probed his nipple again, this time with her thumb, and was surprised and delighted when he cursed and tried to wrench away, as if the sensation was too much to bear. "You're trying to kill me," he accused her.

"No," she said, half in wonder, "I'm learning."

He misunderstood her, just slightly. "I want to learn how to please you, too. Show me."

Even if she knew what to say, hell would get mighty chilly before she found a way to say it. "I…" she began, and halted.

He kissed her again, moving from her lips to her earlobe, inflicting little nips along the path. "Don't be shy," he encouraged. "It's me, Dorian. You can trust me with your secrets. We're all alone and we both—" his thumbs were under the waistband of her skirt, edging it lower "—want this."

Secrets. Oh, God. "Dorian…."

Her feet left the ground, and the mock Persian carpet was under her back. Her skirt was gone. Her satin panties were far from what she usually wore, but she'd bought them just today. She'd be a liar if she tried to convince herself that she hadn't bought them hoping he might see them tonight. That meant she wanted this, right? That meant she was doing the right thing.

Right?

The attention he was paying to her belly, poochy as it was, was damn near worshipful. Inch by inch, he kissed it, making little circles, radiating outward from her navel. It quivered as every kiss landed, until her abdomen was taut in anticipation of the next onslaught. He loomed above on his hands and knees, looking down at her. He seemed so huge, so big and imposing, that she felt like she were lying out in an open field, looking up at the sky while the dark clouds gathered, blocking out the moon and the stars. He lowered himself down, so that he was fully outstretched upon her body.

She wondered if she would be able to breathe.

Something hard dug into her bare thigh, pressing into her skin as he moved against her. Too hard. Too big. Downright painful. "Ow!" She squirmed away from the offending lump.

"What?"

"You…uh…." She wasn't sure how to say it.

He looked bemused, and then laughed. "Sorry." As he reached down between them, she prudishly squeezed her eyes half-shut, but then he fished into the pocket of his pants and withdrew his knife of many uses. "Forgot." He put it down on the coffee table.

Her relief must have been palpable, because he glanced once at her apprehensive face, then back at the large metal instrument on the table, and laughed even harder. "Oh, you're kidding. Surely you didn't think that was…."

"I did *not,*" she lied hotly, feeling stupid.

He didn't believe her, but didn't hold it against her, either. "Sorry, darlin', but I haven't been that blessed. I don't think anybody's that blessed." He peeled off his pants like a snake wriggling out of its old skin, and then settled down upon her again. Blast him, he was still grinning at her idiocy.

Denial of her mistake was useless. Then it became a moot point, because this time, what she was feeling pressed against her was all real, all him. And it felt good.

He touched her body experimentally, moving from spot to spot like a physician trying to identify the site of an elusive ache. "D'you like this? This?"

She did like it. Very much. She bit down hard on her lip in

an effort to remain silent, but her reaction told him all he needed to know.

"Pretty," he commented, as he rolled those bought-for-him panties down over the bump of her bottom and slipped them off her ankles. "Did you get these for me, like your blouse and your skirt?"

How could he tell? Did he think that made her forward?

"You don't need to answer that. And I wasn't being mean. I'm flattered. I'm honored."

She felt more naked than she thought possible. Having nothing to shield her skin was one thing, but having nothing to shield her eyes…. He turned one hand so that his wrist rested just below her navel, and his fingers stretched downward, past the border where the tight curls of hair began. He explored her, lightly, reveling in the texture of the tightly folded petals.

Unbelievable, how he knew to touch her like that. She remembered what it had been like, not half an hour before, when she was teaching him how to dance with her. How to move with her. This time, he didn't need a coach. He knew literally and figuratively where her buttons were, and he pressed them.

Somewhere inside her head, it was the Fourth of July. Starbursts. Light and color. She tried to push his hand away, but he persisted, ignoring her mewling pleas, and enjoying them.

She was knocked off her moorings by a wave of intense sensation, hit unexpectedly from behind, no warning signals, no *Mayday! Mayday!* She went under, holding her breath, praying to retain her sanity until she could rise to the surface for air.

When she opened her eyes, he was smiling down into her face. His hand was still. "I wish you could have seen what I just saw," he told her.

She fought to regain her equilibrium, unable to answer.

He didn't need a response. He took her hand and placed it on the band of his shorts. He whispered a hoarse, "Undress me."

Undress him? She couldn't. She wouldn't know where to look.

"Please. Show me you want me, too."

Her face was crazy hot, hands shaking with fear and excitement and apprehension, but she helped him out of his shorts. He was as naked as she was, as excited as she was.

Wonderful. Frightening.

He tried to catch her eyes, brow furrowed. "Rita?"

"Yes?"

"You okay?"

"Yes." She was okay. She was *okay*. If she told herself that enough....

"Good." He felt about again for his pants, fiddled in his wallet for a condom, and she fixed her eyes on the back of his strong hands as he put it on. Then he reached for her. She went willingly. But as he pressed against her, she stiffened.

He sensed her hesitation at once. "Been a long time?" he deduced sympathetically.

"Actually...." she floundered. Tell him. *Tell him.*

"It's okay," he soothed, kissing her hair. "It'll be all right. Trust me. Trust your body. It'll remember."

She did as she was advised, trusting her body to know what to do, but as he sought entry, something within fought back. He pushed again, more insistently, whispering in her ear soft pleadings for her not to shut him out. For her to relax. Then, astoundingly, he was in.

And it hurt. It hurt so much that she buried her face in his neck to spare him her grimace of pain. She bit into the back of her fist. She was not going to scream. She was not going to ruin this, for him or for her. She tried to think of the pleasure he'd given her moments before. It would get better in a minute.

She was wrong. As he moved inside her, her only sensation was one of invasion, sore flesh stretched beyond its limit until it gave in. Her strangled sob stopped him dead.

"Rita? What is it? Am I hurting you?" He was so genuinely bewildered that she felt sorrier for him than for herself. "I thought you were ready." He withdrew, and the pain was replaced by a ghost of itself. He rubbed his head, trying to get his thoughts in order. "I don't understand."

They both saw the blood at the same time. There wasn't a lot of it, less than she'd been led to expect, anyway, but he recoiled in horror, sitting up with his back against an armchair. "What the hell…?"

"Dorian," she began. She didn't know how to continue.

His gaze was locked on the crimson smears on her thighs, and though she knew it was futile to try to hide the evidence, she rubbed at them with the closest thing at hand: that light, pretty skirt that had so enchanted him. It would be ruined, but she didn't think she'd ever want to wear it again. "Let me explain," she begged. "Give me a chance."

"I hurt you!" He was aghast. "I didn't think I was being rough with you. I thought I was being so careful. I feel like a monster." He leaned toward her, one hand on her leg. "Are you okay? Let me see—"

"No!" She slammed her knees together and tried to wrap that benighted skirt around her like a sarong.

"But if you're hurt—"

"I'm *not* hurt." She wished he wouldn't look at her with such pain and puzzlement.

"But I still don't under…." The penny finally dropped. "Rita, are you…are you a virgin?" The idea defied comprehension.

"Not anymore."

"But that's impossible. You can't be."

"It's not, and I was."

"But you're twenty-seven!" He stared at her as though she'd confessed to being a member of a strange and unproven new species.

"Guess that makes me a late bloomer." Embarrassment made her gruff. "So shoot me."

Hurt was reflected in his eyes. "Why didn't you tell me?"

"I tried!" She had, hadn't she?

"When? When you were dancing for me? When your blouse

hit the floor? When you were lying naked on the rug, with your arms and legs all tangled up with mine, begging for me to—"

"I never begged!" Not true, her conscience whispered, but she was stubborn in the face of her own error.

Her harshness seeped outward, infecting him and tainting his words. "I can promise you, sweetheart, I may be dumb as a rock when it comes to spotting superannuated virgins, but I know sexual hunger when I see it, and you were definitely—"

This was stupid. "I did try to tell you. I wanted to. But every time I tried…." She threw her hands up. "What difference would it have made, anyway?"

"What difference would it have made? For starters, I would have taken more time. I'd have figured out a way to minimize the pain."

"What way?"

"I don't know. Something. I can't say off the top of my head. It's not like I have virgins offering themselves up to me every night—"

There he was again. Did his ego not have any limit? "I was not *offering myself up* to you—"

"Whatever you say, angel. But at least the information would've showed a little respect for me and my feelings. In fact, if you'd told me, I might have decided to wait awhile, make sure we both thought this through."

"There you go."

"What?"

"Now you know why I didn't tell you."

His eyes narrowed. "What's that supposed to mean?"

"If I'd told you, you might have…." She was too miserable to continue.

He had no such qualms. "I might have turned you down? In hindsight, that would've been a pretty good idea."

She hated that he was so angry with her. She wished he'd understand. "But then you would have left me—" she didn't ever want to use or hear the word *virgin* again. It had been an albatross for too long, and now he was reacting as though she'd come to him with an undisclosed medical condition "—the way I was," she finished lamely.

"So what? You put up with it for twenty-seven years. It wouldn't have killed you to put up with it a little longer."

"Twenty-seven years is long enough."

"So you got up this morning, decided it was time to rid yourself of your little inconvenience and made a booty call?"

"It wasn't a booty call. That's an awful thing to say!"

"Did you or did you not set this up?" With a sweep of his arm he encompassed the remains of their dinner on the table, the empty wine bottle, the scattered clothes. "Did you or did you not ask me over, choose the right music, cook the right food, buy new clothes, new panties—"

It couldn't get worse than this.

"—with the express intention that the evening would end up this way? Didn't you plan on seducing me?"

"You're interrogating me. I'm not on the witness stand!"

"Didn't you plan for this to happen?"

"Yes, but—"

"That, my dear, is the definition of a booty call." The disgust on his face was apparent. He got up and began dragging his clothes on.

He couldn't leave like this, misunderstanding her. She tried to repair the damage. "It wasn't just about that. I wanted to be with you—"

"Because I'm special?" he threw at her.

"Yes."

"But not special enough to give me the heads-up before I get the scare of my life to find you bleeding."

"I'm sorry." Humiliated tears burned in the corners of her eyes. She wished she could explain herself, but the more she said, the worse things got. She hopped to her feet, still naked, and tried to hold Dorian by the arm. He was putting away his dangerous-looking knife, the one that had them both laughing just a short time and a whole millennium ago, and refused to look at her. "But I told you, I was afraid that, if you knew, you wouldn't…want me anymore. And I needed to…." She floundered desperately. "Besides, Cassie said…."

He spun around with such ferocity that she staggered back. "You had sex with me because *Cassie* said you should?"

"Not in so many words. She said I needed to get out more, get a love life. That I should buy some hot clothes, and that you and I…. She said if I had a little more, uh, male company, it would improve my writing."

He was the picture of incredulity. "Your editor told you if you lost your virginity your *writing* would get better? Wouldn't night school have the same effect?"

"No! No! She doesn't know about that. Nobody does. She's my best friend, but I couldn't tell her."

"Good thing you didn't. She may be your friend, but she's still your boss. If she found out she was paying a woman who's never had an intimate relationship with a man to give advice *about* intimate relationships, she'd know what you are."

"What am I?" She waited miserably for an answer.

"A fraud." He snatched his jacket up and shoved his arms into the sleeves. "Get dressed, Rita," he suggested. "This is over."

"You're leaving?" Little Miss Obvious asked.

"No reason to stay." He wrenched open her front door and stepped into the hallway. "Be sure and lock up tight. The world's a dangerous place." If the neighbors weren't up, the slamming door stood a pretty good chance of waking them.

Numbly, she did as she was told, then stood with the key still swinging in the lock, fingers interlaced, face buried in her hands, and wept.

This all went so awfully, terribly wrong. She'd made so many mistakes she couldn't identify where the snowball of errors had begun to gather speed. Had it been wrong to call him? Or was the first mistake she'd made inviting him to her home, where she knew they'd be alone? Should she have worn something less suggestive? When things had turned raunchy, should she have told him about her little "problem," and let him make up his own mind? And that underwear! What was she thinking?

So many questions. They, coupled with lingering smell of congealing food, threatened to make her throw up. She reeled toward her bedroom, naked. Her discarded clothes would stay on the floor until she had the chance to throw them out. She wasn't wearing those again.

Her bedroom was dark, and so cold that gooseflesh rose on her skin. Even her gerbil, Wallace, was balled up in a corner, buried deep under a heap of wood shavings. Great. Just what she needed tonight: a busted thermostat. She felt a draft, right on her bare bottom, and whirled around. A breeze ruffled the curtain in one of her windows, the same window she and Dorian had found open that first night. Problem was, she knew for certain she'd shut it. Gingerly, she approached, arms wrapped around herself to keep her thudding heart from bursting through her rib cage.

"Hello?" Nothing. She looked down below, onto a deserted street. Dorian's car was gone, and the only movement was that of fallen leaves whirling along the sidewalks. She eased her head through the crossed metal bars, straining and twisting to look upward to the rooftop. Nothing but an expanse of silence.

She brought her head back in again, overwhelmed by the sensation that something was wrong. That someone had tampered with the lock. Maybe entered her bedroom, even while she and Dorian had been in the living room, lying tangled together. Her stomach lurched. With mingled anger and fear, she pulled the window shut and locked it.

As she did so, something fell from the windowsill onto the floor at her feet. A piece of paper. Her shaking hands could barely unfold it. On that single sheet of ordinary bond paper, a sentence was printed, in the most generic font possible, Times New Roman, 12 point. It said, *Are you afraid of heights?*

Chapter 10

The sleepless night Rita spent after that fiasco did her no good. Neither did the next, nor the next. Her misery at the inept way she handled what should have been a priceless, memorable event with Dorian made her reluctant to leave the house. The eerie feeling that came over her every time she thought about the note on her windowsill made her half afraid to stay. Even Starbucks was off-limits; the possibility of sipping coffee while sitting a few feet away from her tormentor was too creepy.

She thought about calling the police, but was too embarrassed to pick up the phone. With all the bad things going on in the world, her stalker seemed almost trivial. Besides, what kind of complaint could she lodge? Felony note-leaving?

She was afraid to open her e-mail, even though the questions therein were essential to her column. With her deadline approaching, she rummaged through her files, pulled out some of her rejects and answered those instead.

She ended up with a botched job she could hardly be proud

of. Her advice was perfunctory, her prose lacked her usual edge, and, given the fact that the letters she was responding to were weeks or months old—an eon in Internet time—her answers came too late to be of any real use. That gave Dorian's accusation the ring of truth. She was a fraud, in more ways than one.

Dorian. Oh, God, what a mess. He was right; she'd led him on. She burned when she remembered how she'd come on to him. She should call him, try to explain herself. But her cowardice, made more potent by her shame, undermined any conviction she had to set things right. She'd rather go blind than look Dorian in the eye and see, once again, his contempt for her.

But Santa Amata was a small city. Sooner or later, she was bound to run into him, especially if his partner continued to date her friend. Speaking of whom, what was she going to tell Cassie? She wasn't the kind of woman you could keep things from. So, she'd been ducking her. She'd begged off from their morning jog for more than a week, citing a charley horse in her left calf, a painful period, overdue assignments, and, one day when she just didn't have an excuse handy, a case of the blahs.

Cassie had been sympathetic, prescribing ice for the sprained muscle, orange tea and a hot water bottle for the cramps, and romantic comedies and a box of chocolates for the blahs. But Rita knew Cassie was just humoring her. She was smart enough to guess that Dorian was at the heart of the problem, but held her tongue—at least, for now.

Not that Cassie had time to concern herself with anyone's problems. Her romantic whirlwind was getting more serious by the minute. Exactly how serious was a mystery to Rita, until Cassie barged into her living room one morning, yanked apart the curtains, and shouted, "Okay, sulking time's over. Get up!"

Rita was slumped before her computer, in nothing but a grubby T-shirt, a pair of panties and fuzzy gray ankle socks. She'd let Wallace out of his cage to stretch his legs. At Cassie's sudden arrival, poor Wallace, who'd been happily nestled on her shoulder, pressed into the crook of her neck, lost his balance and tumbled over. He saved himself by snagging her neck with his claws.

Rita yowled. "You snuck up on me! You startled Wallace. He scratched me!"

"It'll heal. You got any iodine? Rub some right on there."

"Thanks for being so concerned." Rita patted the scratches on her throat, half hoping to see a tinge of blood to justify her disgruntlement.

Cassie blew her a kiss. "You know I love you, babe. Under any other circumstances, I'd be bandaging that boo-boo myself, but right now we got fatter fish to fry." She poked Rita in the back. "Shake it. Funk's over."

Rita was less than willing to shake it. Sulking was suiting her just fine right now. But she knew better than to argue with Cassie, so she put Wallace in his cage and slumped off toward the shower.

"Good girl," Cassie cooed—and followed her into the bathroom as Rita began to shuck off her grungy clothes.

This was strange. They weren't teenagers. The BFF routine usually stopped at the bathroom door. "Am I on suicide watch, or do you think I need help scrubbing my back?"

Trying to stop Cassie with sarcasm was like trying to stop a train by putting a penny on the tracks. "You look like you need help scrubbing everything, babe. You've got enough dirt on your arms to plant mustard seeds. And how long you been wearing that T-shirt? I caught a whiff of it from out in the hall!"

Rita cracked a smile. "I think I put it on, uh, maybe Thursday."

"Good grief, woman! What're you planning to do with it now? Burn it? Because let me tell you, they're working wonders with laundry soap these days, but…."

Rita stepped into the shower. She had to admit that the water, long forsaken, felt good on her body. She pulled the curtains closed and listened to the admonitions that continued on the other side.

"And that hair. What's up with that? You turn Rastafarian

without telling me? You need to comb all that stuff out and get it retwisted, pronto, before the cooties move in…."

Rita closed her eyes and washed herself carefully, slowly, enjoying the smell of the soap and the cleansing effects of the water on her body and her mind. Cassie was right. She'd been letting herself go to the point where she didn't even look or feel like herself.

Through the shower curtain, she could see Cassie's silhouette as she swayed up and down, humming to herself, occasionally stopping to do a little cha-cha-cha.

Cassie.

In her bathroom.

Doing the cha-cha-cha.

What the…?

"Cass?"

"Dearest?" Cassie's voice was like wine and honeysuckle.

"You sound really happy today."

"Oh, yes. I am."

Since no clarification seemed forthcoming, Rita probed again. "Has it got anything to do with where you're taking me?"

"It's got everything to do with where I'm taking you."

"And that would be…?"

"The wedding store." Cassie dropped her bomb. "I'm getting married."

Rita had a coughing fit so intense she had to shut off the water to catch her breath. "What?"

"Choked on your soap?"

Disregarding her nakedness, she tore open the curtains. "You're getting what?"

"Married." Cassie held up her left hand and waggled her finger, which was adorned by a rock the size of an asteroid. "Rita, meet my new friend Harry…Winston, that is. And if you ask me who gave it to me, you're eating that loofah."

"But you've only known Clark a month. You can't!"

"I can, and I will. A month's long enough when you're in love. And of all people I'd expect to be happy for me, it would be you." There was the slightest edge to her voice. "Was I mistaken?"

Rita heard it and felt like a rat. Cassie was right. A horrified shriek was hardly the response a woman wanted to hear when she announced her impending nuptials. Before Rita could undo the damage, Cassie left the bathroom.

"You planning to stand there with your mouth open and drip-dry, or you going to towel off and get dressed?" she yelled.

In the bedroom, Cassie was waiting, the wave of euphoria that had washed her into the apartment somewhat diminished. She was standing at the window—the window through which Rita's intruder had entered—and looking out onto Jubilee Street.

Rita approached her from behind and wound her shower-cooled arms around her shoulders. "Cass?"

"Mmm?" She didn't look around.

"I'm sorry."

"What you sorry for, girl?" She was hurt enough not to make this easy on her.

"For reacting so badly. I was just…surprised, that's all."

"Why were you so surprised? I see him every day, I talk about him all the time. He's taken me to meet his family. They love me. He loves me."

"I know. It's just that…."

"It's just nothing. Either you're happy for me or you aren't. Which is it?"

That was a no-brainer. "I'm happy for you," she said, and with all her heart, she meant it.

Not one to hold a grudge, Cassie managed a smile. "Then let's go shopping."

"How's them cooties?" Cassie asked.

"All gone," Rita answered. "I feel like a real person again."

"You'd better. You realize we've been in here for—" she took a look at her watch, lifting her hand out of the warm bowl of water in which the manicurist had been soaking it "—three hours? If you don't feel better after a wash, a new 'do, a pedicure and a manicure, then, my girl, you're a lost cause."

Rita had to agree. After half a day at the mall, browsing through wedding catalogs and trying on white gowns, veils, gloves and shoes—"It's gonna be a *white* wedding," Cassie had insisted with a straight face—they'd decided to wind down at their favorite beauty parlor.

Now she was buffed and shiny and squeaky-clean, with fresh twists in her hair, excess hair from other places waxed into oblivion, and her bitten-down nails were being returned to a semblance of decency by a manicurist.

She closed her eyes, enjoying the pampering. "Thank you."

"For what?"

"For this. I needed to get out. I was going nuts in there."

"It showed. You really were slipping."

"I know!" Rita rolled her eyes. "The stinky shirt, the cooties…."

Cassie disagreed. "That's not what I meant—although that shirt was beginning to host its own ecosystem." She sipped on her mimosa before saying, "That last 'Dear Rita' column sucked."

Sucked? It wasn't one of her best, she knew, but, *"Sucked?"*

"Eggs. It was too short, too superficial and never touched a nerve. I'd have sworn you dug it out of your reject pile, dusted it off, did a little window dressing and skated it over to me just under deadline."

"I did not!" Rita exclaimed, although that was exactly what she'd done. "Not exactly."

"Yes, exactly. I've got to put on my editor hat here." She mimed placing a broad-brimmed hat onto her hair, which she'd just had colored a more conservative shade than her usual flamboyant hue. "I'm not happy with your work, lately. If you weren't my girl, you'd probably be on notice right now. Actually, well…."

Cassie looked pained. "You *are* on notice. Sharon called me in yesterday and suggested I talk to you. Unless you can turn things around soon…well, it doesn't look good." Sharon was editor-in-chief at *Niobe*.

"Tell me you're kidding," she begged.

"I wish I was kidding." Cassie put the mimosa down as though she no longer enjoyed the taste of it.

There was a sick, rolling sensation in Rita's stomach. "What can I do?"

"Hit 'em between the eyes with something different. Change your perspective. Shelve the whole über-feminist thing and do something fresh. Something about men—"

"It's a *women's* magazine."

"And women love men. I've got a great idea for a new series on the hottest men in Santa Amata. You know, the eligible bachelors, the good catches. Who they are, what they do and why they're worth writing about. Something smart and upbeat."

The rolling sensation in Rita's stomach intensified. She knew what was coming. "No, Cass."

Cassie barreled on, eagerly selling her idea. "You can do interviews with a new man every month. Hang out with him, follow him around, get to know him and get an understanding of his contribution to society. It'll be fabulous!" She punctuated her assertion by throwing her hand up into the air, sending an arc of soapy water with it. "And I know just who to start with."

Don't say it, Rita pleaded silently. *Don't call his name.*

Cassie was deaf to her unspoken thoughts. "You're doing the first article on Dorian."

Talk to Dorian? She'd rather die. "I can't."

"Rita," Cassie answered carefully, like a patient teacher. "You have to. Don't let me spell out the consequences."

"You'd fire me if I don't do this?"

"I wouldn't, but *Niobe* would."

"Thanks for sticking up for me, girlfriend," she snapped,

knowing she was being unfair. She leaped up from the chair and rushed away, flapping her hands to dry them. Cassie caught up with her.

"I haven't got a choice in this. I'm offering you a way out here."

"But, Dorian? In all of Santa Amata, couldn't you find another so-called hot bachelor for me to write about?"

"Probably loads, but I only came up with this idea yesterday, and Dorian's right in our backyard, and you need to get going on an article to save your butt. Besides, I talked to Sharon. She's willing to let you try."

"Without asking me first?"

"Hey, your tail was on the line, and I had to think fast to save it." Cassie was getting huffy. "Excuse me for yanking you away from the thin ice in the middle of the lake without your express permission."

A little gratitude would have been in order, but then the sound of her door being slammed by a furious Dorian reverberated in her head. "But Dorian's not...speaking to me." Not speaking to her? Too mad to get a word past his throat would have been a more fitting description.

"He will once Clark talks to him," Cassie countered. "And I don't know what got into the two of you. One minute you're like Black Barbie and Cocoa Ken, and the next..." An ugly thought hit her. "Did he do something to you?"

"Nope." Not anything she was willing to discuss, anyway.

"Say something?"

"No."

"Then what's the problem?" Cassie demanded in frustration. "Last we talked, you were gonna call him over to your place and crank up the heat a little, remember?"

"Right. You suggested I sleep with him to improve my writing."

"No," Cassie corrected her painstakingly, "I suggested you sleep with him to improve your *mood*. The writing part was just gravy." Her epiphany showed on her face. "Y'all did it, didn't ya!"

"Cass!"

Cassie's experienced eye picked up on the heat that rushed into her cheeks. "Ah. That's all I needed to know. Oh, you little devil. You took that hunk 'round the block for a test drive, didn't you."

"Did you have to put it that way?"

"Sorry," Cassie said, but didn't look remotely sorry. "Let me rephrase: you and that hunk made sweet, sweet *lurve,* didn't you?"

Until she ruined it, yes. She sighed heavily, but couldn't find a thing to say.

Cassie was doing enough talking for both of them. "Was he lousy?"

No answer.

"A little too quick out of the starting blocks?"

"Cass…."

"Okay, okay! I give up!" She wheeled around and went back to her waiting manicurist. Rita followed, relieved the interrogation was over.

Except that it wasn't. Cassie didn't last two minutes. "He didn't rough you up, did he? Because if he did…."

"He didn't rough me up. But I don't want to—"

"Then what? Aw, baby, was he…." She mouthed the word *disappointing.*

"What d'you mean by that?"

Cassie made an eloquent gesture with her hands, making it only too clear what she meant. "Was God not kind to him?" she explained in a whisper that could be heard under the hair dryers in the other room.

Cassie's audacious and indiscreet question—not to mention her wholly inaccurate assumption—brought an unexpected grin to Rita's face.

Cassie laughed. "I knew that was unlikely. I mean, all you have to do is look at the boy. The way he walks…that kind of self-confidence has got to come from somewhere!" She clapped her hands like someone on the receiving end of a delicious secret.

Then she said, "Anyway," and gave a little cough. "Whatever happened between you that was bad enough for you to be mooning around on your lonesome for a week and a half, while that beauty wanders around unclaimed, you're going to have to get over it. 'Cause you're working with him. 'Kay?"

Working. With Dorian. That thought brought a wave of dread—which was washed away by a thrill of anticipation. If Cassie browbeat her into writing a feature on Dorian—and it didn't seem as if she had any other option—she would be seeing him again very soon. She shivered.

At the memory of his touch, her body flushed hot enough to speed-dry the bronze polish on her nails. Had the evening really been that much of a catastrophe, or was it just the final, awful ten minutes? Hadn't the rest of it been as wonderful as her racing heart reminded her?

It had been wonderful. That wasn't a product of her imagination. They'd laughed together and shared wine. They'd danced long and slow, kissed long and slow. She'd felt him and smelled him, tasted his skin...and that skin had been as sweet as its coffee-darkness had predicted. And he'd held her and stroked her, kissed her as no one ever had, eased sighs and moans from her as no one ever had, and explored her body with all the curiosity of a black Indiana Jones in a Mayan temple.

No, barring the horrible ending, her last encounter with Dorian hadn't been bad at all. Rita passed a hand lightly over her hair, and let it settle against her cheek, trying to conjure up the memory of his touch.

"I see we're coming around to the idea," Cassie said cheerfully. "That's good. That's real good."

"Why?" Rita was suspicious again. Cassie had more tricks up her sleeve than a multi-armed goddess. "Why's that good?"

"'Cause you're seeing him tonight. Clark and I are having an engagement dinner at his place, and Dorian's going to be there. Isn't that wonderful?"

Chapter 11

Clark's elegant home was festooned with the colors of autumn. Pumpkin, cream and gold were in the curtains, on the cushions, in the place settings and the floral arrangements. Baskets of harvest vegetables were everywhere, and on every available surface sat frosted glass dishes filled with floating scented candles. Evidence of Cassie's hand.

The large, sedate house was situated in upscale Belmont, forty-five minutes from the centre of Santa Amata. This evening, it was packed with friends of the happy couple who were seated at the head of the table, hands linked, chatting away, too excited to eat their own engagement dinner.

To Dorian's eye, Cassie's hair color was less startling, and her cleavage was demurely covered by a cream linen jacket. Clark had opted not to wear one of his perennial business suits, but instead sported a long-sleeved, duck-egg green—Clark never wore pastels!—shirt that had, wait for it, a Nehru collar. Dorian had to suppress a smile.

The catering staff kept the glasses filled with champagne. Guests had risen with aplomb to the occasion, even though most of them had had less than twenty-four hours' notice. And what an eclectic mix of friends that was. Bankers and dignitaries, photographers, models and writers, property developers and reggae artists. A few waded across the cultural divide to mingle, but most stuck with their own kind.

Clark's friends gossiped excitedly. Who was this new woman who'd snatched away Clark's heart? Who knew his heart was even available, given the intensity of his grief after he'd lost his wife? And was this happy, laughing man really the stoic, buttoned-down, undemonstrative person they knew?

Cassie's friends were equally stunned. Clark's vanilla house, in its vanilla neighborhood, with its precision-trimmed lawns and air of old money, hardly looked like the kind of place their girlfriend would look to find a partner. He was old enough to be her father. As a matter of fact, what would Cassie's father think?

Dorian said little, drank less and listened plenty. Whether they belonged to Clark's camp or to Cassie's, the consensus of the guests was the same. The happy couple were a mismatch worthy of a morning talk show, but it was obvious to all that they were in love. They'd do okay.

Dorian wasn't so sure. A career in divorce law made him wary of predictions of marital success, even when a couple seemed perfectly matched. When you threw in racial and cultural differences, an age gap, divergent tastes in everything from food to music to books to politics and a whirlwind romance, the potential for disaster was way off the scale. If a bookie were to offer him good odds on the longevity of the match, he'd be keeping his wallet in his pocket.

But out of love for his friend, he remained silent. He'd hugged Clark when he'd broken the news to him this morning, wished him all the best and meant it. There'd be time, when Clark was down from his high and ready to listen, to do what he had to. His duty as Clark's friend, and his attorney.

And although this was an engagement party, the engagement was not foremost in Dorian's mind. Rita was.

He had a clear view of her, on the other end of their table, seated between Makandal, a photographer from *Niobe* and Petal, Clark's legal assistant. She looked beautiful: hair freshly twisted, makeup carefully done, wearing a navy blue sweaterdress that hugged her all over. The shape of her body, clearly outlined by the clingy fabric, brought back memories, both pleasant and ugly. She looked as lovely as she had that last night that he had seen her.

She was hardly eating, but drank wine at a pace that made him afraid for her. She toyed relentlessly with a silver chain around her neck, allowing herself to be engaged in conversations, but Dorian knew she wasn't focused on them.

She was looking at him. Even when he wasn't looking at her, he could feel her caramel eyes on him. When their gazes locked, she let her eyes speak for her, begging him to respond. *I want to talk to you,* her eyes said, *but I can't. I can't take that first step, so you'll have to.* He met her wordless request with a carefully noncommittal stare, holding her gaze each time until embarrassment made her turn away.

She deserved it, his little revenge. After the humiliation she'd put him through, she deserved a taste of her own medicine. Even after a ten-day cooling-off period, he was as mad as blazes. Madder still, perhaps, because in all this time he hadn't heard from her. Not a call, not a note, no attempt to apologize or explain. His sexual pride smarted every time he thought of the catastrophe on her living room floor—and he thought about it often.

But he wasn't just filled with anger. He'd spent all this time turning the same puzzle over and over in his mind: Rita, a few years shy of thirty, and a virgin? How? Why? She was smart, successful and beautiful. What man wouldn't want to date—and bed—a woman like that? Shyness? No, that was one label you couldn't apply to Rita. So what, then?

The specter of abuse came to his mind. Could it be possible

that at some point in her young life some bastard had hurt her? Each time this prospect came to him, his feelings toward her softened. He liked her so, so much. If he shoved aside the memory of that ghastly night, or even just the denouement of an otherwise delightful night, what remained was a collage of enjoyable encounters. Including that first, when they'd gone at each other's throats like two wet badgers in a garbage can.

More disturbingly, he still wanted her. As he looked at her, with her head bent and hair falling in her face, he was assailed by a sensory flashback. He was suddenly surrounded by her scent, both that of the perfume she had been wearing and the warm, natural, womanly smell that had wafted up from her body during their shared heat. The cloth napkin in his hand reminded him of how her long, lemony skirt had felt as he eased it up over her hips. His hands remembered the shape of her breasts as he cupped them. He let the napkin fall, and turned his palms up, almost expecting to see the imprint of her nipples there, like some kind of erotic stigmata.

He could no longer taste the wine he was sipping. Instead, his mouth was filled with the taste of her. He looked across the table again. She was saying something to Petal, lips curved, smiling, and to him it was as though the din and chatter around them were silenced, and all he could hear was the sound of her voice, sighing in his ear.

She had inexplicably, magically, projected her essence up and above her physical self, gliding across the table, unnoticed, to assail him. He felt her near him, around him, above him. Her damn scent was impossible to chase from his nostrils. Her taste clung to his tongue. He found himself shockingly aroused, his whole body so taut his skin hurt, the hairs on his forearms, across his chest and at the back of his neck so rigid they felt like tiny spikes. From all the way over there, she'd gotten to him as surely as if she were standing behind him, naked, enfolding him with her scent and her warmth and her arms. He wasn't sure he liked that.

Rita lifted her head and looked at him again. This time, there was no pleading in her eyes, no sorrowful, pained request. This time, there was a challenge. *I'm done begging,* she let him know. *Put up or shut up.*

She knows, he thought, stunned. *She knows what she just did to me. How could she?* He felt ashamed of the immediacy and the physicality of his response to the mere memory of being with her, and was angered by the sway she held over him. He was responding to her like a stray dog responded to the scent of a female in heat.

Dorian excused himself, pushed his chair away from the table and rose. He prayed fervently that his clothes were well enough tailored, and the other guests distracted enough, that his intense arousal would not embarrass him. He made haste for the large French windows. He didn't have the heart to look around to see if she was following.

She was. He'd not been out there two minutes when he heard a sound and knew it was her. By then he'd had time to suck in huge lungfuls of cold November air and exhale several puffs of misty breath. He'd had time to school his body into submission, managing to calm his restless blood. His mind, however, was another story.

He could smell her, feel her, sense her nearby. She was standing right behind him.

"How's Angela?"

He spun around. "What?"

"How's…your dog, Angela?" The question was slightly less self-assured than before.

The last words they'd hurled at each other when they'd parted had been like bullets in the opening salvo of a war, and now that he was seeing her again, she was asking about his dog? Had she had more wine than he'd thought?

But her eyes were clear and bright. They reflected the thousands of glittering fairy lights draped over every tree, bush and shrub surrounding the patio, and the flame of the citronella torches stabbed into the black earth along the paths that swirled through the garden. Fingers of flickering light played on her skin and on the droplets of silver dangling from her ears and around her throat. In the chilly mist that had rolled in from the East Coast, that glowing light looked like a halo.

Instead of answering her stupid question about the damn dog, Dorian reached for her, pulling her roughly toward him, hands on her upper arms. Squeezing a little too hard, perhaps, but he was afraid that if he didn't hold on tight she might wriggle free. He kissed her.

His mouth remembered hers. It found its way unerringly and seized what it wanted. The last time he'd kissed her, she'd tasted of wine, too. He liked that; the sweetness on her lips enhanced the less definable flavor that was her own. His kiss was both urgent and angry. He was like a thirsty man who'd been offered a drink by his enemy and had given in to the insistence of his parched throat over the objections of his conscience. His body demanded this contact, but his sane self protested. He was still mad at her, remember?

Rita kissed him back, ardently, the way she had that night, when she'd led him on, sucked him down inside herself like a siren drawing a sailor to the rocks with her song. As his body grew rigid again, rose again, so did his ire. His need to touch her, dive into her again struggled with the need to punish and to hurt. The kiss morphed, grew less ardent and more cruel. He stole the breath from her lungs, crushed her lips against her teeth, sank his fingers into the soft flesh of her arms.

She mewled softly in protest, but he didn't want to hear. He turned her slightly, and pushed her backward up against a sweet-scented pine. He leveraged his full weight against her so she was crushed against the rough bark.

She squirmed, resisted, until she tore her mouth free. "Dorian!"

He didn't release her, but didn't attempt to reclaim her mouth. "What?"

"You…you kissed me!"

"I thought that was what we came out here for."

She struggled fiercely against his grip. "Not exactly. Not like this."

"Like what, then?"

"I don't know. Just not…just not like this. You're hurting me."

"Am I?" he asked, although he knew he was.

"Yes!" She twisted like a grub on a hook.

Good, he wanted to say. *You* hurt *me.* But that was wrong. He was heavier and stronger than she was by far. He let her go so suddenly she had to steady herself. She rubbed her arms, scowling up at him.

He wanted to say he was sorry, but his anger had swelled into such a tidal wave of resentment that it swept away reason. "You owe me an explanation."

"For?"

"Don't play games with me. You've played them long enough. Ten days, if I remember correctly. Where the hell have you been?"

"Right where you left me."

"And, what, your phone was out of order? You couldn't send an e-mail?"

"To say what? You made it clear to me you weren't interested in anything I could possibly have to tell you. What would you want to hear from me?" She was still scowling, still defiant.

"How 'bout the truth?"

Her gaze slipped away.

He ran his fingers over his scalp, frustrated. "Rita, please. I have a right to know. I'm entitled to an explanation. First, you flash more green lights at me than an intersection on Independence Avenue—"

"I never—"

He went on relentlessly. "And next thing I know, I'm halfway through making love to you when I discover a tiny, insignificant fact you just happened to leave out—that you're a virgin."

"Was," she corrected automatically. "And you say it like it's a bad thing."

"It's not a bad thing. Surprising, but not bad. I just wish you'd told me. There were two of us there, and both of us had rights. It was your right to do away with your virginity when you chose, but it was my right to know."

"I couldn't."

"I know," he said dryly. "You were afraid if I'd known about it, I'd have passed on the offer. Then you'd have missed out on the opportunity to improve your writing, like Cassie suggested."

She put her hands up over her cheeks. "It wasn't like that. It wasn't about Cassie, or my writing."

He shrugged. "I'm just going by what you told me, sweetheart."

"You don't understand!"

She looked so miserable that his heart softened. He folded his arms across his chest, willed his anger to manageable levels, and said, "Explain it to me."

She slipped past him, away from the tree, and walked back toward the pool. Her high heels clacked on the pavestones. He wanted to follow, but allowed her the space instead. She looked down into the water at the bright white tiles and the patterns the colored underwater lights made on them as the water rippled gently. She was quiet for a long time. He wondered if she'd drifted so far across her mental landscape that she'd forgotten he was there. Eventually, she spoke. "You're right."

"About what?"

"I did set out to seduce you that night. It was just what you called it, a b-b-b-booty call."

"'Booty call' is an ugly term. It's dismissive and disrespectful, and I'd rather we didn't use it."

"*You* were the one—"

Stupid him. He should have bitten his tongue, rather than

insult her like that. "I know what I said and I'm sorry. No matter what the circumstances, it doesn't describe what happened between us, so let's not use it again, okay?"

"Call it what you want to call it. But when I asked you over, I had it in mind to sleep with you."

"Why?"

"Because…I didn't want to be a virgin anymore." She said it as though the memory of the condition rankled.

"Why not?"

"Not for the reason you think. Not because Cassie said. Cassie doesn't even know about my…affliction. She'd laugh herself sick if she did."

It grieved him to hear her talk about herself as though she had some sort of shameful disease. "Cassie loves you. She's way too level headed to have such a juvenile reaction."

She shrugged her elegant shoulders slowly, doubtfully. "Maybe. But I didn't tell her. It had nothing to do with improving my writing, either."

"Glad to hear that," he admitted fervently. He probed her gently for more information. "Why, then?"

She threw up her hands. "Because I was tired of it. I was fed up of all the pressure to be sexually active. It's out there, everywhere. In the music. On the radio, on TV, in movies, books and ninety percent of the ads you see. Even my job, the questions people ask me, and the things I write. It's all about sex." She bit her lip to keep it from trembling.

Again, that insane urge to hold her. He didn't move. He listened.

"I felt like a freak."

"You weren't a freak," he told her gently. "Everyone's entitled to make their own sexual choices, as long as they don't hurt anyone else."

"I was hurting *me*. I had all these desires, and I didn't know what to do with them. And the more time passed, the more ashamed I was. I was surrounded by people who made assumptions about me—you made the same assumptions, don't try to convince me you didn't."

"I won't insult your intelligence."

"I knew those assumptions were wrong. But I played along and tried to blend in."

"I wish I knew why, though. What made you hang on to your virginity until you were twenty-seven?" He stepped closer, wanting to be right there for her if she reacted badly to his next question. "Did somebody…harm you? When you were younger?"

She looked puzzled, then realized his meaning. "You mean, was I abused? Never! Nobody's ever laid a hand on me."

Relief. "I'm glad to hear that. I was worried…."

"Then put your mind at ease. The answer is no." Her gaze returned to the depths of the water, and she rubbed her hands thoughtfully over her arms.

"Good. So why, then?"

"You'll think this is funny…."

"See me laughing?"

"Okay. Fine. I'll tell you. It was the pressure. The constant pressure. My parents—"

Ah, the parents. Probably so full of rules and regulations, scare tactics and bullying that in their attempt to steer their young daughter clear of mistakes, they'd instilled fears within her that lasted well into her adult life. He'd heard that story before. "Overprotective, huh?"

She was incredulous. "Who? My folks?"

"Yes. You said they had you under pressure—"

Her short, startled laugh was like the bark of a sea lion. "*My* parents? Overprotective? Oh, I wish."

"What's that mean?"

"It means that at least I'd have grown up like a normal kid. Normal kids had parents who choked out the birds-and-the-bees story and then darted off when it was finally over. My parents' version of 'the conversation' was fully illustrated with brochures and posters. They started out with the old what's-happening-to-your-body talk, then segued from sex to babies to contraception to HIV. They came at me every few months, cut me some slack, then started up all over again. It got to be like a movie you'd seen so many times you knew it by heart, but still sat through it anyway."

He wasn't getting her. She meant him to follow, but he was lost. "What kind of parents did you have? What were they thinking?"

"What d'you mean? You know my folks. Everybody knows my folks. They're hard to miss, unless you live under a rock." The puzzled look on his face made her pause, and then she asked, "My last name rings no bells with you, does it?"

"Steadman? No, I don't think…." Then it hit him like a thunderbolt. "Beatrix and Torrance Steadman are your parents?"

"You got it."

"The couple who wrote *The Black Man's Guide to Spectacular Sex* and *The Black Woman's Guide to Sexual Bliss?*"

"That's them, all right," she confirmed bitterly.

He struggled to get his mind around it. Rita's parents were probably the most popular black sex gurus in the country. He'd heard them speak in New York City earlier this year and had caught them several times on TV and on the radio. "Those two are dynamite," he blurted. "I've got both their books."

Her expression soured even more. "Wonderful. You realize, of course, that you've probably used techniques on *me* that you learned from my *dad!*" She shuddered. "Oh, ugh!"

He couldn't stifle a chuckle. "Could be, but I came up with a few others on my own."

"That's not funny. That's creepy. And you promised not to laugh." She was both petulant and resentful.

"Sorry, sweetheart. I did. It won't happen again."

"Better not."

He tried to steer the conversation back on track. "So, what kind of pressure could they possibly have placed on you? They're hardly prudes."

"A little prudery would do them some good, if you ask me. When I was growing up, in high school, everybody thought it was so cool to have those two as my parents. They wouldn't have if they'd known what it was like at my house. Everywhere I looked, there was sex. Paintings, books, art from all over."

"Like the ones you have at your apartment."

"Exactly. Some mothers give their daughters sweaters or perfume. Mine gives me erotica. When I was a teenager, I used to come home from school and find my mother holding an encounter session in the living room with twenty middle-aged women, all talking about multiple orgasms and…and…you know, sex toys! I'd walk into the den and my dad would be there with a heap of notebooks, watching footage of water buffalo mating. Oh, and don't ask for mealtimes. Normal families talked at the table about soccer and school concerts and Grandma's arthritis. Mine talked about STDs over breakfast, fertility goddesses over lunch and gestating possums over dinner!"

Now he was beginning to understand. It was bizarre, like nothing he'd ever encountered before in all of his experience with women. Almost funny. But, apart from his solemn vow not to laugh again, there was the stricken look on her face, so his response was more sympathetic than amused. "A little too much, huh?"

She snorted. "Too much? Beatrix wanted to be the 'cool mom.' She thought I needed to 'explore my own sexuality.' She tried to put me on the Pill when I was seventeen. I refused. Other kids got cookies. I got condoms."

How could two progressive, intelligent, educated people be so obtuse and irresponsible when it came to their own daughter? "And the more they pushed, the more you resisted."

"Yes. I dated, of course, and did my share of making out, but I always had a good reason not to go all the way. Virginity got to be a habit. Then I got older. I started feeling there was a huge gap in my life. A hunger that needed to be fed."

"Sexual hunger is the most natural thing in the world," he

interjected. "We all feel it. It's not a bad thing, it's a wonderful thing."

"Maybe, but by then I was aware of the rarity of my…uh…condition. I felt like a freak. I couldn't admit it to anyone, not even Cassie. And certainly not to any man I ever dated. I thought they'd laugh at me, or react like I was some kind of leper. Or that the concept of deflowering a 'superannuatcd virgin'…."

He winced at his own words.

"…would scare them so badly that they'd get the heck out of Dodge."

"Scared of what?"

"Scared that I'd be clingy afterward. That I'd see it as some sort of commitment." Her lips twisted. "Or maybe just that in my inexperience I'd be lousy in bed. Not worth the effort."

"You were wonderful in bed," he said softly, "and worth every ounce of effort."

She searched his face, unsure of how to respond. Then the water had her attention again. "Well, there you have it. My sad little tale. Understand, now?"

"Most of it," he assured her. "There's just one thing you haven't explained."

She looked fearful, as if she knew what his question was going to be. "What's that?"

"Why now? Why me?"

If this had been a movie, the silence between them would have been filled with crickets. As it was, it was filled only by the faint strains of music filtering out from the party and the tinkling of glasses whenever anybody opened the doors. Rita ran her tongue along her lips, a gesture that drew him again to their inviting fullness. "I…." she began. She floundered.

He could have let her off the hook at any time, suggest that it was getting cold out here and maybe they should step back inside. But her answer was more important to him than he was prepared to admit. This time, there was more at stake than his ego. He was acutely aware that his heart rate had leaped to ridiculous levels.

Rita was still trying to frame an answer. "I…."

"Yes?" His whisper was barely audible.

"I…chose you because…the time was right, and you were there, and I knew you'd be kind…."

He hoped he didn't look as crestfallen as he felt. "So it was purely a question of availability?"

"No! No, Dorian, that didn't come out right. It's not about you being there physically; it's about you being there—" she tapped the center of her forehead "—in my mind. I was thinking of you. And wondering what it would be like with you."

"Curiosity, then." His disappointment still burned, but what had he been hoping for?

"More. More than curiosity. Wanting." She swallowed hard. This was difficult for her to admit, but he waited quietly until she was obliged to fill the void of silence again. "And I like you."

Now, that was more like it. He felt the corners of his mouth lift. "I like you, too." Plenty, he wanted to add, but while they were on the subject of scaring people away, that was likely to give her the jitters. So he let her continue.

"And I wanted to be with you, okay? Separate and apart from everything else, whether I was a virgin or not, or whether I'd been with two men or five men or ten in my lifetime, I like you and I wanted to be with you. And when you kissed me…"

"Yes?"

"When you kissed me…"

She was getting defensive, hugging herself again, locking him out of the circle of her arms. He was a good enough attorney to know when a witness had been badgered, and needed a break. It was time to put an end to the Q&A. She didn't resist as he pulled her body against his. She didn't resist as he lowered his head so that their lips met once again.

All cruelty was gone. So were ego and frustration and the need for vengeance. The only things left were desire and warmth, hunger and tenderness, and an aching to be engulfed in her softness once again. She kissed him like a child. She kissed him like a woman. She kissed him shyly. She kissed him audaciously, brazenly darting her tongue out at him, before dancing it away when he attempted to capture it.

He felt her hands under his jacket, around his waist to the small of his back, where she caressed him, roaming up and down his broadness. Slipping her fingers under the waistband of his pants, tugging up the tail of his shirt so that she could make contact with his bare skin. In this chilly night, out in the open air, the effect of her warm fingers was electrifying. He quivered.

She chuckled, but didn't take her hands away. His hands had an agenda of their own. They strayed down her hips to her thighs, and up again. Her muscles, well toned from her daily jog, tensed under his touch. *He* chuckled. He let one lawless hand stray between them, palm outward, wrist just grazing the lower curve of her belly, fingers nestling at the juncture of her thighs. The heat that radiated from her took the chill off the night.

Through the wool of her dress, he stroked her, feeling the faintest indentation of her cleft under the tip of his middle finger. The shock of discovering she wasn't wearing any panties nearly killed him. He took his hand away. She grunted in protest.

He straightened up. His height made it difficult for them to kiss standing up for very long without taking a toll on his spine. Having relinquished her mouth, he was happy to nestle into the pile of twists at the crown of her head. There was just one more thing he needed to know. The words he whispered into her hair were muffled. "Did I hurt you badly?"

"When?"

"That time. When we…." The image of blood smeared across her thighs had come to him in his dreams every night since, an indictment on his cluelessness.

She understood. "Oh, no. Not a whole lot, at least."

"I'm sorry."

"It's okay. Happens all the time, doesn't it? It's normal."

"Mmm-hmm." She smelled so good. She felt so good. He wanted to hold her forever. "Poor Rita," he murmured. "Dear Rita."

"Next time will be better," she told him.

He wasn't sure she was actually saying what he thought—hoped—she was. "What?" he asked cautiously.

"It gets better, doesn't it? Sex, I mean. After the first time. Once you get over that first, uh, hump, if you'll excuse the pun."

"It does." His heart was thumping again. If this cardiac seesaw kept up, he'd have to see a doctor about it.

"And the pain goes away."

"So I'm told."

Rita looked him square in the eye. Her face was a mixture of daring and desire and mischief and anticipation. "Show me."

"We need to get out of here."

Chapter 12

Rita followed half a step behind Dorian. His warm hand engulfed hers. She hoped her excitement and nervousness wouldn't make it sweaty. Inside, dinner had been cleared away. The music was a little louder, and someone had pulled the tables to one side, leaving space for dancing.

The guests, who at the start of the event had been polarized into the Clark camp and the Cassie camp had found common ground in the good wine and hearty dinner. People joked over after-dinner drinks. Others were getting funky on the dance floor.

She couldn't begin to guess how long they'd been outside. For anyone who'd been observing them, it was obvious what they'd been up to.

"Rita!" Cassie yelled from across the room. Several heads turned in her and Dorian's direction. Taking her cue from Dorian, Rita tried to act nonchalant. "You guys! You've been gone for ages. I could have sworn you'd fallen into the pool! You missed Clark doing his Benny Hill impression!"

Clark did impressions?

"Pity," Dorian said warmly. "He'll just have to arrange a command performance for Rita. It's a must-see."

"Yup. Gonna have to." Cassie's volume remained cranked up to eleven. "Where've you guys been? Scratch that, I know where you've been. What have you been up to?"

Oh, Cassie. Just once, just this once....

Dorian was unabashed. "Mending fences," he answered. He squeezed Rita's hand reassuringly.

Cassie beamed. "Good on ya. Now come in and warm up. Have a drink, something to get a little fire going in your belly. It's cold out there."

Dorian said at once, "We'd love to, Cassie, but Rita and I really must be going. We had a great time"

"Oh." She frowned for a second, but then the light dawned, and she grinned. "Got yourselves an emergency at home, huh?"

"Four-alarm," Dorian said smoothly, then smiled from Cassie to Rita. Rita didn't know where to look.

"Well, then, I won't hold you back. I'll tell Clark you said goodbye." She got up on tiptoe, stretched upward and yanked Dorian down by his necktie, so she could peck him on the cheek. Then she threw her ample arms around her friend. "Oooooh!" she squealed into Rita's ear, none too quietly. "Told you he was sweet on you!"

She stood in the doorway waving until they reached Dorian's Weekend Warrior Mobile. Dorian made sure she was comfortable and then climbed into the driver's seat. He let the engine idle for a moment, looking directly at her in the dim light. "Where to?" he asked eventually.

"Hmm?"

"Would you be more comfortable at your place or at mine? Most women are more at ease on their home turf."

How thoughtful. Briefly, she pondered, and said shyly, "Yours, I think. I've been holed up in mine for too long. I was just about ready to go nuts in there." Besides, she didn't need such a tangible reminder of the catastrophe that took place the last time they were together.

She was sure he understood what her real reason was, but all he did was nod, place a light kiss on each of her eyelids, and put the car into gear.

Dorian's place was across town in Augustine, on the other side of Falcon River, an easy twenty-minute drive at this time of night. It was a newer section of Santa Amata than her own, not as exclusive as Clark's Belmont but still very attractive. It was home to a large number of middle-income Black, Asian and Hispanic families. Most of the buildings consisted of condos and townhouses, with a few blocks of single-family homes, complete with picket fences and kiddie play sets out front.

Dorian pointed out a few structures, such as the high school he'd attended, and the financial complex for which Clark had done much of the legal work. But for the most part, neither of them had much to say, and he didn't rush to fill the void with artificial chatter. He just placed her hand on his thigh, covered it with his own and let her be.

She couldn't believe she was leaving the safety of a dinner party to ride out to Dorian's place with the express purpose of making love. Even more unbelievably, she had been the one to suggest it. As they rode across the bridge spanning Falcon River, she had a brief image of herself as Persephone being escorted by Pluto to his lair, but she laughed it off. Dorian was no deity of the underworld and this certainly wasn't a kidnapping. Any anxiety was overwhelmed by relief that she'd finally told him the truth. She felt the kind of calm that a liar felt once the burden of the lie had been lifted.

Dorian swung into a compound. Electronic gates opened at the touch of a button to welcome them. There were maybe a dozen graceful, three-level units, set four to a row. Warm shades such as umber and ochre gave them a distinctly Mediterranean look. Balconies with fancy black-painted iron railings were positioned to welcome the sunrise. Tall evergreens spiced the air with their perfume.

He parked along the second row, hopped agilely out and came around to help her down. Dim lights at ankle level lit their way, and gravel crunched under her feet as she walked with him across the narrow strip that separated the car from his front door.

He found his key, inserted it without looking, and the door opened before them. "After you," he murmured as he gestured into the entryway.

He switched on just enough lights to avoid her tripping across unfamiliar territory, but not enough to hurt her eyes after the darkness of the car or put a damper on their mood. An ecstatic yelp heralded Angela's arrival seconds before the hound came pelting out of the kitchen and hurled herself directly at Rita.

"Angela!" She dropped down onto her knees and gave the quivering, furry heap an affectionate hug. "How you doing, girl?"

Angela was doing just fine, judging from the lickfest that ensued. It was only when she was satisfied that she had appropriately welcomed the visiting human that she turned her attentions to her master, who had tossed his keys into a hand-painted Mexican dish on the sideboard and was watching the two of them with amusement. "Seems she remembers you," he commented, accepting Angela's belated greetings with an affectionate pat.

"Seems like it," Rita agreed. To be honest, she was more than just happy to see the dog for the dog's sake. Angela's arrival provided a buffer between herself and Dorian during those first awkward moments of entering. She was almost disappointed when Dorian said firmly, as though talking to a child who was trying to find excuses to stay up past bedtime, "Okay, Angela, enough's enough. It's sleepy time and you know it. Back into your corner." Angela yapped a farewell and trotted off the way she had come.

Dorian began to remove the small, square platinum cuff links at his sleeves, head bent to focus on his task. He asked, without looking up, "Could I get you something to drink?"

Rita was sure she'd had enough at the party while she was working up the courage to talk to him, so wisdom answered for her. "I'm okay."

The cuff links joined the keys in the dish, and he held out his hand. "Okay. Come with me, sweetheart."

She let him lead her farther in. Dorian's place was everything she'd expected. Neat, but not fussy. High ceilings divided by solid, regular wooden beams. Thick pile carpets and oversized leather furniture. An entertainment center, consisting of a flat-screen plasma TV, a CD player, tape deck and—bless her stars— a bona fide turntable, were all hooked up to an elaborate speaker system. The bass speaker alone was the size of an ottoman. Next to the whole contraption were shelves filled with CDs, tapes, DVDs and vinyl records. She was sure the kitchen lay beyond, since that was where Angela had run to, but instead of leading her that way, he approached a central staircase.

On the first landing, he merely said, "Guest bedroom, workout room and my study," before they went on to the upper floor. The steps led directly to a huge bedroom. The walls were a pale cucumber, and the moldings were trimmed with fern green. The dark parsley carpet was like a forest floor. There was a desk and swivel chair near the main windows, with an open laptop and a stack of paper next to it. Beyond the desk were tall French doors, which she figured led to the small balcony she'd noticed outside. The room was filled with a faint, pleasant scent that reminded her of the way he smelled when he held her close. That scent, too, was somehow green. A single piece of artwork, a charcoal sketch of a voluptuous black nude, took up most of the wall above the bed.

The bed. A king-size affair, fitting for a man his height. It stood on a platform in the center of the room. The top sheet and blankets were pulled back just the way he'd left it when he got up this morning. It was an undeniable reminder of their purpose for being here. Rita drew a sharp breath.

Dorian didn't stop there. "Come," he urged her. Through the bedroom and into the bathroom. This room smelled of him too, only more so. Aftershave combined with cologne, deodorant and soap. In contrast to the array of greens in the bedroom, this room was a stark, blinding white accented with softly glowing pewter plumbing. He let go of her hand, leaned forward, and began to run water into the enormous tub.

"What're you doing?"

"Running you a warm bath."

"Why?" she half joked, "Am I stinky?"

"No, but you're tense." He held his fingers under the stream until the temperature satisfied him, and then stood, letting it fill. He faced her, reaching out to stroke her cheek with his fingers. "I want to help you relax. This isn't supposed to be an ordeal. This is supposed to be all about pleasure. And that's not going to happen if you're afraid of me."

She wished she could have denied being afraid, but that would have been lying. She said nothing. She realized he was undoing the many tiny buttons down the front of her dress.

Even his nimble fingers stumbled. "Good grief! How many buttons are on this thing? Twenty?"

"Thereabouts."

"I thought chastity belts went out with the Round Table." But despite his complaint, her dress was opened, and he eased it off her shoulders. He made quick work of her bra, and then she was standing before him in nothing but a pair of panty hose. He drank in the sight of her, and she told herself she *would not* chicken out and cover her breasts with her hands. She gave him a look that was part defiant, part inviting.

"Attagirl," he murmured. He slipped each thumb under the waistband of her panty hose, knelt and began slowly sliding it down over her hips. She could feel his breath against her skin. "No panties," he commented approvingly. "Was that for my benefit?"

Ah, the arrogance of the male animal. "Get over yourself. This is a wool dress. Ever heard of VPL?"

"What?"

"Nothing. Girl stuff."

"Ouch. Keep your secrets." He got to his feet with obvious regret. "Speaking of girl stuff, I don't have any fancy-smelling girl-type bath whatsits, but I have some mint oil. Would that do?"

"That'll do just fine." But she was a little surprised. How come a man as fine as him, with his obvious sexual prowess and undeniable magnetism, hadn't transformed his home into the ultimate lady-pleasing love pad? As she stepped into the water, she wondered when was the last time he'd "entertained" in that huge bed, or who was the last woman to receive his patented, pre-lovemaking mint-oil bath. But as she lay back and let the water rise up to her breasts, she couldn't think about it, because Dorian had squatted down beside the tub, lathered up a big natural sea sponge, and was making long, rhythmic strokes down her body. She closed her eyes.

"That's it." His lips were close to her ear. "That's it, lovely Rita. Relax. Let me do everything for you. Let me make your first time everything you'd ever wanted it to be."

Her eyes fluttered open. "But this isn't—"

"Shush. I don't want to think about that ever again, and neither should you. Forget it. It never happened. Tonight is going to be our clean slate, and we're going to write whatever we choose, okay?"

He made it sound so easy, as if the power of the mind could erase history. "What d'you choose to write?"

"This." The sponge that had been making insistent circles around her nipples, its roughness bringing them to painful attention, fell into the water. His hand broke the surface, going down, down, down, skimming over her belly and making it quiver. Down, down, down again.

Those fingers. Those knowledgeable, insistent, persistent fingers. They danced a ballet between her legs. They had an electric charge all their own, and the water around her, that great conductor of electricity, made each jolt more powerful than the last. She gritted her teeth and clamped her lips shut, afraid of what would come out of her mouth if she lost control.

"Don't hold your breath," Dorian warned. "You'll hurt yourself."

"I'm afraid…." she managed to gasp.

"Don't be. You're with me. Do whatever you need to do. Give in."

She opened her mouth, expelled a lungful of spent air, and then sucked in fresh air as fervently as if she'd been beneath the surface all this time. Then she did give in, crying out in agonized pleasure. Her nails dug into the back of his hand, half-heartedly trying to dissuade him from his purpose. He would have none of it, and persisted until her cries petered out and she was a limp, soaking wet heap, leaning back against the tub, desperately trying to figure out which way was up.

He delved into the water and gathered her up against him, shirt be damned, and carried her into the bedroom. He toweled her dry with vigorous strokes, and set her down on the bed. She lay back on the firm mattress, head as light as a helium balloon. He had certainly attained his goal. Her tension was replaced by greedy desire, a hunger for him that the appetizer in the bathroom had only whetted.

"Take off your clothes," she demanded.

He was all smiles. "Gladly." He pulled off the wet shirt without bothering to undo the buttons, stepped out of his shoes and sat on the bed to remove his socks.

She sat up and reached for the buckle on his belt. "Let me help you." She was less nimble than him, and fiddled with the buckle and the buttons, but she managed to get the last of his clothing undone and off. He was stark naked—magnificently naked. The blackness of his skin gleamed in the light of a single bedside lamp.

Rita reached out and stroked his flank as if he were a thoroughbred horse. His skin was fine, smooth and warm. She moved to his abs. Under a sprinkling of hair they were hard, corrugated from hours of disciplined workouts. They quivered as she stroked them. He was a huge man. His hips, although narrow in proportion to his torso and shoulders, were nonetheless massive, as were his thighs. And, in between…

Feeling brazen, she touched him. Here, his skin was even finer, even softer, but it sheathed steel. She brushed her cheek, her lips, against his lower belly, feeling the crinkle of hair and inhaling the giddying, utterly sensual scent of him. Then she opened her lips and took him inside.

The effect was astounding. The feel of him, the dichotomy between hardness and softness, strength and delicacy, and the perfect balance between the two. The taste of him, like nothing she had ever experienced before.

It was his turn to catch his breath. He tried to ease away, but with hands on his haunches, she held him fast.

"No," he pleaded, "stop!"

She paused. Had she made a mistake? Was she doing this all wrong? "Don't you like this?"

"Are you kidding? I'm about to have a heart attack. But this isn't about me. It's about you. I should be giving you what you want."

"This is what I want," she answered, and silenced his protests once and for all.

When he could no longer stand it, she relinquished her hold on him. He climbed into bed beside her, smiling into her face. "You're beautiful."

"So are you."

"Are you ready?"

She would never be more prepared than she was now. "Ready."

He put on a condom quickly, without any fuss, and then stretched out beside her once again. There was no need for either of them to say any more. She went to him eagerly.

Whatever pain she felt was soothed away by his kisses. Her excitement made her supple, open, and willing, and he found his way into her with ease. He paused, giving her time to get used to the sensation of fullness, but then, at her insistence, began moving against her. Together, they found their stride.

On and on they rode, with every one of her senses being bombarded. An unceasing stream of endearments poured from his lips. He taunted her with his body, taking her to the edge of reason and then drawing back, denying her that final sanctuary of release, until he sensed that her body couldn't take any more, and let her fall over the edge. She spiraled downward, all control lost, all shame and self-consciousness relinquished. When she was about to crash to the bottom, he was there to catch her.

She fell into his arms, sobbing. Rivulets of tears ran down onto his neck. His hands stroked her back and her hair, and he shushed her, but she couldn't stop. If anything, his kindness and his gentleness made her weep more.

Finally, eventually, she was able to speak, but all she could say was his name. "Dorian, Dorian."

"Here I am. I'm not going anywhere. What is it? Tell me."

She gulped. Tears burned her throat and made her tongue heavy, but she managed, "I think I love you." And she hid her face again, afraid of his reaction.

His soothing, calming hands missed just one beat, but resumed their movement against her damp skin. His seconds of reflection felt like forever, and then he eased her up so that he could search her eyes, looking, perhaps, for evidence that she had spoken the truth. It seemed that he found it, because he let her fall back onto him, pushing her head down against his chest, cradling it in one big hand.

"I think I knew that," he said.

Chapter 13

Rita awoke alone in Dorian's big, rumpled bed. Hazy white light spilled in through half-open blinds, telling her that it was *waaay* past getting-up time. The moment her eyelids fluttered open, she remembered where she was and her reason for being there. She raised her arms above her head and stretched, pointing her toes, flexing her body to rouse it from its contented lethargy. A warm, invigorating buzz ran through her, a glow that could be felt rather than seen. It had nothing to do with the spa day she and Cassie had indulged in yesterday, and everything to do with Dorian's loving last night.

Dorian. Oh, wow, she'd really lost it there, breaking down in his arms, sobbing like a schoolgirl. Telling him she loved him almost before she realized it herself.

It was insane. But it was real.

She pressed back into those huge pillows—how was it that everything this man touched bore traces of his gorgeous scent?—and pondered her predicament. She'd never been in love before, but she was now. She was sure of it. Thanks to her blurting, he knew it, too.

What would he think? What was it that he'd said last night? "I know." Not the mandatory Hollywood staple, "I love you, too." An acknowledgment of her feelings, rather than a declaration of his. But what did she expect? Dorian was experienced in the ways of love and sex, knew what he wanted and how to get it. She, on the other hand, was a novice, a newbie who was floundering in water far too deep for her.

Dorian, handsome and manly, considerate and kind, an expert in things sensual, had everything to offer. He was a perfect target for her girlish, awkward infatuation. It was the attachment a woman felt for the man responsible for her sexual awakening. The attachment a duckling felt for the first creature it laid eyes on the moment it crawled out of the egg.

With that realization, the glow that had filled her a few moments ago dimmed, and she became self-conscious and intimidated. A chasm of unreturned love yawned between them. Rather than lie back and luxuriate, she was assailed by the panicky urge to cut and run. She wondered if—

Speak of the devil. A dark head emerged from within the stairwell, and Dorian appeared bearing a tray. He was dressed in a pair of jeans, feet and chest bare. Angela trotted happily at his heels. "Good morning." He set the tray down on the desk, edging the laptop to one side, and perched on the bed. "Sleep well?" he asked with a hint of devilry, and kissed her lightly.

That one little kiss sent her blood racing so suddenly she felt giddy, as though she had just stepped off the meanest roller coaster. What a weird thing love was. All this man had to do was come close, touch her, and her whole world went out of kilter. It wasn't fair.

That's when she realized she was as naked as the day she was born. Hastily, she gathered up handfuls of bedsheet to cover herself.

"Want something to put on? I've got dressing gowns, but

you'd probably drown in them. Would you settle for one of my T-shirts instead?"

She nodded mutely. He got up, rummaged around in the closet and held out a T-shirt with a reassuring smile. It was the same faded Army Reserve shirt he had worn on the Cancer Fun Run when he'd beat the pants off her and then kissed her in the grass. She pulled it hastily over her head, and felt much better now that her modesty was reclaimed.

"Good," he said, in pretty much the same tone he used to soothe the dog. "It's a little chilly for breakfast on the balcony, as tempting as that idea is. How about breakfast in bed?"

Without waiting for an answer, he drew back the blinds to let the sunshine come pouring in and then busied himself by smoothing out the sheets and laying out their breakfast. Angela plopped down at the foot of the bed, on the off chance that any scraps should come her way.

Rita realized she was starving. Carefully, so as to protect her modesty, she crossed her legs Indian-style, and made sure the tail of the T-shirt was pulled down well below her knees. Dorian sat on the edge, twisting around to face her.

This was no fluffy, insubstantial breakfast. There were pancakes with a pot of warm Provencal honey, grated cheddar and crisp fried bacon, whole grain toast and spicy Irish sausages, pineapple juice, water, coffee and tea. Coffee! Her wonder drug! Just the sight of the steaming stainless steel pot was enough to have her hankering after a fix.

"I thought you'd be hungry," he explained in response to her widening eyes. She half expected him to make a comment such as, "After all your exertion last night," but he only said, "You didn't finish your dinner last night, did you?"

"I didn't," she recalled.

"Then dig in."

Digging in not only filled her empty belly, it gave her something to focus on to deflect the incredible, foreign sensation of awkwardness and awe that came with being this close to him again now that they'd done what they'd done—and now that they both knew how she felt. "This isn't Betty Crocker," she commented, her mouth full of pancake.

"Nope, it's Dorian Black."

"You made these from scratch?"

"Sure. I started cooking for my dad and brothers when I was thirteen."

"It's wonderful."

"Thank you."

He let her eat in relative peace, even offered her one of two daily newspapers that had been folded on the tray. Companionably, they read. But eventually, they finished eating, and she couldn't hold the paper up in front of her face forever. She put it down.

That was when he asked, "Are you okay?"

"Fine," she said hastily, praying he wouldn't push it.

He pushed it. "No, no, sweetheart, 'fine' isn't good enough. You're as skittish as a squirrel in a rat trap. Am I scaring you?"

"Certainly not!"

"That's good to know," he replied, but it was obvious he didn't believe her. "But we need to talk about something."

She wanted to squeeze her eyes closed to shut out his question, but couldn't see any way she could avoid it. "What?"

"About what you said to me last night."

About loving you, you mean?

"About what you told me."

You can't even say it, she thought despondently. *You can't even use the word* love *to me, not even to repeat what I said.* "I meant it," she told him.

"Thank you. I don't know if I deserve it, but thank you." He scratched his head, stalling for words that wouldn't come. "But I don't believe…I can't…" He sighed heavily, and tried again. "I promise you that I will try to live up to your expectations of me" was all he could finally manage.

Now, what was that supposed to mean? Whatever it was, it wasn't what she wanted to hear. She got up. Breakfast was over. "I'm going to take a shower," she informed him and walked away.

Dorian didn't say much on the drive to Rita's place. Beside him, Rita stared out of the window, wearing the same navy blue dress from last night. She didn't say much, either, but her silence told Dorian nothing about her mood. As gifted as he was at reading people, when it came to her right now, he was drawing a blank. She wasn't angry—at least, not overtly so. Not unhappy, either. She smiled back when he smiled at her, and even made an effort to laugh at his jokes. She seemed reflective, maybe even resigned.

He felt like a dinosaur in a flower garden. Bringing up her confession of love with all the finesse of a tenth-grader, and then floundering when he tried to explain his situation. But how could he explain himself? He wasn't even sure he should. After all, which was worse—to let the easy lie of "I love you, too," roll off your lips, just to make her feel better, or to tell her you didn't, not because she wasn't worth loving, but simply because you didn't believe in love?

Love? Please! A warm, fuzzy feeling that accompanied good sex, good chocolate, or both. The point where sexual attraction and affection collided, lust seen through a soft-focus lens. A marketing ploy that sold CDs and made florists rich on Valentine's Day. If you were naive or incautious enough to take it seriously, it usually led to a year or two of bliss, half a dozen years of apathy and rising bitterness, and several very expensive hours in an office just like his. Screaming insanely at that very person while someone like him helped you divvy up the house, the car, the dog and, tragically, the kids. So it had been, every day of his career, for longer than he cared to remember.

He'd seen enough. As surely as second-hand smoke caused lung cancer, the second-hand pain he'd experienced had infected him with the cancer of unbelief. It wasn't as though he was incapable of caring. He cared about Rita. He certainly had every intention of taking her out—and taking her to bed—again…and again, and again. But that was as far as he was willing to go.

"Left here," she told him.

"I remember." He pulled up to the curb and hopped out. She was on her feet before he could make it around to her side. He tried not to take it personally.

Inside, she looked unsure as to what would happen next. Maybe she expected him to turn tail and run, now that his morning-after obligations had been fulfilled. "I had a, uh, wonderful time." She flushed like a schoolgirl.

"So did I," he told her sincerely. "I know you must be tired, so I'll leave you to get some rest." Both out of a desire for her company and to reassure her that he had no intention of pulling a disappearing act, he added, "When can I see you again?"

"When would you like to?" she hedged.

He could let her cool her heels for a few days, then call her midweek, but he was way too old for games. "Tonight. Maybe a show? Anything you'd like to see?"

"You choose," she told him. "I just want to be with you." The flush transformed into a radiant glow, and her simple pleasure at the thought of being with him almost made him ache. Again, he wondered if he could live up to the image of him he saw in her eyes.

"I'll think of something," he promised.

"I know you will. I'll go get changed now. These clothes have pretty much had it. And I've got to feed Wallace, poor fella." She headed up the corridor. "Have a seat," she yelled over her shoulder. "I'll be right out."

Instead of sitting, he went into her living room, the scene of their first sexual encounter, marveling at how little time had passed since then and how much everything had changed between them. The book of lawyer jokes was still on the coffee table, open to whatever page Rita had stopped at. The scarily endowed African carving was still there, and the silken Japanese scroll graced its wooden stand.

He thought of her parents, who had given these gifts to their reluctant recipient, and shook his head. There was so much yet to learn about Rita, so much more he wanted to know. The intensity of his desire to discover more about her was slightly discomfiting. It was just his legal mind, he told himself, his natural curiosity to unravel a conundrum. It didn't mean anything more than—

"Dorian." Her voice was a choked whisper, barely audible in terms of decibels, but thundering in terms of urgency. "Dorian!" it came again, just as soft, but with a note of panic that sent him running down the corridor.

By the time he got to her room he was riding on a wave of adrenaline, his fight-or-flight response leaning heavily in favor of fight. "What is it?" His fists were tightly balled, ready to strike.

She was standing at the foot of her bed, hands pressed to her mouth. He looked hastily around the room, half expecting to see someone in the corner. But everything to his eyes seemed perfectly normal. "What's the matter?"

"The bed." She pointed at it frantically.

He was trying his damnedest to follow, but she'd lost him. "What about it?"

"Somebody's slept in it…and then made it!"

It was obvious that the bed had been slept in; the sheets were slightly rumpled, the pillows creased, but someone had made an attempt to smooth everything out, and a blanket was neatly folded at the foot of it. "You're sure it wasn't like this when you left home yesterday?"

"Yes, of course, I'm sure. It was a mess when I left it. I'm not the neatest person. Plus I'd been out all day yesterday with Cassie. And before that, I was too depressed—"

Over him.

"I mean, I wasn't exactly in the mood for housework, understand? I think I even left my old clothes lying on it. And now…." She shuddered.

He put his arms around her. "Why'd anyone do something like this? It's nuts."

She wriggled out of his grasp, spinning around, looking about her room for other signs of an intruder's presence. "Wallace!" She rushed to the sprawling array of cages.

He followed, dreading what he would see. Please, he begged silently, not some freakish scenario. Rita loved that little rodent. But in one of the feeding stations, an orange heap of fluff moved, and Wallace stood up on his hind paws, nose twitching. The critter looked fine to him. His relief was palpable, but Rita was still distressed.

"Somebody…this…crazy, crazy person, fed my gerbil!"

This was even creepier than if Rita's intruder had trashed the place or harmed her pet. That would point to anger, even revenge. But this guy wasn't playing with a full deck, and that scared him.

Hurriedly, he checked her bedroom windows, convinced that, like the last time, this weirdo had entered there. One was unlocked, but pushed shut. The lock had been gouged open with a knife.

"I made doubly sure I locked it last night," Rita explained. "I had a bad feeling about it. After the last time—"

"Last time?"

"That night, the night we…the last time you were here. Someone was in here. Or at least, got close enough to drop a note on the floor."

"Someone was here? And you didn't say anything?"

"By the time I found it, you'd already left," she defended herself. "And, besides, you weren't exactly in any mood to—"

"Okay, point taken. But honestly, if I'd had any idea you were in trouble, I'd have come right back, regardless of how mad I was."

"Right." She didn't exactly believe him. "Maybe. But I'd rather have been hacked to pieces by an ax murderer than ask you for help."

The memory of his behavior came back to haunt him, but something else she'd said took precedence over his guilt. "You said he left a note? Where is it?"

Rita looked abashed. "I don't have it."

"Did you give it to the cops?"

She shook her head. "I didn't call the cops. And I didn't keep the note. I threw it away."

He couldn't believe what he was hearing. "Let me get this straight. Someone was in your bedroom while we were in the living room, left a note for you, and you threw it away? And didn't call the cops?"

She lifted her hands in explanation. "I didn't think it was worth reporting. It was just a piece of paper pushed through an open window—"

"Three floors up," he reminded her. "Somebody had to want badly enough to get up here to climb up and risk his neck. Didn't that worry you?" He wanted to strangle her for being so careless.

"I guess, a little. But I didn't—"

"What did the note say?"

"It was nothing."

"What did it say?"

"Something about being afraid of heights."

"*What* about being afraid of heights? Did he say *he* was afraid of heights?"

"Well…" Her eyes swiveled upward, as though she were struggling to recall the exact wording. "What it said was, 'Are you afraid of heights?'"

He was aghast, and even more annoyed with her for not having called him back. "Are you serious? Doesn't that sound like a threat to you?"

"What, that somebody's going to toss me off a cliff or something? Come on, Dorian. It was creepy, but it wasn't a big deal. I get hundreds of letters and e-mails."

"Hand-delivered through your bedroom window at night?"

"Not exactly, but I've had my moments."

He couldn't fathom why she was being so nonchalant. Was she

truly unaware of the dangers, or was she trying to be brave? Either way, he felt like a frustrated parent trying to reason with a reckless teenager. If she wasn't going to protect herself, he would.

He snatched her phone up from the dresser and began dialing.

"Who you calling?" She eyed the phone as though he'd picked up a live snake.

"Who d'you think?" he retorted. The more he thought about her silliness, the madder he got. He wished he could shake some sense into her, but he settled for punching out the numbers with almost enough force to crack his thumb. "The same people you should have called the minute that note hit your floor. I'm calling the cops."

Chapter 14

Rita watched as two nonchalant police officers, both fatherly types with graying hair and identical bottle-brush moustaches, worked their way through her apartment. They didn't seem overly excited by The Mystery of the Dropped Note, and in a way, that made her feel vindicated.

But as much as she was trying to act blasé, she was rattled. Not just because an intruder had inexplicably bedded down in her apartment, but because she was the only person in the room who knew the rest of the story—the taunting e-mails and the fact that this person knew her whereabouts.

She didn't want to imagine how Dorian would react to *that* little nugget. He was mad enough that she hadn't told him about the note. What would he say if she told him her friendly neighborhood stalker was practically a pen pal?

The officers tut-tutted when she confessed to throwing away the note and lifted their eyebrows when she explained that the culprit had slept in her bed and fed her gerbil, but did little more than make the usual noises about investigating and getting back to her. Their brief tour took them back into the kitchen—and Rita spotted something that made every hair on her body stand rigid. She cursed, and her hands flew to her lips, too late to contain the expletive. She apologized immediately.

"What is it?" Dorian wanted to know.

The kitchen sink was spotless. Two or three breakfast plates stood straight up in the draining rack, her turquoise and emerald cereal bowls were face down next to them, and her good cutlery, which she'd used to serve Dorian that night, was gleaming. A strawberry-dotted dish towel was folded neatly on the counter, and the stainless steel, coffee-shop-grade percolator, her pride and joy, was half full of her favorite Arabica/Vanilla blend. When she'd left the night before, the kitchen was a mess.

"Someone did the dishes," she clarified for the three men, who were eying her expectantly, having failed to notice anything out of the ordinary. "*And* made coffee." She reached forward to touch the percolator, but one of the police officers, the older of the two, put a firm hand on her arm.

"Miss, I wouldn't. We don't know what beef this guy's got with you or what kind of puppy love he thinks he's in. But that coffee jug's just the thing to help us find out. I'm gonna have them send over a couple of lab guys, let them dust this place down real good, okay? But for the time being, don't you touch a thing, okay, missy?" He seemed a bit happier now that a run-of-the-mill B & E was turning out to be a little more unusual. A bed-making, dish-washing, gerbil-feeding stalker? That was more like it. "Just let us handle this, okay?" he added. Rita half expected him to pat her on the head and hand her a lollipop.

Dorian was nowhere near as excited by the newest twist. "That does it. I've seen enough." He seized her by the elbow and dragged her back to her room, threw open her closet and began rummaging through it.

Hours before, this man had been wrapped around her, naked

and deep in sex-induced slumber, and now he was going through her stuff. The invasion felt more intimate than the sex…and not in a good way. She'd had many personal barriers breached over the past twenty-four hours, and it was beginning to wear on her. "Just what d'you think you're doing?"

If he picked up the note of warning in her voice, he didn't show it. "Where're your suitcases?"

"My what?"

"Suitcases. Luggage. I assume you do travel?"

She bristled at his tone. "From time to time. Why? Are we eloping?"

"So where d'you keep your—" He found a medium-sized suitcase and threw it onto the tidily made bed. "Don't bother." He was back in her closet, haphazardly stuffing clothes into it, pulling out bras and panties with zero percent of the sensual attention he'd paid to her bra and her absence of panties the night before.

Now the brother was really tripping. "I asked you—"

"What's it look like I'm doing? I'm moving you out of here. You're coming home with me."

"Are you serious?"

"Are you? You've got some demented Goldilocks running around sleeping in your bed and eating your porridge, *and* cleaning up after himself, and you're planning on sleeping here tonight?"

The prospect sent her skin crawling all over again, but the idea of cutting and running was almost worse. It felt like cowardice and she'd had enough of *that*. She was changing. She'd been hiding from herself for so long. Hiding from her sexuality, using her inhibitions as a smokescreen. Then, last night, she'd had the strength to look Dorian in the eye and tell him how much she wanted him. It was almost funny that a night of lovemaking—which made one more vulnerable than anything—was making her feel so emboldened, so strong. It brought an incongruous smile to her lips.

"This is funny to you?"

"No, I…it's not funny. I just want to be strong about it. I don't want to be afraid."

"You should be afraid. This is scary stuff. I'm scared for you. And being brave doesn't mean putting yourself at risk. You need to get out of here. You'd be a fool to stay."

Maybe he was right. Maybe it would be prudent to beat a retreat for a while, until she could figure out a solution. If she left, she'd be able to think more calmly, more objectively, about what to do next. Where she did her thinking, though, was a different story. "Maybe I should move out for a while. But that doesn't mean I'm moving in with *you.*"

"Where're you going, then?"

Good question. As much as she loved her parents, they had a way of driving her crazy. After a day at their place, she'd be willing to arm-wrestle her intruder in her own bedroom. That left one solution. "I'm calling Cassie."

"I agree you should call Cassie, and let her know what happened. But she's got a wedding to plan, remember? I'm sure she's up to her ears in fabric samples and caterers and invitations and whatnot."

"You're saying she's too busy for me?"

"'Course not. I'm sure she'd drop everything for you, including her own wedding. But would you really want to make her?"

He was right, damn him. "Santa Amata is full of hotels," she countered.

"It sure is," he said, slipping into lawyer mode, cutting down her arguments with surgical precision. "But why spend money when there's room at my place? And wouldn't you be exposing yourself to this creep even more? Out there, in public, without anyone to protect you. You don't even know what he looks like."

She hated him when he made that much sense. "I've got friends," she lied wearily, knowing he was going to shoot her down again but making the effort anyway.

"I'm your friend, too, aren't I?" He lowered his voice in deference to the presence of the officers, whose muted conversation could still be heard in the kitchen. "Maybe more?"

Little pins and needles ran through her.

He went on, persuasive, cajoling. "Don't think of it as running and hiding. Think of it as a chance for us to spend time together. Learn about each other. Maybe a few days in each other's company might be just what we need to help us find out where this is going."

The problem with that, Rita thought, *is that what "this" means for* me *is oceans away from what it means for* you.

Would she be able to stand being around him day and night? What if her raw, painful emotions became too much for her, and she didn't even have the sanctuary of her own apartment to escape to?

Her troubling thoughts must have showed on her face, because he said gently, "I'm offering you my guest room, sweetheart. You don't have to bunk with me—unless you want to. You can shut the door. Lock it if it makes you more comfortable. I'll give you a spare house key so you can come and go as you please."

He sounded nowhere near as mad. In fact, he was almost back to the Dorian of last night: cajoling, sweet and affectionate. She felt herself being drawn in again, aching to say yes to him—about anything.

"Besides," he added with a generous helping of humor, "we've got this Hottest Men of Santa Amata lark of Cassie's to work on, haven't we?"

Rita gasped. "She told you about it?"

He laughed. "Well, Clark did."

"And you're going for it?"

"I thought it was a joke at first, but he convinced me otherwise, so, yes, I guess I'm game. My rep could do with a boost. When the issue hits the stands, I'll have so many babes clambering all over me I'll have to shake them off…."

She knew he was teasing her, but he still seemed way too enthusiastic. "Clark told you why I have to do this, too, didn't he," she guessed dejectedly.

The laughter left him, and he became sober and compassionate. "He said you were in a bit of a bind."

"She shouldn't have said anything to him. That's my private business."

"Oh, don't be like that. They're in love, it's not likely they've got many secrets. She knew it'd be a hard sell for me, so she probably primed Clark by telling him how important it is for you. Don't be mad, she was just trying to help."

Rita closed her eyes, shutting him out for a minute to give herself some alone time to think. Before she could find another reason not to give in to Dorian's implacable logic, she felt herself being lifted into his arms and lowered onto his lap as he sat on the edge of the bed. His mouth was along her hairline, softly tracing the shape of her ear. "I know you feel things are coming at you hard and fast right now. I just want to be there for you. Come home with me for a few days and regroup. We'll work on this article together. It'll be a laugh, I promise."

When he held her like that, resolve was impossible. In fact, it was hard not to notice the fountain of excitement welling up inside her at the prospect of being with Dorian again. Back at his place, surrounded by his masculinity, in the intimacy of their twoness—or their threeness. Who could forget Angela? She couldn't think of anything she wanted more right now.

She suppressed the urge to wrap her arms around his neck and kiss him back. A serious head-on, soul-searing, ground-zero kiss that would blast a gaping hole through any remaining self-control that she might have. Instead, she simply said, "Yes, thank you."

"Good." He was wise enough, having sold the idea, not to scuttle the sale by talking too much. He just kissed her again on the forehead and held her some more.

Footsteps in the corridor reminded her they weren't alone.

"Miss Steadman?" It was the older cop, coming to see what she was up to.

Rita leaped off of Dorian's lap, adjusting the much-abused blue dress, which she still hadn't changed out of. "Yes?"

"Lab crew's outside. We'll have them look around, and then we'll be off, okay?" His eyes darted from her to Dorian and back. He didn't need a cop's instinct to know he was intruding, and a hint of color rose to his beefy face. "I'm sorry—" he began.

But before Rita could answer, Dorian said easily, "No problem, Officer. Miss Steadman will be right out to let them in." He gave Rita an encouraging smile. It was all the support she needed.

When the ordeal of scrutiny was over, the officers took their leave. While she gratefully changed clothes and packed the way *she* wanted to, Dorian cleaned up the traces of fingerprinting powder and other evidence of the invasion.

Then she was ready. Dorian had his car keys and her door keys in one hand and Wallace ensconced in a small traveling cage in the other and was standing at the door, waiting for her, smiling encouragingly. Rita took one deep breath, centered herself and left with him for his place.

Chapter 15

So much for the guest room. They'd had the best of intentions, installing her bags, unpacking her things and laying out her cosmetics on the counter in the guest bath. But he knew and she knew that, come nightfall, after dinner and a comedy on cable, she'd end up in his room, his bed and his arms.

Downstairs, Angela made soft, scrabbling sounds, doing whatever crazy dogs did after midnight. Outside, owls hooted softly to each other, sending discreet signals across the garden like spies on stakeout. Rita lay with her head on Dorian's biceps, with his naked body curled around her. Her back was so firmly pressed against his chest that she could feel the soft thudding of his heart, and the slowing rhythm of his chest as his respiration returned to normal. His good loving made its effects felt, causing her eyelids to droop and sleep to slowly creep up on her.

She fought it valiantly. The experience was so new to her, so wonderfully fresh, she didn't want to miss a second of it. She stifled a yawn, and Dorian laughed. The rumble rolled through him and into her.

"You can sleep if you want to, you know. I'll still be here in the morning, and so will you."

Damn him for guessing what she was thinking. "I'm not sleepy," she told him, and proved herself a liar by yawning again. Before he could respond, she threatened, "Laugh at me again and you're dead meat."

He nuzzled her neck. "I'm not laughing at you, sweetheart, I'm laughing—"

"At me, with me, it doesn't matter. This is embarrassing enough as it is."

"Embarrassing? Why?"

"I feel like a big, dumb kid who doesn't know her bleep-bleep from her elbow when it comes to sex."

His chuckle made a mockery of her no-laughing rule. "Oh, honey, let me tell you this: (a) you're no kid; (b) you're far from dumb, especially when it comes to sex, because, trust me, your body knows what it's doing; and (c) from where I'm lying, you have a mighty fine bleep-bleep. There isn't a red-blooded male in America who'd mistake it for your elbow." To punctuate his words, he slapped her playfully on her bottom.

"Ouch," she grumbled, but the sensation made every nerve ending tingle.

"You know you liked it."

"Do it again and you'll be on the receiving end of the next one."

"Thanks for the warning." Gently, he eased his arm from under her and flipped her onto her back, so he could look down into her eyes. "Don't worry about disappointing me. Just touching you and hearing your voice excites me. Besides, sex is a journey, not a one-off event. As you move along through each experience, you'll learn things. What you like, how to please a man and how to please yourself. And nothing means more to me than having the honor of being your first teacher."

She smiled back. "Really?"

"Really. And when whatever time we're destined to be together is over, and you move on to someone new, he'll teach you something only he can teach you. It's the way of the world. But your body will always be your guide...."

He was saying more; she was sure of it but she couldn't hear a word. She was still reeling from the part about *moving on,* a concept that hit her with physical force. She'd forgotten this wasn't a love match. It was, at best, a love/like scenario. She'd known when she'd climbed into his bed that this was the case and thought she was strong enough to handle it. But somewhere along the way, she'd let her mind slip for a dangerous moment.

But how could she not? The blame was all Dorian's. He'd thrown himself into their encounter with such intensity and passion that she'd lulled herself into the fantasy that they were making love, not just having sex. Now, consciously or unconsciously, he was reminding her that their relationship was finite.

"Loud and clear," she mumbled. The proximity of his body became claustrophobic. He was aroused again. She could feel him unfurling against her thigh. He wanted more of her, and fifteen seconds before—or, if he'd only kept his big mouth shut—she'd wholeheartedly have given in, but now she only wanted one thing: out.

She wriggled from his grasp, registering the stark surprise on his face but unable to stand the anguish of looking him in the eye. His arms tightened around her, instinctively, as if he was contemplating not letting her go. But almost immediately he relented and she was free.

With dignity, she found her clothes and dressed quickly but calmly, while Dorian watched her quizzically.

"Rita?"

"Dorian?" Her Zen-like cool made her proud.

"What's wrong? I thought...."

What did you think, you clueless fool? That you could slap me in the face, tell me that this…relationship, for want of a better word, has a shorter expiration date than a gallon of milk, and then let you overcome me all over again? Let you fool my body into denying the reality my heart knows is true? Oh, no. I may be green, but I'm not stupid.

But all she said was, "Nothing. I'm tired, that's all. I want to go to bed."

"A minute ago, you were falling asleep on my shoulder. What happened to that plan? It sounded good to me."

She sighed. "I've changed my mind. I'd rather sleep alone, downstairs, if that's all right with you." Her eyes challenged him to try to stop her.

He nodded with obvious reluctance. "Very well. Want me to walk you down?"

Ah, such gallantry. "That's okay. I'm not likely to get lost or anything." Turning her back on him was one of the hardest things she'd ever done, but she wished him good-night and walked out the door.

Breakfast the next morning was served not in bed, but downstairs in the kitchen. Or rather, Rita had her breakfast downstairs while Dorian pocketed an apple and a cinnamon roll, scooped up his briefcase and jingled his keys. The weekend was over, and so was playtime. "Sorry to run out on you," he began:

"That's okay. I know you've got work to do." To be honest, she didn't think she could have withstood a whole day in his company, not with her emotions as raw as they were. She'd spent the night contemplating reneging on her promise to stay, but as Dorian had pointed out, she didn't have many other options. So she'd settle for the Dorian-free hours she'd have during the day and use them to collect herself.

"Would you like to go out for dinner, or would you like me to pick something up?"

She would have laughed if her situation hadn't been so stupid.

They were talking to each other in that civil, formal way old married couples had the morning after a fight. When neither one was willing to back down and admit that they'd made a mistake, but both were reluctant to part in silence.

"Um, maybe eat out?" Damned if she wanted to face the abyss of silence that would follow an in-house dinner, then search for an excuse to slink up to her room. Better to immerse themselves in a pool of "others" who'd protect them from the discomfort of being alone.

His face told her he knew what she was thinking, but he didn't quibble. "I can be back by eight, take a quick shower and then we can head out again. Maybe we can work on your article. I'll try to be a good interviewee. I know you'll make me look good."

At least he was still able to make a joke. "I'll do what I can with the material I have," she said, surprising herself by joking back.

He kissed her on the forehead, patted Angela goodbye with equal affection and left.

The Fortress of Solitude she'd been anticipating once he was gone did not materialize. Instead, it felt more like a crypt. She'd been cooped up for too long in her own place, numbing herself after the Great Virginity Debacle, and was overwhelmed by the need to be outside again, mingling with humanity rather than feeling sorry for herself.

"That does it, Angela, my friend. I'm going out. And I'm taking my laptop. Time to get the lead out. Cassie thinks my writing is lousy? I'm going to give her a column that'll knock her socks off this week."

Angela walked her to the door with a happy grin that said, "I've got faith in you." That was good enough for Rita.

Her taxi dropped her off on Independence. She made a beeline for Starbucks, her home away from home. It smelled wonderful. Fresh-perked, mellow coffee and warm banana muffins. Even the muted scents of brass and leather welcomed her back.

She wasn't able to capture her usual seat by the front window, as three young men had already claimed it. Trying not to get her territorial hackles up, she sat as near as she could to her spot, throwing her coat over the back of her chair and taking a deep, satisfying sniff of her oversized hazelnut-infused cup.

It was fairly late, and some of the old regulars were long gone. William Wadsworth, Senior, the businessman with a penchant for expensive suits, had rushed off to his Monday morning meeting or whatever, having left his paper carefully folded on the tabletop. Sad Uncle Harold had left for whatever lonely pursuit filled his days.

But there were still some familiar faces: firemen who always popped in after their shift, a meter maid taking refuge from the abuse she encountered during her daily rounds, and the scrawny, greasy-haired little Goth girl.

Drucilla, as Rita privately called her, had managed to snag her usual seat. She looked especially shabby, taking the grunge idea to a whole new level. The shoes were falling apart, the gray jeans descending along the color spectrum toward black, and the incongruously twisted hair peeked limply out from under the black hoodie which, as far as Rita could see, was her only protection from the cold outside.

Rita shook her head. The gap between herself and the youngsters nowadays seemed to be widening. What was this girl thinking, coming out in the cold dressed like that? And did she ever get cleaned up? She appreciated that youngsters had a different sense of style, but this was ridiculous.

She turned away from the kid, whose head was bobbing unceasingly to whatever beat was being piped into her ears through the device in her hands. Bolstered by the familiar presence of her fellow caffeine addicts, she opened up her laptop and logged on. A few hundred e-mails poured into her In-box. She rummaged through, weeding out the malignant spam. She declined the opportunity to cash in on must-have real estate in Florida, to improve her sex life—she winced at that—and have her Tarot cards read. That took all of twenty minutes.

She scanned through what was left, looking for messages from friends and family. There was one from Beatrix.

Darling!
Do you ever answer your phone? What's the use of having one? Did you hear us on Late Night Mocha on WNTJ last Friday? Probably not. You never tune in to any of our shows anyway. But that's your choice, dear.
      Your father and I will be in Indianapolis this weekend. Then maybe Chicago. Oprah wants us back on her show. Maybe we can squeeze her in, ha ha. I'll tell you when. If you're not too busy maybe you can tune into that one. Kiss kiss.
You could at least have called.
Bea.

Rita was so used to her mother's little jabs she didn't even take offense. She tapped out a warm reply, apologizing for missing her parents' zillionth radio appearance and for not returning her mother's call.

That daughterly task completed, she moved on to business. The rest of the e-mails were from people with problems who were asking her for help. With her cursor hovering, she hesitated. Dorian's stinging barb rang in her ears, made even more resonant by Cassie's forthright assessment of her recent work. What if, *fraud* that she was, she didn't have the first clue how to help this person?

Oh, God. Could she do this? She clicked, trying not to hold her breath, and the e-mail opened up.

Dear Rita,
I done something awful. My husband's on a tour of duty overseas. We was only married seven months when he left, and it's awful here without him. I live with his folks, and they

don't take to me much. They spend most of whatever he sends over, and that don't leave much for me.

He works at this hardware store. They promised to keep his job open for him till he gets back, but things haven't been good, so last month I went and asked if I could have his job myself till he comes back. The supervisor said he didn't think it was possible, since it was a man's job, heavy things to carry and all, but if I came back later, maybe he could find something else for me.

Yeah, you know what happened. I went back after hours, and we got to talking, and one thing sort of led to the next and we did some stuff. And he gave me a little money.

Rita, I'm not no hooker or nothing, but next week I went back, and he gave me money again. And I've been going over there twice a week most of the time, since summer. Now I think I'm pregnant.

Rita, what do you think I should do?

Lisanne.

Don't print my name or anything, okay?

Rita had to drink half a cup before she could wrap her mind around the problem. She ached for this poor girl. There was so much sadness in the world and so much pain. Why did people have to endure such pain just to get by? Slowly, she began typing, deleting her first few attempts and starting over. The specter of her insecurity watched over her shoulder and whispered doubt in her ear.

Dear L.,

First of all, let me tell you how deeply I feel for you. I know how much you miss your husband. I'm sure he misses you. And I know things have been hard since he left. But first of all, you need to stop seeing this man at the hardware store. He doesn't respect you, and you need to start respecting yourself.

Second, you need to speak to someone—fast. Pregnancy isn't a secret you can keep for long. Do you have a friend you can talk to? A pastor or a priest? Turn to someone you can trust. They'll listen.

You need to find another place to stay. If his parents don't like you, there can only be turmoil and you will be too disturbed to think clearly. Find somewhere safe where you can clear your mind and make the right choice for you.

You also need to speak to your husband. I know it's scary, but keeping this from him is unfair. It will only get worse with time. Write down what you want to say to him. Practice it if you have to, but be honest, even though you know it's going to hurt. You've done a terrible thing, and if you still want him to stand by you, you need to ask him to find it in his heart to forgive. I hope that he can, and I hope that between yourselves, you make the best decision for both of you.

This will probably be the hardest thing you'll ever have to do, but I beg you to be strong.

Blessings,

Rita.

Rita surveyed her work, reading it over carefully. The self-doubt receded a little. Her characteristic sarcasm wasn't there. Neither was the biting tone she used to think was witty and hip. In its place were sincerity and a genuine sense of shared pain. It wasn't so bad. Maybe on the next one, she'd do better.

She opened up a new e-mail. It was a one-liner.

Didn't see you yesterday.

It was unsigned.

Rita froze. She glanced at the e-mail address, but it wasn't the one her tormentor usually wrote from. But the message…it could only be him. There were several e-mails from the same new address. He'd changed providers. Was he afraid that if she spotted another e-mail from him she'd trash it unread?

More curious than afraid, she opened up the next. Where are you? And the next—Are you there? Are you sick? The next two were in the same vein, growing more panicked.

Then she opened one that read I need to know you're all right. I'm coming over there. This one was dated Saturday, the night she'd spent at Dorian's. The night this…person…had slept in her bed.

Oddly, there was none of the rising panic that should have assailed her. She'd had enough. Enough wondering. She needed to know who he was. She hit Reply and was about to ask a question, when she hesitated. If she simply sent off an e-mail, it would sit there until this guy opened his mail—whenever that was. She wanted answers, and she wanted them now. There had to be a faster method.

The e-mail provider was one she used when she wanted to remain anonymous. It not only offered an e-mail service, but Instant messaging, as well. She opened up a window, logged on, and typed Who are you?

With a click, her query was whizzing off. Then, she waited.

Sanity, she reminded herself. Calm. Her cup was empty, and she had no idea how it had got that way. She needed another hit of coffee like a junkie needed a needle, but that would mean having to go get one. What if a message came in, and she missed it?

But that was idiotic. The message would be there until she got back. Paranoia was getting the best of her. She gathered up her wits, her wallet and her empty cup and went to the counter, trying not to look too hurried, ordered a double and returned as casually as she could.

Nothing on the screen.

Oh, no, she thought. He's not getting away that easily. She tapped out another message, and this one wasn't so polite. Who the heck are you?

Whiz.

Beep! She nearly jumped out of her skin as the reply popped up with the speed that only the Internet could provide. A.F.

A.F. All the early e-mails were signed with those initials. But that didn't help much. She replied as fast as she could type. What does A.F. mean? What do those letters stand for?

The answer was sarcastic. A Friend. Don't u kno a friend when u see 1?

She almost slapped her forehead. A. F. A Friend. It was so simple a child could have figured it out. But that information was useless. That doesn't help me. What's your name?

There was a long hesitation, during which Rita completely ruined her still-fresh Saturday manicure. Then, Why u want to kno?

Cheeky. She tapped out, Because I want to know who was in my home on Saturday. I want to know who slept in my bed.

That was accident.

Uh, right. She wasn't buying that. The least he could do was admit that he'd done something wrong. You slept in my house and ate my food by accident?

Had 2.

You *had* to break into my home? How does someone *have* to break into somebody's house?

Had 2. Yes.

Why did you have to?

Why u care?

Because it's my home. Because you've tormented me for a month. Because you've been coming in my window, God knows how, and wandering around my house when I'm not there. Even when I *am* there. And leaving me notes. That's why I care!

> Another pause. Even longer. Poor manicure.
> She typed again. Hello?

Sorry.

Sorry for what?

Had 2.

Why?

Y what?

This wasn't going anywhere. She tried a different tack. Why the nasty e-mails?

The response was bald and jarring. Mad at u.

Mad at her? Did she know this person? Had some guy said something to her sometime and she didn't respond? Had she been unthinkingly rude or dismissive?

Rita's mind skated along the halls of her memory, sifting through any peripheral male that she might have had the slightest contact with. Bag boys and laundry attendants, fellow joggers, staffers at *Niobe*, waiters…anybody she could possibly have had even the briefest, most casual conversation with. Anyone who would conceivably be small enough to have gained access to her apartment, via that ridiculous window, with or without a trained monkey.

Even with stretching her writer's imagination taut, she couldn't come up with a single possibility. It had to be someone she'd never met, and the only way for her to have offended such a person was through her writing.

Rita groaned aloud. In all the time she'd been writing, and given that she was usually rough on men in her columns, she was sure that she could fill a small stadium with men she'd ticked off. But would anybody be angry enough to send threats?

The possibility was truly scary.

She was in this far, and she wasn't turning back. She typed, Why are you mad? What have I done?

What u didn't do. U don't do.

What don't I do?

Listen. U don't listen. Im not good enuf 4 u 2 listen to?

Listen to what? How could she listen to someone when she didn't even know who they were? What made whatever he had to say so special that she'd been singled out for punishment just for not listening? Fear was overwhelmed by outright anger. Nasty e-mails, home invasions and now this insufferable self-importance. Either she was dealing with a lunatic or the most arrogant, self-obsessed guy on the planet. Either way, she was calling him out.

You listen. I'm done playing your games. I'm not saying another word until you tell me who you are.

The reply made her jump. How's the coffee?

He's here. My God, he's here. Nearby. Maybe outside, looking in at me through the plate glass. Lurking behind a street sign, or blending in with the crowd.

She looked through the window out onto Independence Avenue. Two middle-aged joggers trotted by, sporting color co-ordinated sweats. Teenagers, either late for school or brazenly playing truant, walked past as though they hadn't a care in the world. An old man in a gray fedora and a too-thin coat huddled against the plexi-covered bus stop, struggling to read a paper in defiance of a brisk wind. Nobody looked her way. Nobody seemed to care what took place in her unremarkable little coffee shop. And there was certainly nobody using a computer.

She looked up at the building across the street. It was twenty stories high. The entire facade was plate glass: hundreds of identical office windows, housing hundreds of working stiffs, all invisible behind the glass tint. Anyone could be sitting there, hands on his keyboard, looking down. Watching her.

No, that was absurd. A.F. was here, right here in Starbucks, within a few feet of her. She was finding out who it was…right now.

She couldn't call herself a poker player, but she could bluff when she needed to. She typed, I know who you are. I'm coming over, and shot to her feet, twisting, turning, trying to see as much of the coffee shop as she could, seeking a reaction from someone. Anyone.

The three young men were done with their coffee and were rising, loudly bouncing friendly insults off each other, swimming in testosterone at the end of their male bonding session. They didn't even glance her way. A tired-looking woman in a nurse's uniform was turning from the counter with a large latte in one hand and a muffin in the other. An alarmingly fat man was easing his girth through the front door, further hampered by an overladen knapsack.

And then there was Drucilla. Not hunched over, as she

usually was. Not consumed by her music or her never-ending computer games. Her back was pressed against her chair, hoodie down on her shoulders, exposing her pasty face and lank, noodle-thin twists. Her eyes bugged as she stared, transfixed, over at Rita.

Gotcha.

Chapter 16

The truth hit Rita like an oncoming train. Before she could step forward, the girl abandoned her seat and dashed toward the door, sending her PDA flying. Small bits of plastic skated away on impact, and the girl gave a strangled yelp, looking down at it as though it were a beloved kitten run over by a car. But Rita was closing in. She abandoned the shattered device, shoved aside the mountainous man in the doorway and darted outside.

Drucilla! Shock made Rita's mind cloudy. It wasn't a man at all, it was a girl. A weird, strange little girl. How? Why? She had to catch up with her. Her laptop was plugged in and open. There was no time to shut down. She yanked at the cord, her haste making it difficult, fumbling with the many steps of shutdown. Then there was her wallet, and her laptop bag.

And that little girl was getting away.

"Oh, nuts." Laptop abandoned, still on her table going through its final stages of shutdown. She left it to the kindness and honesty of strangers, hoping that it would still be there when she returned.

Wallet in hand, coat hastily snatched up, she ran. The cold outside was bracing, but she couldn't stop to put her coat on.

On Independence, she looked up and down. Which way? Post rush-hour traffic was light enough for her to get a glimpse of a small, black-clad figure a hundred yards to the west, in the direction of her own apartment. Rita ran awkwardly, her coat flapping behind her like a badly hung flag. Endless mornings of jogging served her well. The distance closed easily as her much longer legs gave her the edge over her tiny adversary.

The girl threw a look over her shoulder. As she realized Rita was closing in, she redoubled her efforts. She darted, turning here, twisting there, her route reflecting the one used by Rita and Cassie on their morning jogs. Through the wide eastern gates of De Menzes and down the jogging path they ran, as Rita's superior reach and fitness narrowed the gap between them. Her hand closed over the tail of the hoodie.

"Stop!"

The girl struggled, wriggled, trying to peel the hoodie off to ensure her release, but Rita held her fast. "Stop," she commanded again. "I need to talk to you."

The girl was winded, fighting for air. "Please…." She placed both hands on her knees, thin shoulders heaving.

Maddened by her stupidity at having missed an aggressor who had been right under her nose, Rita was harsh. "What's your problem? You think this is funny?"

Head bent, hair shielding her eyes, Drucilla struggled to master her breathing. No, that wasn't her name. Rita was sure she'd told her. She floundered for a minute. Then it came back to her. Right here, in De Menzes Park, during the Fun Run. She and Dorian had met the girl here—had practically been run over by her, she'd been tailing so close—and the girl had told her her name. What had it been? Laura?

"What's your name?" Words peppered her like bullets in a drive-by. When she got no answer, Rita probed again. "Laura? Laurie?"

"Lauren," was the forlorn reply.

That was it. Lauren. "What's your problem, Lauren? Why are you doing this to me?"

"I haven't done nothing. I didn't do nothing to you. It wasn't me...."

"That's ridiculous. We both know what you did. What were you doing in my place? Why'd you sleep in my bed?"

She didn't try to deny it this time. "That was an—"

"Accident? So you said, but I'm not buying it. You invaded my privacy, and I want to know why." Frustrated at not getting a response, Rita added a threat guaranteed to spur things along. "I called the police, you know. They're looking for you."

Lauren's little face was almost as gray as her watery, horrified eyes. Blotchy makeup and smudged kohl did nothing to hide the dark circles around them, and small, uneven teeth gnawed at the almost lipless mouth. "No, please. Don't let them."

"Then tell me why—"

"I didn't have a choice. I had no choice. It was cold, and I needed...."

Then Rita understood. The child had had nowhere to go. There'd been a cold snap on Saturday. They were descending into winter, and this scrawny, inadequately dressed little girl had had nowhere to sleep. Her rage disappeared like a snowflake in the palm of her hand. She took a closer look at the cowering girl before her.

Grubby clothes, dirty sneakers, no coat, no hat. Cheap gloves that left her fingers exposed. Unwashed hair and skin, conniving with adolescent hormones to provoke acne and worse. Crooked teeth spoke of poor health care. Whoever she belonged with couldn't afford or didn't care to get her to an orthodontist. She certainly wasn't eighteen or nineteen, as Rita had always imagined. Fifteen or sixteen would be a better guess.

And the child was alone. Sleeping somewhere nearby, most likely right here in the park, in or near one of the small utility buildings and gardeners' sheds. Suffering the abuse of the elements, and God alone knew who or what else.

Rita reached out for her again, out of pity rather than anger, and held Lauren's arm. Under the fleece, the girl's biceps were as thin Rita's wrist. Lauren reacted, writhing like a snake on an electrified fence. "Let me go!"

She released her at once. "I'm sorry. I didn't mean to…."

But Lauren wheeled, spun and darted around Rita. Having regained her wind, she was gone again, deeper into the park, off the jogging track, in the direction of the lake.

Rita started after her, but stopped short almost immediately. This was wrong. Chasing a frightened little girl, hunting her down like this, was cruel, even barbaric. She had no authority to do such a thing. She watched the frail, dark shape until it disappeared from view, and then fell dejectedly to her knees in the grass.

Man, did she ever screw that up. The memory of herself thundering after the running girl like a trapper after a frightened rabbit made her feel ashamed. She'd let her anger get the upper hand and had behaved like a bully. She had to fix it. There must be a way to help. But how?

Dorian would know. This was a frightened little girl who either didn't have a family or couldn't bear to be with them. Family was Dorian's specialty. If he couldn't help her, he'd know somebody who could.

She got up, feeling two damp, chilly patches on her knees left by the cold grass. She'd return to Starbucks and gather up her possessions—if they were still there—and then call Dorian.

She was in luck. Her laptop and bag weren't on the table where she'd left them, but a thoughtful attendant had saved them for her, along with Lauren's smashed PDA. After some thought, she collected it, as well.

First, she'd pass by her apartment to drop off her stuff. Now that she knew the identity of the offender, there was no reason to be afraid. Then she'd seek out the one man who could help.

Dear Rita

But fate has a way of changing plans. She wasn't a block from home when her phone gave its familiar chirp. She fished it out from her laptop bag. Cassie's number glowed on the screen.

"Cass! Oh, girl, am I ever glad to hear from you! I've been meaning to call, but so much stuff has happened. I made up with Dorian, first of all—" Then she laughed, remembering their hasty exit from Clark's party. "But I guess you already knew that. And you won't believe this—I'm staying at his place for a while. Only it's not what you think. I mean, it is sort of what you think, because we're, uh, together. Intimate, would be a better description, because as far as he's concerned, we're not really a love match. At least not on his side, anyway. Which really hurts. I have no idea how I'm going to handle that. If he touches me tonight, if he kisses me, I don't know how I'll react. I wouldn't know what to tell him."

That was about when she realized that she was babbling into a void. "Cass? Cassie?"

The static on the other side was replaced by the sound of soft crying. "You want to know what to tell Dorian? You can tell him to go to hell. Him and his partner. They're perfect for each other, with their ugly, suspicious minds. And you know why he doesn't love you? Because to love someone, you need a heart. A human heart, with feelings, not a dime-store pump that does nothing but push blood through your wretched body. To love somebody, you've got to believe in love and those two obviously don't!"

A sharp elbow to the ribs by an impatient passer-by in a heavy coat reminded her that she was standing dead center of the sidewalk. She stepped aside, pressing her back to the wall. "What's wrong?"

"Nothing. The wedding's off, that's all. I'm not marrying anyone who doesn't trust me. I'm not marrying anybody who calls me a low-down, dirty, greedy gold-digging—"

"Clark said that to you?" she asked with a mixture of hand-me-down anger and contagious despair.

"He might as well. Planning for a flash flood when everyone else is planning for a picnic. Betting on a funeral when everyone's celebrating a christening…"

"You're pregnant?" Rita shrieked.

"Don't be an idiot," Cassie snapped. "That's a metaphor. Focus!"

"Focus on what?" Rita pleaded. "Cass, I don't understand. You've lost me. Tell…me…what…happened. Slowly."

"What happened is that my fiancé—my *ex-fiancé*—called me up. Know what your boyfriend did? Your boyfriend's convinced Clark he needs to protect his wealth from a shark like me. Your *boyfriend*—"

Rita hated the nasty way she said that, but she was slowly beginning to understand.

"—talked him into getting a prenup. He wants me to sign a damn document promising to keep my grubby mitts off his wealth. Just in case this is all a scam, and everything I've ever told Clark is a lie."

"Did he really say it like that?"

Cassie hesitated, then admitted, "He might as well have. He called me this morning after a night of loving. The things I did to that man, the only thing he should have to tell me was how he's sore all over. How lucky he is to have me. Morning-after love talk, you know."

Rita didn't know.

"But nooo! What does he tell me? That your *boyfriend*—"

"He's not my boyfriend." And becoming less and less so by the minute.

"Whatever. I've never been so insulted. I told him in detail what he could do with his prenup and trust me, after last night, it's gonna be a little uncomfortable!" Cassie stopped for breath, huffing and puffing over the line as though she'd been running.

Rita stepped hastily into the breach. "Cass, listen. I'm sure Clark didn't mean—"

"Whatever he meant, I'm not buying. It's over. I'm done. I'm going over tonight and I'm giving him back his ring. It wasn't my style anyway." And the anguished stream ended in choking sobs.

Rita felt helpless. Her best friend's relationship was crumbling about her and she was hurting. She gave advice for a living. It was time to step up to the plate and say something. Administer healing. Solve this problem before it got out of hand.

She hadn't the first clue where to start. Her hands were not on a keyboard, tapping out trite, cutting remarks that made for good copy and sold magazines. And the person involved was someone she loved, closer than a sister, not a stranger with a made-up name. Not Depressed in Montgomery or Infuriated in Santa Fe. But she was tongue-tied. Her inadequacy burned.

"Cassie," she tried haltingly. "Clark's a wonderful person. You love him."

The sobs intensified.

"And he loves you."

"Funny way of showing it."

Whatever the document said, whatever it offered or denied Cassie access to was one thing. What it meant to her was another. A contract like that was the embodiment of mistrust, a way of hedging your bets if a marriage didn't work out. It practically verbalized the assumption that it wouldn't.

Trust Dorian to do a thing like that. It was just like him, the cynic. The man didn't, couldn't and wouldn't love her. It was becoming obvious to Rita that Cassie's diagnosis was correct. No matter how well the rest of his anatomy worked, Dorian's heart was a pump and nothing else.

Concern for her friend mingled with self-pity at her own situation and anger at Dorian. Cassie didn't deserve this. Maybe he thought he could hurt Rita and get away with it—and maybe, in the midst of her virginal infatuation, she was prepared to let him. But she wasn't letting him hurt Cassie. "Easy," Rita soothed. "Take it easy."

Which set Cassie off on another rant. "Easy? You want me to

take it easy? My whole life is a mess. I spent half the day yesterday writing up wedding invitations. I ordered my dress. We settled on a lemon sponge cake. Now my life is a mess and you want me to take it—"

"I'm going over there," Rita decided aloud.

"What?"

"I'm going looking for Dorian. And he's not going to like what I have to say to him. I'm going to make him take back whatever he said to Clark. I won't let him and his dim view of humanity ruin your life, Cassie."

Cassie sounded doubtful. "Really?"

"I promise."

"But I told Clark…."

"Forget what you told him. Clark loves you and he's not stupid. He knows you were upset. He knows you didn't mean what you said. I'm going to make Dorian take back that stupid prenup idea, talk Clark back out of it, and…and…." She was improvising wildly as she went along. "And I'm going to make him apologize to you. Got it?"

"I don't…I guess…."

Rita answered with more courage than she felt. "Go fix your makeup and have some chamomile. I'll call you later. But in the meantime, I'm going over. I've got some callous, self-opinionated butt to kick."

Chapter 17

Dorian knew at once that the commotion outside his office door meant trouble. If his receptionist, unflappable sixty-four-year-old Miss Foster, saw fit to raise her voice, somebody was getting on her nerves. Worse, the voices were coming this way.

He wasn't too bothered. Given the nature of his practice, there were usually a few disgruntled clients, or, more likely, adversaries of clients, who took it into their heads to turn up and vent their ire. Miss Foster was a dab hand at calming people down, so he was confident that the hullabaloo would subside any minute now.

The clients sitting before him weren't so sure. A husband and wife—soon to be an ex-husband and ex-wife—sat at opposite ends of his large, comfy couch, with a fragile-looking older man perched between them.

An East Indian man with carefully cut gray hair and remarkably ugly glasses that magnified his small black eyes, he fidgeted with the lapels of his tweed jacket and crossed and uncrossed his legs as though he needed to dash to the bathroom.

Professor Juman, a retired lecturer in relationship psychology at State, now freelanced as a mediator. He had an uncanny ability to solve problems between warring parties with empathy and patience. Dorian brought him in when a divorce was going particularly badly, to pour oil on the couple's troubled waters.

His guests looked mildly alarmed at the ruckus. Not wanting to show his irritation, he said comfortingly, "It's okay. Probably just a client being a little too, um, vocal. My receptionist will handle it."

His receptionist didn't handle it. His door flew inward and in blew Hurricane Rita. Her hair looked as though it had been caught in a gale, her eyes were like lightning, and her voice was a thunderclap. "We need to talk."

Probably the most frightening words a man would ever hear issuing from the mouth of a woman. His muscles tensed and his belly went instinctively cold.

Miss Foster brought up the rear, looking flustered and helpless, like a small craft sucked into the undertow of Rita's storm surge. For Miss Foster, this was rare. She wasn't the smallest of women, and in her severely cut navy skirt suit with stark white collar and cuffs and cold pearl buttons, she looked like a schoolmarm who didn't knuckle under lightly. "Mr. Black, I'm so sorry. I told her you're in with clients. I've tried to reason with her—"

Rita cut her off. "Dorian, I said we need to talk."

She looked crazy mad, and he didn't know whether to be more worried for her, for himself or his clients, whose eyes were fixed on this wild woman. Irritation and embarrassment made him forget the knot of fear that was still making itself at home in his belly. He responded in the most professional tone he could muster, the kind he affected when a judge was giving him a hard time. "Rita, as you can see, I'm in with clients."

"But I need to talk to you!" she protested. She was slapping her heavy laptop bag against her calf like an irritated cat flicking its tail.

Stay calm, Dorian. Stay… "Whatever this is about—"

"You know damn well what this is about. And don't try to weasel out of it."

This was the woman who had snuggled in his arms like a kitten last night and shed tears against his neck after he'd taken her over the edge? This little hellion?

He certainly knew what it was about: that terrible *faux pas* he'd made afterward. Alluding to the inevitable fact that there would be other lovers in her future. He was a realistic man and believed with all his heart that it was true, but that didn't make the gaffe any less forgivable. That had been the wrong place, and certainly the wrong time to bring it up.

And this was the wrong place and the wrong time to discuss it. He glanced at his guests, who seemed slightly less intimidated now that it had become apparent that one, Dorian knew the intruder, and two, she didn't seem to be armed. That intimidation was replaced by an inkling of titillation. This conversation had the sweet smell of scandal.

That wouldn't do. He had his image to maintain. He kept his tone even, but injected a firmness not even this enraged Rita that he hadn't met before could brook. "I'm busy now. My receptionist will escort you back to the waiting room. You'll wait until my session is over. Whatever we have to discuss will keep until then. Understood?"

The blaze in her eyes flickered before the ice in his, but the fire didn't die. She looked around as though for the first time realizing they weren't alone, and her pretty top teeth drew in her lower lip. She was contemplating arguing back, but decided that was a bad idea.

For good measure, he added, "You'll apologize to my guests and excuse yourself."

"I'm, uh, sorry to have interrupted you. Please accept my, uh…" She didn't finish the thought, but allowed herself to be escorted out by a triumphant Miss Foster—but not before she threw him a dark, venomous, this-ain't-over, not-by-a-long-shot look. He tried not to sigh.

When the door closed, he turned to his enraptured audience and added his own apologies to Rita's. It was a long time before he could bring all their minds—especially his—back to the subject at hand.

When his session was finally over, he personally escorted the now mollified couple and serene professor out, rather than have Miss Foster do it. He knew before glancing toward the waiting room that Rita was still there. The same three pairs of eyes that had goggled at her sudden arrival now regarded her with open curiosity. They looked from him to Rita and back again, putting two and two together and getting three million, four hundred and six. He tried to pretend his professional image hadn't taken a blow and resolved to talk himself out of strangling her when he had the chance.

Once his guests were safely out the door, he returned Miss Foster's rolled eyes with an eloquent shrug and approached his infuriated lover. The time spent cooling her heels had done nothing to mollify her. Three empty coffee cups were laid before her in a row and the caffeine junkie was working hard on a fourth. This wouldn't help matters.

"Sorry to keep you waiting." He couldn't eradicate the trace of irony from his voice.

"You done ruining someone else's life?"

He repeated his mantra. *Stay calm.* "As far as I know, their marriage was ruined before I came into the picture, if that's what you're alluding to. I'm just helping them tie up the loose ends so that they can get on with their separate lives."

She snorted. "Huh. So you had nothing to do with screwing up their marriage, eh?"

Was he missing something? "Sorry to disappoint you, but no."

"Not this time, at least," she said to her coffee cup.

"Excuse me?"

"So, what were y'all talking about in there?" She was getting more exasperating, and harder to fathom, by the second.

"I'm bound by privilege not to discuss the personal affairs of my clients. What's this about?"

"You were in there divvying up their loot, right? He gets the TV, she gets the stove? Who got the house?"

"Rita...."

"What's the matter? Didn't they have a prenup?"

"Not that it's any of your business, but if they'd had one in the first place, they probably wouldn't have much need of my services."

"Wouldn't that put you out of business, if everyone got prenups?"

His patience was running out. "Look, Rita, I haven't got time for games. I've another appointment in about ten minutes. I can see you're mad, and I thought I knew why, but I'm beginning to doubt myself. You're really going to have to relinquish this sudden interest in my clients' affairs and get to the point."

If she was getting to the point, she wasn't heading there via the expressway. "So, you think all couples should sign a prenup before they get married, huh? No matter how much in love they are? You think all men should protect their assets from greedy, money-grubbing little hussies who're so unscrupulous they're willing to marry their money, rather than work for it, eh?"

Clink. "Oh, snap," he muttered, more to himself than to her. "That's it. Clark spoke to Cassie, didn't he."

"Don't act like you don't know that."

"I didn't. I haven't spoken to him since early this morning. I don't even think he's in office right now."

"He's probably gone off to cry somewhere, like Cassie's crying right now. You ruined their lives."

Dorian looked around. Miss Foster was busy at her desk, head down, rifling through some papers. Rita's volume was steadily rising—not that Miss Foster needed it. She had the hearing of a foxhound. "Let's take this into my office."

She surprised him by hopping up immediately, squishing the coffee cup in her hand. "Yes. Let's." She led the charge back to the office, still swinging her laptop.

Inside, he shut the door and faced her. "Okay, spit it out."

"Spit what out?"

"Whatever it is you came all the way over here to bash me over. Go on. Get it out of your system."

"Don't patronize me."

"I'm not patronizing you. You said we have to talk. Go ahead. The floor is yours."

She was suspicious, but too mad to bottle it up. "How dare you cast aspersions on Cassie's character? How dare you convince Clark that he needed a prenup to protect his assets from her? Like she's a common swindler."

"I did nothing of the kind, and she's no such thing. I spoke with Clark for ten minutes this morning. As his attorney, I merely offered to handle such a document. *If* he decided he wanted one."

"You're his attorney?"

"And he's mine, yes."

"Why? Why does he need to rely on you? Why doesn't he do his own dirty work? He taught you practically everything you know."

"True. But it's as dumb for an attorney to handle his own affairs as it is for a dentist to fix his own teeth. Besides, you know what they say about a man who has himself for a lawyer."

"Oh, ha ha. So you took it upon yourself to advise him to get a prenup."

"You could say that, but he understands the law enough to know for himself why that would be the prudent thing to do."

"So you two were going to draw up this document from hell and toss it in Cassie's face?"

"Don't be silly." He ran his hand over his scalp. Something told him this was going to be a long day. "That's not how we do things. I told him that if he wanted to invite Cassie over to discuss their mutual assets with me and come up with an agreement that they both were comfortable with, I'd be happy to oblige. And furthermore, a contract like that only has the power you decide to give it. It's no better or worse than any other contract, and it doesn't mean that anyone's planning for a divorce any more than life insurance means that you're planning for a funeral, or that you're setting yourself up for a major coronary the moment you buy medical insurance. You do have insurance, don't you?"

He was half thinking she wasn't going to give in and admit it, but she slowly nodded.

"Good. So maybe you understand my position a little better?"

She boiled down a little in the face of his logic, but refused to be completely mollified. "She broke up with him."

That was disturbing. Clark hadn't mentioned that. "Sorry to hear that."

"You sure look sorry," she sniped.

"But I doubt it's a permanent break. Maybe Clark was a little direct, maybe he didn't handle the request too well. I love him like my own dad, but he's not the smoothest guy when it comes to talking with women. And it's not uncommon for one party to react that way to such a suggestion, especially women. They see it as questioning their motives, their love."

"You think?"

"Aw, please, cut me some slack!"

"You don't deserve any slack. You have no idea what Cassie's been through with men, especially her last boyfriend, who was, by the way, a homicidal lunatic. If anybody deserved to be happy, it was her. You ruined everything."

She wasn't listening. He was sorry to hear that Cassie had taken so badly to the suggestion, but in his experience, objections to these arrangements hardly ever resulted in a genuine breakup. More to pacify her than anything, he offered, "I can have a talk with her if you like."

She scowled. "Good luck. The opinion she has of you right now…."

"I don't doubt. But don't worry, I'm not easily intimidated. I've had scarier people hold much worse opinions of me. I think I can handle it."

Childishly, she clarified. "She totally hates your guts.'

He would have smiled at the inanity of the remark, if Rita hadn't been glowering at him so hard. Instead, he tapped his chest with one finger, just over the heart. "I'm immune to hate, remember? Teflon-coated heart. You pick one up at the front desk your first day at the Bar."

His joke went over like the Hindenburg, and too late he remembered why. She stared at the finger, which had frozen over his heart the moment he realized that his second stupid foot had joined the one he had shoved into his insensitive mouth last night. Hurricane Rita lost her fury, leaving all craft becalmed in a sea of painful silence.

Aw, crud.

Before he could say anything to salvage the situation, she said, "I'm moving back home."

Of all the responses he could have seen coming, that wasn't one of them. "What?"

"I'm catching a cab and going back to your place, and I'm packing up my things and heading back to my apartment. With Wallace," she added pointlessly.

Was she serious? "There's a wall-crawling maniac popping in and out of your bedroom window whenever it pleases him, and you want to go home just because you're mad at me?"

"I'm not going home because I'm mad at you…well, okay, there's that. But I'm going home because I can. There's no danger."

She looked confident, as if she had information. "No danger? What, did the cops call you? Have they held the guy?"

"No. But there's nothing to be afraid of." She swallowed hard, looking less convinced than she sounded. "I'm going home."

He couldn't let her put herself in harm's way like that. "Don't be ridiculous. Not until we talk this out—"

"Talk what out? I don't think we have anything to discuss."

"You know we do."

He knew she heard him, but she gave no outward indication of it. Instead, she turned with a toss of her head that let him know he was dis*missed*. Then, halfway toward the door, she realized she was still holding the scrunched-up coffee cup and began looking for a place to put it. Unable to see his wastebasket, which was behind his desk, and unwilling to ruin her grand exit by asking for something so mundane, she decided to hold on to it until she got outside. "I'll see you, Dorian. You take care."

"What's that supposed to mean?" A rising sense of panic made it hard for him to think.

"You know exactly what it means."

"No, I don't." He hastened to cut off her access to the door. "Not until we discuss this."

"Discuss what?"

"Now you're the one being obtuse. You said we needed to talk, and I agree with you. Don't walk out on me like that, without even giving me a chance to explain myself. That's not fair."

She lifted her brows. "Somebody told you life was fair?"

She was trying to get past him, but he blocked her like a defensive player at the three-point line. "Don't do this to me."

"Why does it always have to be about you, with you men?"

"That's not what I meant." He wasn't getting anywhere, and he hated that. She was hurt and upset and bent on thwarting him at every angle. It was time for a strategic, and very temporary, retreat. But she wasn't robbing him of the chance to fulfill his obligations as a host and as a man. "At least let me drive you over."

"That won't be necessary."

He groaned. "Baby, sweetheart, please. I'm trying to—"

"All about you again." She was triumphant at being proven right.

Maybe he should go bang his head against a wall until he was flat-out unconscious. It would be faster and a lot less painful.

She must have recognized that she was being too harsh, because she offered a slightly more reasonable excuse. "Besides, you've got clients to see, haven't you?"

At least she hadn't said something nasty like "more lives to ruin" and that was a start. He was about to think up a plausible denial, but sometimes, life really did work like it did in the movies; the intercom behind them beeped once, and Miss Foster announced, "Your one o'clock appointment has arrived, sir." Implicit in the statement was the addendum, *Will you be throwing that rude little hussy out of your office, or am I going to have to do it?*

Not defeat, he reminded himself. Ceasefire. "Okay, angel. You win. I advise against it, but if you really feel you have to go home, go ahead. But be careful."

"I know what I'm doing," she assured him.

He was just going to have to take her word for it. "I'll see you, then," he promised.

"You won't." She opened the door. "This is goodbye."

"It's not," he countered, and for the time being, that was all he had to say about that.

Chapter 18

Wallace was happy to be back in his cage again, even though he'd been away for only one night. He trotted along on his exercise wheel until Rita was sure he was going to drop from exhaustion. At least there was one happy camper in the room, Rita thought sourly. She'd spent the better part of the evening over at Cassie's indulging in some cholesterol-laden but highly therapeutic girly post-breakup therapy. This consisted of *Thelma and Louise* and *Waiting to Exhale,* microwave popcorn with extra butter and Swedish beer.

They ate Chinese out of boxes with chopsticks and complained about the crimes of their lovers, picking over the ruins of their relationships and crying, sometimes in turn, sometimes all over each other. Somewhere along the way, Rita found the courage to tell about her formerly virgin state.

Cassie cried a little more. "Oh, Rita, I'm so sorry. I pushed you into it, didn't I? I had no idea. I'm so sorry, girl."

"It's okay," Rita consoled her. "I went in with both eyes open.

It's not anybody's fault. Besides, it's over with Dorian and me. I don't want to see him again."

But she hadn't believed it even as she said it, and, several hours later, in her dark, quiet apartment, she still didn't believe it. She knew with her soul that it was far from over, and that if Dorian didn't seek her out soon, she would, in her weakness, go looking for him. She needed to see him again like she needed to see light when she opened her eyes in the morning. She craved the sound of his voice.

That was the way love worked, she supposed. It had a way of melting anger, letting it drip down and evaporate until all that was left was a damp patch where all that rage had been, leaving you wondering what it had all been about. All she was left with was longing and the memory of the harsh things she'd said.

She looked at the clock; it was almost midnight. Her phone had been silent all night. Where was Dorian? Why hadn't he called? He hadn't taken her seriously, had he? He didn't believe that they were really through, did he? That possibility alone was grounds for panic.

Call him, something said to her. *Call.*

"I can't," she told the silent voice. "I'd feel like a fool."

Then you are *a fool,* it retorted.

Her bed just didn't feel right after Dorian's. His was larger, higher and much more comfortable. It had Dorian in it. She rolled to one side and then to the next. She hit her pillows a few hard thumps. Nothing made her comfortable. She gave up and hopped out.

This was ridiculous. She was a grown woman. She snatched up the phone and dialed his number. If he was asleep, she was damn well waking him up. The phone rang and rang. By the time it went into voice mail, she'd lost the nerve to leave a message. She hung up and went to stand by the window.

The street below was eerily quiet. Apart from the fact that things were seldom hopping on a Monday night, especially in her neck of the woods, the cold snap had driven everyone indoors. Everyone, that is, who could go indoors. As she thought of Lauren, an empathetic shiver made her pull her nightgown closer. The last she'd seen of the weird little creature, she'd been high-tailing it into the depths of De Menzes Park. Rita had assumed that she was living in there somewhere, but surely that would not be right. Not on a night as cold as this. There were shelters out there for people like her, right? Plus, she was a minor. Surely the cops or park security would have found her and taken her, against her will or not, somewhere warm and safe. She couldn't be sleeping in the cold darkness of the park. Not tonight.

She remembered what Lauren had texted her, explaining why she'd spent Saturday night in Rita's home. Had to, she'd said. Because it was cold and she didn't have anywhere else to go? That must be it.

If she gave what she was about to do next too much thought, she'd back down. So she just went ahead and did it. She pulled on her jeans and a warm sweater, shoved her feet into thick socks and leather boots, and found two scarves and two coats. She put on one set and slung the other over her arm.

"See you in a little while, Wallace," she told the gerbil, who had finally worn himself to a frazzle and was too deep in sleep to hear her. "Back in a jiff, okay?"

As she let herself out the front door, she pulled the thick coat even closer around her. She paused on the sidewalk, tilting her head way back to look up at the night sky. It was an astronomer's dream: an endless, crisp black night, with the stars all out and glittering. There were so many of them they had to compete with each other for space. When she'd had her fill of it—and after she'd reminded herself of the folly of standing on an empty street after midnight—she began walking. The dead leaves under her feet crumbled easily, adding their scent to the already sweet air.

In the stillness of the night, the hum of the car behind her was loud. Even though she was well on the sidewalk, she instinctively stepped even further to the right, waiting for the sound to grow briefly louder as it drew near, then softer as it passed. It did no such thing. Instead, it followed her for perhaps ten or fifteen paces—paces that grew faster with her concern—then pulled alongside.

In a few panicky seconds, images flashed across her mind, all of them to do with the nasty things that befell women who wandered around lonely streets at this hour. Her eyes darted around for possible safe havens: store fronts, driveways, anywhere she could take cover. She glanced over her shoulder, wondering if her best bet would be to double back. Surely this man couldn't reverse as fast as she could run.

She stopped dead, but her heart went galloping on without her.

"Where the hell are you going?"

Dorian.

In the darkness, all she could see was a pair of angry black eyes.

"You frightened me," she yelled. What was he thinking, sneaking up behind her like that?

"*You* frightened *me*. I couldn't believe it was you, walking around a neighborhood like this at this hour."

"A neighborhood like what?"

"A dark, quiet, lonely one. Which brings me to my original question—where the hell are you going?"

Ten minutes, fifteen minutes ago, she was longing to see him or even to hear his voice. But now that she got what she wanted, she was mad at him all over again. Woman's prerogative. "What's it to you?"

"Come on. Don't be tiresome."

"I should ask you the same question," she hedged. "I belong here."

"I came looking for you."

"At this hour?" she mimicked.

He shrugged. "I was pretty sure you'd still be up. I didn't expect that you'd be up and *about*."

"Well, there ya go." She started walking again, her mind churning. He'd come looking for her. What did that mean?

The car rolled slowly beside her. "Get in. Wherever you're going, let me take you."

Her hands were already going numb. She shoved them in her pockets, tried to hitch up the heavy coat she was carrying, but was stubborn enough to reply, "That's okay, I've got it."

"Get in, or, God help me, I'm going to come over there, pick you up and toss you in."

"Isn't that assault or kidnapping or something?"

"It's something all right, but it's a whole lot better than the things that could happen to you out here on your own. What could be so all-fired important that it couldn't wait until daylight?"

That was enough to remind her of her mission. Wasting time bickering with Dorian wasn't doing Lauren any good. And the inside of the car looked toasty.

Spotting a softening of her resolve, he hopped out, ran around and opened the passenger door, helping her in as gallantly as always. "Where would Madame like to go?" he asked, with a trace of irony.

"De Menzes Park," she told him, well aware of how stupid that sounded. He stared at her as though she were a madwoman, but didn't comment. Instead, he took the heavy coat and scarf she was carrying, eyed it curiously, and then stowed it in the back.

He waited until he was back in his seat and moving before asking, "What's that about?"

"I'm taking it to my little visitor. It's cold out."

"Come again?"

She enjoyed the shock on his face. She could have played a few more games, strung him along a little longer, but that wouldn't help matters any. So she decided to drop the whole I've-got-a-secret number and explained, "I'm taking it for a little kid I think is living in De Menzes Park. A young girl called Lauren. She's the one who's been breaking in, and she's been doing it because she's cold. Hungry, too, I guess."

"It's a girl?"

"Yep."

"How old's this kid?"

She'd been wondering herself. She shrugged. "I can't honestly say. Sixteen, maybe. Hard to tell under all that messy hair and crumby makeup. But she's thin as a rake. Half-starved. Scared, too."

He thought about this new bit of information in silence for a while, and then pointed out, "Okay, I'll buy that she's cold, and I'll buy that she's hungry. But what's with the note?"

Confession time. She coughed. "Actually, that wasn't the only one. I've had maybe a dozen e-mails from her, too."

"E-mails?"

"Nasty ones. You know, like the note, only a lot more of them. That I think I'm so smart, more of the are-you-afraid-of-heights thing. Like that."

If looks could kill, her parents would be thumbing through the phone book for an undertaker right about now. "You mean you've been getting nasty e-mails from this person and didn't tell me?"

"Pretty much," she admitted and half cringed, waiting for the bawling-out to begin.

Disappointingly, it didn't come. He simply said, "Now I'm glad I turned up. Not only can I provide a little protection if you need it, but at least there's going to be *one* sane person in De Menzes Park tonight. You know, should the need for a level-headed decision arise."

She wasn't as bugged by his sarcasm as she could have been. In fact, she managed to crack a smile. "Should the need arise," she agreed.

"So, this girl's mad at you."

"Uh-huh."

"For what?"

"Because I didn't listen."

Dorian was running out of patience. "What didn't you listen to?"

"I don't know. I tried to ask her this morning. She was in the coffee shop, and I tricked her into admitting it was her. Then she ran out the door. I chased her into the park, but she got away."

"And you're worried about her. That's very compassionate of you, especially given what she put you through."

"She's just a kid," she defended.

"Okay, sweetheart. I'm not too sure I like it, but I'm here with you." They pulled up outside the park. Amusingly, even though it was the dead of night with not a breathing creature in sight, he still obeyed the No Parking sign and parked on the side opposite the main gates. He didn't shut off.

Rita peered outside. It was darker and quieter than she'd imagined. Visibility didn't stretch twenty feet past the entrance. Not even the hansom cabs that frequented the park were around. In the absence of the comforting clop-clop of horses' feet, she was fervently glad he was there.

He unbuckled his seat belt so he could get closer and examined her face carefully. He was so close. He was going to kiss her—but they'd broken up, right? She'd told him it was over. Surely he wouldn't…. She swallowed hard.

He was contemplating it. Had to be. His eyes lingered on her mouth for way too long. But drat him, drat him, he leaned back in his seat and closed his eyes with a gusty sigh.

Leather squeaked under her as she reached behind, snatched the coat and scarf off the backseat, and hopped out. He shot up, startled.

"Where you going?"

"Inside. To do what I came here for." It seemed a whole lot colder than it had been when she'd gotten into the car, but maybe she was imagining that.

"Wait." Behind her the engine went dead and his door opened. She could hear the crunch of his feet in the leaves. "Be careful!"

Be careful of what? The only thing she needed to be careful of was breaking down in front of him. Tears or rage, it could swing either way.

A ghost car swerved out of the darkness, not sure of which

side of the road belonged to it. She heard Dorian bellow her name. The grille looked like a grinning face. It took less than half a second to look at the curb before her and the one behind and decide which one was closer. She twisted, leaped—

And made it to the other side. Dorian was just one step behind her.

A laughing teenager, his upper body hanging out the open window, waved a bottle at her in mock salute. It wasn't a bottle of soda pop. With the other hand he made an obscene gesture as the car banked on the curb and swerved on its way.

Dorian sent a few ripe curses sailing after them. Then he put one hand out. "You okay?"

"Yeah. Driver had lousy aim."

"Damn kids." For a second, he sounded like a Scooby-Doo villain. Then he directed his ire at her. "What were you thinking? You should have waited for me to cross with you."

"Then we'd have made twice the target. Remind me how many points you get for hitting a pedestrian in Grand Theft Auto?"

"That's not funny. You could have been killed. I barely made it to you in time."

Ah, the ego of the man. "You didn't. I saved my pretty little tushie all on my lonesome. I can take care of myself, you know. I don't need a hero."

She might just as well have decked him. He winced. "You could have still waited."

"Why? Time's wasting. A little girl's freezing in there. I was in a hurry to get to her."

"No, you were in a hurry to get away from me."

"That's ridiculous." She shifted restlessly. She needed to get going again.

"No, it's not. I know you."

"Know me? You don't even—"

"There you go. That's why you're really mad."

He snared her with his dark eyes. Desperate to wriggle free, she drew the weapon of obtuseness from her measly arsenal. "I told you why I'm mad. Because you ruined Cassie's life with your cold-blooded, anti-romantic—"

"Anti-romantic?" Dark brows swept upward in bemusement. "That's a word?"

She sniffed. "It is. Trust me."

"I'll have to."

"You'd better. And don't try to change the subject. You, Dorian Black, are anti-romantic, and hard-hearted, and bitter, and you hate to see other people happy—"

He cocked his head to one side as if he hadn't heard right. "I don't like to—"

"You heard me. I'm mad at you because you took your twisted view of life out on my best friend, and now her heart's broken. And you don't even care."

"First off, I care very much, because Clark's my friend. As a matter of fact, I spent most of the evening with him. We had a couple of drinks and talked the matter over. He's really cut up at the way Cassie reacted, but he's going to talk to her as soon as possible. I'm sure it's going to be resolved. He knows what I suggested is an option, not a mandate. Ultimately, it's up to the couple to decide.

"Second, I like Cassie, and I'm sorry to see her hurt, but it was my duty to speak up. I hope when this blows over she'll forgive me." He cracked an ironic smile. "It just won't do to have your partner's wife hating your guts."

She could have said something about the likelihood of that wedding taking place being slim to none, but he was making too much sense. Maybe this would blow over.

"Third, and here's the real sticking point, sweetheart, none of this is really the issue. Not Cassie, not Clark. You're ticked off with me for another reason entirely."

"And that would be?" She tried to look menacing by lifting an eyebrow, but couldn't quite pull it off. She managed to look cornered instead.

He stepped closer, until all she could think about was the nearness of him, his warmth and his scent. She wanted to close her eyes and shut him out, but he grasped one twist of her hair and twirled it gently between his fingers. Although hair was supposed to be dead, insensate, this particular strand was full of nerve endings. Tingles shot through the thick curls and rippled through her, making him impossible to ignore.

The timbre of his voice dropped lower, so that his words came from some deep place inside him. "You're really mad, Rita, because I haven't…I can't tell you that I love you."

Oh, the humiliation. He'd hit the nail on the head with a re-sounding bang. There was the crux of the problem. She knew it, and, embarrassingly, he did, too. Why, oh, why had she opened her stupid mouth and said something so irretrievable? Why had she allowed the tide of emotion and wonder and sexual gratification to rise inside her so high that it had spilled over into those three damnable, never-to-be-taken-back words I love you? She made a halfhearted attempt at denying it, scrabbling around desperately to save face. "I didn't really—"

He cut her off with a kiss, his mouth sealing off the lie before she could dishonor them both with it. Maybe he'd meant it to be just a light pressure, a punctuation mark to bring an abrupt end to her foolhardy remark, but her body wasn't letting him get away with it that easily. It knew instinctively what to do. Her hand found the back of his head, holding him fast. Her mouth blossomed under his. It was incredible that she had been in his arms and his bed less than twenty-four hours ago, kissing him like this, and more. She was starving for him, like a diver craving air after having been submerged way too long.

Somebody had to stop this. He did. "I need to tell you why. I owe you that much."

Why? Wasn't the fact of it enough? "Does it matter?"

"It does to me. I didn't want you feeling that it had anything to do with you."

"Didn't think that for a second."

He'd have smiled at her comeback if this wasn't so serious. "I just can't express something I don't believe in."

"How could you not believe in love?"

"How could I? I spend half my day with people who did. They swallowed the whole idea of raindrops on roses and whiskers on kittens. Where do they wind up? In my office squabbling over property. All these sad, bitter, broken people once said 'I love you' to each other."

"I'm not all those people. I'm different."

"You are different. That's why I want to be with you. And I know you want to be with me. So why not? I'd be good to you, and we could have fun together."

She knew what he was asking. She didn't like it.

He dangled candy before her. "And the sex is great, isn't it?"

"Friends with benefits, eh?"

His lips twisted in frustration. "No, no. More than friends. Lovers. A couple."

"Lovers who aren't in love?"

"It's just a word."

If he really thought that, he needed more help than she thought. "It's not just a word. It's real. I feel it. Why can't you?"

He looked up at the inky sky. He seemed to have a habit of doing that when she was around. She liked that he needed to seek divine help in dealing with her provocation.

Divine help wasn't forthcoming. He struggled, briefly, while she waited in hope, and then he said, "It's all I can offer you." He avoided her eyes.

Surrounded by ruined relationships every day? Oh, please. She knew what that was like. All these people writing her, sad women with broken hearts. Like his clients, they still believed in love. And like him, she'd had her doubts about men and love, too. But loving Dorian changed that.

Loving him had taught her that love was individual, custom-made. As specific to each person as their own individual scent. Her love for Dorian wasn't the same as Depressed in Dakota's for her no-good man or Miserable in Montana's for hers. Hers was unique. Just because it didn't work out for all those people didn't mean it couldn't work out for her.

If she was able to believe that, why couldn't he? If she was willing to take a chance, why couldn't he? "Coward."

"That's not fair."

"It's true." She looked upward into the sky just as he'd done, trying to find strength from the same source he had. Maybe she'd be more fortunate.

The strength was there. A wellspring of it. Enough to let her say, "If I can't hear you say it, I don't want you."

"You can't mean that."

"I do. I want more. I'm worth more—"

"I never said you weren't worth—"

"All or nothing, *sweetheart*." She mocked his term of endearment.

He was thinking hard. His chest rose and fell so slowly she began to believe he'd managed to slow his respiration down to nil.

God, it was cold out here.

When he shook his head, she knew all hope was lost. "I'm probably the only guy on Earth who's had a woman break up with him twice in one day."

Tell me he's not trying to make light of this. She wanted to rant, rave, shout out her disappointment and hurt, but she was as cool as dry ice. "Once. We never made up."

"This isn't over. I'm not giving up on us.'

"That makes one of us." She'd had enough. Saying what she'd said had drained the last dregs of energy from her. She didn't think she could stay in his company much longer, in case fatigue made her weak enough to go back on her word. It was better they did what they'd set out to do and go their separate ways. "Look, it's freezing. I realize it was a dumb idea to come out here in the first place, but I'm here. Might as well do what I set out to do. We have a little girl to find. You coming or not?"

He didn't argue. Instead, he buttoned up his coat and took her arm. "Guess I'd better. It looks dark in there."

Chapter 19

One of the lights atop the huge stone pillar at the entrance to the park was out. The shadows cast by the lone light on the opposite pillar were strange and lopsided. For about three heartbeats, Rita reconsidered. But Dorian was right there at her elbow. He didn't say anything, but spurred her on with a touch.

A migraine was exploding inside her head like a dying star. The weak lighting along the footpath felt like a million candle-power. The soft hooting of night birds, the sound of their footsteps, even her own breathing, were like a battering ram at the back of her skull.

Focus. All she needed to do was stay calm, ignore the pain in her head and her heart, do what she needed to and get out of here.

The park looked different. She'd jogged here almost every day for as long as she could remember, but there was none of the usual comforting, welcome-home feeling she always had. Even the trees looked offended at their presence.

They passed the spot where they'd lain in the grass and kissed while listening to the band. Rita sneaked a peek at Dorian, but he looked carefully ahead.

The bandstand nearby seemed an obvious place to begin their search. In the darkness, a few shapes moved near the stage. As Dorian led her there, she realized she was clutching his arm.

The smell hit them before they were even within speaking distance. It was the smell of unwashed human, alcohol, smoke and despair. Not all of the smoke was tobacco. Five or six people lingered about near the stage, staying close to each other for warmth. There were others stretched out on the benches arranged before the stage in a semicircle.

"Good evening," Dorian said to nobody in particular.

She was glad he'd chosen to speak, because the cat had run away with her tongue. Nobody acknowledged them.

"Can you see her?"

"I don't know. Hard to see in this darkness. Plus they're all bundled up. And I feel awkward staring."

Instead of answering, he walked to within a respectful distance of one of the older men. The man was wearing a large straggly coat that was obviously cut for a woman. A woolen hat was pulled down over most of his face, but from what Rita could see he was white, over sixty, and didn't have that many teeth left.

"Excuse me." Again, bless Dorian for speaking out first. "We're looking for a young girl…." He floundered, and then turned to Rita. "What does she look like again?"

The cat released her tongue enough for her to say, "Small, dark hair in little twists like…mine. High-top Converses, black clothes. Very pale. Very Goth. Lots of bracelets and chains. She doesn't look well, and I don't think she has a coat."

The man's eyes were filled with cataracts and suspicion. "What's it to you?"

"I'm a friend of hers."

"How good of a friend?" The look veered from the suspicious into the realm of the calculating.

Dorian took the cue gracefully. He fished into his pocket, removed his money clip and handed over a bill. Rita hoped fervently that the sight of money wouldn't be mistaken as an open invitation for all and sundry to swarm. Although Dorian looked confident, even relaxed, she could feel the tension in his body and knew he was poised for action if necessary.

Army Reserve, she reminded herself. He can hold his own.

The man snatched the bill, looked it over, and then, satisfied, put it away. "Girl you thinkin 'bout, I think I seen her. But she ain't here."

He looked as though he wasn't going to say any more, but Dorian was intent on getting his money's worth. "Where, then?"

The man pointed into the darkness with his chin. "Try further in, by the lake. One o' them boathouses they got there."

Dorian looked in the direction he had pointed, and said, "Thank you kindly."

"Now, I ain't her pops, mind. I ain't her keeper. No tellin' if she gonna be there tonight or not, understand? So if you don't see her, don't you be coming to ask me for your money back. Hear?"

Dorian smiled. "I wouldn't dream if it. You have a good night now."

"Same to you, son. You and the missus."

Before Rita could deny their relationship to this stranger, Dorian whisked her away.

Deeper, deeper in. Colder, because of the wind coming off the lake. "You okay?" he asked.

"I'm fine," she said stoically.

"Good."

Mist hung over the lake like something out of a Stephen King novel. Rita half expected it to swirl and congeal into living wraiths, and drift over the ground toward them. The shore was dotted with boathouses, small and large. Some were empty, but one or two showed signs of activity.

Before Dorian could make the choice for her, she approached

a group gathered around a fire. She'd die rather than continue to allow him to be in command of this mission.

This bunch was younger. A boy detached himself from the huddle at the fire and walked toward them. He was brown-skinned, short and looked about seventeen or so. His only protection from the warmth was a hoodie, a denim jacket and a cheap scarf.

"Help you folks?" The question was not congenial, but menacing.

Dorian answered for her. "We're looking for a young lady."

"Yeah? What this young lady done to you?"

Rita interjected, "Nothing. I just need to see her. She's small, white, with black hair. High-top Converses. Black clothes. Her name's Lauren."

"What you want her for?"

Rita perpetuated the lie. "She's a friend of mine."

"Lauren got no friends other than us."

Heads were raised, looking at them. A few youngsters stood warily, like meerkats sniffing the air for signs of danger.

Rita said, "Please, we just want to see her for a minute. I want to help."

The boy had been on the streets long enough to know that help in adultspeak meant trouble. He spun around and yelled, "Lauren! Cops!"

A small figure broke away from the fire and started to run along the shore. Rita recognized it at once. "There she is!"

Dorian didn't need any prompting. His medal-winning sprint brought him within grabbing distance of her in ten flat. His arms closed around the girl as she bucked and squirmed but trying to get away from him was like trying to shift the Rock of Gibraltar.

When Rita got there, with the young boy ahead of her by two paces, Lauren was still struggling. "Let me go, cop!"

"I'm not a cop."

Lauren, still struggling, squirming and spitting, recognized Rita. "You called the cops on me? I said I was sorry!"

The young boy pulled on Lauren's flailing arms. "Let her go. She didn't do nothing. We got rights!"

"He's not…."

Something clicked for Dorian as he looked down into the panicked face. "She was in the park the day of the race."

Recognition flicked across Lauren's face, but it didn't slow down her bucking. "Leave me alone. I said I was sorry. Ralph, Ralph!"

Rita tried again. "He's not a cop. He's my…friend. And I don't care about any of that other stuff. I was worried about you."

"I don't need you to worry about nothing. Tell him to put me down."

"Promise you won't run away?"

"I ain't promising you nothing."

She was truly scared. Dorian may have been effective in restraining her, but otherwise, he wasn't doing her any good. "Dorian…."

He set the girl down. Rita half expected her to dash off the second her feet hit the ground, but she brushed off her thin jacket and glowered at them.

"Say the word, Lauren," Ralph warned.

Before things got any worse, Rita tried to explain. "I don't mean you any harm. I was worried about you. I wanted to give you this." She held out the coat and scarf, which now seemed like such an inadequate offering.

Lauren barely looked at it. "I don't want nothing from you. I don't want nothing from nobody."

Rita didn't pull her arm back. "Take it. It's cold."

Lauren looked down at the proffered garments, and her hands went up to finger the jacket she was wearing. She sucked in her lower lip and swayed.

"Take it, Lauren. You can't survive out here without it."

Lauren grabbed the coat from Rita's fingers, shook it out, and put it on without a word.

Ralph wasn't liking this. "You don't need their stinking—"

"Be quiet," Dorian barked.

The boy fell into a sullen silence.

Feeling more in control, Dorian asked, "Young lady, why are you out here?"

Lauren wrapped the scarf around her neck. "None of your business."

"How old are you? Where are your parents?"

"Double none of your business."

This wasn't working. She was a pretty stupid Samaritan, thinking she could change the world with a coat and a scarf. That was like putting a bandage on a bullet wound. Her coat was as heavy as the one she'd given Lauren, but she was still chilled to the bone, and she'd only been outdoors an hour. The kid must be dying.

"Come home with me." It was out of her mouth before she could even think it.

An incredulous "What?" came simultaneously from Dorian and Lauren.

The idea gelled. Rita repeated it, and as she said it, it became real. "Come with me. You can't sleep out here tonight. It's going to get colder." It made perfect sense. Why hadn't she thought of that? A coat wasn't the solution. This was.

Lauren frowned, sideswiped by the offer. To cover her confusion, she chose belligerence. "I don't need you. I'm fine where I am."

"You're not fine. You're going to get sick. You look sick already. I don't know why you're out here instead of being with your family, and I don't want to know. But you've been where I live and you know it's safe. Just come with me for the night. You'd have a warm place to sleep. We can talk about this in the morning."

Dorian cut into her persuasive patter. "Rita, talk to you for a sec?"

She didn't need to be psychic to know what was coming, but stepped aside with him anyway. It was a good sign that neither Lauren nor the young boy took the opportunity to scamper off. They were too bemused to do anything other than stare.

She tried to head him off. "I know what you're going to say."

"Do you?"

"You want to know if I'm crazy."

"Something along those lines, yes. You don't know the first thing about this child. She could be dangerous. Isn't this the same girl who was threatening you?"

"She didn't mean it."

"How d'you know?"

"I know, okay? Besides, what d'you want me to do? She's alone and scared, and she'll freeze to death out here."

"I know. And I don't want that any more than you do. I'm not suggesting we don't help her. I know a lot of people, I could make a few calls. I can find her a safe place for the night. Longer, if she needs it."

"You mean an institution."

Dorian glanced across at Lauren, and then back at Rita. "They're not all that bad. She'd be well looked after, and they'd help find her family. She's a minor. You don't need an attorney to tell you you can't just go taking young girls home with you. Do you have any idea what kind of trouble you could be in for doing this? What if her family objects and claims you've interfered?"

Trust Dorian to be logical. To think when she wanted him to feel. He didn't understand. She'd spent so much time just giving advice to people in trouble. Telling them what to do rather than helping them do it. Couldn't he see she needed this as much as Lauren did? "I'll take my chances."

A dozen possible arguments flitted at the back of his eyes. Some made it to his lips, but not past them. Reluctantly, unhappily, he conceded.

The victory didn't make her happy, but she walked back to where Lauren was standing, watching them curiously. "Lauren, I'm begging you. For your sake. Just for tonight, okay?"

Lauren glanced at the boy who was standing beside her with his arms folded, and then down to the damp earth at her feet. She nodded.

The four of them made it to the park gates in silence. Dorian displeased, Rita hopeful, Ralph scowling, Lauren defeated. As Dorian helped Lauren and Rita into the car, the boy stood on the curb and shouted warnings at his friend. She didn't take her coat off, but Dorian turned up the heater anyway. Ralph stayed on the curbside until they were out of sight.

Rita was quiet next to him. Now that she had what she wanted, she was confused and nervous. What had she done? What if Dorian was right? And had she invited the girl home only out of compassion or because of a need to prove something to Dorian?

"Hungry? Want me to stop? We could pick something up."

He was talking to Lauren, not to her, but Rita answered anyway. "Let's just get her home. There's lots to eat there."

For the first time, Lauren piped up. "And coffee?"

Lauren was a bona fide member of the caffeine junkie sisterhood. They had that much in common. Rita smiled. "And coffee."

Dorian waited in the kitchen while Rita busied herself inside with Lauren, getting her a change of clothes and making sure she had a long, hot bath. Lord knew she needed it. He wondered what she did for simple amenities like bath and toilet. He supposed the public facilities at De Menzes Park would have to do. He was guessing they didn't offer hot water.

He made himself useful, fixing up the fastest, hottest meal he could think of: fried sausages, eggs, buttered toast and hot soup. With coffee. Being busy helped take his mind off Rita.

The girl came out, looking so fresh and clean that he'd have had trouble spotting her in a lineup if he'd been called upon to identify the girl from the park. The ridiculous twists in her hair had been washed out, and it now fell, damp and clean, around her face. She was still quiet, not looking directly at him, as though aware that Dorian didn't like that she was here.

He didn't, but tried his best to disguise it. He couldn't eat a thing himself, but Rita joined Lauren for dinner/breakfast. It was two in the morning. She hoped neither of them would regret it later.

"I've put up a camp bed in my study," Rita told Dorian. Unnecessarily, since he'd heard the commotion of her setting up the thing.

He nodded. "You'll be okay tonight," he promised Lauren. He hoped Rita would be okay, too. As a matter of fact, he was damn well making sure of it.

Lauren took Rita's comment as a signal. She stood up, pushing away the same cheerful ceramic mug she'd used on her unauthorized entry the last time. How she was planning on sleeping with that much caffeine in her system, he didn't know. "Good night," she said specifically to Rita. She threw Dorian a frown and disappeared down the corridor. He considered pointing out to Rita that the kid still hadn't said, "Thank you," but thought better of it.

Rita set about clearing away the dishes, but he stopped her, whisking them away himself and making quick work of them in the sink while she hovered behind him and watched. In the small kitchen, they were separated only by their awkwardness.

She didn't say anything, and he thought it wise not to push her. Instead, he removed his tie with a sigh, settled down in one of her twin armchairs and began to take off his shoes.

"What're you doing?"

He wanted to groan. This had not been a good day and he was bone tired. He answered levelly. "Settling in for what's left of the night."

"Excuse me?"

"Did you think I'd leave you all alone with a complete stranger?"

"She's a child, not an ax murderer."

"I wouldn't be so quick to bet on the last part. Juvie Hall is full of children her age who've committed crimes that would raise your hair."

"Good to know the warm fuzzy feeling normal people get

from doing something nice for someone hasn't dulled your suspicious nature."

She wasn't the only stubborn one there. "You could say that."

When she leaned forward, picked up his shoes and handed them firmly over, he knew the battle was lost. Something sickening lurched inside him. "You're throwing me out?"

"You catch on fast, counselor." His coat and tie were pressed into his hands. "Lauren and I will be just fine." She didn't need to add, *We don't need your help.*

It wasn't about Lauren. It wasn't about protecting Rita. Couldn't she see that? He was scrabbling for one last desperate handhold to cling to her life. After her blunt and brutal rejection in the park, all he had left was the protection his masculinity and superior physical strength could provide. Was she taking that from him, too?

She put her hand to her temple in a familiar gesture, and he knew that her head was pounding as hard as his. This wasn't the time to argue his case. It was time to retreat, regroup and plan a new offensive. She might be convinced it was over between them, but he knew otherwise.

Without any further objection, he let her walk him to the door. She looked surprised—dare he hope, disappointed—that he didn't argue any further. He stood in the doorway, allowing her her small victory. Wondering whether to kiss her good-night.

Better not.

"I'll see you soon," he promised.

"Why bother?"

Chapter 20

Rita was wrist-deep in the entrails of a huge pumpkin when the doorbell rang. It was an evening for soup, and she was feeling particularly domesticated. In the living room, Lauren was lying on the couch watching music videos, a spot and a station she hadn't deviated from in the last three days.

It didn't look as though Lauren was all that keen on going anywhere, and although she was beginning to feel a growing sense of disquiet about the legality of harboring the child, Rita was glad she was okay for the time being. She barely spoke, other than to make basic requests for things like towels, magazines and coffee, but at least she wasn't hostile.

The sound of the bell didn't rouse the girl from her perch. Either that, or the hard-core metal that had been blaring forth from the TV since morning had dulled her hearing. Rita got the door.

Cassie wafted in. "Ay, girlfriend."

"Cass! Where've you been?" Relief at seeing Cassie again was mixed with the kind of irritation a parent felt after worrying over the disappearance of a child, only to discover him playing out back with the neighborhood kids, happy as a pig in mud.

Cassie missed or chose to ignore the trace of irritation in her voice. "Colorado. There was an early snow. You should have seen that powder…." She threw her bag onto the counter and shifted out of her coat. "Ooh, pumpkin soup. Yum. How long before it's done?"

Rita's irritation level went up a notch. She put down the carving knife and carefully picked at pumpkin seeds and flesh stuck to her apron, buying herself time before she said, "I called you a dozen times. I left messages. I practically set up a vigil outside your house, and all you have to tell me is that you went skiing? With who?"

"Who d'you think?" Cassie smirked.

"Clark? But I thought…."

"Oh, come on. You didn't really believe we'd broken up, did you?"

This wasn't for real. She answered slowly, "I did. Because that's what you told me."

"Oh, girl. You take life way too seriously." Cassie nosed around in the fridge, found a tub of cream cheese and popped a frozen bagel in the toaster. "These are organic, right?"

As used as she was to the Jekyll/Cassie routine, she was flabbergasted. She dumped the bowl of diced pumpkin into the soup pot and stirred it a little more vigorously than it needed, before saying, "I take life too seriously? Weren't you the one who called me up crying? How can you act like nothing happened?"

Cassie's flippant tone faded. "Something did happen. But we talked it over and we're cool now. We realize we were rushing into this marriage thing. We love each other, but we need to take it slowly."

Rita wasn't mollified. "What does 'slowly' mean?"

"We put the wedding off for another six months or so."

"And the prenup?"

Cassie examined her nails. "It's actually quite generous."

The soup had taken enough of a battering. Rita tossed the spoon down and covered the pot. Pumpkin wasn't the only thing she felt like battering right now. "Oh, great. You made me go over there and yell at Dorian. I made a fool of myself for you."

It only now penetrated Cassie's brain that their argument was supported by a heavy metal soundtrack. She peeked out the kitchen doorway into the living room and spotted the small figure curled up on the couch. "Who's that?"

The woman had the attention span of a gnat. Rita wasn't letting her meander down another conversational path, not this time. "Never mind who that is. You can't just do things like that, Cassie."

The recrimination in Rita's voice was enough to jerk her attention back to the kitchen and the conversation. "Wait, you're mad because I'm happy?"

Rita tried to explain. "No, I'm mad because you had me worried. You had a crisis on your hands and I went to bat for you. Then you disappear on me for three days, worry me sick, and waltz in here like Holly Golightly. You can't treat people who care for you like that."

"I wanted to call you, but things got hectic. You know."

"Oh, I'm sure phone reception must be awful up on the slopes."

Cassie defended herself. "What's the big deal? Dorian knew Clark was away. Why didn't he just tell you?"

"He, uh, hasn't been here." *Because I threw him out. And he took me at my word.*

"You two still broken up?" Cassie looked as though Rita had revealed that dinosaurs still roamed the Earth.

She'd made sure of that, hadn't she? She tried to sound resolute. "Of course we are. I told you—"

"Right. He didn't fall out of *Jane Eyre* or *Wuthering Heights* or whatever, and protest his love for milady, so you chicken out." The toaster dinged behind Cassie, but she didn't turn around.

"I didn't chicken out. I'm just not prepared to settle for less."

"Settle? You got a fever? You consider being with Dorian Black settling?" She counted Dorian's attributes off on her beautifully manicured fingers. "The man is smart, well-established and a total babe. There're women who'd give up an arm for a chance to be with a man like him, and you dump him because he doesn't love you?"

She put her hand on Rita's shoulder. "Baby, listen to me. I've been around the block a couple of times. You on the other hand, have barely made it to the end of the driveway, so trust me, I think I know a little more than you. You're a damn fool if you give up on that man."

Rita tried to hold on to being mad at Cassie, to avoid conceding she was making sense. "I'm not a fool, and you have no right—"

"You need to get real. Love doesn't always come at once. Sometimes it takes a while. Sometimes it takes a long time. Sometimes it never comes, but that doesn't mean you can't be happy. My folks have been married for forty-two years, and I don't believe I've ever heard my father tell my mother he loves her. But she's a happy woman. You know why?" When Rita didn't answer, Cassie badgered, "You know why?"

Wearily, Rita gave up the guessing game. "Why?"

"'Cause she's got herself a good man who treats her right. Think about it."

Thinking about it was the last thing Rita felt up to right now. "Don't you want your bagel?"

Cassie didn't answer, but, having won their little spat, returned her attention to the teenager in the living room. "Now, like I said, who's the kid?" She jerked her thumb at the kid in question, just in case Rita wasn't sure which one she was talking about.

Of all the topics Rita didn't want to get into right now, that was the second. They'd just been over the first. "She's just… someone I know. From the coffee shop."

"She pop over for a cup?"

"Not quite. She's staying here for a few days."

"You brought home a kid from the coffee shop?"

"No, not exactly. I know her from the coffee shop. I brought her home from the park." Why didn't Cassie just fill her mouth with bagel and not ask any more questions?

"The park? What was she doing in the park?"

"She has nowhere else to go."

A suspicious, dismayed frown passed over Cassie's face. "Oh, no. Not one of those kids who're always hanging around by the lake. Half the time they're hopped up on something or the other. What's she using?"

Through the doorway, Rita saw Lauren turn her head. Then her expressionless face turned toward the TV again. Rita didn't like the idea that the girl knew they were discussing her. Cassie's voice wasn't the softest in the world. She steered her deeper into the kitchen, away from the entrance. "She's not using anything."

"Says the expert on juvenile drug abuse."

"I'm not an expert. I just know—"

"What I know is this—you've got a homeless teenager living with you. That makes you nuttier than an Almond Joy. Where're her parents?"

"She hasn't said. She doesn't talk much."

"Well, you better get her talking. You have any idea the kind of penalty you pay in this state for harboring a runaway minor?"

"No."

"Me, neither, but if you were still talking to Dorian, he'd tell you."

She didn't want to go down that path again. "He's against the idea."

"'Cause he's smart. You call the police?"

That would be a horrible idea, just the thing she didn't want in the first place. "I can't do that to her. She's afraid. What if she's running away from something truly awful?"

"That's up to the police to deal with. She needs help. You're really not equipped to handle this kind of situation."

Rita nodded miserably. "That's what Dorian said."

Cassie gave her one of those looks she reserved for the times when she was especially right. "For someone who's shaken the dust of that man off her feet, you sure call his name often. Look, babe, let me be the agony auntie for a change, 'cause you're not doing such a good job of advising yourself."

Ouch.

"One, get that kid to where she belongs pronto, or let the authorities do it." Cassie was spinning around, and Rita realized she was looking for her stuff. She felt guilty about feeling relieved that her friend was leaving, but the whirlwind visit was proving to be all she could handle.

She put on her coat and slung her bag over her shoulder. "Two, think twice about the Dorian thing. Don't harden your heart. Forgive him for hurting you, but get him back in your life. He's one of the good guys."

He was, wasn't he?

As an afterthought, Cassie swiped the bagel from the toaster, and tossed it from hand to hand to avoid being burned. Rita half thought about offering her the cream cheese to go with it, but she was already out the door. She stopped and threw her a final bit of advice. "Don't let him slip away. You'd be a—"

"Fool if I did," Rita finished for her.

Chapter 21

Rita closed the door behind Cassie and locked it, wishing she could lock out the whole world. She'd never had a migraine that lasted three whole days. Something told her the cure for it couldn't be found in a bottle.

Cassie could truly be annoying. Blithe, selfish, uncaring, bossy—and way too perceptive. The last thing she needed right now was somebody who could see right through her. Sometimes you just needed to find a place to hide.

A place to mourn for Dorian and berate herself for her utter stupidity.

She turned from the door and collided with Lauren. She stifled a shriek. The girl had entered the kitchen with the silence and agility of someone perfectly capable of slithering unseen through her bedroom window. "Um, hi." She hoped she didn't look too flustered.

"What'd she say about me?" Lauren's monotone strove to convey disinterest, but the watery gray eyes were anxious.

"Nothing."

"Not nothing. What'd she say?" Lauren pulled at the drawstring of her borrowed sweats. They engulfed her. She was constantly hitching up the slack, baggy pants and rolling the sleeves up beyond her skinny wrists.

Rita made a note to pick up a few things for the girl tomorrow. Maybe even a cheap new PDA to replace the one she'd dropped in the coffee shop—and then she stopped herself. Lauren wasn't a stray dog she'd brought in from the cold. She didn't have title to her or the authority to keep her here. Cassie had been right. So had Dorian.

"Lauren…."

"Oh, brother. Here it comes." Lauren examined her bare toes carefully.

"No, it's not what you think. We just need to talk, that's all. You've been here three days, and—"

"If you want me to leave, all you have to do is say so." Her words were filled with bravado, but she glanced anxiously out the kitchen window. The light wouldn't last much longer.

"No, I don't want you to leave. I just need to know something about you. Anything. Where you're from. Who your parents are. Your last name."

"Why?"

"So I can help you."

Lauren gave a disbelieving snort. "If I tell you who my parents are, you'll just send me back to them."

Why was the girl so reluctant to return home? There were many possible answers to that question, all of them ugly. So many ways in which parents who should never have become parents could make a child's life unbearable. "Did they hurt you? Did your mom…or your dad…do something to you that you didn't want them to do?"

Lauren looked at her incredulously. "I told you they didn't."

"When? When did you tell me? You've hardly said two words since you got here."

Betrayal was mixed with a look of *it figures.* "I told you. You just didn't listen. You never listen. This is so bogus."

What the heck was the kid talking about? They'd had more conversations about Arabica versus Robusta than anything else. What had she done to deserve Lauren's disgust? "When? When did you tell me? What did you say?"

The thin lips wore an ugly pout. "The letters. The e-mails."

Are you afraid of.... "The ones...."

"No, not those. Those were after. The ones I sent to you three months ago. From ho—the place I used to live."

Three months ago? How could she be expected to remember that? She was lucky if she could remember what she had for breakfast last Tuesday.

Lauren prompted again. "The ones when I told you about me. About them—my folks. And the babies."

"You wrote me about your family? You asked me for advice?"

"Don't you remember? About the babies?" Lauren's eyes were pleading.

Rita got the feeling that if she didn't remember, some part of Lauren would flicker out of existence. She tried, but for the life of her.... "Lauren, I get so many letters. Hundreds. Every day. I'm sorry, but I can't...."

The girl looked crestfallen. "You, too, eh?"

"Me, too, what?"

"You ignored me, too. You didn't think I was important enough. I bought *Niobe* three months running to see what you'd say to me. I checked your Web page every week, just in case. But you never said nothing. You're just like them."

Whatever or whoever Lauren was lumping her with, it didn't sound good. "Lauren, please, just tell me what the letters were about. I'm sorry, I'm trying, but I can't...please, just help me remember."

"They have three new babies."

"Who has three new babies?"

"Who d'you think? The twins are two and the baby is eight months old. Three babies. At their age. That's just nasty. Too old to be having sex, much less to be popping out babies."

Oh, merciful Father, she finally understood. "And you feel left out."

"Duh." Baring herself was too much for Lauren. She sought refuge in pointless activity, opening up the soup pot and peering in—at this rate, it would never cook—and poking about the fridge like Cassie had. She found a plum but didn't bite it. She rolled it around between her palms, concentrating on it like a goddess shaping a new world out of clay.

"It's all about them. Always about the babies. They're hungry. They're sleepy. They need changing. Ooh, look, Elias has a new tooth. Listen, honey, Mary Jane said her first word. Colin made poopy. That's all I hear, every day, all day. What about Lauren? Nobody says Lauren got a B+, or Lauren needs new shoes. What about me?" Frustration made her voice even reedier.

Vaguely, something in Rita's memory stirred. "I remember. I remember your letter."

She didn't look up from her plum-rolling exercise. "Letters. I wrote you three times."

Three? That was beyond her recall. "I'm so sorry."

"No biggie. I'm not important enough for you, either." She gave a brittle laugh. "I'm getting used to it. 'S awright."

She couldn't let her believe that. "That's not it. You have to understand. It's not that you weren't important to me. It's just that…remember how many e-mails and letters I get. And out of those, I can only pick three or four. I don't have the time or the space to answer every one."

Lauren wasn't buying it, at least not all of it. "And mine just wasn't interesting enough."

"It's not like that. *Niobe* is a women's magazine, and most of my columns are about relationships. About men and women."

"So you didn't answer me because my problem wasn't about sex?"

"That sounds worse than it is."

"It sounds exactly like it is. I needed help, and you turned out like all the rest."

The poor tortured plum wound up in the sink, and Lauren stomped off from the kitchen. Rita hurried behind her, following her up the corridor to the study at the end, where the camp bed still lay, strewn with Lauren's clothes. They'd been washed, but even so they were so worn out they were of little use. There was only one way in and out of that room, and Rita was standing in it. Lauren was cornered.

"I'm helping you now," Rita pointed out.

"Thanks a bunch."

She didn't let that rattle her. Rudeness was a normal state of being for teenagers. She pressed on patiently. "And I need to help you some more. Lauren, you have to tell me how to find your folks."

"I told you, no, no, no. I don't wanna see them, and I don't wanna talk to them. Now get out of my room."

Rita had to step hastily back to avoid the slamming door. She stared, robbed of speech, never having been thrown out of a room in her own house before. She had a mind to wrench it open and give Lauren some version of the parental speech that usually began, "Now listen, young lady," but she thought better of it. Instead, she returned to the kitchen and mulled the situation over for a while.

The more she mulled, the more inevitable her only option became. There was only one way to help Lauren without betraying her trust, and that was to bring in someone who already knew of the situation.

This is about Lauren, she reminded herself as she picked up the phone. *Not about me. Not about us.* She dialed the number from memory.

The phone picked up. "Rita." His tone was courtroom neutral.

Before he could get any ideas—before she could get any ideas—she clarified. "Dorian, I need your help."

"Figures. Didn't think you were calling because you wanted to see me."

"Please don't be like that."

"I don't plan on wasting your dime debating what I'm being like. You called me. What d'you want?"

"It's Lauren. She's—"

"Don't tell me she's still there! I told you—"

This wasn't the time. "I know, I know. And you're right. She needs help. But I don't know where to start. You know people, and I was hoping you could…please, Dorian. I know you're mad at me. But for her sake…."

She only had to listen to dead air for a few seconds. "Okay. I can make a few calls. But what she needs first is someone to convince her to accept help. And I know just the guy. I can come take her to see him, if she'd go with me. If I'm allowed in your apartment, that is." He wasn't able to resist that dig.

She didn't respond to it. She couldn't. "I…thank you." There was so much more to say. So many things she needed him to know. But not now, not over miles of empty air. She ended with a lame, "See you soon, then."

He'd already hung up.

She went back to her study. It wouldn't be fair to spring Dorian on Lauren like that, given that they hadn't exactly taken to each other. She could at least prepare her first.

The door to the back room was open. She hadn't even heard it. The kid was as sneaky as a cat.

"Lauren?"

The study was empty.

No one in the bathroom, either.

"Lauren?"

Even with the pounding of the never-ending loop of rock berating her via the TV, there was an underlying stillness that told her she was alone in the apartment. But that couldn't be possible. She'd been standing in the kitchen during the minute or so it took to talk to Dorian. She'd had her eyes on the front door the whole time.

She wouldn't…

She must have.

Rita made a panicked dash to her bedroom, all the while whispering, "No, no, no," to herself. And, in a way, to Lauren, except Lauren wasn't around to hear her.

The draft coming from the window gave her her answer. She stuck her head out and twisted it just enough to see a pair of bare feet on the narrow ledge that ran around the building.

"Lauren!"

"Leave me alone. I'm not going home!"

"Nobody's sending you home. Now get down here. Come back inside this instant. You're three stories up!"

"I heard you talking to that guy. If you try to send me home, I'll jump."

She'd heard? How? Then Rita remembered the extension in the back. There was no use in denying it. "I'm not sending you back. Nobody's going to make you do anything you don't want to. Dorian's just going to take you to see someone who can listen to you better than I can."

"A shrink?"

"A counselor, maybe. If Dorian says he can help, you have to trust him." Her awkward position was making her dizzy. Looking up at Lauren on her precarious perch was making her nervous. "Come down. If you fall, you'll die."

"Maybe I wanna die."

"You know you don't want to do that." She was praying she was right. "Come down."

"No."

"Then I'm coming up." The adrenaline that made her say it also prevented her from analyzing the idea too closely. Instead, she ran into the hallway, taking the stairs rather than waiting for the elevator, and by the time she hit the pavement outside determination had obliterated her fear.

She stood directly below Lauren and looked up. The aging facade still bore the scarred shadows of the angelic busts that had once adorned it. But its architecture could help her. Columns stretched from ground to roof every few yards along the sides. They were decorated with ridges and scrollwork. Much of it was worn away by time and the elements, but enough remained to provide a few footholds. Lauren had made it up via this route at least three times. If she could do it, so could Rita.

She made one last try before beginning her ascent. "Lauren, please come down."

All she could see was the small, pale face looking down at her from what seemed like a long way up. The face shook from side to side, slowly, but resolutely.

Her first attempt told her that shoes were a bad idea. She kicked them off, trying not to yowl when her feet touched the cold concrete. She tried again, regretting not having paid more attention to the rope-climbing sessions that had seemed so pointless in high school gym class.

Carefully, past the first floor. Gingerly, past the second. Up to the third, and bingo. The ledge was even narrower than it looked from the safety of the ground. She sidled next to Lauren, feeling her heart in her mouth. Now that she was there, she wondered what to say. Lauren might cotton to this sort of thing, but she sure didn't.

But the girl was trembling, clenching her fists until her knuckles were white. A soft keening came from between her teeth.

"You okay?" The question sounded ludicrous even as she asked it, but it conveyed her concern.

Lauren couldn't even turn her head. "I'm scared."

"I promise you, things will be okay. I won't let anybody harm you. Dorian and I just wanted you to talk—"

But Lauren wasn't listening. "Sohighsohighsohigh…."

"Lauren?"

"Gonnafallgonnafallgonnafall...."

Are you afraid of heights? "Oh my God." It hadn't been a threat, at least not against Rita. It had been a statement of intent. A promise.

She had to do something. Now. "Don't be scared. Hold on to me."

"I can't. I can't move my arms."

"Just reach out."

"Can't."

She wasn't all that keen on moving herself, but if Lauren wouldn't, she'd have to. She inched sideways until she grasped Lauren's hand. The sharp little nails almost pierced her skin. "Don't look down," Rita advised.

"Down is all there is."

Darkness was falling with a swiftness typical of the season, but they'd already been spotted. A handful of people were gathered below, looking up and pointing.

She tried to reassure her. "They'll get help. Someone will come and help us down."

That turned out to be a bad idea. Galvanized by the idea of a confrontation with any authority figure, Lauren wriggled away— but not so far that she had to let go of Rita's hand.

Rita wondered how long it would be before the cold made her lose all sensation in her feet—or worse, her hands.

Then a familiar green vehicle skated up to the curb. The Weekend Warrior had arrived. He spotted them the second he got out of the car and pushed through the crowd. "Rita! Lauren!"

Had she ever been so happy to see anyone?

Lauren didn't share her joy. "Tell him to go away. Tell him to go or I jump."

Lauren was too terrified to jump, wasn't she? She was sure this was nothing but a panicked, last-ditch attempt to stave off the inevitable, but she wasn't taking any chances. Stuck on a ledge was stuck on a ledge…and this one was distressingly narrow. She yelled down, "Stay away, Dorian."

Either he ignored her, or he hadn't heard. "I'm coming up."

She watched with a mixture of relief and horror as Dorian untied his shoes. The same shoes she'd handed back to him with such smug superiority three nights ago. And he began to climb.

Maybe, sixty or eighty years ago, the facade would have put up with all this youthful nonsense. But like any crotchety old lady, Rita's building had had enough of these shenanigans for one night. Dorian didn't make it to the first floor windows. Chunks of plaster tumbled to the pavement below, and he went with them.

Her mind screamed out his name, but she wasn't sure if her mouth had done the same. The ledge was reluctantly bearing the weight of two people. It wouldn't stand for a third. The groaning beneath her feet told her she was right.

"Don't come up. You'll kill us!"

He heard her this time. Defeated, he stood with the rest of the gathering crowd, looking up.

Again, she had an image of the smashed, cherubic plaster face on the sidewalk. "Lauren, we have to get inside."

"I can't go back down there."

"You don't have to. You can get back in through the bedroom window. Same way you came. You've done it before, remember?"

"I'm sorry."

"That's not important. You need to get in. This ledge isn't going to hold. You saw what happened to Dorian. Hurry!" To her relief, Lauren found the courage to move. Slowly, slowly, she squeezed past Rita, who was closest to the window. She watched with detached fascination as the girl wriggled, becoming near-boneless, and slithered inside through a space that logic insisted was too small for her.

That left her alone on the ledge. She looked at the window, and the thought died before it could be formed. No way was she getting in there. Her shoulders wouldn't make it, far less her hips. Damn Starbucks and their muffins.

There was only one way down, then. She turned around, said her prayers and began her descent, ignoring her own advice not to look down. Dorian's face was directly below her, horror written all over it. Above, Lauren's face, peering out the bedroom window, bore the same expression.

Dorian waved his arms. "Don't do it, baby. Stay there. Don't move!"

"It won't hold me!" she yelled back.

"It will. It will. Just hold on. Help's coming."

She heard the wail of sirens at the same time he did, but she was too jazzed to wait. She was lighter than Dorian. Way lighter. The column was going to hold. One crevice at a time, one foothold at a time, she made it to the point where Dorian had faltered. The holds were crumbly, less reliable, as fresh plaster had been exposed. She hesitated.

But he was reaching up and pulling her down into his arms. The fire engine and police sirens were right there, yards away, and men came pouring out of both vehicles, but all she could focus on was him.

"You fool! Why didn't you wait?"

"I couldn't. The ledge was crumbling."

He didn't argue that point. "You could have died. Why'd you go up in the first place?"

Was he mad? Hadn't he seen what she'd seen? She pulled free of him. "Why d'you think? I couldn't leave her up there like that."

"You could have talked to her through the window until I got here. You knew I was coming."

"Then what would you have done? You were too heavy to make it up there. You saw that for yourself."

"I'd have thought of something."

She knew he was afraid for her, and for Lauren, but the adrenaline that had kept her going up there made her brutal.

"*You* didn't. *I* did. I saw what needed to be done and I did it. I told you—I don't need a hero."

She wished instantly she could take that back. What passed across his face was a combination of pain, bewilderment and anger. Those beautiful lips that were so skilled at drawing a response from her were nothing but a thin hard line. "I guess you don't." He turned away.

She called his name softly, but his stiff retreating back gave no indication whether he heard her or not. She put her arms around herself. It was fully night now, and she was chilled through and through.

Chapter 22

There were just two of them left, after hours of bustling, to-ing and fro-ing as the police came, took statements and went. Dorian was in his element, managing the inevitable questions, shielding her and Lauren from as many as possible. With a few calls he put an end to the investigation into the prowler in Rita's apartment and set in motion a new, more delicate one, into the circumstances surrounding Lauren's disappearance from her home. Thanks to him, Lauren won some respite from the officers she feared so much. Rita knew that she'd be safe in the place where Dorian had arranged for her to stay.

Now that she was down from her adrenaline high, she felt exhausted, morose. Dorian sat at the table before a bowl of pumpkin soup, but wasn't eating any. She couldn't blame him. It was slightly burned. She didn't have any appetite, either.

She watched him, not bothering to do it covertly. Cassie was right. She usually hated it when Cassie was right, but this time, she was right with good reason. Dorian was such a good man.

She was selfish and stupid to turn him away for the sake of three little words. She just needed to find the courage to tell him so.

"I should go." He neither looked up nor moved a muscle.

"Don't."

Something inside the soup bowl seemed to fascinate him. "Why not?"

She got up and went around the table. In perfect humility, she dropped to her knees and put her head in his lap. "I want you to stay."

His hand fell to her nape and twisted one little curl around his finger, but he let her speak.

"I was wrong. Cassie said—"

He let the curl go and cursed. "Cassie said? Is everything that happens between us going to be dictated to you by this woman?" He stood up abruptly, and she had to wrench out of his way as he stalked off. He almost made it to the door.

She got between him and it. "No, no, you're taking it the wrong way. We talked, yes, but she only put into words what's been going on in my head since the last time I saw you. What I'm about to say didn't start with her. It started with me."

If his eyes had been coffee, it would have been bitter and cold. "What are you about to say?"

"I love you. I told you that once before, but that time I was all…" She flushed and stumbled. "I was…emotional. I'm stone sober and logical this time. No…distractions. I know exactly what I'm saying. So I want to tell you again. I love you. And I was wrong to turn you away. I've been aching and aching to call you and tell you I was wrong and to beg you for another chance."

He wasn't going to make this easy for her. "The things you said the last time…"

"That doesn't matter anymore. I know you don't love me back, and I understand why. God alone knows I've made a living talking to unhappy people in wrecked relationships, too. I felt that way myself. You changed that. I know their problems have nothing to do with me. I know you care for me. And we're…compatible. Physically, I mean." Again, those crazy flushes.

That made him smile. The coffee became a little warmer. "More than."

Elated at this small relenting, this little bit of encouragement, she smiled back. "More than," she agreed. "I know you'll make me happy. I want to be with you. That's all that matters."

He stared at her without saying anything.

"If that's okay with you."

Still nothing.

"Dorian, say something. You're scaring me. Yes or no. Maybe. Something. You're *scaring* me!"

"*I'm* scaring *you?* You have any idea what it was like for me to stand there on the sidewalk and look up at you perched on that damn ledge like a pigeon? Knowing that I couldn't get up there to save you?"

"I was okay."

"You weren't okay. You could've been killed. I was sick just thinking of it. I looked up at you and imagined you falling and all I could think of was an endless bleakness without you. Please, please, don't ever do that to me again."

Never go up on another ledge? That was an easy promise to make. "I won't."

He searched her eyes for confirmation. Then he said, "That was when I understood what it must feel like."

"What what must feel like?"

"Love. It's not about promises that may or may not be broken. Or property that has to be shared or fought over. It's about looking into your future and deciding that without this person, nothing else is worth much."

This wasn't what she wanted to hear. Not exactly. "So you love me?"

"Yes."

How disappointing. To yearn for something, only to get it—

sort of—and discover it wasn't exactly the flavor you'd been han-kering after. "You decide you love me because you're afraid not to have me in your life? You don't *want* me. You're just afraid of *not having* me. That's the emotional equivalent of white space around a drawing. It's negative, not positive. No thanks."

He was horrified at her reaction. "No, no. That didn't come out right. I've wanted to be with you practically from the start. I told you that, remember? It's not negative space. It's very positive. I love you and I want you. I was just trying to explain what made it real for me. Forgive me if it didn't sound the way you wanted it to. I'm not a poetic person, but I'll learn."

She searched his face, thinking hard. Her heart was thumping again; for the second time this evening, it threatened to choke her. She needed to give up scaring herself like this.

Dorian had waited long enough. "For heaven's sake, Rita, give me a break. I'm sweating bullets here. I swear to you I've never said anything like that to any other woman. And I mean it. Please, let's start over."

"No."

He crumpled, leaning backward onto the door, body going limp. "What? Why?"

"Let's not start over. Let's move forward. We can't erase our history…but we can build on it."

He looked up and she was smiling at him. His relief made him beautiful. Love made him more so. "You better mean that."

"I do."

"Prophetic words," he murmured as he gathered her up against him.

It was her turn to say, "What?"

"Nothing. One step at a time, sweetheart."

She laughed. It was good to be against him again. So good to feel his touch, smell that incredible scent that emanated from him and him alone. Individual, custom-made, just like their love.

She didn't know how long they kissed; seconds, minutes,

hours. But she broke it eventually because there was something else she had to tell him. "Dorian?"

He murmured, nuzzling her neck, reluctant to interrupt the kissing thing to do more of the talking thing. "Hmm?"

"About that hero business?"

He sighed. "Okay, I get it. I'm not going to try—"

"You were a hero tonight. The way you managed everything afterwards. The police. Lauren. You were smart and professional and compassionate, and totally in control every step of the way. I was impressed."

"You were, huh?"

"Yep."

"Good."

"Know what would impress me even more?"

"What?" he asked, but he was smiling like he knew what was coming. Oh, that dimple in his cheek. She wondered how deep it was, and if she could measure its depth with her pinkie…or her tongue.

"Another demonstration of your skill at getting me out of my clothes. And maybe an encore of the bath trick."

"I think I can do that."

She was up in his arms, held aloft and looking down at him. She squealed in surprise. "You aren't going to carry me all the way to the tub, are you?"

"That's what the hero does in the end, isn't it?"

"Really?"

"Really."

"Guess I've got a lot to learn."

"I'm right here to teach you. I'm even willing to waive my fee."

"You'd better. I can't afford you otherwise. We never did that article on you. I'm probably out of a job."

"We can fix that in the morning." He set her down just long enough to turn the taps on and begin to fill the tub. He had one last thought. "You still sleep with that hamster in the bedroom?"

"Gerbil," she corrected automatically. "He has a—"

"Don't know how I'll feel about that thing being in the audience while I do all the things I plan on doing to you tonight."

She hadn't thought of that. "He's probably asleep by now," she assured him.

"He'd better be," he said, and laughed.

A steamy new novel from *Essence* Bestselling Author

GWYNNE FORSTER

DRIVE ME

Wild

Reporter J. L. Whitehead would do anything for a story—even pose as a chauffeur to newly made millionairess Gina Harkness. But when business turns to mind-blowing pleasure, will Gina believe that though J. L.'s identity is a lie, their untamed passion is real?

"SWEPT AWAY proves that Ms. Forster is still at the top of the romance game."
—*Romantic Times BOOKreviews*

Coming the first week of April wherever books are sold.

KIMANI™
ROMANCE

www.kimanipress.com   KPGF0600408

Model
PERFECT
PASSION

National bestselling author
melanie schuster

Billie Phillips dreams of quitting modeling for real
estate, but she needs mogul Jason Wainwright's help.
Jason's willing to play along to lure her into his bed,
but Billie's all business. With persistence, Jason may
win the girl…but lose his heart.

"Schuster's superb storytelling ability
is exhibited in fine fashion."
—*Romantic Times BOOKreviews*
on *Until the End of Time*

Coming the first week of April wherever books are sold.

TM
KIMANI
ROMANCE

www.kimanipress.com   KPMS0610408

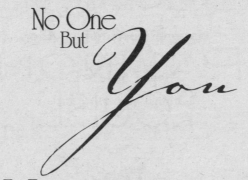

"Never again will I hold onto a Kim Louise book. As soon as it reaches my hot little hands, I will find the quietest spot in my house and lose myself in her work."
—RAWSISTAZ Reviewers on A LOVE OF THEIR OWN

National bestselling author

KIM LOUISE

Sweet LIKE Honey

When Honey Ambrose's online sex-toy business takes off, her brother hires professional organizer Houston Pace to help her out. But when Houston arrogantly insists that anyone who needs gadgets doesn't know what they're doing in bed, Honey takes matters—and her toys—into her own hands....

Coming the first week of April wherever books are sold.

ARABESQUE®

www.kimanipress.com

KPKL0700408

Three powerful stories of
mothers, daughters, faith
and forgiveness.

BESTSELLING AUTHORS

STACY HAWKINS ADAMS
KENDRA NORMAN-BELLAMY
LINDA HUDSON-SMITH

This Far by Faith

The relationships between three women and their
mothers are explored in this inspirational anthology.
As secrets and lies are brought to light, each must
learn about redeeming faith, the power of
forgiveness and enduring love.

*Coming the first week of April
wherever books are sold.*

NEW SPIRIT

™

www.kimanipress.com   KPANTHOL0240408

"I need some help," Kurt said.

"My whole family does. I'd pay you a decent wage, plus room and board. I'd also understand if you turned tail and got out of here as fast as that puny car of yours would take you."

Oxygen seemed to escape Sarah's brain, leaving her dizzy, with bells ringing in her head. Bells of excitement? Or bells of warning?

Had the Lord placed her in the diner at just the right time this afternoon to meet Kurt? Was it the Lord's plan for her to help her heart donor's family by working as a nanny for them for the summer?

There was no way to know for sure. Unless she took a leap of faith.

She drew a shaky breath and lifted her chin. "My car is not puny and I've never in my life turned tail when faced with a challenge. Mr. Ryder, I accept your job offer

CHARLOTTE CARTER

A multipublished author of more than fifty romances, cozy mysteries and inspirational titles, Charlotte Carter lives in Southern California with her husband of forty-nine years and their cat, Mittens. They have two married daughters and five grandchildren. When she's not writing, Charlotte does a little stand-up comedy, "G-Rated Humor for Grownups," and teaches workshops on the craft of writing.

Montana Hearts
Charlotte Carter

Steeple
Hill®

Published by Steeple Hill Books™

STEEPLE HILL BOOKS

**Steeple
Hill**®

Recycling programs
for this product may
not exist in your area.

ISBN-13: 978-0-373-87642-6

MONTANA HEARTS

www.SteepleHill.com

Printed in U.S.A.

And now these three remain: faith, hope and love. But the greatest of these is love.

—1 *Corinthians* 13:13

Special thanks to my agent, Pam Strickler,
for her hard work, dedication and guidance.

Chapter One

Was she on a fool's errand?

Sarah Barkley's stomach knotted and her chest ached on a whole raft of second thoughts. She just had driven two-and-a-half days from Seattle to reach Sweet Grass Valley, Montana.

Now, sitting at the counter of an old-fashioned diner in the small rural town, the only place she could find to eat, she wondered if she'd be smart to turn around and go back home.

Unsure what to do, she mindlessly rubbed the nine-inch scar hidden beneath her cotton blouse. Her doctor had warned her against trying to locate the family that had lost a loved one—and had generously saved Sarah's life. "Unless they specifically request contact, organ donors and their family should remain anonymous," the doctor had told her. "You can cause a grieving family to relive their pain and loss."

She had written the family a letter of thanks, but that seemed like paltry appreciation for the extraordinary gift she had received.

The heart that beat steadily in Sarah's chest had once

belonged to someone's loved one. The gratitude she felt
was as big as the Montana sky. She wanted to find some
way to thank the family.

But how?

There'd be no need for them to know that the heart
that beat so strongly for her now had once known this
town, the streets and sidewalks, very likely even this
diner.

If her research had identified the right heart donor.

Sarah looked up as the waitress arrived with her order
of a turkey sandwich on wheat bread, no mayonnaise,
and fruit. The lunch rush had apparently passed and
there were only a couple of older men lingering over
their coffee in a booth by the wall.

"Here you go, hon. I'll freshen that iced tea for you."
A brassy-blonde in her forties with short hair and a
great smile, she refilled Sarah's glass. Her name tag
read Bonnie Sue. "You just passin' through?"

"I'm not quite sure," she admitted, adding a packet
of sweetener to her tea.

"We don't get many tourists."

"It is a bit off the beaten path." So far off the beaten
path, she'd almost missed the turn off from Highway 2
in the northern part of the state.

"I'll say. I've lived here my whole life. It's a good
place to be if you like neighbors who are good ol' down-
home folks and you aren't interested in living high on
the hog."

"No big city lights, huh?"

Bonnie Sue laughed a hearty sound. "Hon, we don't
even have sidewalks after seven o'clock. We roll 'em up
and tuck 'em away till five the next morning."

Sarah smiled, wondering what it would be like to live in such an out-of-the-way place. Peaceful, she guessed. A far slower pace than Seattle.

The bell over the diner's door tinkled. Sarah glanced in that direction. A long-legged cowboy wearing a sweat-stained Stetson, jeans and boots sauntered toward the counter. His shoulders were far broader than his hips, his movements a symphony of masculine grace.

"Hey, Ryder," one of the men in the booth shouted. "How's it goin' on the Rocking R?"

The newcomer gave the men a casual salute. "It's as dry at my place as it as yours, Mason. If we don't get rain soon, we're going to ask the government to divert the Marias River down Main Street."

The two men laughed, and the cowboy took a seat at the counter one down from Sarah.

She averted her eyes, but her mind was racing. Ryder. *The Rocking R Ranch. Could he be—*

"Hey, Kurt," Bonnie Sue said. "Haven't seen much of you lately." She poured him a big mug of coffee and slid a pitcher of cream in his direction.

Sarah tensed. *Kurt Ryder.*

"You know how it goes. Cattle and kids can keep you pretty busy." He poured the cream in his coffee. "Can you fix me up with a double cheeseburger and some of those good fries you make?"

Sarah winced at the number of calories he was planning to consume and couldn't even calculate how many of those calories would be from fat. If she ate all of that, the calories would either go directly to her thighs or her arteries. In either case, they'd probably give her a heart attack.

She took a bite of her dry turkey sandwich and realized that on some rebellious level she envied the man.

The man who, impossibly, shockingly, seemed to be the Kurt Ryder who had lost his wife in a deadly car crash in Washington just over a year ago.

The man who had donated his wife's organs to total strangers to save their lives. Including Sarah's life, based on her research.

The turkey turned to sawdust in her mouth. Her hand trembled and tears of gratitude welled in her eyes. She put the sandwich back on her plate.

Had God sent her here, to this diner, to meet Kurt Ryder?

She didn't know what to do. How to act. She hadn't made specific plans when she impulsively left Seattle to come here. She didn't know what to say.

In the mirror behind the prep service area, she saw he had taken off his hat, leaving a sweat line that darkened his saddle-brown hair.

Ruggedly good-looking, he had a broad forehead and square jaw. His firm lips were drawn in a straight line that looked as though they'd forgotten how to smile. Sun-burnished squint lines fanned out from his eyes. Even more impressive than his appearance was the way he carried himself, strong and solid, as elemental as the land where he lived.

He looked up, and for a moment their eyes met in the mirror. A shimmer of awareness, like ripples in a pond, danced down Sarah's spine.

She fought to control her expression. To remain neutral in the face of his compelling presence and the deep sorrow she saw in his eyes, the grief that had etched lines in his deeply tanned face.

She broke the connection and studiously focused on her sandwich, although her appetite had vanished.

He'd lost a wife in that accident. His two children, a boy and a girl, had lost a mother. In her search for her donor family, she'd followed the story, *his* story and his children's in the Seattle newspaper archives.

Sarah struggled to hold back the tears of empathy she had shed when she first read of his loss. The sweet taste of her tea was replaced by the bitter knowledge of death and grief.

Bonnie Sue delivered his cheeseburger and fries, and refilled his coffee. "How're your kids doing?"

He took a bite of cheeseburger and talked around it. "Beth's acting like a teenager, Toby's all boy, and they're both driving me and my mother-in-law crazy."

Chuckling, Bonnie Sue said, "Yeah, makes you wonder some days why anybody has kids."

"You got that right. In fact, you know of anybody who'd like a job as a housekeeper for the summer? I'm going to have to do something. I think it's all getting to be too much for Grace. With the kids out of school for the summer…" He shrugged. "Having them around all the time gets overwhelming for her."

Sarah tried not to eavesdrop, but that was impossible. He was sitting too close to her, his voice a smooth baritone that held a heavy note of weariness.

"Don't know of anybody offhand," Bonnie Sue said. "I'll keep you in mind though."

He thanked her with a wave of his hand and she

went off to refill the coffee mugs of the two men in the booth.

A moment later, Kurt said, "Excuse me. Could you slide that ketchup down this way?"

Sarah started. She hadn't expected—

She found the ketchup behind the napkin holder and slid it in his direction.

"Thanks." He gave the bottle a couple of hard shakes and virtually covered his fries with ketchup.

"I sure hope you like lots of ketchup on your fries."

The corner of his lips lifted with the hint of a smile, just enough that Sarah's heart did a pleasant little flutter.

He picked up a drenched French fry and popped it in his mouth. "That your hybrid car parked out front?"

"Yes." As nearly as Sarah could tell, everyone in this town drove pickup trucks, most with rifles mounted across the back window.

"Looks more like a toy than a car."

"I'm getting almost fifty miles per gallon on the highway," she countered.

"Hmm…" He arrowed another fry into his mouth, and licked the extra ketchup off his lips with his tongue. "You'd probably have trouble stuffing a bale of hay in the back."

"I don't know. I've never tried." His implied criticism of her car annoyed her. She didn't need a truck, certainly not in Seattle. "It may look small, but you'd be surprised how much it can carry."

He eyed her in a thoroughly masculine fashion, which brought heat to her face.

"If you say so," he drawled in his deep baritone voice.

He returned his attention to his burger and fries, leaving Sarah feeling slightly breathless and surprisingly intrigued by the man.

Within minutes, he'd finished his meal, while she'd only made it through half a sandwich. He put some money on the counter and picked up his hat.

"Nice talkin' to you." He touched the brim of his Stetson and sauntered out the door.

In spite of herself, Sarah exhaled in relief.

Bonnie came over to pick up his cash and the dirty dishes.

"He's something else, isn't he?" she said, putting the ketchup bottle back where it belonged. "When he lost his wife, I'd never seen a man so stricken. And his two kids." She shook her head. "A real shame, that's what it was. He could sure use all the help he can get."

Sarah glanced out the front window. Kurt had parked across the street, a black extended-cab pickup. He stood talking with another man, one hand resting on the open window of his truck.

"Do you think he really wants to hire a housekeeper?" she asked.

"I imagine so. Grace Livingston, his mother-in-law, is still grieving. Can't get over losing her only child. I don't expect trying to take care of Kurt's two kids is easy at her age."

Sarah waited for a full minute, trying to decide what to do. Taking a chance warred with her fear of hurting people who had given her so much. She'd come here to help the Ryder family. Had she just been presented with a way to do that?

Please, God, let me do no harm.

She dug some money out of her wallet and put it on the counter. "Thanks."

"Wait, you didn't eat all of your sandwich. Was there something wrong?"

"No, it was fine. It's just that—" Across the street, Kurt was getting into his truck. She didn't want him to leave until she had a chance to talk to him.

She left the diner at a dead run.

Kurt slid his key into the truck's ignition. He had to get back to the ranch. Lately, Beth and his mother-in-law had been all but coming to blows over one thing or another. His job was to referee.

"Excuse me, Mr. Ryder?"

The feminine voice startled him. He turned to find the woman from the diner standing next to his truck, her sky-blue eyes filled with an intensity that pulled her blond eyebrows closer together. Her short, sassy hairdo and the way she dressed in slacks and a blouse identified her as a city girl.

"What can I do for you?" He mentally shrugged. Maybe her impractical little car had broken down and she needed a ride.

"My name's Sarah Barkley. I couldn't help but overhear your conversation in the diner. If you're really looking for a housekeeper, I'd be interested in applying for the job."

Kurt's eyebrows shot up, and his mouth went slack. She was the least likely looking housekeeper he'd ever met. Way too slender and dainty to handle any heavy work. A real lightweight. He had to wonder if she even knew how to cook.

"Miss, my ranch is five miles out of town. My closest neighbor is more than a mile away as the crow flies. I've got two kids who can be a handful and are forever tracking dirt into the house, stacks of laundry are always piling up and three meals a day need to be fixed." His wife, Zoe, had grown to hate the isolation, the constant sameness of each day. That's why they'd gone to Seattle, to give her a break. A second honeymoon, they'd said. And he'd as good as killed her with his own hand. The grief, that truth, had been lying in his stomach like a sun-baked rock for more than a year.

"I don't mean to insult you," he said, "but you don't look like you'd be up to a job like that."

A blush traveled up her slender neck and bloomed on her cheeks. "Mr. Ryder, I'm a lot like my car. I may look small but I'm strong and dependable and tougher than you think." She reached into her purse, pulled out a business card and wrote something on the back. "That's my cell number. I'll be in town for a day or two if you change your mind. Naturally, I'd be happy to provide references."

"References as a housekeeper?" Maybe as secretary for a big-city law firm, or even a paralegal. Not a housekeeper. That didn't fit.

"References from people who know me."

With that, she whirled and walked briskly back across the street. In the side mirror, Kurt watched her go, a bundle of energy in a small but very attractive package. He'd give her an A for spunk, too.

He glanced at the number she'd written on the card then flipped it over. Sarah Barkley, Puget Sound Business Services, Payroll & Accounting, Seattle, Washington.

Maybe she'd been laid off or the company went out of business. He shrugged and tossed the card on the passenger seat. No matter. Time to get back to the ranch.

Less than ten minutes later, he drove over the cattle guard and through the entrance of the Rocking R Ranch. His great-grandfather had moved to the northern plains of Montana with his family when he was ten. They'd homesteaded the land, raised cattle, made friends with the Indians and sometimes battled them. His ancestors' blood and sweat and tears had nurtured the land, protected it. Now it was Kurt's turn to protect that legacy for his own children and teach them to love the Rocking R as much as he did.

He pulled past the two-story ranch house and parked near the barn. By noon today, the temperature had topped ninety degrees. Now clouds were forming on the western horizon, but that didn't mean they'd get rain. Not the way weather patterns had been lately.

He climbed out of the truck. Rudy, their aging border collie, ambled out of his favorite shady spot by the tractor to greet Kurt. Automatically, Kurt scratched behind the dog's ears and gave the old guy a friendly pat on his rib cage before going into the house.

He found his daughter in the kitchen grabbing a soda out of the refrigerator, the twelve-year-old's face as red as a flag hanging off the rear end of a truck with a long load.

Sitting at the oak table, Nana Grace's face was almost as red, not from embarrassment but from one of her "spells." A line of perspiration had formed above her lip.

Kurt's heart sank. More trouble at the Rocking R.

"What's wrong?" he asked.

"Nana grounded me! For a week!" Beth's shrill cry pierced the air. "Tell her she can't do that, Daddy. Tell her she can't."

He held up his hand to quiet Beth, like a referee separating two boxers. "What happened, Grace?"

"This morning I told little Miss Smarty Pants that I couldn't drive her into town. I had the laundry to do and I wasn't feeling well." Using a napkin, she wiped off the perspiration from above her lip. "Next thing I know, I see her get into a car with a boy and they drive off. She hadn't even told me where she was going."

"It was Caroline's brother. I was going to go see her, like I told you." Using her hips, Beth smacked the refrigerator door closed. "I wasn't doing anything wrong."

Caroline was Beth's best friend, but it didn't sound like the girl had been in the car. That troubled Kurt. Beth not telling Grace where she was going troubled him even more.

"An hour later," Grace continued, "a deputy sheriff brought your daughter back home. That boy had been speeding, going close to a hundred miles an hour, the deputy said. An seventeen-year-old boy. The deputy gave him a ticket. He thought leaving a girl as young as Beth—"

"I'm almost thirteen!"

"—with someone so irresponsible wouldn't be safe."

Kurt didn't think so either. He knew Caroline's big brother. The kid was too old for Beth and played too fast and loose with the rules. "Is what your grandmother said true?"

"I didn't know he was going to speed."

"But you knew he was going too fast, didn't you?" Kurt asked.

She made a great study of opening the soda can. "I guess."

"Did you ask him to slow down?"

She shook her head. "He wouldn't't've listened to me."

"Then you shouldn't be hanging out with a boy who doesn't care about your feelings or your safety."

"He was just showing off." Her lower lip extended into a full-fledged pout.

Anger and love, fear and frustration tangled in his chest. "I think your grandmother is right to ground you for a week. Maybe that will teach you to respect yourself enough not to allow some kid to put your life at risk. And next time, you tell Nana where you're going and with who."

"You're taking Nana's side?" Beth shrieked, shock and dismay twisting her pretty face into an ugly mask.

"You're grounded, Beth. For a week."

"You can't do this to me!" She let loose a fountain of tears that ran down her cheeks. "I hate you! I hate you both!" She whirled, racing out of the kitchen and thundering up the stairs to her room. A door slammed, shaking the house.

Taking off his hat, Kurt slapped it against his thigh, creating a puff of dust. "I'm sorry, Grace. I don't know what's got into her lately."

"I don't either, son." She used the napkin to dab the sweat from the back of her neck. Her hair looked unkempt. She hadn't had a color job in months, and her hair had turned mostly gray. She'd lost weight in the past year and gained a web of wrinkles that crisscrossed her face. "But I can't take it anymore. It's too hard being around here every day, around memories of Zoe, and that child bickering with me constantly. Every time she goes out, I have to check to make sure she isn't wearing some outlandish outfit. I just can't—" She broke into sobs and put her head down on the table.

Feeling helpless, Kurt's hands hung at his sides. His mouth worked but no sound came out, no magic words of consolation or support. Like a dry summer windstorm, a sense of failure swept over him, sucking the life from him and his family.

"Go on home, Grace." His words were thick with regret, his chest hollowed out with his own grief and guilt. "Get some rest. Take some time off. I'll try to—" He didn't know what he'd do. He only knew that he needed help.

In a hurry.

Chapter Two

In the hour since Kurt had driven away, Sarah had walked the length of Main Street, as far as the glistening white church steeple that rose at the east end of town, then back to her car. She had explored the town where Zoe Ryder had lived, the town that perhaps Sarah's new heart already knew.

Since her surgery she'd worked hard to gain strength and build endurance. In recent months she'd walked three or four miles several days a week and felt stronger because of the effort. She had needed that energy today to work off the adrenaline and distress that flooded her veins and her heart.

She'd walked past buildings constructed in the early 1900s with the brick facades and actual hitching posts left over from an earlier era, making the town look like a set from an old Western movie. Kurt Ryder, with his long legs and masculine swagger, fit like a well-cast actor in this setting.

He still fit into the scene now that horses had been replaced by battered pickups with large dogs standing guard in the beds of the trucks or tied up to the fenders.

He wasn't going to hire her as a housekeeper. She'd seen rejection in his golden-brown eyes and the surprised arch of his brows.

Probably for the best, she thought as she had stood staring off into space, trying to quell her sense of failure. Admittedly, she wasn't the greatest housekeeper in the world. Or cook, for that matter.

She never should have told him she had planned to stay around for a couple of days. He wasn't going to call. She'd been foolish to even consider coming here.

There was no reason for her to stay.

No way for her to help the family who had lost so much.

On a weekday afternoon, no one seemed in a rush in Sweet Grass Valley. Traffic through town was light. The lush scent of sage and grass on surrounding open rangeland drifted on the air along with the smell of hay stacked in the backs of passing trucks.

Zoe Ryder had walked down this sidewalk, past the bakery, dress shop, grocery store and the one-screen movie theater across the way, probably greeting the proprietors by their first names. She'd been a part of this community in a way that Sarah had never been a part of Seattle.

Did the people miss her? Had Zoe left a hole in their lives as she had in those who had loved her?

It felt strange to envy someone who was dead. But Sarah did, at some cavernous level she hadn't realized existed in her soul.

Please, Lord, help those who loved Zoe and miss her to find peace within Your loving embrace.

Sarah had seen a decent-looking motel about twenty miles back in Shelby, on the highway the way she'd come. She'd stay there tonight and then head home to Seattle tomorrow.

As she got into her car, her cell phone rang.

She froze, momentarily paralyzed. It could be her friend who was waiting on the results of her CPA exam and handling Sarah's accounting business while she was out of town. A simple business question she could answer.

Or it could be...

With a shaking hand, Sarah flipped open the phone. She didn't recognize the number.

Her throat tightened and her mouth went dry. "Sarah Barkley," she answered.

"Ms. Barkley, this is Kurt Ryder. If you're still interested in the housekeeper job, I'd like to talk to you."

"Yes..." Her voice caught. She squeezed her eyes shut. "Yes, I'm still interested."

"Good. I think it would be best if you came here, to the ranch. Then you'd know what you're getting into."

That sounded a bit ominous, as though she'd agreed to work for the local ax murderer. "I can come there."

She propped the phone against her shoulder and searched for a notepad and pen in her purse while he gave her directions to the ranch.

When he finished, she closed the phone and took a deep breath. Her insides quivered with a combination of excitement and trepidation. Second thoughts assailed her like the bugs that had spattered her windshield on the highway.

This is what she wanted. This is why she had come to Sweet Grass Valley. To help those who had given so much.

As instructed, she took Second Street north out of town. Residences on modest lots quickly gave way to open prairie. Scattered clusters of cattle grazed on rolling hillsides and horses stood head-to-tail in pairs beneath shade trees, switching flies with their tails. A gentle breeze rippled the fields of tall grass like waves on a summer-green ocean.

Soon she spotted her destination. She turned off the road to drive under the arched entrance of the Rocking R Ranch. In the distance, a two-story house appeared through the rising waves of heat. Several outbuildings were also visible including a large red barn and a corral. The Rocking R appeared to be a profitable enterprise.

In front of the house, a white gazebo sat in the middle of a lawn surrounded by flower beds that had been left untended for some length of time. Weeds had invaded the plots where rosebushes and irises had gone scraggly. Sarah suspected Zoe had kept her garden a showpiece. Since her death, the family had let the beauty wither away.

A porch with two wicker rocking chairs and a cedar porch swing stretched the width of the house on the western side. She imagined sitting there at the end of a day, drinking iced tea and watching the sun set behind the distant mountains.

A black-and-white dog wandered out of the barn and barked at her.

As soon as Sarah came to a stop, the front door of the house opened. Kurt waited for her on the porch, his thumbs hooked in the pockets of his jeans, his legs wide apart. The cuffs of his blue work shirt were rolled to his elbows, revealing muscular arms lightly covered in dusky hair.

The dog had kept track of her as far as the corner of the house, where he stood guard.

"Thanks for coming," Kurt said as she reached the porch steps.

"You have an amazing place here. How much of this land do you own?"

"About all you can see plus a little bit more." She sensed he wasn't bragging. He was simply stating a fact.

Sarah's small cottage on a city lot didn't bear comparison.

"Come on in. Beth's fixing some iced tea. I wanted you to meet my kids."

He held the screen door open for her. As she passed him, she suddenly realized how tall Kurt was. He stood well over six feet. At five foot four, she barely came up to his chin.

She stepped inside and caught the faint scent of lemony furniture polish.

The Western decor was immediately obvious, maple furniture with floral print upholstery. A large fireplace made of river rocks bisected one wall, a variety of riding trophies displayed on the oak mantel. The opposite wall contained family photographs, grandparents and probably great-grandparents in old black-and-white shots, the history of the Rocking R Ranch down through the decades. In the center of the collage stood Kurt and his beautiful blonde bride, Zoe.

With a lump in her throat, Sarah quickly looked away. Guilt burrowed like a garden gopher into her midsection, as though she were responsible for stealing Zoe's life. Not just exercising her heart.

Sarah struggled to regain her composure.

Kurt introduced his son, Toby.

She extended her hand to the boy, the resemblance to his father striking. "I guess some of those trophies are yours."

"Yep." Dressed like his father in jeans and a work shirt, he shook her hand firmly. "Calf roping for ten and under."

"Congratulations." She felt overdressed wearing slacks and a fussy cotton blouse when the uniform of the day seemed to favor jeans.

"Have a seat, Ms. Barkley." When she sat down on the chintz-covered couch, Kurt said, "How is it you happen to be in Sweet Grass Valley?"

"I'm on vacation, taking some time off to see the countryside." She wondered what he would say if she told him the truth. How she had ferreted out the death of his wife. And why.

Sitting in the adjacent armchair, Kurt appeared to consider her answer. "Did you lose you job or quit?"

She smiled, realizing he thought she was an employee of her company. "A friend is filling in for me. I do have to be back in Seattle by September first, which means I can stay here through the rest of July and most of August." That was the date of her next doctor's appointment. In the meantime, she took a whole phalanx of pills to keep her body from rejecting her new heart.

Nodding, he glanced at Toby, who had plopped down on a colorful plaid pillow on the raised hearth of the fireplace. "Son, go find out what's taking Beth so long with the tea. And have her put some of Nana's cookies on a plate for our guest."

"'Kay." He hopped to his feet. "But she'll probably bite my head off."

"Just don't start anything."

When Toby left the room, Sarah said, "He's a good-looking boy."

A flash of pride flared in Kurt's eyes and he smiled. "Smart like his mother." He glanced over his shoulder to make sure the boy was out of sight. "When I got back from town earlier, my mother-in-law was in quite a state. She and Beth don't get along well. Today things were so bad, Grace grounded Beth for a week, and I had to agree. I'm guessing it's part women's troubles and part that Grace still misses my wife, Zoe. She was Grace's only child."

"I'm sorry for your loss." She was sorry, even while she felt guilty that Kurt's loss had been her gain.

"It hasn't been easy for any of us," he admitted. "I thought the best thing for Grace was to take some time off. That's why I called you."

"I understand."

Beth appeared from the kitchen carrying a cherrywood tray with a pitcher of tea and two glasses. A slender, pre-pubescent girl, she had her long blonde hair pulled back in a ponytail and wore a tank top and jeans.

Toby strolled in behind her, a glass of cola in one hand and a plate of cookies in the other.

Her expression sullen, Beth set the tray on the coffee table. Her eyes appeared puffy as though she'd been crying. "You want anything else?"

"I'd like you to meet Ms. Barkley. My daughter, Beth."

"Hello, Beth. It's nice to meet you."

"Yeah, right." She turned to her father. "Can I go now?"

Kurt glared at his daughter. "You can stay right here and be polite for a change. I'm talking to Ms. Barkley about being our housekeeper for the rest of the summer."

Beth's eyes widened. "What about Nana?"

"You know Nana Grace isn't as strong as she used to be," Kurt said. "She tires easily and that makes her cranky, I know. That's been hard on both you kids." He gave his children a weary smile. "Since your mother's been gone, I guess I've been cranky, too, and not a whole lot of fun to be around."

"It's okay, Dad," Beth said. "Toby and me, we understand you miss Mom, too."

"Yeah, I do. And so does Nana Grace. So I thought we ought to give her a break. If Ms. Barkley agrees to work for us, she could do the cooking and cleaning and chauffeur you kids for a few weeks, till school starts again. Of course you'd still have to help out with chores. She wouldn't be your slave. More like a new member of the family."

Toby shrugged, and Beth said, "I don't need a babysitter, Dad. Or a prison warden! I mean, I can cook 'n stuff. We don't need anybody else."

"Wait!" Toby cried. "You can't even fry an egg, dummy. We'd all starve. Or be poisoned! Grrrggh…" Making an inarticulate croaking sound, he stuck a finger in his mouth and flipped onto his back, his legs up in the air like a dying bug. "I'm dead! My sister—"

"Cut it out, son," Kurt said, trying valiantly to hold back a smile.

Beth stuck out her tongue at her brother. "You're such a jerk."

Suppressing her own smile, Sarah considered all the joy she'd missed by being an only child. Perhaps her dream of having a sister to play with would, in reality, have turned into a nightmare.

Kurt crossed to the fireplace and helped Toby to his feet. "Get outta here, son. You, too, Beth. Go outside and play or something. And no more bickering!"

Shrugging out of his father's grasp, Toby headed up the stairs to the second floor.

"You never listen to me, Dad!" Beth's voice rose in pitch to a shriek, the volume increasing with each syllable until the entire house shuddered with her distress. "I don't want anybody else around. I want my mom back!"

Like a summer storm, a volley of tears exploded. She whirled and raced up the stairs, trying to escape herself. Escape emotions she couldn't control.

Tears of empathy jammed together in Sarah's throat. Drawing a breath made her chest ache, and she pressed her palm against the pain. Against the scar that hid there.

Beth needed so much help dealing with the loss of her mother. Dealing with the changes in her own pre-adolescent body and emotions. Needed so much love.

Who could give her that love?

From whom could she accept that love?

Standing at the foot of the stairs, his legs wide apart as though poised for battle, Kurt speared his fingers through his hair. His expressive features twisted into a mask of anger and confusion, his lips a straight line, his brows lowered to shadow his eyes.

"That went well," he muttered. His fingers rhythmically flexed and unflexed.

"I'm sorry." For him and for his loss. For his troubled child. Despite his anger, Sarah didn't doubt for a moment that he loved his daughter. And his son. No one could show that depth of emotion without caring deeply for them.

His chest expanded on a long intake of air followed by a harsh exhale. "What you see before you is a desperate man."

"A desperate man, who is grieving for the wife he lost and trying to deal with a menopausal mother-in-law and a hormonal adolescent."

His head whipped around and he blinked at Sarah. "Beth's hormonal?"

"She's the right age. Have you talked to her about—"

"No!"

No matter how hard she tried to stop herself, a smile vaulted to Sarah's face and she laughed at Kurt's horrified expression.

He sank down on the arm of the couch. "This is no laughing matter."

"I know. But you really should have seen your face. You had terror written all over it. In neon lights."

The slightest hint of a smile curved the corners of his lips. "Well, if nothing else you know what you'd be getting into if you take the job." He scratched the day-old whiskers on his square jaw. "I need some help. The whole family does. I'd pay you a decent wage, plus room and board. I'd also understand if you turned tail and got out of here as fast as that puny car of yours would take you."

Oxygen seemed to escape her brain, leaving her dizzy with bells ringing in her head. Bells of excitement? Or bells of warning?

Had the Lord placed her in the diner at just the right time this afternoon to meet Kurt? Was this the Lord's plan?

There was no way to know for sure. Unless she took a leap of faith.

She drew a shaky breath and lifted her chin. "My car is not puny and I've never in my life turned tail when faced with a challenge." Confronted with childhood leukemia and years of radiation and chemo, which damaged her heart so badly she'd needed a transplant at the age of thirty-two, she'd never stopped fighting. She didn't plan to stop now.

"Mr. Ryder, I accept your job offer."

His smile broadened, squint lines appearing at the corners of is eyes. "Why don't you call me Kurt? It'll be easier that way." He stood and extended his hand. "Welcome to the Rocking R, Ms. Barkley."

"Thank you, Kurt." His hand was broad and warm and calloused, not at all like those of the businessmen who were her Seattle clients, but far stronger and more compelling. "Please call me Sarah."

Chapter Three

Kurt gave Sarah a brief tour of the house, then showed her the very large, modern kitchen.

"You could feed an army from this kitchen," Sarah commented. Miles of granite counters and oak cabinets lined one side of the room. The window over two extra-deep stainless steel sinks looked over a fenced backyard with grass and flower beds that needed care. Beyond that a row of poplar trees formed a bright green windbreak.

A round oak table and chairs were placed on the opposite side of the room with a view to the east.

In the center of the room was a butcher-block counter. Above that dozens of gadgets hung from a rack, some of them Sarah couldn't even identify.

"Zoe really liked to cook," Kurt said. "She had the kitchen remodeled and expanded several years ago so she could have bigger parties."

"Very impressive." Sarah rarely entertained. Until recently she hadn't had the strength.

"Your bedroom with a private bath is back here." Kurt led her past what she took to be a pantry and supply room. "Originally this room off the kitchen was for a servant, but Zoe turned it into a guest room. My brother and his family come to visit once in a while. They live in Denver."

Sarah drew a quick breath as she stepped inside. Though simply decorated, the room had a homey feel to it. A handmade quilt covered a cherrywood double bed and there was a matching dresser with a vase of artificial daisies sitting on it. Sheer curtains covered the one window and on the walls, original watercolor paintings featured Western scenes. An oval hooked rug brightened the hardwood floor.

"This is lovely," she said. "Your wife had very good taste."

"Yeah, she did." He backed out of the room. "I'll help bring in your things, then you can start dinner. I checked and it looks like Nana Grace defrosted some steaks."

Steaks? Sarah rarely ate red meat but she supposed tonight could be an exception. Assuming she could figure out how to cook them.

An hour later, she'd unpacked her bags and stood staring at four huge T-bone steaks wondering what to do with them. She'd managed to find some shredded lettuce and tomatoes, and cut up some baby carrots to add to a salad. She figured Kurt was a big eater, so she put a loaf of bread and butter on the table.

But for the life of her, she couldn't find a broiler pan big enough to hold all the steaks.

Willing to admit defeat, she went in search of Kurt.

Toby was sprawled on the living room floor watching television.

"Toby, do you know where your dad is?"

He continued to stare glassy-eyed at the antics of comic characters determined to lop off each others' heads with laser swords.

"Toby?" When he still failed to answer, she shrugged. She'd find Kurt herself.

She turned down the hallway that led to his office. She found him there staring at the computer screen in much the same way Toby was watching TV. A disorganized pile of invoices sat on his cluttered walnut desk and old magazines and farm catalogs covered half of the nearby couch.

She knocked on the doorjamb and he looked up, a frown tugging his brows together. She opened her mouth to ask about cooking the steaks, but before she could speak, he said, "Do you know anything about computers?"

She blinked, caught off guard by his question. "Some. What seems to be the problem?"

"Beats me. I'm supposed to be able to pay my bills online. I clicked on something and the whole screen went blank. It's just plain gone." He glared at the screen as if he could, by force of will, make the device do what he wanted it to do.

"Would you like me to try?" Fortunately, her computer skills were considerably better than her cooking prowess.

He moved out of his dark leather chair, and she took his place. A few quick clicks of the mouse and a spreadsheet appeared.

"Is this what you were looking for?"

As he bent over to peer at the screen, she caught the

scent of sage and wild grass on the prairie. The essential perfume of both Kurt and his land.

"That's incredible. How did you do that?"

"You must have accidentally hidden the whole work sheet. All I did was unhide it. You should be fine now."

They traded places again.

"Did you want something?" he asked, his attention back on the computer screen.

"I was looking for a broiling pan to cook the steaks. I couldn't find one."

"Grace grills them."

"Oh." His answer wasn't very helpful. She guessed he was referring to a barbecue grill she'd spotted on the back porch.

It took a couple of tries to light the propane but finally Sarah dropped the steaks on the grill.

Back in the kitchen, she set the table and poured milk for Toby and Beth and water for herself. She wasn't sure what Kurt would want to drink with his dinner, so she held off on that.

Beth came stalking into the kitchen, a cell phone in her hand. "Isn't dinner ready yet? I'm starved." She plucked a cookie out of a rooster-shaped cookie jar with one hand while the thumb of her other hand nimbly sent a text to someone.

"The steaks should be ready any minute."

Beth glanced at the stove, then toward the back door. "Something's on fire!"

Sarah's head snapped around. "The steaks!" She grabbed a plate, a long-handled fork and raced out the door.

Flames leaped up around the steaks. Grease sizzled and sputtered. The rank air smelled of burned meat.

Sarah stabbed a blackened steak and dragged it onto the plate. She speared the next steak, singeing her wrist in the process. She jerked back and the steak slid off the fork onto the porch.

"Turn off the propane!" Beth screamed. "You're gonna catch the whole house on fire."

Sarah ceased her efforts to rescue the steaks. Burning down the house was a real possibility. She turned the knob on the propane bottle, but that didn't immediately extinguish the flames.

Beth's shouting had rousted Toby away from the TV.

"Hey, a bonfire on our porch. That's cool."

Kurt shoved past his son. "I'll get it." He twisted the propane knob again, starving the flames of fuel. They sputtered one more time before vanishing.

In the silence that followed, Sarah took a deep breath. Her heart was rata-tat-tatting so fast she thought it might leap out of her chest.

"I am so sorry," she said.

Kurt took the plate from her and piled the rest of the steaks on it. "No real harm done except to these steaks."

The poor things looked like lumps of charcoal. "I've never barbecued before. I didn't know how long—"

"Talk about being stupid," Beth complained.

Kurt nailed her with a look that would have terrified anyone else. It didn't seem to faze Beth.

"One more word out of you, young lady, and you'll do without dinner altogether."

"Fine," she snapped. "Nobody can eat that stuff anyway." Head held high, ponytail swinging, she stomped back into the house.

Sarah suspected Beth's attitude was more self-defense than rebellion.

Dear Lord, show me a way to help this child, who is so desperately crying out for love and understanding.

They'd all survived dinner, barely, by scraping off the charred layer on the steaks. Even so, Sarah thought eating the meat was like chewing hardtack.

With Kurt's help, she'd cleaned up the kitchen. Then he'd vanished back into his office to work on the accounts. Beth was still upstairs, pouting. Toby had resumed his place in front of the big-screen TV. From her perspective, the show he was watching looked too violent for a nine-year-old. Or an adult, for that matter.

The family ought to be doing things together, she thought. That's the only way they'd heal their grief.

She went to her room to retrieve her oversize tote that contained her ventriloquist's dummy. Dr. Zoom came fully equipped with a white lab coat, stethoscope, wire glasses and a Pinocchio nose.

For the past several years, when she was able, she had volunteered one morning a week at the University of Washington Medical Center. She donned a costume and became Suzy-Q, clown extraordinaire, visiting the pediatric oncology ward. Dr. Zoom told silly jokes and listened to his own heart instead of the patient's. She'd spent hours in front of a mirror making sure her lips didn't move when she spoke in Dr. Zoom's voice.

As Suzy-Q, Sarah also did face painting. All of this in an effort to pay forward some of the kindness that she had experienced as a child.

The best medicine she could give a sick child was a chance to smile and laugh, a few minutes of simply being a normal kid.

Maybe she could give the same gift to Kurt's children.

Returning to the living room, she sat on the couch and adjusted Dr. Zoom on her lap, his legs dangling over her thigh.

"Vhat's dat kid doing?" Dr. Zoom asked in a fake German accent.

"He's watching TV," she responded.

"Vaste of time, I say."

Toby remained glued to the TV show, not so much as looking over his shoulder to find out who was in the room.

"Well, what should we do?"

Dr. Zoom looked up at her, his long nose quivering. *"Ve could drop a bomb on the boy?"*

"No. That wouldn't be very nice." Sarah wasn't at all sure Toby would even react to a ton of TNT going off.

"Hee hee hee. KABOOM!"

Very slowly, Toby turned his head and frowned. "What'a'ya doing?"

"Is the boy alive? Let me listen to his heart."

Sarah manipulated Zoom's stethoscope to the middle of his own chest.

"Oh, no. I hear nothing. Nothing! The boy is—"

"You're trying to listen to your own heart and you don't have one," Sarah pointed out.

She definitely had Toby's attention now. His glassy, hypnotized look had been replaced by a note of interest.

"Vhat? No heart? Vhy don't I have a heart?"

"Because you're a dummy."

Dr. Zoom twisted his head around to look at Sarah. *"It's not nice to call people names."*

"I'm not. You really are—"

"Don't say that."

"But you—"

The quick exchange between Sarah and Dr. Zoom started Toby laughing. He shifted his position to watch her, the violent TV show forgotten.

"Way cool. How do you do that?" he asked.

"Do what?" she asked innocently.

"Make the dummy talk."

"You mean ventriloquism?"

"Now see vhat you've done?" Dr. Zoom shook his finger in Sarah's direction. *"Tell him it isn't so. I'm not a—you know—vone of dose."*

"Yeah, you are," Toby insisted.

"Is zat what you think? Huh. I vill show you. You know vhat you get when you cross a pair of trousers with dictionary? Huh, you know vhat?"

"Naw, I don't know. What?"

Dr. Zoom did a little hop on Sarah's thigh. *"You get a smarty-pants, that's vhat. A smarty-pants like you, huh?"*

Toby's giggle was infectious, and he had a wicked, little-boy gleam in his eyes. "Hey, Sarah, can you teach me how to do that?"

"But of course, young man. I am the greatest teacher in the world."

"What's she going to teach you, son?"

They both looked up at the sound of Kurt's voice.

"Sarah's a ventriloquist, Dad. It's really cool. Her lips don't move at all. An' she's gonna teach me."

Just like his son, Kurt cocked his head to the side. "Ventriloquist?"

Her face flushed and she shrugged. "A little hobby I have."

"Really? I used to love stuff like that when I was a kid." He sat down cross-legged opposite her, his grin as eager as Toby's. "Show me."

Dr. Zoom proceeded to conduct a ridiculous conversation with Kurt about being a bowlegged cowboy. Kurt laughed and so did his son, the cares and battles of the day forgotten.

Sarah hoped her botched dinner would be as quickly forgotten.

Toby made an effort to speak without moving his lips, which left the words unintelligible. "Hey, I don't get it."

"If you really want to learn, let's start with some easy exercises. There are lots of sounds you already make without moving your lips."

"Like neighing like a horse?" Kurt asked.

The realization that Kurt was interested, too, gave Sarah's heart a little jolt. She couldn't help reacting to the mirthful twinkle in his golden-brown eyes. Her mouth felt dry and she had to lick her lips. "It'll be easier if we start with the vowel sounds, A, E, I, O, U. Try making those sounds without moving your lips."

Toby gave it try, slipping only on the O and U sounds. Kurt repeated the exercise with the same level of success.

She grinned. "I can see you're both going to be great students. You practice and we'll work on lesson two after you feel comfortable with those sounds."

Later in the guest room, she sat down and opened her laptop. First she sent an email to Tricia Malone, who was handling her business in Seattle while she was gone. Without providing any details, she explained she'd be staying in Sweet Grass Valley for the summer and promised to call her soon.

Then she ordered a couple pairs of jeans, casual tops and some sturdy shoes online. Her city clothes weren't at all suitable for the rough wear and tear of ranch living.

That task accomplished, Sarah slipped between the crisp sheets on the bed and picked up her Bible-study book as she did every evening. Tonight's passage was from Colossians 3:12. "Therefore, as God's chosen people, holy and dearly loved, clothe yourselves with compassion, kindness, humility, gentleness and patience." (NIV)

Sarah would certainly need patience with Beth, compassion with Kurt, who was still grieving, and gentleness with Toby. She prayed she would be up to the task the Lord had given her.

And do no harm, she warned herself as her eyes closed and the book slipped from her fingers.

The following morning, Kurt recruited Toby to help him move the mother herd to the north section to graze on the fresh grass. Beth, who could handle cattle well enough when she wanted to, claimed a headache. He didn't press the issue.

"Come on, Ellie Mae. Let's keep the girls moving."

Speaking in a calm, easy voice, Kurt reined his horse Pepper closer to the lead cow and her young calf, who had slowed their pace. His approach caused Ellie Mae to accelerate to her previous speed, and the rest of the mother herd followed suit, their calves trotting along beside them.

"That's my girl," Kurt murmured. "You remember how sweet the grass is in the north section, don't you?"

On the opposite side of the moving herd, Toby held his position so the cows wouldn't wander off track and mosey down into the gully that cut through this section of the Rocking R Ranch. As young as he was, Toby had been riding since before he could walk and held his seat well on Longtail, a dun-colored gelding Kurt had broken to saddle a decade ago. He remembered how Zoe had watched him work the horse during those late summer evenings, the setting sun streaking her blonde hair red and gold.

The image of her shimmered in his memory like a distant mirage. His breath caught in his throat, his heart lunging an extra, painful beat.

He touched his heels to Pepper's flanks and forced thoughts of Zoe away. She'd been gone for over a year. A stupid accident, a wrong-way driver hit them while they were on their way to a second honeymoon in Seattle and had nearly killed him, too.

In those early days, with Zoe in a coma and barely

alive, Kurt had almost wished he had died first. He wouldn't have had to make the most difficult choice in a man's life—to let the woman he loved go. He'd prayed. He'd railed at God. Pleaded. Bargained. Cursed. Blamed Him.

Brain dead. Vegetative state.

Those words thundered in his skull like a depraved farrier banging a horseshoe into shape around a villainous anvil.

How could Kurt blame God when he'd been the one who had agreed to remove Zoe's respirator?

In the course of a year, he'd gone from that catastrophic moment to having another woman living in his house. A tidy package of spunk whose silly antics with a dummy had made him laugh again. Even now, the memory of the prior evening brought a smile to his lips.

When they reached the north pasture, Kurt eased away from the herd to let them graze on their own. With the cows stopped, the calves didn't need a formal invitation to start suckling their moms.

Past the boundary of the Rocking R, Kurt noticed a surveying crew at work. Curious, he wondered what Ezra Stone, his closest neighbor and owner of Double S Ranch, was up to.

"Can I go back home now, Dad? I told Joey I'd ride over to his place today. He's got a new Nintendo game."

"Sure, son. Just be sure you're back for supper."

"'Kay." Reining his horse around, Toby touched his heels to the gelding and took off at a gallop.

Kurt could only hope the horse had enough sense not to step in a prairie dog hole and break his leg.

Deciding to check on the surveying project before he went back to the barn, he trotted over to the fence. A pickup owned by T&K Engineering of Billings, MT, was parked nearby.

"Morning," he called to the closest man, who was wearing an orange safety vest and a Seahawks ball cap.

"Morning." A young guy, he tipped the bill of his cap. His sideburns reached all the way to his jawline.

"What's the survey for?"

"Don't know. We're just mapping the elevations and putting corner stakes in."

Kurt lifted his Stetson then resettled it on his head. "Ezra didn't tell you what he's planning to do?"

"Nobody named Ezra hired us." He checked his clipboard. "Looks like an outfit called Western Region Cattle Feeding hired us. They're headquartered in, uh, Cheyenne."

Dread landed in his chest with the weight of a boulder. Adrenaline surged, readying him for a fight. He tightened his hands on the reins, which made his horse back up a few steps.

He knew that outfit. There'd been talk of them on the ranchers association website and articles in the Billings newspaper. They ran concentrated animal feed lots and had a reputation of not caring what sort of environmental damage they did as long as they showed a profit.

"Are they going to put in a feed lot here?"

The surveyor lifted one shoulder in a half-hearted shrug. "No idea. I just measure and note, that's all."

"Have they gotten a permit already?" Kurt pressed. He hadn't been notified by the authorities or read anything in the newspaper. Maybe it was still pending.

"Beats me." The guy switched his ball cap so the visor was in the back and sighted his equipment toward his partner, who stood a couple hundred feet away.

If a feed lot so close to the Rocking R wasn't properly drained, it could turn the nearby spring creek into a polluted garbage dump. Kurt's herd wouldn't be able to drink the water. He'd have to fence it off. Maybe even need to dig a new well if he wanted to keep cattle grazing this northern section.

Why on earth would Ezra sell or lease his land to an outfit like Western Region Cattle Feeding? And how could Kurt make sure the feeding operation was either stopped or forced to comply with environmental water quality rules? And monitored.

He wheeled Pepper toward home in a slow walk. Given the tension in his household—Beth on a razor edge of rebellion and his new housekeeper—and now the threat of a concentrated feeding operation butting up against his land, Kurt knew the summer was going to be filled with nothing but trouble.

To Sarah's dismay, she'd learned that ranchers get up before dawn to start their day. She'd barely had a chance to dress before Kurt and Toby finished their breakfast and were out the door.

She cleaned up the dishes, then took a moment to sit at the kitchen table, drink a cup of tea and watch the eastern sky change from the pink of sunrise to the baby-blue of a summer day.

Beth came into the kitchen wearing a nice pair of designer jeans and a stretchy top that bared an inch or two of skin around her midsection. A little mature for a twelve-year-old, Sarah thought, but she didn't say anything.

Without acknowledging Sarah's presence, Beth dropped a couple of pieces of white bread into the toaster and found a jar of peanut butter in the cupboard.

"Good morning, Beth. Looks like it's going to be a beautiful day."

"Huh."

"After I put on a load of wash—" which she had discovered in an overflowing laundry hamper "—and do a little dusting, I thought I might pull some weeds in the flower beds out front."

"My mother took care of the flowers." The toast popped up, and Beth spread peanut butter on each slice.

"It's a shame to let the garden go. I'm sure the flowers were beautiful when your mother was alive."

"I guess." Beth took a bite of toast, then got out a pitcher of orange juice from the refrigerator and poured herself a glass.

"I'd love to have you help me pull some weeds."

"Can't. I'm going to ride my bike into town. I'll be home in time for supper."

Beth's casual announcement stopped Sarah in her mental tracks. "I thought I heard your father say you were grounded."

She washed down the first piece of toast with a big gulp of juice. "Dad won't care. He just said that 'cause Nana was so upset, having one of her stupid spells."

Sarah had the niggling feeling that she was being conned by a budding expert. "Let's check with your dad, okay?"

"He's way out in the north pasture. There's no way to reach him. And I'm tellin' you, he won't care." She tossed her long hair behind her shoulder and started on the second piece of toast.

"Doesn't he have a cell phone? We could call him."

Beth stopped eating. Her gaze darted around the room, looking everywhere except right at Sarah.

"You don't know anything about living on a ranch, do you?" she said in a disdainful way. "There are dead zones out here where you can't get any cell service."

"I saw you texting on your cell last night."

Beth's fair complexion bloomed with a spark of anger. "That was here at the ranch. Not way off in the north section."

"Well, then, we have a problem, don't we." Picking up her tea cup, Sarah walked over to the sink and set the cup down. "I can't let you go anywhere unless I'm sure you have your father's permission."

Stunned, she widened her eyes. "You've gotta be kidding me!" she screeched.

Sarah winced. She really didn't like confrontations. "No, I'm not, Beth. If there is no way to reach your father, then we'll simply have to wait until he gets back home."

"No way!"

Sarah knew her response wasn't what Beth had hoped for. She was equally sure Kurt had grounded his daughter. Until she heard otherwise, she'd do whatever she could to keep Beth at home.

As calmly as possible, Sarah rinsed out her cup and set it on the drain board.

"You can't do this to me," Beth protested. "You're not my mother."

Sarah dried her hands on a paper towel. "Do you know where the furniture polish is kept?"

Making a growling sound like a angry bear, Beth threw up her hands. "Okay, you win. We'll get Dad back here, and he'll tell you that you're not in charge of me." She stormed toward the back door.

Not knowing what the girl was up to, Sarah followed her outside. The border collie she'd seen yesterday met them on the porch, his tail sweeping the air that still smelled of burned steak.

Beth stood in front of a large bronze gong hanging from an overhead beam. Fancy scrollwork made it look as though it had originally come from China.

"Hit this as hard as you can." The muscle in Beth's jaw flexed, her eyes narrowed as she handed Sarah the hammer. "He'll hear it wherever he is. Then you'll see."

Using a gong to communicate seemed primitive to Sarah, but she gave it a solid whack. The metal vibrated, sending out waves of sound that echoed inside Sarah's skull and started the dog howling.

Chapter Four

The sound of the emergency gong rang out over the prairie.

Kurt froze in the saddle. Intended to warn of a grass fire, no one had used that gong in years. Not since his mother had knocked over a kerosene lamp and...

Digging in his heels, he spurred Pepper toward the ranch house. Had Sarah tried to barbecue something on the back porch again? Maybe Beth had been messing around with candles in her room and caught the curtains on fire.

Or maybe a tourist had tossed a cigarette butt out a car window into the drought-dry grass and started what could end in an inferno.

Grimly, he urged his horse to a gallop.

Fire. Always a dangerous threat but more so when you lived far from town with only a few nearby ranchers to help put out the flames.

As his horse raced across the rolling landscape, Kurt searched the horizon for any sign of smoke. Nothing. Not a single puff of smoke in sight.

Nerves bunched his shoulders. He gripped the reins

so hard they nearly cut through his riding gloves into his palms. The horse's ears were turned to listen for his commands, and he knew the animal's eyes were wide with a fright that reflected his own fears.

If there was no smoke and no fire, what other emergency could there be? Any number of dangers existed on a ranch, from mountain lions and wolf attacks to someone falling out of the hay loft.

The ranch house came into sight. No smoke. No fire.

Two pickup trucks were roaring down the road toward the Rocking R. They'd heard the gong, too. And responded.

The volunteer fire truck from town wouldn't be far behind them.

In ranch country, neighbors helped neighbors.

Kurt unlatched the final gate separating the grazing land from the ranch house and barns, and sped the remaining yards to the back of the house. He reined the lathered horse to a halt in front of Beth and Sarah.

"What is it? What's wrong?" He was as winded as his horse, his lungs pumping hard.

Beth gave her ponytail an insolent flick with her hand. "Our new housekeeper," she said in a snooty voice, "wouldn't let me go into town unless you said so."

Gaping at his daughter, Kurt shook his head. "You're telling me you rang the emergency gong for that?"

"I did it," Sarah said. "Beth told me there was no other way to reach you. I was under the impression you had grounded her."

Anger built in Kurt's chest. He forced himself to stay

in control as the two pickup trucks roared up to the barn and four hands from neighboring ranches piled out of the vehicles.

"Both of you, stay right where you are," he said. "Especially you, Beth."

He reined his horse toward the arriving men. Still agitated, the gelding danced around, and Kurt had to reassert control over the animal.

"Sorry, fellows. A false alarm. But thanks for coming."

Larry Hicks from the Skyline Ranch thumbed his hat farther back on his head. "You sure everything is okay?"

No, everything was not okay. "A little misunderstanding. Sorry for the inconvenience."

"No problem. Boys were lookin' for a little excitement anyway. They got the summer doldrums." Larry grinned at his buddies.

"Could you call the dispatcher in town, ask 'em to call off the volunteer fire truck?" Kurt asked.

"Will do." Larry resettled his hat and all the men climbed back into their trucks.

Kurt dismounted and walked his horse to the back of the house where Beth and Sarah were waiting for him.

Before Kurt had a chance to say a single word, Beth laid into him.

"Daddy, this is so wrong. I knew you didn't really mean I was grounded. That was only for Nana's benefit so she'd get off my back. And Beth wouldn't believe me, so I—"

"You're not only grounded, Beth, you're going to do

chores all day. Starting with cooling off Pepper." He patted the horse's sweaty neck. "And giving him a good rubdown. Cleaning out the stalls comes next."

"Dad...dy!" she wailed. "You can't mean—"

"I do. Every word." He handed her Pepper's reins. "Now get busy, young lady. When the stalls are clean, come tell me, and I'll think of something else for you to do. We've let a lot of things go around the place this past year." Including him letting his daughter slide by when he should have been paying more attention to Beth and less to his own feelings of guilt and grief. That was going to change.

The daggers Beth glared at him had sharp points, and they hurt at some deep level he hadn't felt in a long time.

She yanked on the reins and walked Pepper to the barn, her ponytail swinging like the swishing tail of a raging bull.

"I love you, angel," he said under his breath, and exhaled a weary sigh.

"I'm sorry," Sarah said. "I didn't know that the gong would bring the entire county out here to see what was wrong."

"Yep. That's what it was meant to do." He plucked his cell phone from the holster on his belt. "Of course, nowadays using one of these is a lot more efficient."

Her eyes widened and pink colored her cheeks. "I asked about you having a cell. She said where you were was a dead zone."

Taking off his hat, he wiped the sweat from his fore-head and sat down on the top porch step. Rudy joined him, sitting on his haunches, his ears alert, his eyes curious.

"There're a couple of dead zones," Kurt said. "But three years ago the cell company put up three towers, one on my property and the other two nearby. My cell works most everywhere on the ranch. I should've thought to give you the number."

"That's a good idea." She eased herself down to a step one below his. "I don't think Beth meant any harm. I think she's troubled."

Gazing off into the distance, he idly petted the dog. "Yeah, I get that. And I haven't been much of a father lately."

"It's never too late. I suspect that's why she's acting out. She wants you to pay attention to her even if it means she's getting yelled at."

"I figured that out. But what do I do? I'm trying to run this place without a hired hand. The price of beef keeps dipping and the bills keep getting bigger. I don't have time for fun and games."

Sarah reached down and plucked a weed from the ground by its roots. "I've never had children, so I'm certainly not an expert, but I'd say if you don't spend time with her now you'll regret it later."

He grunted a noncommital sound.

Rudy deserted Kurt to sit beside Sarah. She patted his head and scratched behind his ears. "Nice dog."

"Rudy used to help me round up the cattle. He herded the kids, too, when they were little and tried to wander off." He smiled at the memory. "Now he's too old and he's got arthritis."

"Poor guy." Continuing to pet the dog, she said, "I

was never allowed to have a dog. My parents were afraid I would catch something from an animal."

Kurt detected a note of both regret and nostalgia in her voice.

"Well, I've got laundry to do and some dusting. I'd better get busy."

She stood and brushed the dirt from the back of her slacks. Not jeans, like the local women wore. But fancy, city-girl slacks. Kurt would guess they weren't bought out of a catalog either, which is what Zoe had had to do except on their rare trips to Great Falls or Helena where she could shop.

No wonder she'd hated living out here.

Brooding, Kurt sat on the porch step for a long time. Finally, when no great revelations came to him, he strolled into the barn. Beth was in the middle of mucking out one of the stalls.

"What do you want now?" she asked. "I'm gettin' it done, just like you said."

He walked past her and picked up a second shovel. "I was thinking if we worked together we'd get this dirty job done a lot faster. And maybe we could talk."

Sarah moved a load of wash into the dryer, shut the lid and pushed the start button.

Realizing she shouldn't put off calling Tricia Malone any longer, she stepped into her bedroom and closed the door for privacy. The young woman was taking care of her accounting service while Sarah was away. Although she trusted Tricia's accounting skills implicitly, she wanted to make sure her clients continued to be happy with the service they received.

She picked up her cell phone. For a moment she marveled how cleverly a twelve-year-old girl had conned her into believing there was no cell service out on the range. Beth certainly had a chip on her shoulder. But what pre-teen wouldn't be upset, the loss of her mother coinciding with the onset of her own puberty. *Poor kid!*

Punching in the number for Puget Sound Business Services, she waited for Tricia to pick up.

"Oh, hi, Sarah. I got your email. How's our world traveler?"

"Traveling pretty slow at the moment." At a dead stop, as a matter of fact. "How are you doing?"

"I'm good and so is your business. I haven't insulted a single client yet and nobody has walked away muttering about your help being incompetent."

Sarah chuckled. Tricia had recently taken her exam to be a CPA and probably knew more about accounting practices than Sarah did. While Tricia was waiting for her test results, she'd agreed to handle Sarah's business.

"I called to let you know I'll be staying in Montana for a few weeks."

"That's what your email said. What's the attraction? I hadn't envisioned you as a cowgirl."

"Nor had I. I'm helping out some friends." The family who had generously provided the heart to replace Sarah's failing organ.

"You're still coming back by September first?"

"Oh, yes. Maybe even sooner." If Beth convinced her father Sarah didn't belong on his ranch for any reason, she'd be packing her bags early. "But if there's a problem, all you have to do is call. I can drop everything and be back in Seattle in a couple of days."

"Don't even think about coming home early. After all you've been through for the past year or so, you deserve more than just a change of scene. Maybe you can find a Montana cowboy who'll put a little sparkle in your eye."

"Tricia!" she scolded, heat flooding her cheeks as the image of Kurt Ryder instantly popped into her mind. "I'll settle for lots of sunshine for a change. That alone will do wonders for my spirits."

By mid-afternoon, her household chores under control, Sarah located gardening tools and a wheelbarrow in a shed behind the barn. She piled the tools in the wheelbarrow and pushed it to the front yard. The flower bed around the gazebo had gone to seed. Ignored and abandoned.

Sarah envisioned Zoe tending a wealth of bright flowers circling the white structure in an explosion of color all year long.

Except during winter when snow covered the ground, she reminded herself. That was rarely a problem in Seattle.

Although she owned only a small cottage on a postage-stamp-size lot, she kept two window boxes filled with colorful flowers to drive away the perpetual gloom of the city.

She'd found an old horse blanket in the shed and knelt on that to keep the knees of her slacks clean. She could hardly wait for the jeans she'd ordered to arrive.

Using a trowel and a two-pronged weed puller, she

set to work. Weeds released their roots from the hard-packed ground only reluctantly, allowing the scent of untended soil and dry earth to escape.

The sun, still high in the summer sky, beat down, and sweat crept down the back of Sarah's neck.

"Dad said I'm supposed to help you."

A spurt of hope zipped through Sarah as she looked up, shading her eyes in order to see Beth. Maybe she could find a way to help the child. "I could sure use a hand. Thanks."

Without comment, Beth grabbed a pointed trowel, dropped to her knees and starting attacking a weed with a vengeance. A reluctant volunteer.

Sarah winced as the girl whacked off the weed without getting any of the roots, then assaulted another victim.

Rudy came over to investigate the gardening project. He sniffed halfheartedly around the pulled weeds, then lay down near Beth.

After a few minutes of silence—and a few more decapitated weeds—Sarah asked, "Did you used to help your mother in the garden?"

"Some."

"Good. I'm sure she appreciated your help." Sarah continued her own de-weeding efforts, including getting up as many roots as she could. Leading by example. "I was thinking, after we get the flower bed pretty well cleaned out, I'd like to go to a nursery and pick out some flowers to plant."

"Closest nursery's in Shelby."

"That's not too far. Maybe you'd like to come with

me. You can show me which flowers your mother liked best."

"I'm grounded." Beth jammed her trowel into the ground with the force of an exclamation mark.

"It'll take a couple of days to get this flower bed in any kind of condition for new plants. By then, maybe I can talk your father into letting you come with me."

Turning her head, Beth eyed Sarah for a moment, then shrugged. "Whatever."

Sarah decided to take Beth's response as one baby step forward. *Thank You, Lord.*

When it was getting close to time to start dinner, Sarah called the weed pulling to a halt. Her back, hands and knees ached from the unfamiliar exercise and she was hot, sweaty and very dirty. She needed a hot shower before she set foot in the kitchen.

Beth readily agreed to put away the tools and dump the weeds in a compost pile out back.

Sarah had barely gotten to her room and started to undress when she heard the slap of the screen door on the back porch and a woman's voice.

"Hello! Anyone home?"

Mentally groaning, Sarah rebuttoned her blouse and went to find out who had arrived.

She stepped into the hallway. "Can I help you?"

An older woman wearing a cotton housedress and carrying a baking pan covered with foil halted abruptly. She gaped at Sarah. "Who are you?"

"Sarah Barkley. I'm Mr. Ryder's housekeeper. Is there something—"

"Really?" The woman's voice rose on the question, and she looked Sarah up and down.

Aware of her disheveled state and the dirt streaks on her blouse, Sarah felt her cheeks warm. "Yes, ma'am."

"No grass growing under Kurt's feet, I'll say that," the woman said. "I'm not gone twenty-four hours and he's got a live-in housekeeper. Too bad he didn't do that for Zoe when she was alive. She worked herself to the bone around here."

Her words sounded bitter, but Sarah tried to give her some slack. "You must be Zoe's mother, Kurt's mother-in-law. I am so very sorry for your loss."

The woman didn't acknowledge Sarah's words of sympathy.

"I brought over a pan of lasagna so the family wouldn't starve, but I guess I needn't have bothered."

"That's very thoughtful of you, Mrs...."

"Livingston. Grace Livingston." She thrust the baking pan at Sarah.

She caught the aromatic scent of ground meat and oregano. "I was going to start dinner as I soon as I cleaned up. I'm sure the family will appreciate your lasagna."

"They will if you don't cook any better than you clean." She glanced toward the back door. "The mud-room needs to be swept every day. Kurt and the children do nothing but track in dirt and somebody needs to clean up after them. Zoe knew better than to leave dirt to be tracked farther into the house."

Mrs. Livingston marched past Sarah into the kitchen.

Stunned by the woman's ire, Sarah tried to remember

Grace Livingston had lost her only child and was now confronted by a stranger she imagined was trying to replace that child. Which was not at all true.

Granted, Zoe might have been a better housekeeper and cook than Sarah, but she believed there was more to life than domestic chores. And she had no intention of replacing anyone.

She followed Grace into the kitchen. "Would you like a cup of tea? It would take me just a minute to brew a pot." She placed the lasagna on the stove top and went to the cupboard to retrieve the teapot.

"Don't bother." Grace appeared to be examining the kitchen for any wayward spot of dirt that had escaped Sarah's notice. "Where is everyone?"

"I think Kurt's in the barn working on one of the horses. Toby isn't home from his friend's house yet, and Beth is putting away the gardening tools we'd been using."

Without making a comment, Grace looked out the window toward the barn as though looking for evidence that Sarah had spoken the truth. Or lied.

"I'm sure they'll all be happy with your home cooking," Sarah said. "I was going to roast a chicken that was in the freezer tonight. But that can wait until tomorrow."

Grace turned to face Sarah. "Zoe always made Southern fried chicken, not roasted. Fried chicken is one of Kurt and the children's favorite dishes. They like it real crispy like I've always made it."

"Yes, well…" Sarah had strict doctor's orders to watch her diet, which included avoiding fried food and limiting the amount of red meat she ate. A heart-healthy diet. Not that she planned to explain the reason for her eating preferences to Grace.

Apparently restless, Grace edged toward the living room. Sarah wondered if the woman was going to count how many dust mites she'd missed that morning. Then she remembered she'd left the clean laundry folded on the bottom step for the children to take upstairs to their rooms. Probably forbidden in Grace's world.

"Would you like me to tell Kurt you're here?" Sarah asked.

"No need. I should be on my way. There's a meeting at church tonight that I should attend."

"I wish you could stay for dinner. I'm sure there's plenty of lasagna for everyone, and I'll throw a Waldorf salad together." She'd found some apples in the bottom bin of the refrigerator and raisins and nuts in the cupboard. Tomorrow she'd make a run to the grocery store to stock up on fresh veggies. And chicken breasts, if they had them.

"I'll just say hello to Kurt before I go."

Without a goodbye, Grace strode out the back door and let the screen slam behind her.

Sarah winced. That did so not go well. She hadn't anticipated a confrontation with Zoe's mother. While she hadn't exactly expected to be welcomed into the household, she would have thought Grace would be pleased to get a break from caring for Kurt and the children.

That was obviously not the case.

Holding up the horse's hind leg, Kurt used a pick to clean mud from the animal's hoof. He really needed to get the farrier out to shoe all his horses. They were overdue.

"A, E, I, O, U," Kurt murmured under his breath, still feeling his lips move on the U. "U, U, U," he repeated, trying to get it right.

"Where did you find that woman?" his mother-in-law demanded in a strident voice.

One more scrape of the horse's hoof, and he released the leg and stepped away.

"Hello, Grace. I didn't expect to see you today."

"I'm sure you didn't, young man. Who is that woman?"

"Calm down, Grace. I needed someone to take care of the house and keep an eye on the kids. It's only till school starts."

"She's not a local girl. Who is she?"

"She's from Seattle. Just passing through."

"She'll probably steal you blind. She surely can't clean worth a lick. The mudroom hasn't been swept and she left clothes piled on the stairs. One of the children is likely to break their neck falling over them."

"Then they better watch where they step." He took off his work gloves and placed them on top of the stall wall. His mother-in-law had always been kind and loving, until Zoe died. Over time, her grief had turned to anger at the whole world. He didn't know how to fix that or help her. "Come on, Grace. You know I can't take care of the chores and watch out for the kids all the time. She's only temporary."

She sniffed. "If you say so. But I'd be careful, if I were you. She's got that look about her."

He did a mental double take. "What look is that?"

"She's a predator, Kurt Ryder. I can see it in her eyes. She spotted a good-lookin' rancher who owns a lot of land and she's set on hooking him for herself."

"I'll be careful," he promised, not believing one word Grace said. The only look he saw in Sarah's blue eyes was a quiet patience with both of his children. An ability to draw them out, just as he'd been drawn in by her silly Dr. Zoom antics. When he'd spotted Sarah and Beth working together, peacefully, in the garden, he'd wanted to hug Sarah. Beth needed a woman to look up to, to talk to, and Sarah was trying to fill that role.

Kurt wasn't going to fault her for that.

Not for a minute did he think Sarah had set her cap for him.

No woman would set her cap for a struggling rancher with two kids who still couldn't forgive himself for what he'd done to his wife.

Especially not if she found out the truth.

With dinner over and the kitchen once again spotless—Sarah hoped—she took her cup of tea out to the porch. She leaned against the railing, watching the slow descent of the sun behind the distant mountains. Clouds that had formed during the afternoon were edged with pink that soon bled into a deeper rose. The final shards of sunlight streaked the sky in a dramatic light show.

"I never tire of watching the sunset. It's different every night."

Sarah turned and smiled at Kurt. "It's truly beautiful. Seattle is so often overcast, it's easy to forget what a real sunset looks like."

He joined her at the railing. "I suspect my mother-in-law gave you a hard time."

"She didn't, not really. She was mostly surprised that I was here. I didn't take it personally."

"I'm glad."

"I did invite her to stay for dinner. She said she had a meeting to go to at church."

Kurt cocked a brow at her. "Odd. I don't think Grace has gone to church since Zoe's funeral."

If that was true, Sarah felt doubly sorry for the woman. She might have found some solace for her grief if she'd sought God's help in His house.

But Sarah wouldn't judge her. Losing a child must be the most profound loss anyone could face.

Kurt hitched his hip over the railing. "Toby's up in his room with the door shut talking to himself."

"Oh?"

The hint of a smile curved his lips. "I think he's practicing being a ventriloquist."

She grinned and laughed and felt warmed by Kurt's pleasure. "Good for him. That's how I learned, in front of a mirror."

"Yeah, it is good for him."

They remained silent, watching the play of light across the sky. The sound of horses moving in the barn drifted on the still air. A pair of swifts darted past the house in search of the last meal of the day. In the distance, a wolf howled and was answered by another.

Sarah shivered.

"Have you ever been on a ranch before?" Kurt asked.

"No, never. I'm a true city girl." Her parents had

always been too afraid to take her far from her doctors. Not that they had a great deal of money to spend on frivolous activities like vacations or sending her to camps after paying for Sarah's medical bills.

"I used to think of this as God's country."

"I can see why." Glancing up at Kurt, at his rugged profile, she realized he'd used past tense. "You don't feel that way now?"

He hesitated, then shoved his hands in his pockets. "How 'bout horses? You ever been around them?"

Recognizing he'd changed the subject, she laughed uneasily. "Not a whole lot of horses where I grew up."

"Well, I've gotta put the horses to bed. Come along and I'll introduce you."

As they walked to the barn, Rudy stood and stretched, then fell in beside Kurt. The smell of hay and manure grew stronger with each step they took, though Sarah didn't find the scent unpleasant. If she'd been dreaming of living on a ranch, this is the way it would have smelled—of fields of grass and large animals.

It wasn't a dream she'd ever imagined. Now, in reality, it felt right to be here.

The barn had held the day's warmth, and the scent of leather in the tack room added to the bouquet of aromas that plucked at Sarah's innate connection to the earth on a much grander scale than her small cottage in Seattle.

One of the horses neighed in his stall and stomped his hoof.

"Hold on, Pepper. You'll get your treat." From his pocket Kurt produced a quartered apple. He held out his palm and Pepper delicately scarfed down the snack, his lips all but smacking together.

"You want to feed Peaches?" Kurt asked.

"I don't think so." From Sarah's perspective, the horses looked gigantic. While the stalls appeared sturdy, she wasn't anxious to get close and personal with any creature that large. "I'll just watch."

"Come on. Peaches is as gentle as a baby. She won't hurt you. Will you, girl?" The fawn-colored mare nodded in the affirmative and he rubbed the white blaze on her face.

A quiver of unease made her stomach flip. "You go ahead."

Kurt eyed her in a way that made her stomach flip again. "I thought you said you never backed down from a challenge."

She said that? In the future she'd have to choose her words more carefully.

Drawing a steadying breath, she took a step forward. Peaches snorted and shook her head. Sarah retreated in haste.

Kurt laughed. "Coward," he teased in a low, seductive voice.

Her cheeks flamed. "I am not a coward." Well, she might be when it came to horses. But that didn't count.

Squaring her shoulders, she marched over to Kurt's side and snatched the apple quarters from him. "If Peaches bites me, I'll…get back at you."

Her hand shook as she held the apple pieces in her palm and stretched her hand toward the horse.

The soft caress of Peaches's lips on the sensitive skin

of her palm amazed Sarah. It was the lightest of kisses. As tender a touch as a mother stroking her baby.

Withdrawing her hand, Sara closed her fingers over her palm in an effort to hold on to that sweet sensation.

"There. That wasn't so bad, was it?"

"I had no idea." She gazed into Peaches's soft brown eyes, wondering if the horse was as stunned by the experience as she had been.

"I'm thinking by the end of the summer you'll be an old hand at riding a horse."

Her head snapped around and her jaw went slack. *Riding? A horse?* Not in this lifetime.

Chapter Five

The following morning, Sarah drove into Sweet Grass Valley and discovered Main Street Grocery was a world apart from any supermarket she'd shopped at in Seattle.

Still, despite the limited selection in every department, the produce was fresh and locally grown, and the meat well trimmed. Sarah loaded up her cart, including a good-looking apple pie from the bakery and some freshly baked whole-wheat rolls.

As she wheeled her cart toward the cash register, she heard a familiar voice.

"Hey, hon. I didn't expect you to still be in town."

It took Sarah a moment to recognize Bonnie Sue from the diner without her name tag on.

"I'm working for Kurt Ryder this summer. Housekeeper."

"Is that a fact? My, my…" The woman's blue eyes gleamed with curiosity, and Sarah feared Bonnie Sue would spread the news around town as fast as a YouTube video going viral.

"It's just temporary," Sarah assured her.

"Well, I'm glad Kurt found somebody to help out." Bonnie Sue turned her cart toward the cash register. "Last time I saw Grace Livingston, she looked exhausted."

The last time Sarah had seen Kurt's mother-in-law, she'd looked angry. She sincerely hoped Grace would get over her temper soon.

Bonnie Sue reached the store's one cashier first. "Hey, Angus, I want you to meet a new gal in town. She's workin' this summer for Kurt Ryder." She turned to Sarah to make the introduction. "Well, sakes, I don't even know your name, hon."

"Sarah. Sarah Barkley." She produced a smile for the middle-aged gentleman. She didn't like being the center of attention.

"Welcome to Sweet Grass, Miz Barkley." Without missing a beat, he scanned the two gallons of milk Bonnie Sue had purchased.

"Angus's daddy opened Main Street Grocery way back when. He still comes in a time or two a week to make sure Angus is doing his job right."

Angus punched in the price for a head of lettuce. "His back's been bothering him somethin' fierce lately so he's been leaving me alone." He flashed a grin that suggested he was pleased with the situation, if not his father's pain.

With her groceries bagged and back in her cart, Bonnie Sue said, "Come on by the diner if you've got the time. We've got strawberry shortcake this week."

"Sounds delicious, but I think I'd better get back to the ranch."

"Well, you drop in when you can." She started to

push her cart away, then halted again. "Say, there's a potluck social at church this coming Sunday evening. Everybody's welcome to come. It'd give you a chance to meet some of the ladies in town."

Sarah considered the idea for a moment. She didn't want to be pushy about it, but she would like to be part of a church fellowship while she was living at the ranch.

Finally she said, "I think I'd like that. Maybe Kurt and the children would like to come along, too."

A peculiar expression crossed Bonnie Sue's face and she exchanged a look with Angus, who shrugged and rang up Sarah's apple pie on his register.

"That'd be real nice if they came." Bonnie Sue's voice resonated with a dispirited note of skepticism.

Sarah was left wondering if the entire Ryder family had turned their backs on the Lord following Zoe's tragic death. Or had they never been churchgoers?

In either case, Sarah's heart ached for them, and she rubbed the scar that hid beneath her blouse. Without the Lord at her side, she never would have survived the trials brought on by her leukemia.

When Angus finished checking her groceries, she told him to put the total on Kurt's tab, as her employer had suggested.

Maybe the Lord had brought her here not simply to thank the family for their generosity but to witness to her faith, as well.

Sarah arrived back at the ranch to find both Beth and Toby pulling weeds in the flower bed around the gazebo.

While that was a shock, Sarah was delighted they

were both helping, apparently in peaceful coexistence. She stopped the car in the driveway and rolled down her window. "That's beginning to look great. You two are doing a good job."

"We're keeping out of Dad's way," Toby said.

That didn't bode well. "Are you in trouble?" she asked.

"Dad's in a really bad mood," Beth said.

"Do you know why?" Sarah hoped it wasn't anything she had done.

"He's been on the phone all morning," Beth volunteered.

"Mostly yelling at Ezra," Toby added. "He's our neighbor." He thumbed over his shoulder toward the east.

Beth struggled to get the roots up on the weed she was pulling, and finally yanked them free. "He's a really old guy. I don't think Dad should be yelling at him."

At least the problem wasn't something Sarah had done. Or, apparently, his mother-in-law. Or his children, for a change.

"Thanks for the warning. I'll tread lightly."

Sarah parked her car near the back of the house and carried her grocery bags in through the mudroom. Kurt was on the house phone in the kitchen, pacing the room, stretching the curling cord around with him. Speaking in an agitated voice, he didn't acknowledge Sarah's arrival.

"Ezra, you had to know Western Region Cattle Feeding doesn't care if they pollute the water table as long as they're making a profit."

He paused to listen, then said, "I know the price of

beef is down. Who doesn't know that? But if I have to keep my cows off the north section—"

Sarah placed the grocery bags on the counter and went back to the car to get the rest. When she returned, Kurt had hung up the phone.

He plowed both of his hands through his hair, making it look as though he'd just gotten up from bed. "I don't know what's gotten into that man," he muttered more to himself than to Sarah.

"Problems?" She set the vegetables aside to be washed and began putting away the whole-wheat bread and rolls she'd purchased.

"Yeah, potentially a big problem." Picking up cans of diced tomatoes and mushroom soup, he put them away on a pantry shelf. "My neighbor is leasing some land adjacent to mine for a cattle feed lot. The company has a bad reputation. They cut corners and don't follow state laws about polluting the land."

"Don't they get fined or something for doing that?"

"Sometimes. But not until after the damage is done."

She ran water over the head of lettuce then did the same for the tomatoes. "Isn't your neighbor worried they'll pollute his land, too?"

"The section he's leasing lies above mine. That means the natural drainage will bring all the contamination onto my property unless they take measures to redirect it to a holding pond. The Western Region Cattle Feeding company never spends that kind of money." Kurt poured himself a mug of coffee, downed a gulp and wrinkled his nose in distaste.

"I can make you a fresh pot, if you'd like."

"Don't bother. This suits my mood just fine." Mug in hand, he paced across the room to the window. "The real problem is, I understand why Ezra thinks he has to do this. He's an old guy, in his eighties, and his sons have all moved away, which means he's running hardly any cattle at all. He's got to produce some kind of income or he'll lose the ranch."

Knowing he was equally worried about his neighbor as he was anxious to protect his land pleased Sarah. His heart was in the right place. "Does sound like a difficult situation."

"Yeah, you got that straight."

She dried her hands on a paper towel. "What about the state or county regulatory agencies? Can't they come down hard on the cattle-feeding company? Make them obey the rules?"

"They only act after the fact. They want proof of contamination before they'll close down a feed lot." He sat down at the kitchen table and stretched out his long legs, hooking one booted foot over the other. Deep worry lines etched his suntanned face. A muscle ticked in his jaw. "By then it's too late and the damage is done."

That seemed strange to Sarah. She had a client in Seattle, a small businessman, who opened a car wash recently. The city planning department and building inspectors were all over him to make sure he complied with all the regulations.

"Maybe if you talked with the county people, you could alert them to the problem and ask them to enforce the rules."

His disheartened head shake was a clear sign of his

discouraged mood. "I guess I can try. Not sure it will do any good, though."

"If you can build a strong enough case against West-ern Region Cattle Feeding, based on their past perfor-mance, they'll have to listen to you and won't issue a use permit."

Lifting his head, he eyed her skeptically. "Just how do I go about doing that?"

Confident of her own abilities to research and build a case, she folded the paper grocery sacks neatly and smoothed them out. "On the internet."

For dinner Sarah roasted the chicken she'd planned for the prior evening and served it with a zucchini cas-serole and apple stuffing. She knew she was serving dishes that Zoe had never prepared, and anxiety about the reaction she'd get from the family burned in her stomach. Maybe she should have gone for fried chicken and asked Grace Livingston for her recipe. That might have been a wiser choice.

Once the family was seated at the table, Sarah said a silent grace before asking Kurt to carve the chicken.

"Sure. I can carve." He picked up the knife and fork and went to work.

"Can I have a drumstick, Dad?" Toby asked.

"You got it, son." He sliced off a leg and thigh, put it on a plate and passed it to the boy.

Beth looked at the bird on the platter with obvi-ous reservations. "Nana and mom always made fried chicken."

"Yes, your grandmother mentioned that when she dropped by yesterday. I thought you might like roasted chicken for a change of pace." A much healthier choice than fried, in her view.

Sarah asked for a slice of white meat, and Beth did the same, leaving Kurt with the second drumstick.

"Help yourselves to the stuffing and casserole," Sarah said. "But be careful. That dish is hot."

Toby peered at the casserole. "This stuff looks like…" With a questioning expression, he looked up at his father.

"Try it, son. You might like it."

Toby put a teaspoonful of the zucchini-mushroom mixture on his plate, then shoved the dish toward his sister.

She wrinkled her nose. "It smells funny."

Pulling the dish closer, Kurt ladled a large serving onto his plate. "Looks good to me." He forked a bite into his mouth. "Hmm, tastes good, too. What is it?"

The burning sensation in Sarah's stomach cooled. "Zucchini and mushrooms in a light cream sauce."

"This stuff on top tastes like cheese." He swirled his fork above the serving on his plate. "Eat up, kids. You'll like it." He dug in again, then reached for the stuffing.

Sarah felt like she'd just passed some massive gourmet cooking test at Le Cordon Bleu in Paris and smiled in relief.

The children's reaction wasn't quite as enthusiastic as Kurt's, but they did eat some of everything. Without Kurt's endorsement, Sarah was sure dinner would have been a complete flop. Kids were so reluctant to try something new.

Accepting her into the family, albeit temporarily, seemed particularly difficult for Beth.

"Beth, do you know how your mother made her fried chicken?" Sarah asked.

"Not really. Just flour and stuff."

"Tell you what," Sarah proposed. "If you'll get the recipe and directions from your grandmother, next time we have chicken, you and I can try to make it like your mother did." One small piece of fried chicken wouldn't hurt her, and establishing a better connection with Beth would be a positive step.

Beth cocked her head to the side. "You think we could?"

"I think we can try."

Staring at Sarah for a long moment, Beth finally shrugged. "Okay. I'll call Nana later."

Quietly, Sarah exhaled the breath she'd been holding. Maybe sharing recipes with her grandmother would help ease some of the tension between them.

The apple pie for dessert was a hit with everyone.

As the others were eating their pie, Sarah said, "Toby, I understand you've been working on your ventriloquist talents."

"You mean he's been admiring himself in the mirror all day," Beth chided.

"That's how you learn, dweeb," Toby countered.

"So how's it going?" Sarah asked, hoping to avert a spat between the siblings.

The boy's forehead furrowed, lowering his brows. "I think I've got it pretty good." Concentrating, he repeated the vowel sounds she'd asked him to practice.

"Excellent!" Sarah gave him a thumbs-up.

"That's easy. I can do it without spending half the day

practicing." Beth recited the vowel sounds controlling her lips about as well as Toby had.

"Hey, my kids have talent." Clapping his hands, Kurt laughed. "Maybe we can get you two on TV as a ventriloquist duo and you'll make a bundle of dough."

Beth rolled her eyes, and Sarah repressed a smile. Not a bad idea for the family to perform together. Maybe at church socials...

"Have you been practicing, Kurt? You could make it a trio," Sarah suggested.

A horrified look crossed his face and a blush raced up his neck to stain his suntanned cheeks. "Thanks, but no, thanks. Cattle is the only audience that'll ever hear me perform."

"You're just chicken." Toby's accusation came with a smile.

Kurt shot the boy a mock look of censure.

"Are you ready for lesson two?" Sarah asked the boy.

"Sure."

"Okay, keep your jaw relaxed and say the whole alphabet."

Toby frowned in concentration again and raced through the letters at breakneck speed.

Shaking a finger at the boy, Beth said, "Your lips moved. I saw 'em."

"It's all right," Sarah said. "Some letters are impossible to say without moving your lips. Like *B* and *F* and *M*. So that's when a good ventriloquist has to fool the audience just a little."

"How?" Beth asked, showing at least a modicum of interest in process.

"You're going to learn to substitute other sounds that don't require using your lips."

As Sarah explained what sounds to use as substitutes and gave Toby some practice sentences to work on, Kurt cleared the table and started to rinse off the dishes.

"I'll do that," Sarah told him.

"No, I'm good. You go ahead with the kids."

Sarah had found ventriloquism a great way to entertain sick children at the hospital. A way to help them and feel good about herself.

She'd been given a talent, a gift from God. If she could pass that on to Kurt's children, she'd feel doubly blessed.

After the children went to bed and Kurt holed up in his office, Sarah went to her room. Despite the fact she'd awakened early that morning, she wasn't sleepy.

Instead, a sense of restlessness plagued her, a feeling of heightened awareness of her own needs as a woman, as though she'd been given an extra dose of hormones.

Which was peculiar. As a rule her emotions remained steady with no wild mood swings. She was in control—control that seemed to be slipping.

To divert herself and her thoughts, she decided to do an internet search to find what she could about Western Region Cattle Feeding and their feed lot activities. With a little luck, she could build a strong case for Kurt to present to county and state authorities about the company's lax feed-lot practices.

Curling up on the bed with pillows propped behind her, she opened her laptop. With a few keystrokes, she found thousands of references to the company. She narrowed her search and began methodically working her way through the websites that appeared the most informative.

She downloaded the most telling reports to a flash drive—complaints and suits filed against the company in a half-dozen Western states, photos of environmental damage caused by Western Region's practices, copies of internal emails the management had exchanged that had been provided as evidence in subsequent litigation. Finally she located the company's annual report to stockholders.

Leaning back, she rubbed her tired eyes. Kurt was right. The chances that Western Region Cattle Feeding would pollute the water table on his land were extremely high. He had to stop them.

She checked her watch. A little past ten. If he was still in his office, she'd show him all this evidence tonight and he could begin building his case to present to the county.

Taking the flash drive out of her computer, she went in search of Kurt. She found him in his office, tilted back in his desk chair, his stockinged feet propped on a drawer he'd pulled out. A newspaper lay open in his lap, and he was sound asleep, snoring lightly.

She started to back away from the door.

He opened his eyes. "Did you need something?"

"I'm sorry. I didn't mean to wake you."

His feet hit the floor. "I wasn't asleep. Just resting my eyes."

Yeah, right, she thought, wondering if he always snored when he was awake. "This can wait until tomorrow."

"No, come on in." He stretched and rolled his shoulders. "What's up?"

"I was checking Western Region Cattle Feeding on the internet. I think I've come up with enough material for you to make your case to the county."

"Really?" He sat forward, wide-awake now, and waved her into the room.

Plugging her flash drive into his computer, she brought up the files she'd found, summarizing and explaining the importance of each discovery in terms of his case. He paid close attention, nodding often, and asking probing questions as they went along.

When she'd finished, he stared at the computer screen and said, "You're an amazing woman, Sarah. It would've taken me a hundred years to ferret out all this stuff."

She glowed in his praise. "Chalk it up to a misspent youth. I've always loved research."

He leaned back. "All I have to do is put this stuff together in a coherent way and arrange a hearing in front of the county planning department."

"I can help you with that, if you'd like."

His smile made her flush with pleasure. "I'd like."

When Saturday night arrived, Sarah asked Kurt and his children about going to church the following day. The looks they had exchanged and Kurt's comments spoke volumes about the distance they had put between themselves and the Lord since Zoe's death.

The next morning, Sarah got up early to make pancakes and sausages for the family, then dressed and headed into town by herself, heartsick that Kurt and his children had turned their backs on God.

As she pulled into the parking lot of Good Shepherd Community Church, the bell in the steeple played a clarion call to worship. Slipping inside, she took a seat near the back and centered her thoughts and her emotions.

The church was small, holding a maximum of a hundred and fifty worshippers seated on simple wooden pews, which were three-quarters full this morning. A pulpit made of oak stood at the front of the church. High windows marched the length of the sanctuary leading to a single stained glass window depicting the Crucifixion. Angled morning sun caught the glass, sending shards of rainbow color across the far wall.

As the last notes of the clarion call ebbed, the congregation stood and the organist struck the opening notes of a familiar hymn. The minister, an older gentleman with silver hair and the whip-thin body of a distance runner, stepped out onto the stage and held up his hands to welcome the congregation.

Peace and comfort washed over Sarah. She felt at home. As though worshipping in this sanctuary was where she belonged. Forever.

Tears stung at the back of her eyes. *She'd only be here for the summer.*

She chided herself for the maudlin thought. She'd never intended to stay *forever.* Seattle was her home.

The preacher's voice filled the sanctuary with hope and faith. The choir, though not large, echoed the joyous message. The congregation nodded their agreement and joined in singing hymns with enough enthusiasm that Sarah didn't feel embarrassed to add her wobbly soprano voice to the mix.

When the service ended, Sarah stood to exit the pew. The woman sitting in front of her turned to greet her.

"Hello, dear, you're new here, aren't you?" In her sixties, the stranger wore large glasses with blue-tinted rims that magnified her striking lavender eyes. She extended her hand. "I'm Alexis Hoffman, the pastor's wife. Welcome to our little church."

"Thank you." Sarah introduced herself and said she was working for the Ryders.

"That dear man. His family has experienced a terrible loss. We pray, in time, his grief will not be so difficult to bear and he and his children will return to our little church, and to God."

"So do I."

Together they edged out into the aisle, joining the departing parishioners. Bonnie Sue was among them.

"Hey there, hon. I was hoping to see you this morning." The waitress-cum-town-welcoming-committee gave her a hug. "I see you've met Alexis. This lovely lady is not only Pastor Hoffman's wife, she's also the Director of Volunteers at the hospital in Shelby. That's where we get most of our medical help unless we're terrible sick and have to go off to Great Falls."

Excitement pinged through Sarah's chest. She hadn't thought there would be an opportunity for Susie-Q and her Dr. Zoom to volunteer at a local hospital. But why not…?

Alexis tilted her head. "Our little hospital is growing all the time. I'll have you know, we now have our very own cardiac specialist on staff. A dear young man. Very skilled. Studied at Johns Hopkins."

Sarah took special note of that information as well,

although she sincerely hoped she wouldn't need his services.

They reached Pastor Hoffman, who was greeting his flock at the door. Alexis introduced Sarah.

"I advise you to stay clear of my wife, young lady. She's a fanatic about recruiting volunteers for the Shelby hospital. It's an article of faith for her."

Alexis laughed and squeezed her husband's hand. "Dear, you know I try not to recruit new people when I first meet them. I wouldn't want to scare this poor young woman off." She winked at Sarah. "The second time our paths cross, however, she'll be fair game for my rousing recruitment speech, which no one can possibly resist."

The pastor laughed and so did Sarah, who stepped away to allow others to speak with him.

"Actually, Alexis, I would be interested in talking about volunteering. I have to get back to the ranch now, but if you're coming to the potluck tonight, perhaps we can get together."

In dramatic fashion, Alexis slapped her hand to her chest. "Bless you, my dear. Of course I'll be there this evening. We'll have a nice chat and see where you'll fit into our little program."

Chapter Six

Kurt lifted his Stetson and used a bandanna to wipe the sweat from his forehead. The midday sun beat down hard, stealing the shade of the barn and making the job of unloading bales of hay from his truck all the more challenging.

He leaned against the truck's tailgate. When Zoe was alive, they used to make it a point to take Sunday off. After church, they'd ride to a natural swimming hole on a tributary of the Marias River where cottonwood trees shaded the bank and have a picnic lunch. The kids would go swimming.

Sometimes Kurt did, too.

The tug of regret and loneliness tightened his throat, and he swallowed hard. He missed those days.

Hefting the last bale of hay, he shouldered the weight and carried it into the barn. Beth was in the house, probably texting her friends. Toby had gone off to be with his buddies.

Without Sarah around, the ranch seemed exceptionally quiet. He only had the lazy buzz of flies, horses shifting from one foot to another and a sleeping dog to keep him company.

Odd that in less than a week he could feel the absence of Sarah almost as much as he missed Zoe.

He shouldn't let himself get used to having a woman around. Not an attractive woman with a slender figure and quick smile that made her eyes light up.

No, he shouldn't let that happen. Not when she'd be leaving at the end of summer.

He heard the crunch of tires on the driveway and knew Sarah was back from church. In spite of himself, his heart picked up a beat, and he strolled as casually as he could out of the barn to welcome her home.

She got out of her car and waved. He touched the brim of his hat in return, continuing to walk toward her, toward her welcoming smile.

"How'd you like Good Shepherd Church?" he asked.

"Very nice. I had a chance to meet Pastor Hoffman and his wife. I'm going to talk to her this evening about volunteering at the Shelby hospital."

He did a mental double take. "Volunteering?"

"Well, me and Dr. Zoom volunteering. In Seattle I try to visit pediatric patients once a week to entertain them."

A generous thing for her to do with her time, though it didn't surprise Kurt. She had that kind of giving heart. What did surprise him was that she didn't have kids of her own. Or a husband.

That thought gave him pause. Had she ever been married? If so, what had happened?

"I'm going to go change and then I'll fix you some lunch."

"Don't worry about me. I'll grab something myself." Feeling awkward and strangely adolescent, he tucked his fingertips in his hip pockets. "How 'bout after you eat, I give you a riding lesson?"

Her blue eyes rounded to the size of saucers. "Riding? As in on a…horse?" Her voice cracked.

"Sure, you've been teaching the kids ventriloquism. Now it's my turn to teach you something. Can't have you living on the Rocking R all summer without ever getting on a horse."

"Oh, no." She shook her head, which made her blonde hair shimmer at her jawline. "No need for you to teach me to ride. Besides, I have to make a macaroni-and-ham salad for the church potluck tonight."

She turned to go inside, and he caught her hand, her fingers slender and soft in his work-roughened palm. She halted abruptly.

"You aren't afraid, are you?"

Her head came up, a frown tugging her brows together as her eyes locked onto his. "A little, maybe. It's silly, I know."

"Tell you what. We'll stay inside the corral. I'll walk you around on Peaches so you can get the feel for sitting on a horse. It's not scary at all. We won't leave the corral and we can stop anytime you give the word."

Without breaking eye contact, she pursed her lips, then licked them. They glistened the lightest shade of pink in the sunlight. "You promise?"

"I promise. Scout's honor." He held up three fingers.

"Were you ever really a Scout?"

The corners of his mouth twitched with the threat of a smile. "Nope. 4-H. But they've got the same sort of rules about honor and doing one's duty. Besides, you don't want Toby to think you're chicken."

Her eyes narrowed, and she withdrew her hand. "All right, I'll try. But you'd better keep your promise or you'll be eating charcoal steaks the rest of the summer."

Laughter rose up in his chest like a bubbling spring in a sun-parched prairie, refreshing and lifting his spirits.

UPS had delivered Sarah's package of jeans and boots the previous day. Now she pulled the pants on and snapped the waist closed. Definitely a snugger fit than her usual slacks. The lace-up boots made her feet look two sizes larger than usual.

"You're not vying for a beauty-queen title, so don't worry about it," she reminded herself. Instead she was going to climb onto the back of an animal that out-weighed her by eight-hundred pounds. *Terrific.*

She should've told Kurt no, thanks. But the burning intensity of his eyes, the purr of his masculine voice, and the feel of her hand in his, had made her a little dizzy. She'd agreed before she could stop herself.

Then his husky laughter had totally undone her. *Foolish woman.*

Her heart beat hard against her rib cage as she walked toward Kurt, who already had Peaches saddled and ready to go in the corral. Zoe had no doubt been an excellent rider. Sarah couldn't compete with her. She had no reason to.

But she hated the thought of looking like a fool.

Kurt eyed her up and down as she reached the corral fence. His lips quirked into a half smile.

"What's wrong?" she asked.

His smile broadened. "Not a thing. Climb on over the fence and we'll get started."

She tried to recall the last time she'd climbed a fence and remembered she'd been about ten years old. She'd followed a neighbor boy over a block wall fence. He'd jumped to the ground on the other side. She'd slipped and scraped both of her elbows and ripped her jeans. Not an auspicious beginning for fence climbing.

Gathering her courage, she climbed to the top of the corral fence, swung a leg over and teetered there for a moment awkwardly trying to get the other leg over.

At the exact instant she was about to take a header into the dirt, Kurt's big hands closed around her waist. He lifted her high above the top rung, then set her safely on the ground.

Heat flooded her face, and the warmth of his grip on her waist radiated through her midsection.

"Easy does it." His voice was low and slightly rough. "I've never had the fence buck anyone off. Don't want to start now."

She swallowed hard and took a step away. "How about Peaches? How many riders has she thrown?"

"Not a one. She'll be as gentle as your own mother."

As overprotective as her mother had always been, Sarah doubted her mother would approve of her going anywhere near a horse, much less ride one.

Maybe that's precisely why she needed to do just

that. She no longer needed or wanted the suffocating concern her mother—understandably—had lavished on her. She needed to assert her independence, savor her good health, try new things.

She looked up at Kurt, his golden-brown eyes focused steadily on her. *And take a risk?*

"All right, cowboy, let's do it," she said, her voice strangely breathless.

"Atta girl." Taking her hand, he led her to Peaches's left side. "Give her a pat and talk to her. She likes to know who she's carrying around."

Barely able to see over Peaches's back, Sarah petted the horse's neck. The horse's withers rippled in response. She caught the strong, though not unpleasant, smell of horse flesh. "Hi, Peaches. Remember me? I gave you a bite of apple the other day."

Peaches turned her head and eyed Sarah, then nodded her head twice.

"See? She remembers you," Kurt said.

"If you say so."

As though drawn to the upcoming spectacle, Rudy came out of the barn and lay down in a shady spot to watch. Maybe a good laugh would make his doggie day.

"I'll help you mount. Grab a handful of her mane with your left hand and put your left foot in my hands. I'll boost you up. Then you swing your right foot over the saddle. Nothing to it."

She doubted it was as easy as Kurt tried to make it sound. Wiping the perspiration from her palms on her jeans, she took hold of Peaches's mane and carefully placed her foot in Kurt's cupped hands. He lifted—

"Ooh!" Suddenly unbalanced, she made a grab for the saddle horn before she went flying off on the other side of the horse. Peaches danced around, her rear end sidling toward the fence.

"Whoa, Peaches," Kurt said, his hand on the bridle.

Sarah hung on for dear life and squeezed her eyes shut.

"You're okay, Sarah. Relax while I adjust the stirrups."

Relax? She was sitting ten feet in the air on a moving creature that maybe didn't want her there, apple treats or not.

She opened one eye to see what Kurt was doing. "I don't think I like this."

"You'll be fine."

He fussed with the stirrup, then slid her foot into it and moved to the other side to do the same. She could only see the top of his cowboy hat but she sensed he was smiling. Probably trying not to laugh his head off.

"How does that feel?" he asked.

"Like I'm doing the splits. I think Peaches needs to go on a diet."

He did laugh then, but it wasn't taunting laughter. More like a shared moment of amusement and not at her expense. A responding smile crept up her cheeks.

"You're enjoying this, aren't you?" she asked.

"Yes, ma'am, I am. If I'd known teaching a city girl to ride would be such fun, I would've started years ago."

His eyes had a playful sparkle in them that made her heart tingle and a lump form in her throat. She'd had no idea riding a horse would be so...entertaining.

He handed her the reins and showed her how to hold them. "If you're going to be doing a lot of riding, we need to get you a hat and some gloves."

Sarah didn't think that would be necessary. A trip or two around the corral would be more than enough riding for her. No sense to overdo attempting new ventures.

Somehow that thought made her sad. That and the knowledge she'd be leaving the Rocking R long before she'd learn to be a competent rider.

While she held the reins—and the saddle horn—Kurt walked beside Peaches using a lead line. "Let yourself settle into the seat. Relax. We're taking this nice and easy."

Easy for him to say. She was used to riding in a car, enjoying a *smooth* ride, not sitting in a swaying saddle that loosened the bones in her spine.

Meanwhile, he strolled casually along, his long legs striding with ease across the ground. Even when Peaches bumped him with her nose, as though she either wanted to be done with this exercise or be given another apple snack, he seemed unfazed. She envied him the comfort he felt in his own skin.

"When you want to turn," he said, "all you have to do is drag the reins in the direction you want to go. Give it a try."

They were approaching the far end of the corral so she pulled the reins to the left. Peaches reared her head and nearly ran into Kurt.

"Not so hard," he said, reassuring the animal. "Use a gentle touch. She has a soft mouth. She's trained to respond to the lightest touch."

"Sorry."

They reached another turn and he said, "Try it again."

She did, barely easing the reins to the left this time. To her surprise, Peaches responded and they headed back to their starting point.

Kurt glanced over his shoulder and smiled. "Good job. You're getting the hang of it."

Sarah wasn't quite that optimistic.

The next thing she knew, Kurt had unhooked the lead line. "I'll keep walking beside you, but you're in charge now."

"Kurt, I don't think—"

"You'll be fine."

This was so not a good idea. Particularly if she got sick to her stomach and had to throw up from a bad case of nerves. Driving the freeway from Seattle to Tacoma during rush hour was less stressful than riding a horse.

She held the reins even more tightly in her left hand, the saddle horn in her right. The horse kept plodding along. Sweat formed on her nape and trickled down her back.

Suddenly there was a commotion behind her. She half turned in the saddle as Toby came galloping up to the corral on his horse. Her foot came out of the stirrup.

"Hey, look at you, Sarah. Yahoo! You're riding Peaches." The boy waved his hat in the air.

She tried to right herself, managing to lose the other stirrup in the process. She pulled on the reins. Peaches started to back up.

"No, don't do that!" she cried.

Kurt reached for the bridle but missed.

She yanked on the reins. "Whoa!"

Peaches reared up on her hind legs.

Sarah lost her grip and screamed. She slid off the back of the horse and landed hard on her rear end. She looked up to find Peaches staring down at her with the most puzzled expression she'd ever seen, almost as if she was asking "What are you doing down there?"

Bursting out in laughter, and thoroughly embarrassed, Sarah buried her face in her hands.

Kurt knelt beside her. "Are you okay?"

Choking on a laugh, she said, "Is that how all your riding lessons end?"

He cupped her chin to lift her head. Their faces were close, his breath sweet, his lips only a few aching inches from hers.

"Definitely a first."

He smiled, a warm smile that deepened the color of his eyes and softened his rugged features. The flutter in Sarah's stomach told her there could be more lessons ahead that might end quite differently.

As Sarah pulled into the church parking lot, she wished again that Kurt and his children had agreed to come to the potluck social. Kurt seemed dead set against going anywhere near a church and assured Sarah they could manage their own dinner.

She was sure that was true. But after the riding lesson, the intimacy she'd felt with Kurt, their shared laughter, she had hoped he'd choose to come with her.

He had chosen otherwise.

She prayed that as time passed that Kurt would eventually find the Lord again.

Picking up the covered macaroni-and-ham salad from the passenger seat, she got out of the car and groaned. The muscles in her legs ached. Her rear end hurt from the fall. And her spine still felt like a wet noodle.

How in the world did cowboys ride all day?

Carrying the salad, she followed a couple from the parking lot toward the social hall at the back of the church. Although the sun was still well above the horizon, the air had cooled and a light breeze brought with it the scent of sage and alfalfa.

In the social hall, folding tables were arranged in rows and covered with bright yellow paper tablecloths. A pot of daisies in full bloom decorated each table. At the back of the room near the kitchen, a long table held the potluck dishes. Dodging youngsters playing a rambunctious game of tag, Sarah headed toward the potluck table.

"Hey, hon!" Bonnie Sue swooped in on Sarah. "I'm so glad you made it. Come on. I'll show you where to put your dish."

"Potlucks are one of my favorite things. So many new dishes to try."

Moving with the energy of a small tornado, Bonnie Sue forced their way through gaggles of chatting church members. They smiled at Sarah, a hint of curiosity in their eyes.

"We got hot dishes over on that end," Bonnie Sue told her. "Salads in the middle and desserts down at that end. Coffee and punch are on the table in the corner."

Sarah found a spot to place her pasta salad on the middle table.

"You couldn't talk Kurt into coming, huh?" Bonnie Sue asked.

"Afraid not. He said they'd be fine on their own for supper."

Her cheery smile faltering, Bonnie Sue shook her head. "Maybe next time."

Sarah hoped so, though she wasn't optimistic.

Alexis Hoffman, the pastor's wife, appeared at Sarah's side. "Hello, dear. It's Sarah, isn't it? I'm glad you could join us."

"I've been looking forward to it all day." Except for that brief period when she sat on Peaches's back, her emotions bouncing between terror and a growing admiration…and affection for Kurt.

"Oh, good." Alexis glanced around the increasingly crowded room through her blue-rimmed glasses. "Let's find us a quiet spot and I'll tell you all about the wonderful help the volunteers at Shelby Community Hospital provide for our patients and the staff."

Hooking her arm through Sarah's, Alexis herded her to the far side of the room, chatting all the way about the various volunteer opportunities.

"Mrs. Hoffman," Sarah interrupted over the hum of conversation in the room.

"Do call me Alexis, please."

"All right, Alexis. I've been volunteering at Washington University Hospital for several years." When her own health permitted. "I visit the pediatric unit and entertain the children, particularly those in the oncology unit. I'm a ventriloquist and dress up like a clown."

Alexis eyes widened. "A ventriloquist?"

"Yes, I use a dummy I call Dr. Zoom. He tells

ridiculous jokes. The youngsters seem to enjoy the diversion."

"My, my." She seemed both surprised and taken aback by Sarah's revelation. "We've never had a ventriloquist. Or a clown entertaining the children. We don't have a pediatric oncology unit, per se. I don't know..." Her forehead pleated as she considered the possibility.

"Each hospital is set up differently, I'm sure. The arrangement, or how your medical units operate, may not be conducive to using someone like me. Hospital procedures always come first."

Alexis squared her shoulders. "I like the idea. Yes, I do. And just because we've never had a clown doesn't mean we can't do something special for our children. But it does mean I'll have to clear it with the administrator."

"I can provide references from University Hospital, if you'd like. And assuming Mr. Ryder approves, I'm thinking a half day per week would be all I could volunteer."

"That sounds lovely, my dear. And Kurt had better approve and give you that much time off or he'll certainly hear from me."

Unable to repress a grin, Sarah was quite confident Alexis Hoffman could be very persuasive.

Sarah gave Alexis her cell number and reminded her that she'd only be staying in Sweet Grass Valley until the end of summer.

They finished their discussion and joined the line at the potluck table. The selections varied from meatballs in a tomato sauce, to a dozen different types of salads and decadent chocolate eclairs from the bakery.

By the time Sarah finished gorging herself on all the delectable treats, she'd met a half-dozen parishioners, had traded recipes with three women, and knew she'd have to diet for the next week if she had any hope of getting into her new jeans again.

Chapter Seven

As the following week progressed, Kurt found himself looking forward to having his morning coffee with Sarah sitting across the table from him. Her hair was generally mussed, and she didn't wear makeup at that early hour. The natural look suited her. Nothing pretentious about how she acted or the way she spoke.

A down-to-earth kind of woman. He liked that.

She'd also been great with his kids. Although Beth was no longer grounded, his daughter was still helping Sarah clean out the flower bed around the gazebo and in front of the porch. They'd bought flowers from the nursery in Shelby and would be planting them soon.

The ventriloquism lessons were going great. In fact, Toby had practically stopped talking in his own voice, sounding instead like some John Wayne cowboy dude turned town sheriff. Great, except it was weird when the kid's lips barely moved.

Friday morning he finished shaving, ran a comb through his hair and headed downstairs, his spirits high as he looked forward to seeing a sleepy-eyed Sarah.

He came to an abrupt halt at the kitchen doorway.

"You're dressed." Unintentionally, he'd spoken the words like an accusation.

Carrying a plate of pancakes to the table, she stopped to look down at herself. Her hair was combed, her makeup in place and she wore a simple cotton dress that buttoned up to her neck.

"What is it?" she asked. "Am I buttoned wrong?"

"No, it's just that..." He strolled toward the table. "I mean, you usually... You must've gotten up early this morning." He missed her sleepy eyes, the way she often mumbled, her efforts at conversation minimal, as she served him breakfast.

"I'm going into Shelby today, to the hospital, after I clean up the breakfast dishes and do a load of wash. I want to get there by ten. Usually the doctors have finished their rounds by then."

"Oh, yeah." He slid into his chair. "The ventriloquist business. I'd forgotten. How long do you think you'll be gone?" Odd, knowing she'd be away, he'd already started to miss her.

"I'll stay at the hospital through lunchtime. The kids usually take a nap then or their families visit."

He stabbed a couple of whole-wheat pancakes—which weren't bad—spread butter on them, then covered them in maple syrup. "It's nice of you to do that for the kids."

She sat down opposite him. "I was sort of a sickly kid and spent some time in the hospital. I'm just paying forward some of the nice things that I enjoyed as a child."

He wondered how sick she'd been, but figured it was none of his business. She seemed healthy enough now.

"I'm sure the kids will love you and Dr. Zoom."

"I hope so." She forked up a bite of pancake, no butter and only a drop or two of syrup. "Will you be around if Beth and Toby need you?"

"Yep. I'll hang close to home. I've got some tack to repair and the tractor's carburetor is acting squirrelly."

"Remind Beth we're going to make fried chicken tonight using her grandmother's recipe."

He downed a gulp of coffee. "Great. I love it really crunchy."

"Your arteries probably won't, but one night won't hurt."

He lifted an eyebrow. He'd noticed from the beginning that Sarah was into healthy food. He'd never had so many salads in his life since she'd hired on to be his housekeeper. Or so much baked chicken. He was a cattle rancher. Cattle ranchers ate beef.

But he was getting used to a lighter diet. In fact, he'd lost a pound or two, and his pants were fitting better these days.

Shelby Community Hospital squatted on several acres of former open prairie at the edge of town. The two-story concrete building wasn't even a third of the size of the Washington University Hospital in Seattle where Sarah had volunteered and had her heart transplant surgery.

The size of the hospital didn't matter to Sarah as long as there were children there who needed to laugh and smile.

Before she'd left the ranch this morning, she'd called Tricia in Seattle to see how everything was going at the office. As usual Tricia was upbeat about everything except the long wait to learn if she'd passed her CPA exam. Sarah sympathized, assured Tricia she'd pass with high marks and promised to call again next week.

Carrying her tote, Sarah walked into the air-conditioned building. She shivered at the contrast between the blazing mid-morning heat outside and the cool interior of the hospital.

She took the stairs to the volunteer office on the second floor. Alexis Hoffman was sitting behind her desk. Photographs of various events and dignitaries hung on the wall behind her and leafy green potted plants lined the windowsill.

"Good morning, Alexis. I thought I'd check in with you before I change into my costume and go looking for the pediatric unit."

Taking off her reading glasses, Alexis looked up from the file she was reading. "Perfect. I've cleared everything with the administration and pediatrics knows you're coming. They're very excited about your visit."

"So am I." A little nervous, too, her adrenaline pumping high energy through her veins. She'd be working with new staff personnel and new children in an unfamiliar environment. She prayed everything would go well.

Alexis handed her a name tag identifying her as a volunteer. "Pediatrics is at the end of the hall on your right. Lori Tame is the supervising nurse on duty. I may pop down later to see how it's going."

"You're welcome to. I'll go change now."

She found a nearby restroom and stepped inside to

transform herself into Suzy-Q, hospital volunteer and clown extraordinaire.

Standing in front of the mirror, she slid a red ping-pong ball over the end of her nose, painted her lips and circles on her cheeks a bright red and pulled on a ridiculous orange wig covering her blond hair. A pinafore apron decorated with colorful appliqued balls and her new volunteer pin completed her costume.

"You rock, Suzy-Q," she said, doing a little jig in front of the mirror.

She fluffed her outrageous wig one last time before heading to the pediatric unit. Years ago she'd been a patient in a pediatric oncology ward. Leukemia had nearly felled her at the tender age of four. All those chemo and radiation treatments she'd had as a child had taken their toll, eventually weakening her heart to the point that she'd needed a new ticker.

As she walked down the hallway toward the pediatric unit, she caught the all-too familiar institutional scent of antiseptic and floor wax that had perfumed so much of her life.

At the nurses station, the nurse on duty stared at her a moment. A slender woman with dark hair wearing light blue scrubs, she laughed. "They told me a clown was coming, but wow! You look great. The kids will love you."

"I certainly hope so." Sarah dug into her tote and handed Lori Tame a badge to pin on her brightly colored nurse's jacket. In bold red letters it read MY HERO.

"Hey, thanks."

"You're welcome." Sarah had the greatest respect for nurses and all they did, particularly pediatric nurses. It could be a tough, heart-breaking job. "Anything special I need to know about your patients before I make my rounds?"

"We have eleven patients on our census this morning. If you have the time, the little boy in two-seventeen could use some extra attention. Shane's our only cancer patient at the moment and he's on a chemo drip. His parents both work long hours so he doesn't get many visitors."

"I'll make the time," Sarah promised.

One room at a time, she visited the children. For adolescents she demonstrated Dr. Zoom and gave them a few tips about ventriloquism. She had a ton of groaner knock-knock jokes for kids in their middle years. Younger children she gave finger puppets that she'd made, doctors with silly glasses and patients in gowns that flapped open just like the ones the children were wearing.

When she reached room two-seventeen, she peered around the door. Her lungs constricted on painful memories of her own childhood chemo experience and her heart went out to the youngster in the bed. No more than six or seven, his bald head and face looked like a full moon, but much paler. He appeared small and fragile, vulnerable as he stared transfixed by a cartoon show on the television. An IV hooked up to his arm pumped poison into his bloodstream in the hope of curing whatever cancer afflicted the youngster before it had a chance to kill him.

Before stepping into the room, she took a deep breath, forced her fear for the child's future to the back of her mind and locked it there. Giving him a chance to smile, a laugh or two, could help him win his life-threatening battle.

"Hey, there. Somebody told me the cutest kid on the floor was in this room. Have you seen him?"

Startled, he blinked and glanced toward Sarah. "Nuh-uh."

"You haven't seen him?" She gestured broadly, arms held wide, as though she were in the circus big top playing to an audience of thousands. "He's got to be here somewhere."

"I don't think so." He spoke in a tiny, almost fearful voice, apparently unsure what to make of her.

"Maybe he's under the bed."

His eyes widened. He shook his head.

Making a big deal of it, she got down on her knees to look, then quickly duck-walked to the other side of the bed and popped up, surprising the boy.

"My name's Suzy-Q and I'm a clown. Are you sure you haven't seen that cute kid they told me about?"

Thoroughly puzzled, his gazed darted around the room in confusion. "I'm the only kid here."

"Well, let me think." She placed her fingertip on her chin. "They said he was about six or seven years old and bald as a cucumber."

He nodded slowly. "I'm bald."

She intentionally waggled her head, making her orange curls bobble back and forth. "Hmm, so you are. I hadn't noticed. How old are you?"

"Six-and-a-half."

"What a coincidence! Maybe Dr. Zoom can help us out." She dug into her tote and pulled out the dummy, holding him on the security rail of the boy's bed.

"Vhat are you doing, waking me up from my nap?" Dr. Zoom complained in his fake German voice. *"Vhat is this place?"* His head spun around, and the little boy giggled.

"It's a hospital," Sarah said.

"Vhat? Am I sick? Nobody told me I vas sick." He grabbed his stethoscope and put it to his chest. *"Oh, my, this is very serious."*

"What's serious, Dr. Zoom?"

He looked up at Sarah, then dropped his head. *"I haf no heartbeat."*

"Of course not. You're a dummy."

"I'm a vhat?"

"A dummy, but we need your help. We're looking for a little boy but I don't know his name."

"So?" He leaned over toward the boy. *"Vhat's your name, kid?"*

The child giggled again. "Shane."

"He's Shane! Dr. Zoom, you've found him." She feigned amazement. "Shane's the cute kid I was looking for."

Shane grinned, a smile broad enough that it reached his big blue eyes and made them twinkle. The spark of delight she saw was more reward than most people got from a lifetime of work.

"Dat is good. Now I can go back to taking my nap, ya?"

"If you insist, Dr. Zoom. And thank you so much for your help."

She slid the dummy back into her tote. Shane peered over the edge of his bed to watch Dr. Zoom vanish.

"He's silly," the boy said.

"Yes, he is. Look what I brought you." From her tote she pulled out a CUTE KID sticker. "Where do you want this. On your gown? Or right in the middle of your forehead where everyone can see it."

"I dunno."

"Tell you what. I'll put the sticker on your gown and paint a pretty flower on your face."

His forehead furrowed above what should have been pale eyebrows but were now as hairless as his head. His bloodless lips turned upside down. "A flower?"

"What? You don't like flowers? Hmm…" She did her little jig and twirled around. "Ahoy there, matey! How 'bout a pirate flag instead? Hardy-har-har," she sang in her best pirate voice, twirling a make-believe mustache.

"Yeah." He grinned, a positively wicked little-boy smile that made Sarah want to pump her fist in the air and cheer. "A pirate flag instead," he echoed.

"You got it, cute kid."

For the next half hour, Sarah used face paint to create two pirate flags, one on each of his pale cheeks. She talked as she worked, telling him how she'd had chemo, too, and look at her now.

"Will my hair come in orange like yours?" A giggle escaped and he rubbed his bald head as though making a wish on a Yoda doll.

Laughing along with him, her heart did its own little dance of joy. She gave the boy a quick hug before calling it a day and heading home.

Home to Kurt and the Rocking R.

Later that afternoon as dinnertime approached, Beth stood at the kitchen counter dressed in shorts and a tank top. She stared at her grandmother's fried chicken recipe that she'd written on lined notebook paper.

"It says to dredge the chicken in flour. What does that mean?" she asked.

"You roll the chicken pieces in flour." Not that Sarah thought she was a great cook, but she'd figured that one out sometime ago. She'd changed into shorts and a tee when she returned from the hospital. The kitchen was really too warm to fix anything for dinner except a light salad, but she'd promised Beth.

"Why don't they just say roll in flour instead of dredge?"

"Beats me, honey. I think cooks have a secret code or something."

Beth shot her a grin. "Mom was a pretty good cook."

"So I understand."

Using her finger to mark where she was on the recipe, she said, "Wonder why Mom didn't teach me how to cook?"

Interesting question. "Maybe she thought you had other things you'd rather do. But now you want to learn. Using your grandmother's recipes is a good way to begin."

"I guess." She studied the recipe again. "It says we need to melt a bunch of butter and lard in a big skillet. Ugh. Lard is gross."

Too true. Sarah could feel her arteries hardening already. "Let's follow the recipe as best we can this time. Then, if you want to, next time you can make some changes."

Agreeing that would work, Beth proceeded to roll

the chicken in flour, followed by eggs and crushed corn flakes. The messy process resulted in gobs of the mixture blobbing onto the counter and the floor.

The chicken sizzled and spattered when Beth dropped chicken pieces into the hot fat. As she added more pieces, she had to crowd them into the frying pan.

"Careful, don't burn yourself," Sarah warned, too late.

"Ouch!" Beth sucked on her wrist where a splatter had caught her.

"Better turn down the fire a little."

Taking a step back from the stove so she wouldn't get burned, Sarah eyed the overly full pan. How would the chicken fry up right with so many pieces not in the hot fat? Maybe she'd bought too much chicken. But Kurt had such a big appetite. So did Toby.

"Hello! Anybody home?" The screen door on the back porch slammed shut. A moment later, Grace Livingston swept into the kitchen. Her gray hair had been recently trimmed and she wore a summery housedress in a flower print. "I thought I'd come by to show Beth— oh, you've already started."

"Hi, Nana."

Sarah gave Beth's grandmother a welcoming smile. "Beth's doing a really good job. She's going to be an excellent cook like you and her mother."

Grace sniffed and eyed the chicken. "She won't have anything but soggy, uncooked chicken using that pan. It's too small. You should have told her to use the big cast-iron skillet Zoe kept in the pantry."

"Cast-iron? I didn't know—"

Ignoring Sarah, Grace marched back to the pantry.

Deflated, Beth's shoulders slumped. "I guess I should've remembered which pan Mom used."

"It's the first time we've tried to fry chicken. Everyone makes mistakes." Grace's autocratic attitude wasn't likely to motivate Beth to try a second time.

Huge black frying pan in hand, Grace stormed back into the kitchen. She gave Sarah a look that was anything but friendly, then edged Beth aside.

"Let me take care of this," Grace said.

Beth stepped out of the way. Her gaze met Sarah's and the girl shrugged, disappointment written all over her young face.

It was all Sarah could do not to throw Grace Livingston out of the kitchen on her keister, she was so angry at the woman for bullying Beth and not giving her a chance to learn. Instead Sarah bit her tongue. It was not her place to come between Beth and her grandmother.

Grace managed to transfer the chicken and the hot fat into the larger pan without burning herself. She fussed with it, turning the chicken pieces and then placed a lid on the pan.

She faced Sarah and placed her fist on her hip. "Young lady, you need to explain yourself. The door was open to the guest room. I wasn't prying, mind you, but I saw all those pill bottles on your bed table and I want to know what kind of a druggie you are."

"Na...na," Beth wailed.

Sarah felt the blood drain from her face. Just before starting dinner, she'd been sorting her meds into her daily portions so she wouldn't miss any doses. A prospect that could lead to disaster, including organ rejection.

She steadied herself. "I don't believe I have to answer to you."

Kurt chose that moment to saunter into the kitchen. He looked hot and sweaty, the knees of his jeans covered with mud. "Hey, Grace. I thought I saw your car drive up."

He glanced around at the three females in the room, finally focusing on Sarah. "What don't you have to answer?"

"It's personal."

His brows shot up. He turned to Grace for an answer.

"This woman—" Her hand shaking, she pointed a finger at Sarah. "This woman you hired to replace me, to replace your wife—"

"I'm not here to replace anyone," Sarah interjected.

"—is a druggie. I've seen it with my own eyes."

"That's not true. I'm not a druggie or anything of the sort." She felt trapped. She didn't want to reveal her real reason for coming to Sweet Grass Valley. The real reason she had to take so many pills. She'd vowed to remain anonymous. To do no harm.

"Go take a look for yourself, Kurt Ryder." Her voice rising, Grace shook her finger toward the guest room. "You'll see what I mean. There must be a dozen pill bottles on the table beside that woman's bed. You'll see."

"Daddy?" Beth's eyes were round and frightened as she tracked the conversation among the adults.

Kurt held up his hand. "Sarah, are you taking a lot of pills?"

"They are prescription medications. Grace would

know that if she'd looked more closely." Although Sarah wouldn't have appreciated the woman nosing around in her room. "I need them to maintain my health."

"She's probably addicted to pain pills," Grace decided. "I've heard about people like that. All those famous movie stars and the like. You shouldn't allow a woman like that around your children. She could be dangerous."

Sarah squeezed her eyes shut. Grace Livingston obviously watched too much television. Although Sarah suspected Grace's underlying motivation continued to be her fear that she—and her late daughter—would be replaced in the eyes of Kurt and his children.

"I'm not a danger to anyone. I am not addicted to anything and I do not take pain medications." She'd hated that mentally foggy, out-of-control feeling when she took pain meds after her surgery. She'd weaned herself off of them as soon as she could. Now she rarely took an aspirin and only then when she absolutely had to.

Folding her arms across her chest, Grace glared at her from across the room.

The chicken on the stove continued to sizzle, little puffs of steam escaping from under the lid.

"Why do you take so many meds?" Kurt asked, his voice subdued but with a hint of steely resolve.

Sarah's heart sank. He didn't trust her. She'd been here, living in the same house with him for almost two weeks, laughing with him, caring for him and his family. She'd started to have feelings for him. Yet he hadn't come to believe in her.

Tears of disappointment and regret pressed at the back of her eyes. Her chin quivered.

"I didn't want to tell you."

"Tell me what, Sarah?"

She swallowed hard and licked her dry lips. She could simply pack her bags and leave. They wouldn't know who she was. Or why she'd come to Sweet Grass Valley. They wouldn't be any the wiser.

But her heart—or maybe it was Zoe's heart—wouldn't let her do that. In ways she couldn't yet quite understand, Sarah felt she belonged here.

She cleared the lump from her throat. "I'm a heart-transplant recipient. I take the pills so my body doesn't reject my new heart."

Chapter Eight

Except for the chicken cooking on the stove, the only sound Kurt heard was the hammering of his heart. His breath locked in his lungs. Spots appeared before his eyes and a wave of dizziness swept over him.

Neither Grace nor Beth had spoken. The shock written on their faces reflected the same stunned sensation he'd felt in his gut.

Sarah Barkley. Heart-transplant recipient. From Seattle. His housekeeper.

He'd donated Zoe's organs in Seattle. That couldn't be a coincidence. Could it?

He forced himself to exhale and draw in a lungful of air to clear his head.

"Why did you come to Sweet Grass Valley? Why agree to be my housekeeper?"

A flush colored Sarah's cheeks. Unable to look at him, her gaze darted around the room. "I was taking time off from work. I was just passing through—"

"No. Don't lie to me." She was hiding something. He could tell. He fisted his hands, not to throw a punch but to keep himself under control. His thoughts, his emotions, were jumping around like a horse that had gotten into some locoweed. And like a loco horse, he jumped to one crazy yet obvious conclusion. "Did you come here because you got Zoe's heart?"

"There's no way to know that for sure." Her words were barely above a whisper, her expression distraught.

Grace gasped, her hand flying to cover her mouth. Half staggering, she collapsed onto a kitchen chair. "My baby girl…"

"Please, Mrs. Livingston—"

"Have you really got mom's heart in your chest?" Beth asked, near tears, her voice quaking.

"Please. I didn't want you to know." Sarah raised a hand toward Kurt in what appeared to be supplication. "I only wanted to help you, the whole family, to thank you in some small way for the sacrifice you've all made."

As she spoke, Kurt studied the woman he'd known for less than two weeks. Except for having blonde hair, she looked nothing like Zoe. She didn't act like Zoe either. The two women couldn't have had more different personalities. And yet—

"You do think you have Zoe's heart or you wouldn't have come here," he said.

"It's a possibility," she admitted.

"How did you— What made you think—" His thoughts stumbled as though he was on uneven ground and couldn't keep his balance.

"The timing was right. Your car accident. The length of her coma before you…let her go."

Still covering her mouth, Grace sobbed a great, soulful sound filled with pain. Tears edged down Beth's cheeks.

Remembering that terrible day, the painful decision he'd had to make, Kurt thought he might throw up. His throat ached with the despair he still felt at the memory.

"How did you find out?" he asked. "Did the doctor tell you?"

"No. Absolutely not."

"Then how?"

She shook her head. "It doesn't matter. Obviously, I've upset you. Upset you all." With remorse in her eyes, she looked at his daughter and his mother-in-law before returning her focus to Kurt. "I'm so very sorry. I shouldn't have come."

"Tell me. Tell me how you found out about Zoe," he insisted.

She stepped to the stove and turned off the chicken, the smell of burned meat suddenly sharp and acrid in the room.

"Research," she said. "The internet. Old newspaper stories. Organ transplants are generally done within a specific geographic region. I knew whoever's heart I had, had to have died somewhere in the northwest, probably the result of an accident and very near the time of my transplant."

He plowed his fingers through his hair and paced to the window before turning around. "There had to be other fatal accidents, other possibilities. Zoe can't have been the only organ donor in the whole state of Washington."

"No, I'm sure she wasn't."

"Then you can't know—"

"No, I can't. That's what I've been trying to tell you."

"Does it *feel* like it's mom's heart?" Beth asked in a small, unsure voice.

"Oh, honey, it beats like any other heart. Better than my old one, of course. But it's a muscle. It does its job, for which I'll be eternally grateful."

Grace stood, her hand on the table to help keep her balance. "Zoe's heart is why you wanted to learn to fry chicken just like she did."

Sarah shook her head. "No, I wanted Beth to—"

"And why you've worked so hard restoring the flower beds out front that she loved so much," Grace continued. "It's because Zoe's a part of you now. It's almost as if she's still alive inside you." Tears spilled from her eyes. "It's a miracle."

Sarah blanched, and Kurt stepped across the room and put his arm around the older woman.

"Grace, don't carry on so. Sarah isn't Zoe. She's nothing like Zoe."

"She has my daughter's heart," Grace cried. "A part of Zoe is still alive because of her. Thank the good Lord. Zoe's still alive."

"No, Grace," Kurt said. "That's not how it works."

The back door slammed shut and Toby tromped into the room. "Howdy, partners. Looks like it's chow time," he said without moving his lips.

Kurt frowned at his son. The kid's crazy ventriloquist business was going too far.

The boy looked around, finally sensing something

was going on. "What's up? Is Nana having a spell or something?"

Beth spoke up. "Sarah's got Mom's heart in her chest. She had a transplant."

Toby swiveled his head to look at Sarah. "Really? Hey, that's cool."

"I don't know for sure whose heart—"

"If you had a transplant," Toby said, grinning, "you've probably got an awesome scar. Pete Wilson had his appendix out and he's got—"

Kurt hushed the boy. "Toby, that's enough."

"I was just saying…" He lifted his shoulders in an I-don't-know-what-I-did-wrong shrug. "Is supper ready yet? I'm starved." Unconcerned with the emotional tension in the room, he opened a cupboard, got out a bag of chips and ripped it open.

Toby's arrival and his request for dinner animated the room.

Sarah removed the lid on the chicken and frowned. Devastated that she'd been forced to reveal her secret, a storm of regret and hopelessness churned in her chest.

"It looks like the chicken is ruined." She stabbed a fork into a blackened drumstick, lifting it above the frying pan.

"Here, let me see if I can rescue dinner." Grace moved to the stove. "Not the first time someone's burned a bit of chicken, dear. Don't you worry yourself. You'll get it right next time."

Grace's cordial, forgiving tone was so in contrast with her usual treatment of Sarah, she had the impression Grace had morphed into a different person.

Or, more likely, in her grief she had imagined her beloved daughter Zoe was in Sarah's body.

Stepping back from the stove, Sarah tried to think what she should do. She'd never been anyone but herself, whatever talents and weaknesses she had. She certainly didn't intend to become Zoe simply to feed Grace's heartbreaking fantasy that Zoe had in some way returned to her.

Toby had gotten a cola from the refrigerator and plopped down at the table munching on the bag of chips, oblivious to what was happening. Sarah considered warning the boy not to spoil his dinner, but that seemed useless.

Standing in the farthest corner of the room, her arms crossed, Beth continued to stare at Sarah. Mentally x-raying her in the hope of finding her mother inside, Sarah suspected. *Poor child!*

Kurt had turned his back on the room. Standing ramrod straight, he stared out the window. Sarah couldn't fathom what he might be thinking. But even though he stood tall and strong, she knew he was vulnerable. Her revelation had rocked his foundation, the life he'd tried to rebuild for himself and his children.

Dear Lord, please help him. Help his family.

"We'll just scrape off this burned part," Grace said, fussing with the chicken. "At least the chicken is cooked through. It will be fine. Did you start the potatoes, dear?"

Sarah blinked, returning to the more practical problem. "Uh, no. I was going to serve brown rice with the chicken and a salad."

"Zoe used to love serving mashed potatoes and gravy

with her fried chicken. A thick, white gravy. Of course, since everything burned, the fat and leavings in the pan wouldn't make a very good gravy. We'll do that next time." Without looking in Sarah's direction, Grace continued her scraping effort, placing the slightly charred chicken pieces on a serving plate. "This will be fine for now."

Still bewildered about how to deal with Grace and the rest of the family, Sarah got down a box of brown rice and set a pan of water on the stove to heat. She desperately wished she could talk to Kurt alone. Ask him what he was thinking. What he wanted her to do, stay or leave.

But she couldn't do that in front of Grace, who seemed determined to take over dinner preparations.

She'd have to wait until she could get Kurt alone.

During dinner, Sarah noticed Beth ate very little and spoke even less.

In contrast, Grace talked almost nonstop, recalling stories about Zoe. How she'd won a barrel-racing contest at age fifteen and had been the high school homecoming queen her senior year. She'd won a chili cook-off at the county fair and took second place with her cinnamon-apple-peach crisp in the dessert division. Based on Grace's account, Zoe had been the epitome of a perfect daughter.

No one could live up to that high standard. Certainly not Sarah.

Kurt spoke only when he was forced to. When Toby managed to get a word in, he reported on his buddy's latest video game.

With supper finished, Grace was on her feet first to start the cleanup. Toby headed upstairs to his room. Kurt ducked out, claiming he had some paperwork to do. Beth's help in the kitchen was lackluster at best, and she escaped out the back door at the earliest possible moment.

Grace dried her hands and brushed her gray hair back from her flushed face. "I should be going now." She tilted her head and smiled at Sarah. "I am so pleased Zoe brought you here. I feel as though a terrible weight has been lifted from my shoulders."

"Mrs. Livingston, please. You shouldn't—"

"Would you mind if I hugged you, dear? It's been so long." She held out her arms.

Sarah couldn't refuse the pleading look in the woman's eyes. "Of course. Hugs are always welcome."

The awkward hug wasn't quite right. They didn't quite fit together, their heads searching for a comfortable match, their arms akimbo and graceless.

When Grace stepped back, tears glistened in her eyes. "Good night, dear."

As Grace left, Sarah sighed and looked around the sparkling-clean kitchen. The damage she'd done today remained unseen. Even so, the brittle shards of pain and unresolved grief were as palpable as the electricity in the air after a summer storm.

Her soul flayed by guilt, she lowered her head and closed her eyes. *"Please, Lord, tell me what to do. I didn't mean to hurt these good people. Show me how I can repair the damage I've done."*

No answer came to her. Her instinct, however, told

her the person most at risk of emotional trauma was Beth. Sarah went out the back door to search for her.

The sun was still above the range of the distant mountains, casting long shadows across the ground. The air had cooled considerably since midday, and a soft breeze blew off the prairie to caress Sarah's overheated cheeks.

She spotted Beth grooming her horse in the corral. Tentatively, she strolled in that direction. The horse was larger than Peaches. Reddish-brown in color, the horse's white stockings on all four feet made it look like he was dressed for prancing in a parade.

Sarah stepped up on the lower rung of the fence and hooked her arms over the top. "He's a pretty horse."

Beth ran the brush over the horse's rump. "It's a she. Her name's Princess."

"In that case, she's beautiful."

Remaining silent, Beth continued to brush her horse.

"I never meant to upset you or your family," Sarah said.

For a moment, Beth continued grooming her horse then stopped, her hand resting on Princess's mane.

"It feels weird, you know, thinking you've got Mom's heart inside you."

"It could be someone's else's heart. I can't be sure, and the doctors never tell the patient who the donor was."

"But you came here because you thought it was."

"True." Against her doctor's recommendation, which she should have listened to more closely. "I could be wrong."

Brushing the horse's mane smooth, Beth seemed thoughtful. "Did it hurt a lot? When got your new heart?"

"I was heavily sedated during surgery and didn't feel a thing. After I woke up, yes. It hurt like crazy. But it doesn't anymore." Sarah wasn't entirely sure how much Beth wanted to know or should be told. She wanted to tread gently.

"Did it start working right away?"

"The doctors told me I'd gotten a strong, healthy heart, so I assume so."

"Mom was healthy—until the accident. Then she—" Her voice broke.

"I'm so sorry, Beth. If I could change what happened to your mother, I would."

"But then you wouldn't have gotten a new heart and you'd be dead."

"Possibly," Sarah agreed. Somewhere along the way, another suitable donor might have appeared. In any case, for her to get a new heart someone had had to die. She would always live with that knowledge and the sense of guilt that went with it. A sense of awe and gratitude for the sacrifice the family had made, as well.

In the fading light, Sarah saw tears form in Beth's eyes. She ached for the youngster, her pain and grief.

"If Mom had to die like that, I'm glad you got to live."

"Oh, sweetie…" Before she could think about it, Sarah climbed over the fence, dropped down on the other side and took Beth into her arms.

It felt like the most natural thing in the world to hold this young girl, now on the cusp of womanhood, in her arms as she cried. She soothed her and smoothed her hair. Whispered that she understood the girl's pain. Felt the dampness of her tears soak through her tee and welcomed the baptism of the girl's grief.

Somewhere inside her, near her heart, a feeling of love bloomed for this half child, half woman, and she didn't want to let go.

For more than an hour, Kurt had studied the information Sarah had discovered about Western Region Cattle Feeding and tried to organize his presentation to the county commissioners. The hearing was scheduled for next week.

But he couldn't concentrate.

He couldn't get his head around Sarah being a heart-transplant recipient. She didn't look like someone who'd needed a new heart. She didn't act like one either. She'd ridden a horse. And been thrown off.

Sweat slicked his palms when he thought about what could have happened. Maybe a heart attack. Or the incision could've split open. Why on earth would she take a risk like that?

Because he'd teased her into it. Challenged her.

The possibility that she'd gotten Zoe's heart made the situation even stranger. He didn't know how he felt about that. One minute he was grieving over Zoe's death. The next, he was glad Sarah was alive.

Talk about feeling conflicted. It was like having two teams in the Super Bowl and wanting them both to win. In football and heart transplants there were no tied scores. Someone lost; someone won. That's how the game was played.

He ran his fingers through his hair and leaned his elbows on the desk. This whole business was making him crazy.

At a knock on the door, Kurt looked up. Sarah stood in the open doorway. Her face looked drawn with fatigue, her complexion pale.

"May I come in?" she asked.

"Sure. Of course." Wiping his palms on his jeans, he stood and stepped toward her. "Are you all right?"

"Outside of feeling guilty about hurting your family, I'm fine." Her voice sounded as weary as she looked.

He led her to the couch on the wall opposite his desk. It was half full with papers and magazines he hadn't gotten around to reading. He shoved them aside.

"Here. Sit down." A spurt of panic shot through him. Had the whole ordeal, the revelation that she might have Zoe's heart, been too much for her? "Can I get you anything? Coffee? One of your pills?"

Her lips lifted in a half smile. "No. Really, I'm fine. I've just had a rather emotional conversation with Beth and I'm pretty well drained."

He scowled. "Did she give you a hard time? If she did—"

"Not at all, Kurt. She's upset about the situation I've put you all in but she'll be all right."

Sitting back on the edge of his desk, hooking his hands over the edge, he said, "I'm pretty much in shock myself. If I'd any idea you'd had a heart transplant, I'd never would have let you get on a horse. Something terrible could've—"

"Kurt, I'm healthier now than I've ever been in my life. If it weren't for me being a coward and my mother being overprotective, I probably would've ridden horses and skied down hills and maybe even taken off in a hot air balloon. But I wasn't healthy and I'm still a coward. The first problem is taken care of and now I'm working on not being such a wimp."

Her spirit, her courage, amazed him. He couldn't imagine all she'd been through—and survived.

"Are your parents still around?" he asked.

"Dad died several years ago. Mother passed away in February. I think having a sick child stole years from both of their lives."

Blaming yourself was a bad habit to get into, one that was hard to break. "What happened that you had to have a new heart? If you don't mind me asking."

"It's a boring story, actually." She told him about her childhood leukemia, chemo therapy and radiation. "By the time I approached thirty, all the damage they'd done to keep me alive caught up with me. My heart began to fail. There weren't many choices left so I was put on a heart-transplant waiting list. And the rest, as they say, is history."

"Zoe's heart."

"Possibly. But that doesn't change who I am. I'm not Zoe and never could be."

He pushed away from the desk. "I know that."

"I'm not sure your mother-in-law does."

"There are a lot of things Grace doesn't know. Like how Zoe wasn't the perfect wife. Not that I was the perfect husband, either," he admitted. They'd married too young. Neither he nor Zoe had given themselves much chance to grow up, to discover who they were before they started to grow apart. He'd loved Zoe. He thought she had loved him, too. But it was an adolescent love that wasn't strong enough to last during the tough times. Ranchers had a lot of those.

"I feel as though I've put you all in a very awkward position. If you'd like, I'll leave. It wouldn't take me long to pack. I could be on the road within the hour."

"No." The panic he'd felt a moment ago was mild compared to the mental alarm set off by her words. "No, I don't want you to leave. I'm sure the kids wouldn't want you to go. You've been great with them. I mean, how would Toby ever get any good with that ventriloquism business you've taught him?" He chided himself for making such a dumb statement. Toby and his clowning around wasn't the reason he wanted Sarah to stay. He wanted her to stay because...

Because he liked the way she'd smiled at his stupid comment.

"I'm reasonably sure Toby and Sarah will adjust to the situation," she said. "But I'm less sure about Grace. Or you."

"I'm fine with you staying." More than fine, he thought, as he went back to his desk chair and sat down. "As far as I'm concerned, you're the person I hired to be our housekeeper and I still need your help with the kids until school starts. Let me worry about Grace."

A frown creased Sarah's smooth forehead. "At dinner, Grace seemed...I don't know. Maybe determined to plant Zoe's memories in *my* head so I would *become* Zoe. I don't think that's healthy for her. I can't replace her daughter."

"She'll get over it."

"I'm not so sure. Has she—or any of you—received any grief counseling?"

"Hardly. I sure don't have time for that sort of nonsense. Plus, Sweet Grass Valley isn't exactly home to a whole lot of psychologists. Around here, if we've got a problem, we grit it out on our own."

She shook her head. "I'm sure you think you're strong enough to handle emotional trauma and the loss of your wife. But Beth and Grace could certainly use some help. Maybe Toby, I don't know."

Picking up a pencil, he tapped the eraser on his desk. His jaw muscle clenched. "It's been more than a year. We're doing fine."

"Perhaps if they talked with Pastor Hoffman."

He snapped the pencil in half. "Sarah, I'll take care of my family. If you're going to stay, great. Right now I've got work to do."

Her lips tightened into a straight line. Her blue eyes darkened with disappointment. She stood, graceful, her head held high.

"I'll have your breakfast ready for you at the usual time in the morning."

His chest tight with regret, Kurt watched her walk out the door. He wanted to call her back. To tell her he was sorry. But he couldn't.

God had deserted him once. He never planned to let that happen again.

Nothing Pastor Hoffman could say would ever change that.

Chapter Nine

The following day, as the heat rose and storm clouds formed over the distant mountains, tension mounted at the Rocking R Ranch.

Kurt had barely spoken to Sarah at breakfast. Right after that he'd ridden off somewhere in his truck without telling her or the children where he was going.

Feeling let down and restless, Sarah cleaned up the kitchen and put a load of sheets in the washer. She stood in the laundry room staring out the window as the washing machine agitated the sheets in a hypnotic rhythm. Swish-swish. Swish-swish.

She'd heard wolves howl in the night. The distant cry of the pack had stirred her and deepened the sense of loneliness she'd felt since her conversation with Kurt last night. Maybe she should leave, go back to—

Beth popped into the laundry room. She'd changed from the nightgown she'd worn at breakfast into a tattered pair of jeans, tank top and flip-flops.

"I thought I'd start planting those flowers and stuff we bought the other day."

In the face of Beth's energy and enthusiasm, Sarah's

spirits lifted. "Good idea. Give me a couple of minutes and I'll join you."

"I'll get the tools from the shed." With that, Beth went out the back door, letting the screen slam behind her.

Invigorated, Sarah finished the chores she needed to do.

Once outside, she found Beth already digging a hole for one of the two climbing rosebushes they'd bought. By the end of summer they'd both be covered with baby-pink blooms, which according to Beth was one of her mother's favorite flowers.

Rudy had assumed his watching position in the shade of the front porch.

"How big should I dig the hole?" she asked.

"A few inches deeper and wider than the pot. We want to be sure the roots can take hold and spread and won't get bound up. I bought some soil amendment that we can use to replace some of the dirt."

Under Beth's firm tutelage, the hard-packed soil surrendered to the shovel a few inches at a time. For a young girl, Beth was strong and not afraid of getting dirty or building up a sweat.

Together they'd decided to plant sunflowers on the south side of the gazebo. As the flowers grew, they'd attract birds to feed on the seeds. Sarah picked up a trowel and two of the six-inch pots of sunflowers. She was more than happy to let Beth do the heavy lifting with the shovel.

They worked in companionable silence, commenting occasionally on the weather or the movie that was playing in town, a G-rated show. Beth wanted to go to the matinee with her friends. Sarah saw no problem with that.

"We don't have to plant everything we bought in one day," she said, realizing that would be an impossibility without more willing workers. "We'll keep the pots well watered and take care of the rest another day. I'll drive you to town when you're ready to go."

"Great. Thanks. Maybe Caroline's mother can bring me home."

"Fine. Just call and let me or your father know what's happening."

Toby appeared from the barn. "I've mucked out the stalls and spread new hay, like Dad said. Can I go now?"

Sarah sat back on her haunches and wiped the sweat from her forehead. "Where to?"

"Billy's house. There's a vacant lot by him where the guys play baseball 'n stuff. I can ride my bike."

"Will you be home for lunch?"

"Naw. Mrs. Morgan usually feeds us something."

Sarah wished she knew the families in town, but it sounded as though Toby was used to visiting the Morgans.

"You'd better clean up before you go," she said.

He looked down at his dirty jeans. "Why? I'm fine."

"You smell like you've been rolling in manure, little brother," Beth said. "Phew!"

Sarah suppressed a smile. "Go change. And wash your hands good. I'm sure Mrs. Morgan doesn't want any smelly little boys in her house."

He pulled a face, then marched around to the back of the house to go inside.

A sense of pleasure filled Sarah as she realized both children were responding to what she told them without an argument. Only a niggling feeling that they might be responding to her because she had their mother's heart dampened her delight.

Surely they'd begun to realize she was their friend, someone they could count on. That knowing about her heart transplant hadn't changed the situation.

A few minutes after Toby left, Beth leaned on her shovel before attacking the next hole to be dug.

"Are you planning to go to church tomorrow?" she asked.

Sarah looked up from her work, curious about the girl's seemingly casual question. "Yes, I plan to. Why do you ask?"

"I don't know." She shrugged and jabbed the shovel into the ground. "It's just that Mom and Dad and us kids all used to go. I kind've missed it. I mean, a lot of my friends go to church."

Nerves tingled along Sarah's scalp. After Kurt's reaction to the mere mention of Pastor Hoffman, she'd have to be careful what she promised.

"I'd be happy to have you go with me, but we'll have to ask your father if it's okay."

Beth grew thoughtful for a moment, then shrugged again. "I don't think he'll care."

Sarah's confidence wasn't quite that high.

After delivering Beth to the movie theater in town, Sarah returned to the ranch. She fixed herself a sandwich and iced tea, and sat on the side porch gazing at the dark clouds roiling in the distance.

The parched ground could certainly use some rain.

Rudy joined her, sitting down right in front of her. The dog studied her with his big, brown eyes, his tongue hanging out. Lots of gray whiskers showed around his muzzle.

"You're begging, aren't you, ol' fellow?"

His tail made a sweep of the porch.

She pulled off a bit of chicken from her sandwich. "You won't tell Kurt, will you?" She offered Rudy the chicken, which he neatly plucked from her fingertips.

He resumed his begging stance.

"No, no more for you. This is my sandwich."

He didn't look convinced as she consumed the remainder of her lunch under the dog's watchful gaze.

At the sound of Kurt's truck returning, her heart rate accelerated. Rudy left her to welcome Kurt home.

Not knowing what his mood might be, Sarah intentionally kept her expression neutral.

He pulled to a stop beside the house. When he climbed out of the truck he was carrying a plastic shopping bag from the general store in town and his rifle.

Eyeing the rifle, a ripple of unease skittered down Sarah's spine.

"I stopped in town and got you something." He stepped up onto the porch and handed her the shopping bag.

Curiosity replaced her dread. "For me?"

"It's nothing much. Open the bag."

She did and found a straw hat with a powder-blue grosgrain ribbon wrapped around the crown. She placed it on her head. "Thank you. This is very thoughtful of you."

His lips hitched into a smile. "Looks good on you. The sun around here can bake your brains if you're not careful." His voice, his cordial body language, held no hint of their conflict last night or his sour mood this morning.

Inordinately pleased with his considerate gift and improved mood, she said, "I could have used this hat earlier today. Beth and I spent the morning planting flowers around the gazebo."

"I noticed when I drove in. There're some gloves in the sack, too. Your hands are too soft to be digging in the dirt bare-handed."

The gloves were a light blue like the ribbon on the hat and had little yellow daisies printed on them. A color-coordinated gardening ensemble, she thought with a smile.

She slipped one hand into a glove. "They fit. Thank you again."

Lifting the rifle, he held it at angle across his body and sat on the porch railing. "Next time I'm in town, I'll get you a pair of riding gloves at the tack store."

"You don't have to do that. I can pick up a pair when I'm in town."

He cocked an eyebrow. "Meaning you're willing to get on a horse again?"

A flush heated her face. "Next time I plan to hold on much tighter."

"Just don't pull on the reins so hard. Peaches thought you wanted her to back up."

"Not likely. I was having enough trouble going

forward." She eyed his rifle again. "Are you planning to shoot something?"

"You hear the wolves howling last night?"

She nodded. The memory of the eerie, compelling call of the pack still had the power to send gooseflesh down her back.

"I thought they were after my cattle, but there was no sign of them."

Relieved the wolves had not hurt his cattle, she picked up the plate and glass she'd used for lunch, and scooped up the shopping bag.

"I'd better get on with my chores. Thank you again for the hat and gloves."

"You needed them." He waved off her thanks.

She headed inside and stopped at the door. "Beth would like to go to church with me in the morning. Would that be all right with you?"

His eyes narrowed. "Was that your idea?"

"No. I didn't prompt her, if that's what you're thinking. She asked on her own."

Silent, he lowered his rifle, barrel down. "I guess she's old enough to decide for herself about going to church. If that's what she wants…"

He turned and walked down the steps, setting out for the barn.

Sarah shuddered as a cold wave of regret swept through her. She wondered if he'd ever make his way back to the Lord again.

Attendance seemed light at Good Shepherd the next morning when Sarah and Beth arrived. Beth looked particularly sweet dressed in a sundress and wearing a hint of lip gloss.

Beth spotted her friend, Caroline Buttons, and her parents, sitting in a pew in the middle of the church. She slid into the pew next to Caroline, a dark-haired girl her own age, and Sarah followed Beth into the pew. The girls giggled and Beth made hushed introductions.

As the organist played a soft prelude, Sarah sat back and focused on the wooden cross mounted on the wall behind the pulpit. A sense of peace settled over her. Meeting Beth's friend and her parents gave Sarah a feeling of acceptance. She reached out to the Lord in thanksgiving and gratitude. If she could lead Beth back to the church perhaps, in time, Kurt would follow.

Pastor Hoffman walked out onto the stage and the congregation rose for his opening prayer and the service began.

Later, when the service ended, Sarah led the way to the aisle, joining the departing parishioners.

Alexis Hoffman caught up Sarah outside. "I must tell you, young lady, you and your Dr. Zoom are the absolute talk of the hospital. The pediatric nurses are trying to bribe me so you'll come visit the children every day."

Sarah laughed, pleased her efforts had been well received. "I'm afraid Dr. Zoom would run out of silly jokes if I dragged him to the hospital that often. But I do plan to return again next Friday."

"I certainly hope so. And this time you're likely to draw an audience of doctors and nurses as well as the children in the unit."

"In that case, I'll plan to bring extra face paint," Sarah said with a smile.

An elderly woman approached Alexis, wanting to talk with her. Sarah excused herself and looked around for Beth.

Somewhat to her surprise, Beth and Caroline were standing near the edge of the parking lot talking with two boys. The girls were giggling, fluffing their hair self-consciously and doing those things girls do to attract the attention of the opposite sex. Behaviors that Sarah had never mastered as a teenager and still hadn't acquired.

Her eyebrows rose. Perhaps Beth's motive for attending church had more to do with those boys than learning the gospel message.

She strolled toward the young people. "Beth, are you ready to go?"

The girl turned, her face flushed. "Yeah. I guess."

"See you later, Loopy-Lizzy," one of the boys teased.

Beth grimace, but Sarah suspected it was in mock protest of the nickname he'd called her.

Once they were in the car, Sarah pulled out of the parking lot onto Main Street.

"Are those boys in your class at school?" she asked casually.

"No, they're a year ahead of Caroline and me. They're real dorks."

"Really? It looked to me like that taller boy, the one who called you Loopy-Lizzy, might like you." She glanced toward Beth, whose face had turned bright red.

"I dunno," she mumbled, making it a point to look out the passenger-side window.

Sarah smiled to herself. If Kurt hadn't talked to Beth about boys and dating, she thought he'd better soon. His little girl was growing up fast.

As she pulled into the driveway at home, Kurt was loading an ice chest in the back of his pickup.

"Hurry up and change clothes, ladies," he said as they got out of the car. "We're going on a picnic."

"Really?" Beth squealed. "We haven't gone on a picnic in forever!" She raced into the house.

Sarah moved more slowly. "You're a man of many surprises."

"I am, huh?" His spirits seemed high and he looked quite pleased with himself. "I figured it's time that we did more family stuff together. So I made some sandwiches and there're cold sodas in the ice chest. Cookies, chips, even some healthy fruit just for you."

"I'm impressed." And pleased he'd included her in a family outing.

"There's a place not too far from here where we always used to go. It's right on a creek, big ol' shade trees, and it has a nice, private swimming hole. So bring your swimsuit if you brought one along."

"No, I'm afraid that's something I didn't think to pack." She choked and shook her head. She hadn't owned a swimsuit in years. Which was just as well since she'd never learned to swim. She had no intention of baring her nine-inch surgery scar for all too see.

"You can always roll up your pants and go wading, I guess."

Toby stepped out of the house carrying a beach towel and his iPod. "Hey, I thought we were gonna ride horses to our picnic place."

"Not this time, son. I don't think Sarah's ready for that long a horseback ride just yet. We'll take the truck."

For that, Sarah was ever so grateful.

Bouncing along in a pickup truck across the open prairie wasn't exactly Sarah's idea of comfortable transportation, but Kurt had been right about the picnic spot he'd chosen. Cottonwood trees stretched out to meet their neighbors across a creek that rushed by, the water so clear Sarah could see the rocky bottom. In the shade, a slight breeze cooled the air and fluttered the leaves on the trees.

Kurt had spread an old quilt on the ground, though Toby and Beth had no interest in sitting down. They were already splashing in a nearby pool of crystalline water despite the fact that they claimed it was freezing cold.

Stretched out on the quilt, Kurt braced himself on his elbows. "During the spring thaw, the creek rises up its banks and sometimes overflows. By September, if we don't get some decent rain, this will only be a trickle."

"It's a beautiful spot, though." Sitting with her legs beneath her on the quilt, Sarah admired both the countryside and Kurt's strong profile. He looked more relaxed at this moment than he had since she'd met him.

"My dad used to bring us out here, me and my brother and mom."

"You mentioned your brother the day I came to the ranch."

"Hmm, Ralph. Two years older than me. He lives in Denver with his wife and a couple of kids a little older than Beth and Toby. They visit once in a while."

"I'm surprised as the older brother he didn't stay on the ranch."

"Nope. He's a stockbroker. His wife, Terri, doesn't want anything to do with ranching."

That struck Sarah as sad. Living here in the middle of such wide-open spaces made her feel especially connected to the wonders of nature and the Lord's creations.

"Guess you've already figured out living on a ranch is a lot different than living in the city," he said.

"Different, yes. But that doesn't make it better or worse. Though it does take some getting used to the thought of sitting on the back of an eight-hundred pound animal instead of riding in a nice, comfortable car is a stretch for me."

He chuckled, a deep sound that vibrated through his chest and found a matching response in her heart.

Watching the children playing in the water and listening to their laughter, they sat in silence for a time. The buzz of insects accompanied the click of leaves brushing together in the cottonwood trees. Overhead, a hawk circled in an updraft. On the far side of the creek, a gust of wind rippled the grass creating a golden wave across the landscape.

"Beth and her friend Caroline found a couple of boys to talk to after church this morning," she told him.

He lay all the way down, tucking his hands behind his head so he could look up through the tree branches to the blue sky. "Yeah?"

"She's growing up fast, Kurt. Have you talked to her yet about boys and dating?"

He bolted to a sitting position. "Was she doing something with those guys? Who were they?"

His horrified expression nearly made her laugh. "Shh, calm down. She wasn't doing anything wrong. But one of the boys did seem interested in her, and I think she may be interested in him."

"She can't date yet. She's only twelve. Seventh grade."

"Almost thirteen, as I recall. The boys were a little older. It would be better to talk to her now instead of waiting until—"

"I can't talk to her about boy-and-girl stuff." He glanced toward his children. "I'd get all tongue-tied. Why don't you talk to her? She'd listen to you."

His suggestion stunned Sarah. "It's not my place to talk to her, Kurt. For one thing, I'm only here until school starts. She's going to need to have more than one conversation on the topic. And for the other…" A lump formed in her throat and an ache filled her chest. She had to look away. "I'm not her mother."

When she looked back, Kurt was staring at her intently with an unreadable expression on his face. His golden-brown eyes had turned nearly to black.

The intensity of his demeanor, the look in his eyes, created a hunger in her she'd never before experienced.

A hunger that had nothing to do with going on a picnic.

He held her gaze for a moment longer, then glanced away. "I think I'll go cool off." He pulled off his boots and socks. Standing, he stripped off his shirt, jogged toward the swimming hole and did a cannonball right between his two children.

Beth screamed. Toby laughed.

Surfacing from the bottom of the creek, Kurt came up sputtering. "Man, this is *cold!*"

Sarah smiled at his antics. It was good to see Kurt playing with his children. Good for them and for Kurt.

So why did she feel a strange emptiness somewhere near her heart?

By midafternoon, the children had had enough swimming and enough sun. They packed up the remnants of the lunch Kurt had prepared and drove back to the ranch house.

"Hey," Toby said from the cramped backseat of the truck's extended cab. "Isn't that Nana's car in the driveway?"

Sarah glanced at Kurt. "I hope there isn't anything wrong."

He shook his head. "With Nana Grace, you never know."

As Kurt parked near the barn, Grace stepped out of the house and waved.

"Hello, you people," she said. "I wondered where you had gotten to."

Sarah got out the of the truck cab and Toby tumbled after her.

"We went on a picnic," Toby said. "Out at the ol' swimming hole. Dad did a cannonball and practically drowned Beth."

"He did not drown me," Beth said.

Holding her hands together as if in prayer, Grace

said, "Wonderful! Your mother loved picnics. How nice Sarah remembered."

Sarah started and shook her head. "I had no idea—"

"Well, come on in, children." Grace beckoned them inside. "I've a special treat for you. You'll see. It's in the freezer."

Nonplussed that Grace thought *she* had remembered something of Zoe's past, Sarah turned to Kurt. "I think your mother-in-law is having some sort of a nervous breakdown. She's confusing me with her daughter."

Kurt hefted the ice chest out of the back of the truck. "I'm sure it's just wishful thinking. She'll get past it."

Not confident that was the case, Sarah snared the damp towels in the truck bed and carried them into the house, dropping them off in the laundry room.

"I stopped in town on my way here and bought some peppermint ice cream." Grace retrieved a gallon container from the freezer. "That was always Zoe's favorite flavor. I thought you'd all enjoy the special treat." She busied herself getting out bowls and spoons, then scooped generous servings of the ice cream into bowls.

Grace's strange behavior raised the hair on the back of Sarah's neck. "Just a spoonful for me, Grace."

"Don't be silly, child. You love peppermint ice cream." She held out two bowls of ice cream to Sarah. "Now, everyone sit down at the table. We'll have a nice chat. I have another surprise for you."

For a moment, Sarah froze with the two bowls of ice cream in her hands. "Grace, I've never tasted peppermint ice cream."

"You'll love what else I brought for you to see," Grace said, ignoring Sarah's comment. "It's Zoe's scrapbook, from when she was a tiny baby all through high school."

Kurt tried to intervene. "Nana, the ice cream's great, but I don't think Sarah wants to look at Zoe's scrapbook."

"I do. I love looking at Mom's baby pictures." Beth picked up a couple of servings of ice cream, carried them to the table and plopped herself down at her place. She shoved the second bowl in Toby's direction.

Reluctantly, Sarah sat down at the table. Almost immediately Grace sat down between her and Beth and produced the scrapbook.

"Maybe we should wait until after we eat the ice cream," Sarah suggested. "I know the scrapbook is precious to you, Grace, and I wouldn't want anything to spill on it."

"Oh, you're always careful, dear," Grace blithely said.

Opening the brown faux leather scrapbook to Zoe's first baby pictures, Grace began a monologue that covered every high point in her only child's life. She rarely took a bite of ice cream, far more engrossed in her daughter's past than the present.

Beth—and sometimes even Toby—seemed to eat up the stories, some of which they'd probably heard before.

What troubled Sarah was Grace's apparent mental confusion. Several times she asked if Sarah remembered a particular incident then shrugged off her denials.

Even Beth looked at her occasionally as though Grace were talking about Sarah, not her deceased mother.

Only Kurt, who frowned or shook his head occasionally, seemed to share Sarah's concern about his mother-in-law's behavior.

While it was good for the children to learn about their mother's life, Grace appeared to be creating a fantasy world where Zoe still lived, or a part of her did, in the heart that now beat in Sarah's chest.

For everyone, mentally and emotionally, that was an unhealthy fairy tale.

Chapter Ten

The next several days were surreal.

One afternoon, Nana brought a batch of snicker doodles she'd baked to the house, Zoe's "favorite" cookie. After a shopping trip to Shelby with a friend, she brought Sarah a turquoise tank top with a scalloped, scooped neckline.

"Zoe always looked good in turquoise," Grace said with a large dose of nostalgia. "I thought you might like something cool to wear on these warm days."

The brushed cotton fabric felt soft in Sarah's hands; the style was impossible for her to wear.

"It's very thoughtful of you to think of me." She handed the top back to Grace. "I really don't wear tank tops."

Grace's eyes widened in surprise. "Why on earth not? You have a lovely figure and the color is perfect for you."

Sarah took Grace's hand. "Look at me, Grace. You know I had major surgery, a heart transplant. I have a scar from my breastbone to my belly button. I'd be embarrassed to wear something that showed my scar."

Her eyes blinked a half-dozen times in rapid succession. "Yes, of course, what was I thinking?"

"You were thinking of your daughter. I'm *not* your daughter. I'm Sarah Barkley from Seattle. You know that, don't you?"

Grace withdrew her hand and stood up to her full five feet three inches. "Of course I know that. Whatever you may think of me, I'm not a ninny." She whirled and marched out of the house, her back as straight as a fence post.

Sighing, Sarah went back to folding the clothes that she'd taken out of the dryer. She hadn't handled that very well. But she desperately wanted Grace to face reality. Her daughter, the daughter she had loved and raised, was dead.

Zoe was never coming back.

Grace wasn't the only person who'd been acting strangely this week. Since the picnic, there'd been something different about Kurt.

Any number of times, Sarah had caught him looking at her with a singular glint in his eye. Masculine interest? Or curiosity? She couldn't tell.

In either case, the glances he'd sent in her direction had unnerved her. Once she'd even dropped a glass on the kitchen floor. He'd hurried to help her pick up the broken shards of glass, giving her another her one of those looks.

She'd been left breathless and with a bad case of palpitations that had nothing to do with heart failure.

The night before the county hearing on the Western Region Cattle Feeding permit, Kurt sat at his desk, so frustrated with his computer he was ready to throw it out the window.

He gritted his teeth and leaned back in his chair, closing his eyes. Ever since the picnic, he hadn't been able to concentrate. The image of Sarah kept popping into his mind—the way her silky hair skimmed her chin, the soft curve of her lips, the sparkle in her eyes when something amused her.

He'd had other thoughts, too. Thoughts he hadn't been able to articulate, yet they continued to haunt both his waking hours and his dreams.

Opening his eyes, he sat forward again. Maybe Sarah could figure out what he was doing wrong on the computer.

He found Sarah in the living room, sitting on the couch, her legs curled up under her, reading her Bible.

Kurt felt a stab of…what? Envy? Or regret that she was so comfortable with her faith and he had lost his?

He cleared his throat. "Excuse me. I hate to bother you."

Keeping her place, she looked up and smiled. "No bother. What do you need?"

"A computer guru, or at least someone who can help me print out copies of my statement to the county and backup material for tomorrow's hearing."

She used a blue ribbon to mark the page where she'd been reading and closed the Bible, setting it on the end table. "That shouldn't be a problem. Let me see what I can do."

In his office, she sat in his chair. Kurt stood behind her, peering over her shoulder at the computer screen as she worked. He'd noticed lately that her hair had a faint scent of citrus. A surprisingly provocative fragrance that made him think of fresh laundry hanging on an old-fashioned clothesline blowing in a breeze. A fragrance he wanted to capture and put in a bottle so he could enjoy it morning, noon and night.

"How many of these exhibits do you want to print out?" she asked.

"Five of them, plus my statement. I've been trying to combine them into one file but I keep messing up. I get seven copies of my statement and nothing else."

"Okay." Her slender fingers flew over the keyboard, switching from file to file. Her fingernails were short and, despite the gardening she'd been doing lately, well trimmed.

"There, I think I've got it." She looked up and he could see the reflection of the overhead light in her blue eyes. "Would you like me to print out one copy to see if I've got it right?"

"Sure." He forced the word past the tightness in his throat.

She held his gaze for a moment, and he had the uncanny urge to stroke her cheek with his fingertips, to feel the softness of her flesh. In the weeks that she'd been here, the Montana sun had deepened the color of her skin from creamy-smooth to a ripe, golden peach he hungered to touch.

She blinked and broke eye contact, turning back to the computer. A few more keystrokes and the printer started to spit out sheets of paper.

Forcing himself to step away, to distance himself from the scent of citrus he found so enticing, Kurt retrieved the papers from the printer as they appeared.

Nodding, he glanced through the presentation. Everything he wanted seemed to be there. "I don't know what I was doing wrong or what you did, but this looks good."

"Wasn't too hard, really. I just started over and moved everything into a new file. You want me to print out the rest of the copies?"

"That'd be great. Thanks." He sat on the edge of the desk as the printer went to work again. "All I have to do tomorrow is convince our honorable commissioners that Western Region has a history of messing up the environment wherever they operate a feeding program. Therefore, they shouldn't be granted a permit on my neighbor's property."

"You can do it. I'm sure you can. You'll make a good case, they'll see that."

Kurt wasn't so sure. The three county commissioners had a lot of contacts in the business community as well as ranching. Sometimes it was hard to know which way the wind would blow.

An inspiration struck him, a way to spend the better part of the day with Sarah. "How 'bout you coming along tomorrow to give me moral support? Western Region is bound to bring their big guns in to counter my arguments. It'd be nice to know someone there was on my side."

She pondered his question a moment. "I'd like to come, but what about the children? Who'd keep an eye on them?"

"Maybe they can arrange to hang out with one of their friends."

"All right." She seemed pleased with that arrangement.

"They can call their friends first thing in the morning. If it all works out, I'll come along to be your cheering section."

Feeling like a kid who'd been granted his deepest wish, Kurt nearly pumped his fist in the air.

The county commissioners met in the county health department conference room at noon. The room had seating for fewer than fifty people and was only half full when Sarah and Kurt arrived. Kurt handed copies of his statement and backup materials to the clerk, and they found chairs near the front.

Sarah had worn the one quasi-business outfit she'd brought along, a straight gray skirt, white blouse and navy blazer. From her perspective, Kurt looked quite dashing in his yoked Western shirt with a bolo tie, slacks and dressy boots.

Kurt leaned toward her. "Those three guys in pinstripe suits have to be from Western Region, probably from the Cheyenne headquarters." He gestured toward the men in the front row. "I'm betting attorneys."

Sarah agreed, though she thought they had the look of hatchet men rather than members of the bar. Anxiety knotted in her stomach. She didn't want Kurt to lose his case.

As the meeting got under way, she studied the three county commissioners, all of them slightly overweight, as if they'd spent too much time on the chicken-and-pea-dinner speaking circuit with their constituents. Dressed casually, they wore no jackets or ties and had rolled their shirtsleeves up. She sensed they'd all grown up around Shelby and knew almost everyone in the county.

She hoped their local ties to community paid off for Kurt, not for the big out-of-town moneyed interests.

The commission chairman announced, "The next item of business is a request for a feed lot permit on property owned by Ezra Stone and leased to Western Region Cattle Feeding." He looked toward the three businessmen in the front row. "We'll hear from Western Region first. Then, if there are any objections, we'll allow time for those."

The company representative who stood at the podium was smooth, Sarah had to give him that.

With a professional PowerPoint presentation, he covered all the economic benefits to the community that would flow from issuing a permit for the feed lot, including increased taxes to the county and employment opportunities. He failed to mention any negatives about the company's past performance and frequent violations of environmental regulations.

When the gentleman completed his remarks and sat down, Kurt whispered, "How do I beat a pro like that? He made it sound like Western Region is as pure as a summer sunrise."

She squeezed his hand. "You beat him with the facts, Kurt. You know they'll destroy your land. Tell the commissioners the truth."

He took a deep breath, walked to the podium and introduced himself.

As he spoke, a sense of pride grew in Sarah's chest. He was forceful without being confrontational. He cited case after case where Western Region had failed in their obligations to the land owners and the communities.

When Kurt thanked the commissioners for their

attention, Sarah knew he would have convinced her of the truth. Now it was up to the three elected officials sitting at the front of the conference room.

The one on the right spoke up. "My dad and grand-dad ran cattle over Sweet Grass Valley way. Water was always a problem. They dug more dry wells than I care to remember." He glanced pointedly at the three company representatives. "From what Mr. Ryder has told us, chances are pretty near one hundred percent your operation on Stone's land would pollute Ryder's water table and make a whole section of his land unusable for cattle."

He turned to the commission chairman. "Peter, unless we get a whole lot more assurances and over-sight for their operation, I have to vote against issuing the permit."

Sarah grabbed Kurt's arm. He'd done it! He'd convinced the commissioners—

"Aren't you convicting Western Region before they've committed any crime?" the commissioner on the left said. "We sure could use the increase in taxes they'd pay and the jobs they'd bring into the county."

Air escaped Sarah's lungs. She wanted to leap to her feet and tell the commissioner he couldn't do that. Couldn't vote for granting the permit that would ruin Kurt's land.

The commission chairman tapped his gavel to quiet the murmured comments buzzing around the room.

"Looks like it's up to me to break the tie," he said. "In all honesty, I'm surprised our county staff didn't research Western Region more carefully. Mr. Ryder took the time to discover their feed-lot business practices, and I'm grateful he did."

Kurt took Sarah's hand. "Should I tell 'em it was you?"

She gave a quick shake of her head, pleased he wanted her to share the credit for the report he'd put together.

"But knowing that now," the chairman continued, "means I can't, in good conscience, vote to approve the permit with its present parameters."

Yes! Sarah grinned at Kurt.

"If you gentlemen would like to resubmit your request, I'd suggest you build in plenty of government oversight and mitigating measures so that Mr. Ryder's property is not negatively impacted. We'll take a vote now."

The roll call went as expected. Kurt won, two-to-one.

As soon as they could make their exit, Kurt hustled Sarah out of the meeting room and to his truck. The sun beating down on the vehicle had turned the truck cab into an oven. Kurt turned on the air conditioner. Sitting sideways facing her, his smile was as broad as a Montana sky.

"We did it," he said. "*You* did it. Without you—"

"You were magnificent. They couldn't vote against you, not after they learned the truth."

His eyes lasered in on hers. Her heart rate skipped a beat as he leaned forward. She felt herself moving toward him. Wanting him closer. Wanting…

His lips covered hers, at first tentative then with more feeling. She responded in kind. Emotion rose in her chest. And joy. It felt so right, so perfect, to be kissing Kurt.

He reminded her of the great outdoors, a combination of rugged individualism and masculine pride. The sensation sent her head spinning and her heart pounding. Her breathing labored and she felt as though she was standing on a high mountain where the air was too thin to sustain any rational thought.

His fingertips caressed her cheek. She threaded her fingers through his hair, the strands damp from the heat of the day.

When he finally broke the kiss, she inhaled deeply. Her body trembled.

"I've been wanting to do that since the picnic." His hoarse voice was barely a whisper.

"You have?" She'd been thinking similar thoughts but hadn't dared to pursue them.

"Yeah." He hooked a few strands of her hair behind her ear. "We make a good team, Sarah."

She smiled. "You go into battle and I'm your backup."

"More than that. Much more." He touched his lips to hers again, a brief kiss that sent shivers of desire through her body. "I've been thinking…" He hesitated, visibly searching for the words he wanted. "I think you and I…I know this isn't the most romantic place for this, or maybe not even the right time, but I've developed feelings for you. I think we might have a future together."

Shock snapped her head back. A future? Together? She hadn't expected, hadn't dared to hope, had only dreamed he might…

And yet she knew in her soul, a painful reality, that a future with Kurt was an impossibility. Not that she hadn't grown to care about him. Maybe even love him. But there was one obstacle she couldn't ignore.

"I'm sorry, Kurt. So very sorry." Tears of regret, of longing, burned in her eyes. "I don't think that's possible."

Chapter Eleven

Like a horse that had kicked him in the ribs, Sarah's rejection of him drove the air from Kurt's lungs. His chest ached. Drawing a single breath took all of his strength.

"You don't have to decide now." His throat tightened, making the words sound ragged to his own ears as he backtracked to save face. He wasn't going to beg. "My timing's off. I shouldn't have rushed you."

"That's not why I don't think it will work." She raised her hand as though to touch his face, then dropped her hand back to her lap.

"I know we haven't known each other long." He'd grown up with Zoe. Why would he expect any woman to agree to marry him when they'd only met a few weeks ago? "I can wait. We'll spend more time together getting to know each other better. I care for you, Sarah. Very much. I think you care about me."

Her eyes softened, glistening with new tears. "I do care about you, Kurt."

"And you get along great with my kids. It was a little rough there at first with Beth, but she's come along."

"Your children are wonderful. You're very lucky to have them. I envy you."

He shifted his position and stared out the windshield. Ripples of heat rose off the asphalt parking lot. Disappointment and a sense of futility weighed his spirit down like someone had handed him an anvil to carry.

"I guess I understand why you wouldn't want to live on the Rocking R permanently. It's okay for a summer maybe, but I imagine you're already missing city life." Zoe had, and she'd never lived anywhere except Sweet Grass Valley.

"That's not why I don't think that us as a couple is a good idea."

He turned his head. "Okay, then why not?"

"My faith is extremely important to me, Kurt. I'm sure you're aware I read my Bible and go to church whenever I can."

"Hey, that's fine by me. I'd never stop you from going to church or whatever you wanted to do. I didn't stop Beth when she wanted to go, did I?"

"No, you didn't. But I believe in marriage both the husband and wife should share the same faith in the Lord. You've lost your faith, Kurt."

A muscle clenched in his jaw and he gripped the steering wheel with both hands. "So what if I've lost my faith in God? I have my reasons. But if it's that important to you, I'll go to church with you."

"It's not the same," she said, her tone filled with a regret he couldn't understand. "I'm sorry."

"Then I guess there's no point in talking about it."

When she remained silent, he cranked the key and headed home. *No point at all.*

* * *

After a few days, Sarah knew something had to change.

Kurt had been avoiding her. That hurt almost more than she could bear. She ached with the loss of his presence, his deep voice, the quick flash of his smile. His rare moments of laughter.

The memory of his kiss tormented her.

She prayed for a miracle, for God to take matters into his own hands. To touch Kurt's heart.

When that didn't happen, she went about her business of caring for his children. Caring for them when they were at home, which wasn't all that often.

Friday rolled around. She took Dr. Zoom to the hospital to entertain the children. That evening she served the family a chicken-and-noodle casserole, whole-wheat bread and a fresh green salad for dinner.

She couldn't let this tension between her and Kurt continue any longer. With a little extra effort, she thought she could break through the wall he'd built around himself and do something good for the children at the same time.

She sat down at the table, bowed her head for a silent grace, then looked up.

"It seems to me you two children spend a lot of your time at your friends' houses." She glanced at Toby and Beth. "I think it would be a nice idea if you reciprocated by having a party for them here at the ranch."

Kurt frowned at her from across the table, but said nothing.

"What kind of a party?" Toby asked. "It's not anybody's birthday."

"It doesn't need to be a special occasion. You invite your friends and I can help you organize games. Maybe a treasure hunt in the barn. Or some sort of riding contest. You'd get to pick."

"One time at Billy's he had a blindfolded calf-roping contest. Most of the guys fell off their horses and the calves got away."

That sounded a little dangerous to Sarah, but she let it go for the moment.

"Beth, do you think your friends would enjoy face painting? I could get extra supplies and show them a few tricks. Then you could paint each other's faces."

The girl perked up. "Yeah, they'd like it better than blind calf roping."

"None of her dumb friends are gonna paint my face," Toby announced.

"They wouldn't want to, gopher boy," Beth countered in a teasing voice.

Sarah swallowed a laugh. "Toby, you could entertain everyone with your ventriloquism. How does that sound?" She'd helped Toby create a sock dummy with a big red mouth, a purple tongue hanging out and green button eyes, which he named Mervyn the Monster.

He shrunk down in his chair. "That sounds scary. I've never shown anybody—"

"You're becoming quite skilled, Toby. I think you're ready for prime time."

He shrugged, then shoveled two quick bites of casserole into his mouth. "Okay," he mumbled. "But you gotta do Dr. Zoom, too. I'm not gonna get up in front of the guys all alone."

Sarah was happy to agree to that condition. "We can serve watermelon, ice cream and cake—"

"I think Nana would make a cake for us," Beth said.

"Dad's got a hand-cranked ice-cream maker we used to use a lot," Toby offered. "If you can get that out, Dad, the guys will crank the wheel."

"Good idea, son." Although Kurt had remained silent until now, he seemed to be on board with the party idea.

They set the date for a week from Saturday.

The following morning shortly after breakfast, Sarah heard banging and clanking on the back porch. She followed the noise to find out what was going on.

Kneeling on the porch and muttering under his breath, Kurt appeared to be in a wrestling match with an ancient ice-cream maker.

Shoving it aside, he muttered, "Worthless!"

"It might make a big hit on *Antiques Roadshow,*" she suggested.

His head jerked up. When he saw her, a reluctant smile tilted his lips. "You might be right. This thing has been in the family since I was a kid."

"It looks like it served you well."

"Yeah." He picked up the ice-cream maker and stood, his expression somber. "Nothing lasts forever."

Her breath hitched. Was he talking about more than the ice-cream maker? Suddenly, he looked vulnerable. She wanted to hold him, feel his arms around her. But she couldn't do that. She didn't dare.

"Kurt, I'm sorry if I've hurt you. I didn't mean to."

"Hey, no sweat." He held up the ice-cream maker. "I'll order an electric one this time. It'll do a better job and won't be such hard work."

He walked off the porch toward the barn and never looked back.

Sarah wasn't that strong. No matter where she went or how long she lived, she'd always look back on this summer and remember how she'd fallen in love.

Preparations for the party kept everyone busy the following week.

Beth and Sarah worked on activities for the girls—Beth had invited a dozen of her friends—and they selected goodies for the treasure hunt in the barn.

Toby wanted to take his buddies out to the swimming hole, but Kurt convinced him that excursion would be better done some other day. So they decided on blindfolded calf roping, but not from a horse. The boys would keep their feet firmly on terra firma. Or so Sarah hoped.

When Toby wasn't working with his dad, he rehearsed for Mervyn the Monster's big performance with Sarah or up in his room.

Nana promised to do her part by providing two sheet cakes, one strawberry and one chocolate.

"I'd love to help out," Grace had announced. "Zoe loved hosting parties. Usually for adults, though. Too many children made her nervous."

In contrast, Sarah was looking forward to the party because so many youngsters planned to attend. As a child who was almost constantly in ill health, Sarah had been allowed to attend few parties. Come Saturday, she planned to make up for that.

On Friday, she volunteered at the hospital with Dr. Zoom. When she returned home, makeshift tables made of plywood resting on saw horses were arranged beneath the tree in the backyard. Paper table covers and matching plates were ready in the laundry room to be taken outside in the morning. Treasures had been hidden in the barn, little trinkets and candies that didn't cost much but would be fun to discover. Kurt had brought two calves in from the north section to serve as subjects for the calf-roping contest.

The only possible hitch in their plans came from the weatherman. He predicted Saturday afternoon thunderstorms throughout the area.

"If that happens," Kurt said, "we'll move the boys into the barn and the girls can come inside. It'll be fine."

Excitement kept Sarah awake most of Friday night, and she woke feeling extra tired and a little achy. Ignoring the feeling, she dressed and prepared for the party.

A little after noon, carloads of youngsters began arriving. She wished she'd thought to get them all name tags so she could tell one child from another. She'd remember that next time, she thought before realizing there wasn't likely to be a next time.

The end of summer was approaching all too swiftly. She'd be gone soon. Gone from the Rocking R. Gone from Kurt.

The thought brought an ache to her chest and sent a shudder down her spine. She'd miss Kurt and his children. More than she dared to admit even to herself.

Blinking away the sudden burn of tears, she went outside to greet the arriving guests.

One of the mothers approached her. "Hi, I'm Jayne Morgan, Billy's mom. All these boys can be quite a handful. Would you like me to hang around and help out?"

"If you'd like to stay, I'd love to have you. The more helping hands the better." Only half of the boys had arrived so far and it already looked like a gang of wild creatures had invaded the Rocking R Ranch. The girls were much more subdued, though their giggles were so high-pitched and shrill, it sounded like a flock of screaming eagles had joined the party.

She wondered if she'd been that silly as a preteen. She supposed she had wanted to be even if her mother hadn't approved.

By one-thirty, Sarah had developed a headache and began to wonder if the party had been such a great idea after all. Not that the youngsters weren't having a good time. They were. But she felt both drained of energy and flushed.

That wasn't like her. She'd been extraordinarily healthy since her surgery. All those pills were doing their job.

So far, the weatherman's clouds had remained at a distance. She hoped it stayed that way until after the party.

Nana, Beth and Jayne Morgan served the cake, and Kurt handled the ice cream while Sarah went inside to get Dr. Zoom. She and Toby planned to perform while the youngsters ate their dessert.

She picked up her tote bag, glanced in the mirror

and frowned. Overnight she'd grown dark bags under her eyes. Her cheeks looked puffy. Lack of sleep, she told herself, and went back out to the party. She blamed nerves for the slight case of nausea unsettling her stomach.

Kurt had constructed a small, foot-high stage for them between the two makeshift tables and had placed two chairs in position.

"I'm kind of scared," Toby said under his breath.

"You'll be fine," she told him, taking her seat. "Just remember to speak loudly enough so they can all hear you." She winked and pulled Dr. Zoom out of her tote.

"Whoa! Vhat are all deez kids doing here?" Dr. Zoom asked, looking around.

Toby held up Mervyn and stuck him in Dr. Zoom's face and growled in Mervyn's voice. *"They're having a party, dummy. And they didn't invite us."*

"Vhy would they invite you? Nobody vants a monster at their party."

Slowly the youngsters began to realize something was happening. As Mervyn and Dr. Zoom carried on their nonsensical conversation, they began to listen.

"Hey, doc, knock-knock," Mervyn began. *"Who's there?"*

"I don't know, monster. Who's there?"

"Boy, you must be a real dummy. Anybody can see it's me, Mervyn the Monster."

Sarah twirled Dr. Zoom's head around as though he was going to attack the monster. *"Who you calling a dummy, huh? Look in the mirror, vhy don't ya?"*

As Dr. Zoom and the monster sparred, Sarah began

to feel even worse than when she'd gone into the house. Maybe it was the heat added to her lack of sleep. The clouds were approaching, too. She could see streaks of lightning slicing through the black sky.

She shouldn't feel this bad. Fatigued. Nauseous. Flushed. Those were symptoms the doctor had told her to watch for. Potentially fatal symptoms...

"You're so smart, doc. Tell me what you get from a pampered cow?" the monster asked, followed by laughter from their audience.

Sarah had trouble concentrating. Her stomach roiled like the oncoming clouds and she felt breathless. *"You get..."* Her body starting shaking. *"...spoiled milk."*

Like a window shade being pulled down, everything turned dark. She felt herself sliding off her chair in slow motion.

The next thing she knew she was on the ground looking up at Kurt as big, round drops of rain began to fall on her face. Toby stood behind his father, his concerned expression a twin to Kurt's deeply furrowed forehead.

Why now, Lord? Why now?

Kurt touched her forehead. "You're burning up with fever. You must be coming down with something."

"No." She licked her lips. Her throat was so dry, she barely had any moisture in her mouth at all. "My heart. My body's rejecting my heart."

Panic slammed into Kurt's gut. *She was rejecting Zoe's heart?* He couldn't let that happen. He couldn't lose Sarah, too.

"Dad!" Beth had raced to Sarah's side the moment she'd collapsed. "What's she saying?"

He forced himself to remain calm, act calm, in spite of the churning in his belly and his urge to scream out his anger. His anger at God. Why would a benevolent God allow this to happen again?

"It'll be all right, honey," he said to Beth. "I'm going to take her to the Shelby hospital. She'll be all right," he repeated like a mantra.

Sarah's hand touched his cheek. "I'll be fine. There's a new cardiologist at…" Her hand fell to her side. "Tell him to call my Seattle doctor. His name's…"

"I'll find him, sweetheart." He'd find her doctor if he had to call every cardiologist in Seattle. In the whole country, if that's what it took.

Slipping his hands under Sarah's slender body, he lifted her in his arms. "Grace, can you and Jayne take care of the kids? I'm taking Sarah to the hospital."

Wide-eyed and red faced, Grace appeared on the verge of hysteria. "This can't be happening. Not again. My poor baby." Her voice rose to a screech.

Beth wrapped her arm around her grandmother. "Come on, Nana. Let's go inside. I'll make you some tea." She met Kurt's eyes, and he realized what a remarkable young lady she was becoming.

He nodded in approval.

Jayne Morgan stepped forward and shooed the children away from Kurt. "Okay, kids. No more gawking. Everything's under control. Let's get in out of the rain before you all get drenched. We're going to play charades in the barn till your folks come to pick you up, and I think the girls will beat the boys."

"No way!" the boys shouted, rising to the challenge.

Kurt wasn't interested in who won the charade game. He knew he had to get Sarah to the hospital fast.

He lifted her into the truck cab and buckled her in. "Stay with me, sweetheart. Stay with me."

Racing around to the driver's side, he leaped into the truck, cranked over the engine and barreled down the driveway. A trail of dust rose behind him. Rain splattered on the windshield.

Once on the highway, he floor-boarded the gas. He hoped a cop would spot him and give him an escort to the hospital. But no such luck. What he got instead was a downpour that the wipers could barely handle and gusts of wind that threatened to push him into the ditch.

He felt the warmth of Sarah's palm on his thigh. He risked a glance and saw that her fingernails were tinged in blue.

"Slow down, Kurt," she whispered. "It won't do anyone any good if we're both killed in a crash."

He eased his foot off the accelerator. She was right. But the terror of losing her was worse than the thought of dying himself. He hadn't realized until now how much he loved her. His pride hadn't allowed him to admit the depth of his feelings to himself, much less to Sarah.

And now, one way or another, he was going to lose her.

He started to pray. He'd prayed for Zoe's life and God had failed him. He had to try again. Maybe this time…

The downpour had kept people inside waiting for the storm to pass and leaving the streets of Shelby empty of traffic. Kurt sped through a blinking red light and pulled into the hospital parking lot. He drove up to the Emergency entrance, hit his horn to alert the staff, and jumped down from the truck.

In a matter of seconds, a torrent of rain had drenched him.

A nurse in her mid-forties and a young orderly pushing a gurney met him at the passenger door. He yanked it open.

"What's the patient's name and problem?" the nurse asked, all business.

He unbuckled Sarah. "Sarah Barkley. She's a heart-transplant recipient." His breath came in anxious gulps as he lifted her from the truck and placed her on the gurney, trying to shield her from the rain. "She's rejecting her heart."

The nurse gaped at him, momentarily stunned.

Sarah struggled to speak. "Call Dr. Allan Jennings. Seattle."

That broke through the nurse's temporary paralysis. "Let's get her into E.R., stat. Hook her up to oxygen." She and the orderly wheeled Sarah into the hospital, Kurt following behind at a near run. "What meds is she on?" the nurse asked over her shoulder.

Kurt didn't know and Sarah wasn't able to answer.

"I'll call home and get a list." He pulled out his cell phone and speed dialed his house, praying that someone was inside to answer.

As the nurse passed the Emergency Room reception desk she told the clerk, "Get Dr. Trevor in here in a hurry. Tell him we've got an organ rejection for him."

Listening to the ring of his home phone, Kurt tried to

follow Sarah beyond the door to the Emergency Room but the clerk stopped him.

"I'm sorry, sir. You'll have to wait out here for now. They'll let me know when they're ready for you."

Grace picked up the phone. "Hello?"

"Grace, I'm at the hospital." He kept his eye on the closed door as if he had X-ray vision and could see through the wood. See into that place where they'd taken Sarah.

"Is Sarah all right? We're all worried sick about her. Beth and Toby, everyone."

"I don't know." And he didn't have time to chat. "I want you to go into Sarah's room and find all of her medicine bottles. They want to know what meds she's taking."

He snatched a piece of paper from the clerk's desk and a pen. Pacing, he waited for Grace to return. Water dripped from his hair onto the floor.

Outside, a flash of lightning lit up the sky. An instant later, a thunder clap shook the building and the overhead lights flickered. Kurt hoped to goodness the hospital had a backup generator.

"I've got the bottles," Grace said in his ear. "I'm going to have to spell the names of the medicines. Most of them I couldn't possibly pronounce."

"Go ahead." He printed the medications as she spelled them out. Words he'd never heard of. Meds that had kept Sarah alive. Until now.

When he'd finished the list, he handed it to the clerk. "The nurse wanted this in a hurry."

She glanced at what he'd written. "I'll get it to her right away."

She vanished beyond the door into the Emergency Room. When she reappeared, she gave him what he took as an encouraging smile.

Then there was nothing left for him to do but wait.

Chapter Twelve

Time passed with the speed of a desert tortoise.

Kurt had moved his truck away from the emergency entrance, then hurried back to the hospital lobby. There'd been no need to rush.

He picked up a newspaper he found abandoned on one of several orange, molded plastic, miserably uncomfortable chairs. When he tried to read, his eyes blurred and he couldn't decipher the words. He switched to staring at an overhead TV but the news didn't hold his attention.

He kept having flashbacks to the hospital where Zoe had died. Shelby Community Hospital might be smaller than the one where he waited a year ago, but there were still patients' loved ones who passed through the lobby with the look of strain and fear on their faces.

He imagined his grim expression was the same.

Every time the door opened to the Emergency Room, his heart lurched. But no one came to talk to him.

After what seemed like an interminable amount of time, a doctor who looked like he was right out of med school strolled out into the lobby. Blond, about six feet tall and slender, he wore a white jacket over a Broncos

T-shirt, jeans and cowboy boots. A stethoscope hung half out of his jacket pocket.

"Mr. Ryder?" he asked.

Kurt jumped to his feet. "That's me. How's Sarah?"

"Doing as well as can be expected."

Kurt's heart sank. That didn't sound good.

The doctor extended his hand. "I'm Dr. Trevor. I'll be treating Ms. Barkley while she's here at the hospital."

"I don't mean to insult you, but how much experience do you have with heart-transplant patients?" He'd have a qualified doctor flown in to Shelby, or get a medevac plane to take Sarah to a major hospital, if that's what it took to get her back on her feet again.

The doctor smiled. "No insult taken, Mr. Ryder. If you're asking if I'm a heart surgeon, the answer is no. But I'm a board-certified cardiac specialist and I've talked to Dr. Jennings in Seattle, Ms. Barkley's surgeon. Together I think we can manage her condition."

"Just manage? Not fix?"

"She's in very critical condition, Mr. Ryder. In order to prevent organ rejection, we have to suppress her immune system. That makes her vulnerable to infection. We'll be running tests in the morning to see exactly what's happening. Dr. Jennings and I are both hoping the rejection is reversible."

"And if it's not?" Fear clawed at his belly and he tried to tamp it down.

"Dr. Jennings tells me Ms. Barkley is a strong and very determined young woman. Let's wait for the test results before we make any decisions about the next step."

Kurt nodded, although he would have felt better if the doctor had told him Sarah was going to be fine. But a lie wouldn't have done him or Sarah any good.

"I do feel it necessary that I warn you," the doctor continued, "the outcome may not be as positive as we'd like. If her current heart continues to fail and her condition worsens, she may need a second transplant."

Kurt's knees nearly buckled.

"May I see her?" Grimacing, he rubbed the back of his neck as though he could erase the doctor's words.

"Yes, briefly. I've moved her to the Intensive Care Unit. She'll get the best care there. They allow family members a ten-minute visit every hour."

Kurt didn't correct the doctor. As far as Kurt was concerned, he was Sarah's family. He was all Sarah had. He'd knock down a few doors if that was the only way he could see her.

The doctor directed him to the ICU, located on the second floor. He had to wait at a locked door until a nurse admitted him to the unit. The smell of medication and antiseptic mixed in the cool, dry air, forcing him to breathe through his mouth and fight off memories of Zoe's last days.

After making him put on a paper gown over his clothes, the nurse led him to a glass cubicle where Sarah lay propped up in a hospital bed. A bunch of wires and tubes were attached to her, and she was getting oxygen through her nose. An overhead monitor kept track of her vital signs.

Dread filled his chest as he approached Sarah. He took her hand and found it dry and limp. When he squeezed, she didn't respond.

"Please, Sarah," he whispered, his throat so tight he could barely speak. "Don't die. I don't want to lose you. The kids love you. I know they do." So did Kurt. More than he'd thought possible.

Slowly, she opened her eyes.

"Hi." His voice cracked with emotion.

"Sorry...to ruin the party." She licked her lips, which looked dry.

He held up a cup of water and let her take a sip through the plastic straw.

"You didn't ruin anything," he said. "Everybody's worried about you."

"I'll be...fine. Little setback."

It was crazy that she was trying to reassure him, not the other way around. But he couldn't. Not when she looked so pale, so vulnerable and small in the hospital bed.

Could her body possibly survive another heart transplant?

"They're going to run some tests in the morning," he said.

"I know. Doctors do that a lot."

In her voice he could hear a weary note echoing her years of going through one test after another. How hard it must have been for her as a child, and then as an adult, when her heart started to fail. No wonder she had wanted to get away for a few weeks, leave doctors and hospitals behind. Visit Montana.

Now Kurt had brought her to a new hospital, and the tests would start all over again.

Would God fail her like He had failed Zoe?

The nurse stuck her head into the room. "Time to go now. She needs her rest."

"I'll wait outside," Kurt told Sarah. "They only let me see you for ten minutes at a time."

She squeezed his hand, although she was so weak he could barely feel it. "No, go home. Tell them I'll be fine."

How could he tell them that when he wasn't sure himself? Neither was the doctor. "I can call them."

"No, go home," she ordered, the bravest woman he'd ever known. "Take care of your family. Tomorrow." She struggled to draw enough breath to speak. "The doctor will know more."

The nurse grew impatient, and Kurt knew he'd have to leave.

Bending over, he brushed a kiss to Sarah's lips, so soft and warm he wanted to linger.

He wanted to tell her that he loved her, but what good would that do?

Most of all, he wanted her to be well.

In the hospital parking lot, he sat hunched behind the steering wheel of his truck for a long time. Helplessness and futility stalked him. He longed for the power to help Sarah. If it were possible, he'd give her his heart. Let his heart beat inside her chest and keep her alive.

Resting his head on the steering wheel, tears came. He couldn't stop them. Didn't try.

His chest heaved with sobs that rose from deep in his soul. He ached from the pain that ripped through him. Found nowhere to go for solace to ease the anguish. "Sarah, I need you. Don't leave me."

Almost dark when Kurt got back to the ranch, the

storm had passed and all the lights were on in the house.

He pulled up near the back door. Toby was the first one on the porch to greet him, quickly followed by Beth and Grace. Even ol' Rudy came out of the barn to find out what was going on.

Kurt's children pummeled him with questions.

"Is Sarah okay?"

"What happened to her?"

"Are they gonna give her a new heart?"

"Why did Mom's heart quit?"

"Is Sarah gonna die?"

"No!" Kurt swallowed hard and pressed his way past the children. He couldn't, wouldn't tell them how perilous her condition was. He'd lie because he couldn't, wouldn't face the truth. Not until he had to. "She's going to be fine. The doctor's doing some tests in the morning and then he'll know what he has to do next."

He halted in the middle of the kitchen, gathering his kids to his side, wrapping an arm around each of them. He met Grace's concerned gaze. "Sarah doesn't want you to worry. She's a strong woman. We all know that. So she'll be fine in no time."

"Word has spread about Sarah and people have been calling." A tremor shook Grace's voice. "They're all worried about her. Bonnie Sue from the diner. Pastor Hoffman and Alexis. They're all saying prayers for her."

If Kurt thought prayers would work, he'd get down on his knees and stay there until Sarah came back home. Home to his ranch.

"I'm going to say a prayer for her, too," Beth said.

Smoothing his daughter's hair, Kurt figured her prayer couldn't hurt and might make Beth feel like she was helping.

His prayers hadn't helped Zoe.

Not hungry for the dinner Grace offered, Kurt went out to the barn to get the horses settled for the night. By rote, he tossed hay into the stalls, added oats to their feed bags.

Later he tried to sleep, but he barely closed his eyes all night, and he was up at first light. He drove back to Shelby. As he was entering the hospital, Pastor Hoffman was coming out.

"Hello, Kurt. Good to see you," the older man said.

"Pastor." Kurt took the hand that was offered.

"I've just come from seeing Sarah. I came early so I could get back in time to give my sermon, not that the congregation couldn't use a break from my weekly harangues."

Kurt didn't much care about his sermons one way or another. "How is she?"

"Alert but weak. In good spirits, though. She has an amazing faith, Kurt. I think she'll pull through."

"I hope so." Kurt started to step away.

"They just took her for some tests," the pastor said. "She'll be sorry she missed you."

"I'll wait."

The pastor placed a hand on Kurt's shoulder. "If you want to talk later, call me. I can come back to the hospital. Or you can come to the parsonage. I should be there all afternoon."

Kurt shook his head. "No, I'm fine. Thanks."

He walked upstairs to the ICU. Sarah wasn't there. He

told the nurse he'd wait and asked her to let Dr. Trevor know he was there.

Then he sat down on a pale green couch in the ICU waiting room and began his vigil.

When Dr. Trevor came out of the ICU, he was wearing green scrubs and something like a shower cap covered his hair. His expression was grim.

A spurt of fear shot Kurt to his feet. "What happened?"

"We took her into the O.R. this morning and performed a myocardial biopsy. The results were inconclusive."

"What does that mean?" Kurt didn't understand myocardial anything but inconclusive wasn't the word he'd been hoping for.

"It means we're not sure if the rejection Sarah is experiencing can be reversed. We'll keep watching and waiting and hoping her body can heal quickly. If not…"

The tightness in Kurt's chest nearly exploded.

"We're increasing her meds," the doctor explained. "Stopping the infection that caused the rejection is critical at this juncture. If we can do that, her prognosis improves considerably."

"Keep her inside a sterile bubble if that's what she needs."

The doctor chuckled. "Maintaining her in an ICU setting should be sufficient." His expression turned sentimental. "You're a lucky man, Mr. Ryder, to have such a tough, determined woman love you so deeply. She seems more worried about you and your family than herself."

The doctor's revelation stunned Kurt. *Sarah loved him?* If that was true, why had she not wanted a relationship with him? Had she had a change of heart?

He shook his head. Maybe he just plain didn't understand women.

"There's one other thing I did at Sarah's insistence," the doctor said. "I consulted with Dr. Jennings and your late wife's physician here in Shelby. Sarah was not the recipient of Zoe's heart."

As though his legs had been yanked out from under him, Kurt sat down hard on the couch.

"Not Zoe's heart?" he questioned, baffled by the doctor's announcement. "That's the whole reason she came to Sweet Grass Valley." To the Rocking R Ranch.

"It doesn't matter. Your late wife's blood type wouldn't have been compatible with Sarah's. She would have instantly rejected the heart, assuming some doctor was foolish enough to transplant the organ into her body."

Kurt's head spun like he was on a carnival Tilt-A-Whirl. "Then whose heart does she have?"

"I don't know nor does Dr. Jennings. And if we did know, we wouldn't be permitted to reveal that information to you or to Sarah."

"Did you… Does Sarah know?"

"Yes, I told her this morning."

The Tilt-A-Whirl came to a jarring halt. "How did she react?" Was she mentally packing to return to Seattle to start her search for the donor family all over again?

"I'd say surprise was her primary reaction. Plus some concern about you and your family and how you'd respond to the news." He shrugged. "I have to get on with my rounds. If you have any questions, give my office a call and page me. The nurse will let you know when you can visit Sarah."

Kurt stood, his legs still a little shaky. "Thank you, doctor."

"The time for thanks is if and when I can release her and let her go home." Giving Kurt a casual wave, the doctor vanished behind the ICU doorway.

It was a long time before the nurse granted Kurt permission to step into her inner sanctum. She garbed him in a paper gown again.

Not sure what to expect, he approached Sarah with caution.

"Hey, there," he said. "The doctor says you're doing good."

"Liar," she said with the hint of a smile, lifting her hand to him. She still looked pale, and there were bruises of fatigue under her eyes.

He ran his thumb over the back of her hand, her skin smooth and soft and warm. Caressable.

"Did Dr. Trevor—" she drew a breath "—tell you about my heart?"

"You mean that it's not Zoe's?"

She nodded. "Grace, the children. It might upset them." Although she didn't ask, her eyes seemed to be asking him how he was reacting.

"I don't care whose heart is inside your chest. I just want it to keep on beating for a long, long time."

She pursed her lips together. Tears sheened her eyes. "Thank you."

She glanced around the room, then patted the bed next to her. "Sit down. I want to tell you a story."

"The nurse is probably going to throw me out in a minute. You can tell me another time."

When she patted the bed again, he lowered the guardrail and did as she'd asked, then took her hand again.

"Do you know the story of the man who was walking along the beach...with the Lord?"

"I don't think so." He didn't particularly want to hear it now either. He wanted her to rest and get better, not wear herself out by talking.

"I know you think God deserted you. He didn't."

The remembered pain of Zoe's last days stung him for the millionth time but not as painfully as it used to.

"It's like the poem. You're like the man walking on the beach with God. The man saw his past and saw two sets of footprints in the sand during those times that he and the Lord were walking together." Closing her eyes, she rested a minute. "There were other times when there was only one set of footprints. The man asked God... why He'd left him during the worst days of his life."

Kurt focused on Sarah's hand clasped in his. Not on whatever message she was trying to communicate.

"That's when God told him that where he saw only one set of footprints those were the times he was carrying him. He didn't desert you, Kurt. He was there all the time."

"That's hard for me to believe, Sarah."

"I know. But I believe the Lord has carried me much of my life or been right at my side. I believe He brought me here to Sweet Grass Valley, to you, for a reason." She forced a wry smile. "Evidently it wasn't because I had received Zoe's heart."

"Then why?"

"I think you know the answer in your heart, Kurt. But you have to *believe* God has had a hand in it. Please try."

Chapter Thirteen

Kurt waited around to see Sarah again. But the nurse strongly encouraged him to leave. Sarah was sleeping. Let nature and the meds do their work, she told him. Come back later.

So Kurt got in his truck for the drive home.

Sarah wanted him to believe in God and His power. All of his life, he had done just that. He'd gone to church almost every Sunday for as long as he could recall. Like most ranchers, he'd prayed for rain during droughts and prayed the snow wouldn't get too deep for his cattle to find food during hard winters. He prayed for his family, for their health and happiness.

Then Zoe died. He'd prayed as hard as he knew how and God didn't answer.

As though his faith had been no more than an illusion made of papier-mâché, his belief in God's power crumbled.

He didn't know where to find a switch to turn his faith back on.

As he reached Sweet Grass Valley ready to turn toward home, the sun caught the glint of the steeple above Good Shepherd Community Church, reflecting back in his eyes. Squinting, he went past the turn off to the Rocking R.

Instead, he continued down Main Street toward the church.

Sunday service was long over, the parking lot empty.

Kurt pulled up near the white stucco building. The last time he'd stepped inside any church was for Zoe's funeral more than a year ago.

Pastor Hoffman said the door would be open.

Not sure what he'd accomplish, if anything, Kurt climbed out of his truck. The main entrance had arched double doors stained a dark walnut, each decorated with a cross inside an oval. The effect was classic, the message ancient.

He grasped the wooden door handle, worn smooth from the grip of many churchgoers, and pulled the door open.

Light filtered into the church through a stained glass window. A single spotlight focused on a cross on the wall behind the pulpit.

Somehow the silence comforted Kurt as he walked down the side aisle to the front of the church. Two large vases of flowers had been placed on either side of the choir area, scenting the air with a hint of rosebuds, white carnations, purple iris and colorful zinnias.

He slid into a pew and waited. Searching within himself, he tried to find the words he wanted, the words that God would hear coming from him and heed. The words that would make Sarah well again.

Time slipped by bringing memories of Sarah—when

she'd nearly burned down the house trying to barbecue steaks, using the emergency gong to call him home, her help with the hearing before the county commissioners, her endearing routine with Dr. Zoom.

Her collapse at the party yesterday.

Fear crashed in on him as he relived that moment. Fear that squeezed his chest and turned his mouth as dry and parched as a summer drought.

Leaning forward, he gripped the pew in front of him.

Still, the words wouldn't come.

Out of the corner of his eye, Kurt caught a movement. Pastor Hoffman sat down beside him.

"I saw your truck outside," he said. "I'm glad you came."

Kurt shook his head to drive his fears away. "I'm not doing much good here. I can't even remember how to pray." Much less have faith that his prayers would help Sarah.

"It will come back to you, son." The pastor placed his hand on Kurt's shoulder. "Let's start with something you know. We'll pray together."

Hesitantly at first, Kurt joined the pastor in The Lord's Prayer. One word, one phrase at a time, Kurt felt the tightness in his chest ease until they said in unison, "Amen."

The pastor patted his shoulder. "I know after Zoe died, you gave up on the Lord. But He hasn't given up on you. He's still there. If you speak to Him, He'll listen."

Kurt bowed his head again as Pastor Hoffman exited

the pew. He was on his own now. No, that's not what Sarah had told him. The Lord was beside him, even carrying him, when his pain grew too great for him to bear alone.

And so he prayed.

He didn't know how much time passed as he sat there praying, but finally he rose to his feet. He'd drained himself of every prayer he could think of, asking the Lord to help Sarah get well. His body ached with fatigue but the burden of defeat he'd carried for so long seemed lighter.

When he turned to walk up the aisle, he was stunned to see so many people in the church. Close to thirty people, so silent he hadn't heard them entering the nave.

Frowning, he identified Bonnie Sue from the diner, Ezra Stone, his neighbor, Angus from the grocery store, Alexis and Pastor Hoffman sitting together. Ranchers with whom he'd shared good times and bad had driven into town to sit in church with him.

Then he spotted Grace with his two children. Grace hadn't been inside a church for as long as Kurt. Now she was there. Praying for Sarah? Even though she knew Zoe's heart wasn't the one struggling to keep Sarah alive.

As he walked by, his friends reached out to him, taking his hand and whispering their good wishes.

"We're praying for Sarah," Jayne Morgan, Billy's mom, said. "And you."

"She'll pull through."

"Count on the Lord."

"We've all come to love Sarah," Bonnie Sue said in a voice much softer than her usual brash holler across the diner.

Having trouble keeping his emotions in check, he stopped beside Grace. "Thanks for coming and bringing the kids."

"Beth convinced me this is what Sarah would want."

He smiled at his daughter and nodded.

Toby squirmed in his seat. "Beth told me Mervyn the Monster would eat me if I didn't come pray for Sarah. I didn't believe her, but I came anyway."

The boy lifted his shoulders in a "no big deal" gesture. Kurt knew the truth; it was the biggest kind of deal a nine-year-old macho kid could muster.

As he left the church, stepping out into the sunlight, Kurt marveled at the impact Sarah had made on the townspeople in a few short weeks, the friends that she had made.

He shouldn't be surprised, he realized. In the same short period of time, he'd been thrown, as though by a bucking bronco, all the way to his knees in love with her.

Now he had to figure out how to convince her that they were meant to be together. *If* she recovered from this "small setback" as she called her body rejecting her heart.

As he drove to the ranch, he noticed the rainstorm had awakened the landscape, tinting the grass green in nature's rebirth of life.

Rebirth for Sarah was his prayer.

* * *

For the next three days, Kurt rose early to do his chores. Without being asked, both Beth and Toby helped out, and Grace came around to be with the kids when Kurt went to the hospital.

Every day after Kurt visited Sarah in ICU, he went by the church to pray. Every day someone else was there praying for Sarah. He finally asked Grace about that.

"They've set up a vigil for Sarah," Grace explained. "Friends signed up in shifts from six in the morning until nine at night. Almost everybody in town is taking a turn. They did that for Zoe, too."

Kurt hadn't known that. He'd been in Seattle, hospitalized himself for several days, then at Zoe's bedside until he'd made the final decision to let her go.

The fact that so many others had been praying for her both awed and humbled him.

Now they were doing the same for Sarah.

Would the Lord hear their prayers this time?

On the fourth morning, Kurt headed up the stairs to the second floor of the hospital and walked directly to ICU.

The nurse shook her head. "She's not here."

His stomach took a plunge. *Not here? Dear God…* He swallowed painfully before he could speak. "What happened?" She'd looked much better yesterday. He'd hoped…

Instead of her usual stoic, all-business expression, a smile enlivened the nurse's face, making her suddenly look beautiful. "The doctor had Sarah moved to a regular room early this morning. Room 211. She's going to make it."

He would have sent up a cheer louder than the fans at the end of a championship football game but his lungs had compressed on a huge sigh of relief. The room spun crazily. He put out his hand to steady himself.

"Can I see her?" he finally asked.

"I suspect she's been waiting for you all morning."

He whirled and hurried down the hallway. He almost lost his balance when he turned sharply into room 211 and had to abruptly halt. Sitting up in bed, Sarah was the most beautiful sight he'd ever seen. She'd combed her hair and put on some lip gloss. But it was her naturally rosy cheeks and the sparkle in her blue eyes that told him what he needed to know.

She wasn't going to die.

He stepped farther into the room, his focus entirely on Sarah. "Hi, gorgeous."

She chuckled. "You probably say that to all the girls."

"I've never meant it more in my life." When she held out her hand, he took it and bent over to kiss her lips. "The whole town's been praying for you."

Raising her brows, she said, "The whole town?"

"Pretty much. They set up a vigil for you, including Grace and the kids." He drew a breath. "And me."

She squeezed his hand and tears formed in her eyes. "Thank you."

"I don't know whose prayer worked, but somebody's did. You're going to be all right."

"God was listening, Kurt. He heard you."

Maybe Kurt wasn't one hundred percent sure about that but he intended to keep on praying. Hard.

"So the remaining question is, when is Dr. Trevor

going to let you out of this place so you can come home?"

"He wants to keep me here a day or two to make sure I'm stable."

Two days. Kurt could wait that long, although he'd be counting the hours.

"Can the kids come visit you now? They don't let children into ICU."

"Of course. I'd love to see them. Grace, too. Maybe she could pick out some clothes for me to wear when I'm released. Oh, and I really need my cell phone. Tricia Malone, the young lady I told you about who's handling my business this summer, must think I've dropped off the end of the earth by now."

The reminder that Sarah had a home somewhere else and a business of her own stuck in Kurt's throat like he'd swallowed a rusty nail. He had the urge to find her cell and stomp it into little pieces.

Conscious of every steady beat of her heart, of every cleansing breath she drew, Sarah waited the next day for Kurt and his family to visit her.

She'd had her breakfast and a refreshing shower. Though she was weak from so many days in bed, she knew each day she'd regain a little more strength. Soon she'd be taking long walks again.

In Sweet Grass Valley? Or in Seattle?

She heard Beth hushing her brother out in the hallway before Kurt arrived at the door to her room.

"Hope you're decent," he said, grinning. "Because I'm going to have a small riot on my hands if the kids can't see you."

Her heart fluttered in a very nice way. She sat up straighter in her bed. "Bring 'em on!"

Kurt stepped aside, replaced by Beth, who was carrying a large vase filled with cut flowers. She smiled shyly from the doorway. "Hi."

"The flowers are beautiful."

"Dad bought them for you but he said to tell you they're from all of us."

"Then I thank all of you." Especially Kurt, who was grinning like mischievous boy who'd just pulled a prank on everyone. "Is a 'hi' all I get from you, Beth?" Sarah opened her arms. "How about a hug?"

Still hesitant, the girl came closer and put the flowers on the bed table. "I don't want to hurt you."

"You won't, I promise."

Leaning forward, Beth put her arms around Sarah, who hugged her back. Stiff at first, Beth finally relaxed enough to give her a proper hug.

"I was so scared," Beth whispered, her head next to Sarah's.

"I was, too. But I'm okay now." She patted Beth's back and stroked her blond ponytail.

Sniffing as though fighting tears, Beth said, "I prayed for you to get better."

The girl's admission touched Sarah deeply. She knew how hard it had been for Beth to lose her mother. Sarah's relapse could have broken her spirit. She was grateful to God that it hadn't. "Looks like your prayers worked, honey. Thank you."

"I prayed, too." Toby stood on the opposite side of the bed.

"Well, thank you, Toby. I can't tell you how much I

appreciate your prayers. Sounds like the Ryder family has been keeping the Lord busy lately."

The boy grinned. "Look who I brought along." Growling, he showed Sarah his Mervyn the Monster dummy. *"Why do gorillas have big nostrils?"*

Sarah choked back a laugh. "My goodness, I don't know why gorillas have big nostrils."

"Don't ask," Beth said. "It's really gross."

Toby ignored his sister. *"Because gorillas have big fingers."*

Beth groaned. So did Sarah, but she laughed, too. "Good one, Toby." Just gross enough to be perfect for a nine-year-old boy. "Dr. Zoom will have to remember that one."

"He's told that joke so many times in the past twenty-four hours," Kurt said standing at the foot of her bed, "that we've all memorized it and are dreaming about gorillas in our sleep."

Grace had slipped into the room last and was putting some clothes in the narrow closet provided for the patients. That was a favor Sarah hadn't been able to ask of Kurt. One serious kiss and a couple of pecks on the cheek didn't mean their relationship had progressed that far.

"I brought you a nightgown, too." Grace didn't look at Sarah as she spoke, instead she opened the drawer below the closet to put away the gown. "I'm sure you hate wearing those drafty hospital gowns as much as I do."

"Thank you, Grace. I know…" Sarah didn't quite know what to say. Clearly, Grace more than the others had wanted to believe a part of Zoe had come back to her. Learning that Sarah's new heart had belonged to someone else must have caused her to grieve for her daughter all over again. "I'm sorry," she finally said.

Grace closed the drawer and looked up. "No need to be sorry, child. I'm a silly old woman who had trouble letting go of Zoe. I've made my peace with the Lord now." She glanced at Kurt. "I think we all have."

Kurt hooked his arm around his mother-in-law's shoulders. "We're getting there, aren't we kids?"

Tears of gratitude flooded Sarah's eyes, and she wiped them away.

Kurt visibly took a breath and cleared his throat. He pulled her cell phone from his shirt pocket and put it on the bed table beside the flowers. "So when does the doctor say you can escape this place?"

"Tomorrow, assuming I continue to do well."

"You will." Coming from Kurt, the words sounded like an order. "I'll be here first thing in the morning."

"Not too early." She laughed at his determined expression. "Dr. Trevor will have to sign my discharge papers before they'll release me."

"No problem. If he doesn't show up by noon, I'll just kidnap you."

Toby cheered. Beth and Grace seemed delighted with his plan, too.

But what would happen next? The end of summer was quickly approaching, the time for her to return to Seattle. How could Sarah ever leave this family that she'd come to know and love? How could she leave Kurt?

She squeezed her eyes shut. Somehow she'd have to trust the Lord and leave the answer up to Him.

After they all left to go back to the ranch, Sarah

checked her cell phone and discovered she'd had several messages from Tricia in Seattle. She punched in her business number.

Tricia answered on the second ring. "Puget Sound Business Services."

"Hi, Tricia. It's me."

"Sarah! Thank goodness you called." Her voice rose in excitement. "I've been worried about you."

"Sorry to be so out of touch." Sarah had been checking in with Tricia at least once a week until she'd fallen ill, though she had complete confidence her friend wouldn't have any problem handling the workload. "I did have a small setback, but I'm fine now. How's it going with you?"

"Great. Everything is under control here. I'm getting to know some of your clients pretty well, and they're really nice people. They always ask about you and how you're doing."

Thinking of the small-business clients she'd worked with for so many years, she smiled. "Tell them 'hi' from me."

"Will do. And the best news of all…" Tricia paused for effect. "I passed the CPA exam!"

"Whoo-hoo! Congratulations! I never doubted for minute that you'd nail that exam."

"Then you were more confident than I was. What a monster."

"So what are your plans?" Sarah asked.

"I'd sent my resume to a bunch of places and had a few interviews. I got a really good offer, too." She named one of the most prestigious accounting firms in the city.

"Wow, you're going big-time. Did you accept?"

"I did but I told them I couldn't start until September first."

The date Sarah was supposed to be back in Seattle for her three-month doctor's appointment and to take over her business again. "Were they okay with that?"

"They said fine, although earlier would be better. It's a great opportunity for me." Tricia laughed. "But it's a huge company with offices all across the country. I'll be just one of about a dozen junior CPAs in the Seattle office trying to scramble up the promotion ladder, and that could mean transfers to other cities as time goes on."

"I'm betting you'll be the smartest and work the hardest of all of them." Sarah wanted the best for Tricia. Raised by a single mother, she'd put herself through school and achieved outstanding grades.

"It does seem like a dream come true, and the money is great. Anyone would be dumb to pass up a chance like that, wouldn't they?"

Not wanting to unduly influence her friend, Sarah hedged her answer. "You're the only one who can answer that, Tricia."

"Great. Now you're sounding like my mother."

They chatted for a few more minutes, then Sarah hung up. She'd had a dream when she came to Sweet Grass Valley—to find a way to help the donor family whose courage and compassion had given her a new heart. She'd failed that mission.

And somewhere along the way, her dream had changed.

She didn't know yet if her new dream would come true.

Or what would happen to her business clients if her new dream came true and she didn't return to Seattle. Her conscience wouldn't allow her to leave them totally in the lurch.

Chapter Fourteen

The hot summer day and the scent of sage drifting in from the prairie mixing with car exhaust in the hospital parking lot spelled freedom for Sarah.

A woman in her sixties who wore a royal-blue hospital volunteer jacket had brought her downstairs in a wheelchair while Kurt went to get the truck. Sarah carried her vase of flowers in her lap.

The volunteer stood beside her, one hand resting on the back of the wheelchair. "Now, you take your time getting your strength back before bringing Dr. Zoom in to see the children again."

"I will." She'd walked down the corridor to pediatrics yesterday afternoon, peeking inside the rooms, and was very much looking forward to getting back to entertaining them again.

"The youngsters surely have enjoyed having you come visit."

"I'll be back as soon as I'm able," she said as Kurt pulled the truck up next to the curb.

He hopped out of the truck and came around to the

passenger side. "I tried to rent a chariot with six white horses but they were all out of them today."

"Your truck will be just fine." Chuckling, she handed the flowers to the volunteer and started to stand up. Before she knew what was happening, Kurt had scooped her up into his arms.

She squealed. "You don't have to carry me."

"You may have entered the hospital on a gurney, but the least I can do is carry you out." With the ease of a man who was used to bulldogging calves for a living, he placed her on the passenger seat. He reached back to retrieve the flowers from the volunteer and gave them to Sarah.

"I'm not an invalid, you know."

"Maybe not. But I intend to take very good care of you."

She mentally groaned. Kurt was going to be more overprotective than her mother had been. Sarah would have to do something about that. She hated being coddled.

He drove away from the front of the hospital building, went about fifty feet and stopped, shifting the truck into Park.

"What's wrong?" she asked.

"Nothing." He turned toward her, cupped her face with his calloused hand and brought his lips down on hers. He tasted of the warmth of Montana, the heat that had been trapped in the cab of his truck.

Her heart responded with a heavy beat and she ached for him to hold her, not just for this kiss but forever.

With her hand, she caressed his smooth-shaven cheek,

his square jaw, memorizing the rugged angles and planes of his face, features she would always remember.

He broke the kiss. His eyes had darkened almost to black. "I don't know about you, but I feel a whole lot better now."

She wasn't sure *better* was how she felt. But she certainly felt more alive than at any other time in her life. *Thank You, Lord.*

A half hour later, they drove beneath the arch announcing they had arrived at the Rocking R Ranch. A feeling of homecoming soothed Sarah and she welcomed the sense of relief that she had survived the threat of organ rejection. She knew that her situation had, at one point, been touch and go, though she wouldn't reveal that to Kurt and his family.

Not for a moment did she doubt the many prayers that had been said for her, including Kurt's, had tipped the balance toward recovery.

Buds on the climbing rosebushes she and Beth had planted by the gazebo had blossomed and the sunflowers looked like they'd grown a foot in the week she'd been gone. The heads of brightly colored zinnias beckoned in a light breeze.

Kurt stopped the truck near the front porch, which surprised Sarah. Usually he parked by the barn.

Rather than risk having him carry her inside, she got out of the truck as quickly as she could. She didn't want the children to think of her as an invalid anymore than she wanted Kurt to.

His eyebrows shot up when he discovered she had

gotten out on her own. He took the vase of flowers from her. "You're going to be stubborn, aren't you?"

"It's one of my finest attributes." Chiding him with a smile, she fluffed the tips of her hair in a flirtatious gesture.

"Impish today, are we?" Scowling, he took her elbow to help her up the steps. He had a stubborn streak, too.

Opening the door, he let her step inside first.

Beth, Toby and Grace greeted her with a shout. "Welcome home!" A homemade WELCOME HOME, SARAH! banner in red letters on white butcher paper was strung across the living room. A dozen red-and-white balloons bobbed above two baskets filled with matching carnations.

"Oh, my!" Her eyes widened and she covered her mouth in surprise. Heat burned her cheeks. She turned to Kurt. "Look what they've done."

He rested his hand on her shoulder. "Guess you could say they're glad to have you back. We all are."

"I'm glad, too. More than you could possibly know." She gave the children hugs, Grace, too. "Thank you. All of you."

"I made you a chicken salad for lunch," Beth announced. "There's walnuts and dried cranberries in it."

"Sounds delicious."

"Nana and me made whole-wheat rolls," Toby added. "They're supposed to be healthy for you but they taste good anyway."

She chuckled, ruffled Toby's hair and sent Grace a grateful smile. "Thank you for being so thoughtful."

"It's time we took care of you for a while, instead of you taking care of the children," Grace said.

"Which means she needs to rest." Kurt squeezed her shoulder. "I don't want her to overtax herself. She should take a nap and then have—"

Sarah stepped away from him. "Folks, I have an announcement to make. As much as I'm grateful for your concern, and as much as I appreciate the trouble you've gone to, I'm not sick and I haven't turned into the mental equivalent of a turnip." She eyed Kurt. "What I'd really like to do right now is fix myself a glass of iced tea—"

"I've already made up a pitcher for us," Grace said.

"—and take it out on the porch, sit down and enjoy the great outdoors before lunch. After lunch, I may take a nap...or go for a horseback ride," she added by way of jerking Kurt's overprotective chain.

"No!" he sputtered. "You'll do not such thing. You can't go riding."

"All right. If you insist, Dr. Ryder, I'll put that off for a day or two. But I will go riding—outside the corral— one day very soon."

Sarah left one very stunned, openmouthed cowboy gawking after her as she went to the kitchen to pour her own iced tea. She grinned to herself. A long time ago she'd learned how to handle well-intentioned people who wanted to turn her into a chronically dependent invalid.

Sarah did take a long nap that afternoon, glad to be away from the hustle and bustle of the hospital, and all the pokes and prods and needle stabs that went with being a patient.

As promised, she skipped the horseback ride, although she did walk out to the corral to feed Peaches an apple she'd cut up. Getting used to being around the horse would pay off later. She hoped.

Sunday morning there was no question about what she'd do. She was going to church.

To her surprise, Kurt announced he planned to attend church as well and so did his children.

"Grace will be there, too," he assured her.

Had Kurt truly found the Lord again? she wondered. Or was he going to church only because he knew she'd insist on attending?

So they climbed into his truck dressed in their Sunday best and drove into town. The parking lot seemed quite full. Sarah rolled her eyes when he pulled into a Handicapped spot.

"You can't park here," she said. "You don't have a placard for your truck. You'll get a ticket."

"Don't worry about a thing. I've already cleared it with Pastor Hoffman."

Sarah hadn't heard that ministers had been granted the legal right to make decisions about who was or wasn't handicapped. She felt sure that was solely a doctor's prerogative.

"Well, don't ask me to pay for the ticket if you get one," she said.

He simply grinned at her before climbing down out of the truck. She made it a point to exit on her own.

As the four of them walked down the side aisle to join Grace in a pew, Sarah began to hear a small ripple of applause. The sound increased as they drew near Grace, and members of the congregation began to stand and clap.

The organist switched from the quiet prelude she'd been playing to a booming rendition of the "Hallelujah" chorus.

Sarah tugged on Kurt's sleeve. "What's going on?"

He leaned close to her ear. "I think everybody's glad to see you back and on your feet."

"Oh, dear..." Blushing furiously, she ducked into the pew and scooted across to sit next to Grace.

Beth came in after Sarah, followed by Toby and then Kurt. As they sat down, Sarah was struck by how much they looked like a family sitting together. Her heart did a little ratta-tat-tat, and she put her hand to her chest.

"Are you all right, dear?" Grace asked, concern in her eyes.

"I'm fine. I just didn't expect so much attention."

Grace patted her arm. "Everyone is simply glad you're feeling better."

To Sarah's relief, the pastor walked onto the stage, drawing the congregation's attention, and raised his arms high. "All rise and give thanks unto the Lord."

Lifting her heart up to the Lord, Sarah's prayer of thanksgiving spilled out from the depth of her soul. Starting with her renewed good health and the love and friendship she'd found here in Sweet Grass Valley, she had much to give thanks for. Her cup indeed runneth over and she praised God for all He had given her.

When the service was over, Sarah turned to Grace. "Would you like to come to the house? We can have a light lunch."

"No, dear." She patted Sarah's hand. "You go on with Kurt. I have some things I need to do."

"Come by another day, then."

Standing, Sarah edged toward the aisle. Kurt had let the children go on ahead and waited for Sarah to join him. In a proprietary gesture, he slipped his arm around her waist.

"Did you hear the pastor mention the New Member Class that's going to start next week for folks who want to join the church?" Kurt eased her through the crowd to a side door and they stepped out into the bright sun and the heat of midday.

"I wasn't paying too much attention." She glanced up at him.

"I'm going to sign up. This whole business of you being so sick and everyone praying for you made me realize I not only turned my back on God. Even before that, I'd let my faith slide, not giving it any thought. I'm going to do something about that."

Goose bumps of pleasure and excitement rose on the back of her neck. "That's wonderful, Kurt. I'm thrilled you're rediscovering your faith."

"You could say I'm highly motivated." He winked and gave her waist a little squeeze that sent a shimmer of awareness through Sarah, warming her heart.

They'd started toward the truck when Kurt came to an abrupt halt. "Uh-oh."

She glanced around. "What's wrong?"

"Beth and Caroline are talking to a couple of guys." He gestured toward the far side of the parking lot.

She spied the youngsters laughing, the boys throwing mock punches at each other. "Oh, yes, those are the two boys they were talking to that time I brought Beth to church."

Kurt started off at a fast clip across the parking lot toward the preteens.

Sarah hurried to catch up with him. "What are you going to do?"

"I'm going to talk to my daughter, that's what."

Grabbing his arm, Sarah pulled him to a stop. "You go over there now and talk to Beth in front of those boys, you'll embarrass her and her friends. She'll be madder than one of your cows who has been separated from her calf."

"I'm her father."

"Which is exactly why you need to talk to her in private, not in a public place. I know I would have been mortified if my father confronted me in front of my friends." Not that Sarah had had many occasions to talk with boys at that age. Which didn't change the fact that she would have been embarrassed beyond reason.

Tightening his jaw, Kurt pulled a pouty face like one Toby would make. "I should still stop her."

"No, you shouldn't. She's not doing anything wrong." Tugging gently, she urged him back toward the truck. "She'll come on her own when she sees we're ready to go home."

Once back home, Kurt went out to the barn to work on some tack that needed repair—and to think.

He knew what he wanted to do. *Had* to do. He'd even gone shopping in Shelby while Sarah was in the hospital. That had been an act of faith that she would recover.

Now it was time for action.

The very thought turned his mouth dry and caused his hands to sweat on the broken harness he was trying to stitch back together. He wiped his palm on his jeans.

A man didn't just pop something like this on a woman out of the clear blue. He had to lead up to the big moment. Get her in a receptive mood.

With Zoe it had been easy. Almost from the beginning, they'd known where their relationship was going.

He and Sarah hadn't even gone on a date yet. Going to the county commissioners' meeting with him didn't count. Although their kiss after the hearing certainly got him thinking about the future.

For him, the future without Sarah looked bleak.

How could he ask her to give up her home in Seattle and her business to live on a ranch in Montana with him?

He had to be crazy to even think she'd stay.

After lunch, Sarah rested for a while. She was still weaker than she liked and knew the best way to recover was to let nature and the Lord do their work.

When she woke, the house seemed unnaturally quiet. She freshened up and brushed her hair, then strolled through the house. The kitchen was spotless. So was the living room. No work left for the housekeeper to do, for which she was grateful.

Stepping outside, she found Kurt sitting in the shade of the porch, his chair tipped back, his booted feet propped on the porch railing, and his Stetson pulled down, hiding his eyes. An empty iced-tea glass sat beside his chair.

For a moment, she simply took in the sight of Kurt in a relaxed state. Between running the ranch and seeing to his children, he rarely had a chance to stop and catch his breath.

What he needed was a woman to look out for him for a change.

He snorted and coughed, shifted his position.

"Ah, the master of the house is alive after all," she said.

Startled, his feet dropped to the porch with a bang and he righted the chair. Pushing his hat back up on his head, he said, "I didn't hear you come outside."

"You were pretty well gone."

"Just resting my eyes."

Right! She leaned back on the railing. "Where are the children?"

"They're both doing sleepovers at a friend's house."

"Oh." A prick of disappointment needled Sarah. While she was in the hospital, she'd missed the children almost as much as she'd missed Kurt.

"I asked them to arrange the sleepovers," Kurt continued, "because I'm going to take you out to dinner."

"Oh," she said again, thinking the children could just as easily have come with them to the diner in town, the only place to eat in Sweet Grass Valley. "I could've fixed them something here."

"Nope. Not this time." He stood, forcing Sarah to look up at him. "There's an old farmhouse this side of Chester that a couple have remodeled and turned into a B and B. They serve dinners, too. Nice white tablecloths, fancy silverware, the whole big-city thing. That's where I'd like to take you on a date tonight."

Her jaw went slack. "A date?"

"Yep. Assuming you feel up to going, of course."

"I feel fine. I'm surprised, that's all. I didn't expect—"

His brown-eyed gaze snared hers with its intensity. "A lot of things have surprised me lately. Will you go out to dinner with me? I made reservations for us."

She moistened her lips with her tongue. A quiver of joy arrowed into her heart. "That sounds wonderful. Thank you for inviting me."

The corners of his lips hooked up in a self-satisfied smile that made Sarah wonder what besides a fancy dinner might be on the menu tonight.

Kurt had not exaggerated. The interior of the Old Yellow Farmhouse B and B was tastefully decorated with antiques displayed on bookshelves and in glass-fronted cabinets. Each cozy room had a theme—Victorian, Federalist or Civil War era with furniture to match the time period.

Evelyn Couch, the gracious owner of the B and B, ushered them into a private dining room with a single table set for two. The walnut chairs were upholstered in red velvet. Framed period prints decorated the walls and silver serving pieces lined a walnut buffet, and there was a delicate porcelain vase of pink roses on the table. A single window covered with sheer curtains provided a view of the prairie north of the town of Chester as the sun slanted toward evening shadows.

Kurt held the chair for Sarah, then seated himself.

"May I bring you both some iced tea?" the hostess asked.

"Yes, please," Sarah said. Kurt nodded in agreement.

When Mrs. Couch left them with their menus and a promise their server would be there shortly, Sarah leaned forward, and whispered, "How many cows did you have to sell to afford dinner here?"

Kurt chuckled. "Don't worry about it. I want this to be a special evening for you."

"It already is." She'd never seen Kurt look so handsome or so commanding. He wore a beige silk Western shirt with white trim and a brown-and-gold tigereye bolo tie that matched his eyes. His height and muscular physique seemed to dwarf the delicate Victorian furniture. In this setting, with this man, Sarah felt like a storybook pampered princess.

A young waitress wearing a long skirt and white blouse brought them their iced tea and a basket of warm rolls. "Do you need a little more time to study the menu?"

"Yes, please." Sarah hadn't even glanced at the menu, she'd been too enthralled by Kurt.

When the waitress returned a few minutes later, Sarah selected a Cornish game hen with new potatoes and fresh vegetables on the side, knowing full well she wouldn't be able to eat a full dinner. Kurt chose a T-bone steak, baked potato and dinner salad. She smiled, suspecting before she had started preparing his meals, he would never have chosen a salad with his meal.

They spoke of inconsequential things as they ate. Bonnie Sue's daughter was visiting from Chicago. Kurt needed to order some new parts for his tractor. He'd be moving the mother herd closer to the ranch house soon.

Beth wanted to pierce her ears, which troubled Kurt and endeared Sarah for his concern.

By the time they'd finished dinner and the waitress cleared the table, Sarah was totally stuffed. She wouldn't be able to eat another bite for days.

Kurt cleared his throat and straightened his napkin as though he was suddenly nervous. "A couple of weeks ago, I said we should be a couple and you turned me down. That was the right thing for you to do."

Her meal suddenly turned into a rock in her stomach. Was he telling her goodbye? Sending her back to Seattle? Did he no longer want a heart-transplant recipient around to remind him of Zoe? She felt like a prisoner who'd just eaten a last meal before being led to the guillotine.

"When I told you that I'd come to care for you, I didn't know the right words to say how I felt about you. And my faith in the Lord wasn't strong enough." He produced a small blue velvet box and placed it on the table between them. "I think I've found the words now, and I'm working hard on the faith part."

Barely able to breathe, her heart pounding hard, she stared at the velvet box, then lifted her gaze to his.

"I love you, Sarah. I never thought I'd feel this way about any woman. When you were so sick, I thought I was going to lose you. That made me realize that I want you to be my wife. To stand beside me for the rest of my life." His eyes filled with his plea. "Will you marry me, Sarah?"

Her heart soared. Her head spun. Although she'd dreamed of this moment, she'd never let herself believe it would happen. She wanted this man as her husband more than anything else in the world.

"I know there are some things about living on a ranch that might bother you," he added. "The isolation of living so far from a city. The winters here can be killers."

She extended her hand across the table to stop his babbling, and he took it.

"I love you, Kurt. More than I can possibly say. But there are some things you need to know."

He frowned as he rubbed his thumb back and forth over her knuckles. "I know all I need to know about you."

"I'm not guaranteed tomorrow. My heart could fail at any moment or I could go into rejection again."

"One day with you as my wife would be worth a thousand days without you."

Self-consciously, she glanced away. "The transplant operation left me with a gigantic scar on my chest. It's… ugly," she admitted, hating that she'd been so scarred while still grateful to be alive.

"It doesn't matter. You're beautiful on the inside, where it counts."

She squeezed his hand, ready to make the most difficult admission of all. "Because I'm on anti-rejection drugs, I can't have any babies. I couldn't carry them to term."

"Sarah, honey, I've got two kids who are already a handful. I don't need any more."

For years, Sarah had longed to have children of her own with a man she loved. A man like Kurt. The transplant had made that virtually impossible, and she had grieved for that loss.

"Besides," Kurt said, grinning. "If you marry me, then you could talk to Beth about all that boy-'n-girl stuff that scares me spitless."

She laughed and tears sprang to her eyes. "Coward!"

"You know I am about stuff like that."

"There's one other small hitch. Tricia, who's been running my business, has gotten a job offer she can't pass up. I'll have to go back to Seattle and try to arrange something for my clients. I can't just leave them in the lurch."

"Does that mean you're going to say yes?"

She nodded and the tears began to flow. "What about Beth and Toby? How will they feel? Beth isn't over losing her mother yet and I don't want—"

"They're great with us getting married. In fact, Beth told me that if I blew the proposal she was never going to speak to me again."

Sarah gasped. "You told them you were going to propose to me?"

He shifted in his chair as though suddenly uncomfortable. "I had to, Sarah. I was pretty sure they'd both be okay with it. And they are. But the three of us sort of come as a package, and I didn't want to put you in an awkward position."

"You're a good father, Kurt Ryder. I love you so much and your children. I can't wait to become Mrs. Kurt Ryder."

He opened the velvet box and showed her the diamond engagement ring, a beautiful solitaire mounted on white gold. Simple in its elegance. "If you don't like it, we can take it back for another one."

"Oh, Kurt..." She covered her mouth with her hand. "It's perfect. More that I'd ever hoped for."

Taking her hand, he slid the ring onto the third finger of her left hand and smiled, looking relieved. "You're perfect, sweetheart. In every way."

Epilogue

Saturday, early September

The heat of August had given way to the cooler temperatures of September and the flowers circling the gazebo in front of the ranch house were in full, magnificent bloom. The scent of the floral bouquet they created provided the perfect atmosphere for a wedding.

Both Kurt and Sarah had opted for a small wedding with only family and their closest friends attending. Pastor Hoffman would officiate and his wife, Alexis, would provide the music on a portable keyboard. Toby was to be the best man, Beth the junior bridesmaid and Grace the stand-in mother of the bride.

In the ranch house guest bedroom, Tricia Malone, CPA and maid of honor, fussed with Sarah's hair and the short veil she wore. Both of them concentrated on Sarah's reflection in the full-length mirror on the back of the bedroom door. Her simple wedding dress was street length with a high collar and long sleeves of white organdy over pale pink satin, camouflaging the scar on her chest.

"We really should have gotten you a hairpiece so we could pile it up on top of your head in a fancy do," Tricia said.

"If we had, Kurt probably wouldn't recognize me and he'd go running for the hills."

"I doubt it. That man looks at you like a man head-over-teakettle in love. I should be so lucky."

"You will be one day." Tall and slender with incredible dark eyes, Sarah was surprised some fellow hadn't already set his sights on Tricia.

When Sarah had called Tricia to let her know about the wedding and her plans to return to Seattle long enough to close down her business, Tricia had been more than a little surprised. She'd just learned that her mother had been diagnosed with cancer at the same time the high-powered accounting firm announced they wanted Tricia to start work at their Los Angeles office, not in Seattle.

Tricia couldn't bring herself to leave her mother and move away when she was facing such a difficult time in her life. She'd been struggling with the career decision she'd have to make. Given Sarah's news, Tricia knew it was a gift from God and instantly offered to buy Puget Sound Business Services from Sarah. A happy resolution for them both.

A knock on the door was followed by Beth's voice. "Are you guys ready yet? Dad's having a nervous breakdown waiting for you."

Grinning, Sarah met Tricia's gaze in the mirror. "Come on in, sweetie. We're just finishing up."

Beth opened the door and stood stock-still, looking adorable and almost grown-up in her sleeveless pale blue satin dress. She and Sarah had shopped for their dresses together, giggling as though they were both schoolgirls.

"Wow, Sarah, you look gorgeous. When Dad sees you he's gonna drool."

"Oh, dear, I hope not." Tricia adjusted Sarah's veil one more time. "The rental place will charge him extra for cleaning his tux."

Beth sputtered a laugh. "I didn't mean *really* drool."

"She knows that," Beth assured her about-to-be stepdaughter. "Tricia has a rather dry sense of humor."

"Okay, ladies," Tricia announced. "It's showtime."

From calm one minute to being a nervous wreck the next, Sarah walked out of the bedroom to her future. Her hands shook as Beth handed her the small bouquet of mixed flowers they'd picked together that morning.

"You're gonna be a great mom," Beth whispered. "I think my mother would be glad Dad found you."

Sarah's heart seemed to expand with the love she felt for Beth as well as for Toby. Most of all for Kurt. Trying desperately not to cry, not *before* the service, Sarah kissed Beth on the cheek. "Thank you, honey. I'll do my very best, I promise."

Beth and Tricia preceded her out the front door.

When Sarah stepped out onto porch, her breath caught. Kurt, standing tall and strong in a Western-cut tuxedo, his son standing beside him, waited for her at the bottom of the steps. He extended his hand. Their eyes met and they both smiled.

All of Sarah's jitters vanished in that moment. She knew from the depth of her soul this was why the Lord had sent her to Sweet Grass Valley. Not to find the donor family who had given her a new heart.

But to bring her to this place where her heart and Kurt's could join in a love that would last throughout eternity.

* * * * *

Dear Reader,

Sarah's story is purely a work of fiction; the need for organ transplants is all too real.

According to the Mayo Clinic, 101,000 people are waiting for an organ transplant, the gift of life, and the list grows by three hundred people every month.

Each day, approximately seventy-seven people receive an organ transplant. However, each day nineteen people die waiting for a transplant.

Becoming a donor is easy:

- Register with your state's donor registry.
- Sign and carry a Uniform Donor Card, or indicate your willingness to donate on your driver's license application
- Talk to your family members about your wish to be a donor.

My driver's license indicates I'm willing to be an organ donor, and I've talked with my husband about my wishes.

For more information about becoming an organ donor:
http://www.mayoclinic.org/transplant/organ-donation.html

Charlotte Carter

QUESTIONS FOR DISCUSSION

1. Have you or anyone you know been a recipient of an organ transplant? If so, how is that person's health now?

2. Do you think people who receive an organ transplant take on elements of the donor's personality? Why or why not?

3. Do you or any of your friends have religious objections to giving or receiving an organ transplant? Why or why not?

4. Have you discussed with your family members your wishes about donating your organs should the situation arise? If yes, what was your family's reaction? How do your family members feel about donating their own organs in a similar situation?

5. Do you think Sarah was right to contact the family of the woman she thought her new heart came from? Why or why not?

6. In this story, Sarah became a hospital volunteer in order to "pay forward" the blessings she has received. What motivates you and others to volunteer in your community?

7. Has guilt or loss of a loved one ever caused you to

lose faith in the Lord? If so, how have you sought to restore your faith?

8. What strains exist in a marriage if one partner has a strong religious faith and the other doesn't?

9. Would you enjoy living on a cattle ranch? Or in a small town? Why or why not?

10. The lovely poem "Footprints in the Sand" by Mary Stevenson has inspired millions of people since it was originally written in 1936. http://footprints-inthe-sand.com. What poem inspires you?

11. Sarah enlisted Beth in the effort to restore the garden her mother had loved. Have you used your love of gardening to touch the hearts of others?

12. Do you think it would be fun to entertain children as a ventriloquist? Or by doing face painting? What skills do you have that you'd like to share with children?

13. How would you feel if you had agreed it was necessary to take a loved one off life support? How would you reach the decision?

14. Montana is a land of blue skies and beautiful sunsets. Where were you when you saw your most memorable sunset?

15. The people in the fictional community of Sweet Grass Valley and the members of Good Shepherd

Community Church were close to one another.
What can you do to strengthen the ties within your
community and your church family?